SCOTT CIENCIN

"ONE OF TODAY'S FINEST FANTASY WRITERS."
Science Fiction Review

"The ultimate art of the novel is the art of storytelling, and there are too few writers today who can weave a tale the reader simply can't put down. Scott Ciencin is such a storyteller."

Stuart M. Kaminsky, EDGAR Award-winning author of *Lieberman's Day*

"SCOTT CIENCIN IS SOMEONE TO WATCH OUT FOR."
Cemetery Dance

"Takes readers on a wild tour of some of the darkest, fear-filled landscapes . . . Enjoy the ride!"
Rick Hautala, *New York Times* bestselling author of *Dark Silence*

"I WANT TO SEE MORE. A LOT MORE."
R.A. Salvatore, *New York Times* bestselling author of *The Dark Elf Trilogy*

THE ELVEN WAYS

Book 1

THE WAYS OF MAGIC

SCOTT CIENCIN

AVON BOOKS • NEW YORK

THE ELVEN WAYS, BOOK 1: THE WAYS OF MAGIC is an original publication of Avon Books. This work has never before appeared in book form. This work is a novel. Any similarity to actual persons or events is purely coincidental.

AVON BOOKS
A division of
The Hearst Corporation
1350 Avenue of the Americas
New York, New York 10019

Copyright © 1996 by Scott Ciencin
Cover art by Darrell Sweet
Published by arrangement with the author
Library of Congress Catalog Card Number: 95-95178
ISBN: 0-380-77980-3

First AvoNova Printing: May 1996

AVONOVA TRADEMARK REG. U.S. PAT. OFF. AND IN OTHER COUNTRIES, MARCA REGISTRADA, HECHO EN U.S.A.

Printed in the U.S.A.

RA   10   9   8   7   6   5   4   3   2   1

To my amazing wife, Denise—I love you
and I'm proud of you, sweetheart.

Special thanks to Bob Salvatore, John Douglas,
eluki bes shahar, and Jim and Alicia Hanlon.

There is nothing holier in this life of ours than the consciousness of love and the fluttering of its silken wings.

—HENRY WADSWORTH LONGFELLOW

Every angel is terrifying.

—RAINER MARIA RILKE
Duino Elegies

Prologue

THE DAY OF EXODUS HAD FINALLY ARRIVED. THROUGH-out the city of Hampton, the citizens prepared to leave their old lives behind. Cherished places were visited one last time. Grievances that had severed neighborly bonds were put aside. Former friends and lovers gathered.

History was coming to an end.

Some greeted the prospect of their new lives with optimism. They had sinned, but not fatally. This day they would pay for their trespasses by leaving behind the homes and businesses they had built over the years. A new future beckoned—one filled with shining possibilities and endless wonder.

Travest Mulvihill was not *quite* that optimistic about the future. True, he had served the government well as a tailor. In his possession were letters of introduction to people of means in many other cities. Those documents would allow him to forget all this unpleasantness and rebuild his business with his son in a climate of their choosing. Fortunately, he was one of the few making the Exodus who owned a wagon, and so he could take the tools of his trade and a great deal of his supplies with him.

As Travest packed the last of his belongings into his wagon, he thought of his workers, who would not fare so well. Like so many other immigrants in the city, they had accepted their fate grudgingly. They had made the perilous journey from far-away lands with the promise of a better life. What they had found was countless hours of labor with little to show for it. Now even their meager gains were being taken from them. They were shopkeepers, builders, metalsmiths, fishermen, and more—the invisible laborers without whom the city would crumble in a heartbeat.

The future was most in doubt for the small group remaining behind. Among them were the handful that had been the direct cause of Hampton's troubles, a body of men who had advocated "freedom" from the "tyrannical rule of the *so-called* Heavenly Host." Each was a charismatic speaker, a natural-born leader. That they had managed to go so far as to draw up a "Petition of Formal Separation" from the Host and gained fourteen thousand signatures was in itself a miracle; or so it had seemed at the time. Later, it became clear the avatars of God had been aware of their exploits the entire time. The faith of the people of Hampton had been tested and found wanting.

The Separatists would face their final judgment soon.

Also remaining in the city were those deemed the most pious, whose reward it would be to stand in the halls of a City of Heaven and glimpse at last what would come for most only when the Rapture finally descended. They guarded the Separatists.

The group that waited for the moment of Convergence was a study of extremes. Theological arguments abounded. The prisoners were beaten into submission. A few sobbed and claimed they were repentant. The time for such pleas was long past.

As Travest packed the last of his materials and called once more for his son to join him, he considered the small faction of malcontents who had escaped the Great Purge. During that unusually dark and bloody time, all who had signed the petition and all who were known outwardly as supporters of the Separatists' cause were put to the Question by the soldiers of God's Army. The pale-skinned shining avatars of the One True God had carried out their work solemnly, with the public forced to look on. When it was over, the earth beneath Public Square, once a gathering place for minstrel shows and the newest works of the Bard Continuance, was stained crimson. The malcontents had been on hand to witness the demise of so many who shared their views. Only their own limitless ability to loathe their existence but do nothing to change their lives, had saved them.

"Sorry I'm late!" a young voice called, jarring Travest from his revery. He turned to see his son Lileo, who bounded up to take his place beside Travest on their small perch at the front of the wagon.

The Exodus began. People closed the doors of their houses for the last time. A few set fires. Looting quickly became rampant. The soldiers of God had already left the city. Whatever foolishness the humans wished to commit at this point would be on their heads at the day of the final judgment.

Travest was a tall man, thin, with short, perfectly groomed auburn hair. His eyes were a perfect sky blue, his clothes fashioned in the styles steadily gaining popularity from the Mexicas of the southwest: A frock riddled with odd, interlocking patterns of turquoise, lime, and orange; quilted black leggings originally meant to protect warriors in battle and instead only chafed those who could afford them; and crimson boots that he personally viewed as an eyesore, though his clientele paid top prices for them. He wore silver earrings with bright plumes and his rings were shaped like eagles.

The style had begun with the Azticas, a race of savages who once performed human sacrifices in the name of their heathen gods; now they were among the favored people of the Host. Travest hated wearing this outfit, but he knew it marked him as a man of importance, and told brigands that God's wrath might fall upon any who harmed him. His son, with his shock of long brown hair and his handsome features, was dressed much the same.

Above the cacophony of screams and shouts rose the voices of human choirs who walked the streets of the city, singing hymns of divine praise. The gates of the city were thrown open and people flooded outward. Those who had horses rode into the freezing cold of a winter that was coming to an end, but not soon enough. The handful with wagons carted their belongings, while the majority of the people left with whatever they could carry.

Travest's wife had died giving birth to their only child and the tailor had raised the boy alone. Wives had been offered to him—he had even been pressured to marry on several occasions. That part of his life was over. He lived for his son, and the boy had turned into a very promising young man under his tutelage.

They had lived in Hampton for ten years. The port city, one of the oldest in the Virginia colony, was far too close to the north. Travest was tired of the cold. Perhaps a warmer setting would be pleasant. He would have to make a decision soon.

Most people had loaded their wagons early this morning, when the heavenly guard was still around to offer escorts. Travest had wished to leave the city with the soldiers, as had so many others, but his son had delayed them with his need to say good-bye to his many friends scattered throughout the city.

They were fortunate. No one accosted them as they passed through the gates and rode to a clearing in the distance.

"I want to see it," Lileo said breathlessly.

"It would be better if we rode out now," Travest said wearily. It was just after daybreak, and if they headed out now, they would be well on their journey to a new life when dozens of others were still trying to leave behind the mad tangle of people he could already see ahead.

He had been having this discussion with his son for days, and he knew what the outcome would be. Still, he had at least to attempt to exert some control over matters. "Everyone from Hampton will be stopped to watch the Convergence. If we ride now, we won't be caught in all the confusion later as people try to leave this area once and for all."

"If you say, Father," said Lileo, a bright-eyed boy. The child did his best to hide the disappointment in his voice, but it was impossible to mask it completely.

Travest sighed. "If you promise to take first watch for the next week while we are on the road—then we can stay."

"I'll do it!" Lileo cried.

"And you'll have to worry about both our laundry."

"Anything! Just say it."

"I will when I think of it."

"Tell me and it'll be done."

Travest smiled. He knew he could take his son at his word. Every day, Travest thanked God that despite his inability to say "no" to his son, the ten-year-old had not turned out to be a spoiled, whiny brat like so many of the children paraded into his shop each week for fittings. This one thing, staying behind to watch the coming of the City of Heaven, was all he had asked for in months.

Travest thought of his own childhood. He and his father had always been moving to avoid creditors. His father had lived hard and died young, leaving Travest, then only fourteen, responsible for paying off the debt. Doing so had taken ten years. During that time, Travest swore that if he was ever fortunate enough to be blessed with a family of his own, he would give them a stable home. In Hampton, he had made that dream a reality. Now he was being forced to leave, and it was very hard. A part of him wanted to break with his former home as quickly as possible. Lingering only made it worse.

Travest sighed. He knew that he had, in no way, contributed to the expulsion of Hampton's citizens. Nevertheless, he felt terrible that his son was now going to learn many of the hard lessons taught to him during his days on the road. The least he could do was allow his son this one indulgence.

The road was clear, but on either side of it were thousands of people crowding before the edge of the woods. Many were on their knees, lost in prayers of deliverance. The Curacas of Hampton, the city's highest-ranking government official, and all of his associates had been placed under house arrest by the Separatists. The leaders of the Separatists abolished the duties of the Curacas. No more would a member of the Church keep watch to ensure that a family's taxes were paid in gold and labor. Never again, they vowed, would a Curacas enter a household and chide a wife for not keeping the place spotless, or force arranged marriages upon his subjects. A man's labors did not need to be constantly scrutinized and criticized by the Curacas, the Separatists proclaimed. Hampton would now be a free place, and all would work to better themselves.

The Host had made no formal judgment against the Curacas and his fellow officials for becoming prisoners of the Separatists. In fact, after the Curacas and his associates had been freed, the task of maintaining order outside the city while the Convergence took place had been given to them as a sign that they had been forgiven.

A man belonging to an order of enforcement officials known as the Arrow Riders came forward, and stopped Travest's wagon. He wore a costume that had its roots in the armor of the Roman Centurions. New Rome, it seemed, would always be the Host's key seat of power for the European-based colonies. Travest didn't know much about the Asian and African nations, except that the Host managed to reach a peaceful accord with them after some early and unfortunate bloodshed. The wars still raged in pockets of land throughout the world. Heathens never seemed to learn.

"Staying?" the man asked.

Travest nodded. The Arrow Rider, a young fellow with long, flowing golden hair and hawklike features, pointed to a position before a group of onlookers.

"Put down over there," he said.

"Those people won't be able to see anything," Travest said.

"They're rabble. They'll manage to get a look. You're not a commoner, like them. There's no reason for you to have to pull your wagon to the back, like everyone else."

Travest nodded. He did as he was told. The Arrow Rider was joined by two other heavily armed companions who cleared the way for the tailor and his son. As he came closer, Travest thought that the trees were alive. Then he saw children perched upon every branch, apparently for the better view it afforded.

He asked the Arrow Rider about this and learned that no adults had been allowed into the trees. Only children.

That made sense, Travest supposed. Children were lighter, more agile. Certainly more prepared for things like tree climbing than a man of his years. He was only forty, but at times he felt much older.

As Travest expected, the people who were being moved off from the front of the crowd by the Arrow Riders did not appreciate giving up positions they had held for hours. As he passed them, Travest muttered apologies, but that didn't help. He reached his place and the Arrow Riders departed. The horses drawing his wagon seemed to dislike being around such a crowd. They chuffed, dancing menacingly toward a few commoners who got too close. Travest controlled them.

The tailor sighed. At least this way he would be able to watch "the blessed event" at his son's side.

"Lileo!" someone shouted.

The boy spun and cried, "Father, that's Fermin and Lanny in the tree right behind us. Do you see them? Tell me you do, tell me you see them!"

Travest turned and saw two young boys waving frantically. They sat on a branch about twenty feet off the ground.

"Can I go see them?" Lileo asked.

"But I thought—"

"I'll be right there!" Lileo called. He turned to look at his father. "Is it all right?"

Travest considered objecting, then he shrugged and said, "If you like."

Lileo loosed an enthusiastic cry and hopped down from the wagon.

"Be careful!" Travest cried. The boy was already halfway to the trees.

Travest watched as his son climbed into one of the oldest trees on the outskirts of the forest. Its trunk was wide, its branches thick.

The tailor was struck by a sudden vision of disaster. He imagined his son sitting on the tree trunk, roughhousing with his friends, and suddenly falling to the ground, snapping his neck.

"Stop it," he chided himself in a low voice. He had always pictured such things and they had never come to pass. For that reason, he ignored his every instinct that told him to gather up his son and leave this place now, before it was too late.

Travest looked around. People were glaring at him because his wagon impaired their view. He climbed down from his seat at the front of the wagon and walked over to a family with very small children.

"Your children can take my seat on the wagon, if you like. I don't know how the beasts will react to what's about to come. I'm going to put spikes into the ground and attach the reins to hold it steady. Your children should be safe enough. Just tell them not to touch any of my things."

The mother and father thanked Travest for his generosity. The children climbed up as he drove the last of the spikes home. Travest went to stand with the horses, talking to them, stroking their manes and soothing them with his gentle tone.

The flood of people leaving Hampton had become a trickle. It was impossible to tell the looters and the thieves from decent folk. As the stragglers went past on the road, Travest decided that those who were hurrying away, dropping things as they went and not bothering to go back and get them, were probably the offenders.

The Arrow Riders let the looters go. At this point, their actions hardly mattered, so long as no one was hurt.

Again, Travest thought of his son. He turned and saw Lileo playing with his friends. The boy was fine.

Travest wished that he could stop worrying, but that seemed to be the essence of parenthood on days like today.

In the distance, a trumpet sounded. Travest turned his attention back to the city of Hampton. He had heard stories of what it looked like when the Cities of Heaven made their way to earth, and he had told himself that it mattered little to him. He was a pragmatist; open displays of unearthly power, of heavenly mysticism, did not interest him. The creation of his son, the first cry of the child that struck at exactly the same moment as his wife's final breath—that was a magic he understood, one that made him a believer that God existed and was good. Though he missed his wife so very much over the years, Travest was grateful not to have lost his son with her.

The trumpet sounded again.

Despite all his inner protests, Travest was enthralled. He watched as the people fell to their knees and felt an undeniable compulsion to follow them. The trumpets were joined by voices. A heavenly choir filled the air with an odd trilling sound. Travest felt the hairs on his arm suddenly tickle his flesh. His eyes began to ache. He felt dizzy and thought of Lileo.

The sight before him drew away his compulsion to check on his son. Brightly glowing figures gracefully circled above the city of Hampton, held aloft by invisible wings.

The angels burned with heavenly fire.

Hampton had stood for over three hundred years. It had begun as a village called Kecoughtan, transformed into Fort Algernourne, and finally renamed in honor of Henry Wriothesley, Third Holy Earl of Southampton, a patron of letters and member of the Virginia company.

The seaport had quickly gone on to acquire wealth and standing. Thousands of buildings, some more than four stories high, were erected. The style of architecture was largely attributed to the Goth influence that had been embraced by Europeans during Hampton's early years and through its first major expansion. Soon it had gained a formidable look and feel of its own. Walls had been erected to protect the city and its people.

Hampton had withstood terrible storms and two failed invasions. Today it would be destroyed for what amounted to an ill–thought-out letter writing campaign—or so it seemed to the now homeless tailor.

Such is the will of the Host, he thought. He had learned a long time ago not to voice opinions that even vaguely appeared to ridicule the ways of their lord. It had been centuries before his birth, in what had been known by the old calendar as the year 1500, when the angels had first come to mankind. They appeared in every country of the world and announced that the Millennium, the thousand-year Reign of the Almighty, would soon begin. The angels asserted that God's word had been maligned and misinterpreted by many of the religions throughout the world, though all held a certain amount of truth.

Some believed; others did not. A thirty-year war began, and when it was done, God's Army had triumphed. The Lord chose nine Vessels in which to reveal Himself to the people, nine beings within whom resided the many aspects of His will and power. The Vessels helped to usher several Cities of Heaven to the mortal plane.

In the beginning, the locations chosen for the Cities of Heaven were invariably where human cities already stood. The people of Milan, Rome, London, Paris, Madrid, and so many other cities had set themselves against the One True Way. Their sites were declared unclean. It was decreed that only the presence of a dwelling place for the Host could scour such tainted earth. When this occurred, the people were usually given warning, such as today. It was rumored, though, that some cities had been supplanted with no prior notice, the residents vanishing into the celestial maelstrom of energies released during the Convergence.

Today, it was very rare for one of the world's thriving meccas to be destroyed. Generally, when the Host decided to take up further residences on the world of man, their cities appeared *close* to places of power by human reckoning. The people of Hampton had sinned grievously, and their expulsion had been the result.

Travest once listened to a poet who claimed that all human cities had souls. The cities carried the dreams and fears of all who had ever stepped into their reaches, and all who ever would. If that was true, the soul of Hampton was about to be harvested.

The shining beings flew in strange arcs, leaving trails of crackling, many-hued energies in their wakes. For an instant, Travest thought he saw symbols where the angels had flown, as if they were painting runes into the very air with their divine flames.

A rumbling came from deep within the earth. Travest got to his feet and stood between his horses, doing his best to calm them. Ahead, the shapes of the city began to shudder and lose consistency. The walls surrounding the city fell, veins of blinding white energies rippling through them. Buildings shook and the tallest began to crumble. The earth itself shimmered and seemed to be possessed of an eerie light that rose up and began to etch new forms in the air. Spires. Twisting staircases. Minarets with beautifully carved balconies.

Elaborately designed palaces, some with domed roofs, sprang from what had been Hampton. Towers grew to impossible heights, seeming to graze the clouds, while arches defined themselves, linking them. All these shapes pulsed with a blinding, flickering energy, a sparkling rain of mystical forces that glittered and flashed as if they were alive.

The people, Travest thought, *what is happening to the people who remained behind?*

Inside the rapidly changing city, the humans who had been left to face judgment and their keepers huddled together in fear. Half their number had already died. Two had been felled by falling stone. The others had taken their own lives out of a feeling of unworthiness to stand at the nexus of such an amazing event. All but two of the others had gone irrevocably insane.

Wilson Smith, the fifty-year-old gray-haired leader of the Separatists, and Ulrich Rutherford, a talented student of the Aubrick Order who had only just marked his eighteenth year, stood together. Rutherford was a cleric best known for his ability to see the spirits of the dead and communicate their wishes. Smith had made a fortune overseeing matters of finance for Hampton.

They clung to each other.

The courtyard in which they stood was a blazing sea of primal chaos that did not hold any one form for long. In one instant the two men were surrounded by statues of perfectly round eyeballs, in another they were standing above a lake of fire.

Madness beckoned, but neither man surrendered.

"TURN TO FACE US," called a voice that seemed to be many voices at once.

Both men trembled as they obeyed the command given them. What they saw affected them in dramatically different ways.

"It can't be," Rutherford said as he stumbled back. The cleric covered his eyes. "We trusted you. We believed in you. . . ."

"WE SEE NO REASON TO HIDE THE TRUTH FROM YOU ANY LONGER. YOU WILL NEVER LEAVE THIS PLACE. NO HUMAN WHO ENTERS A CITY OF THE CHOSEN EVER FINDS THEIR WAY BACK. SO IT HAD ALWAYS BEEN, SO IT ALWAYS SHALL BE. . . ."

"There they are," Smith, the former merchant of finance, said with a glee he had not felt since he was a child. He grabbed at the young man's hands, peeling them from his face. "You wanted to look upon the true faces of the beings you served. What's wrong? You don't find the Vessels pleasing? I do."

Twisting away from the older man, Rutherford fell to the ground. He cried and screamed. He begged for God's mercy, praying in his mind for the rationale behind this impossibly dark jest to make itself clear to him. His prayers were not answered.

Instead, there was a roar. One of terrible hunger.

Smith sat back on his haunches, laughing until he also cried and his stomach pained him, laughing as the Host came forward and collected him along with their faithful servant.

On the outskirts of the city, Travest watched the transformation of Hampton in absolute wonder. He had no idea what kind of horrors the men inside the city had faced.

He only knew that what he saw was a miracle.

Pagodas came into view, then buildings that were egg-shaped while others were flat like boxes. Some seemed to be nothing more than waffle-thin rectangles fitted together like a madman's vision of a house of cards. The shapes changed, reconfigured, introducing styles of architecture he could not understand.

For one incredible moment all these forms drew themselves into sharp relief, displaying an incredible array of colors and forms, then, as if a cloak of mist had been dropped before the onlookers, the City of Heaven became an indistinct mass.

Travest stepped away from his horses, his legs weak, his heart racing. Hampton was gone.

"Father?"

Travest turned to see his son standing before him. He lifted the boy off the ground and hugged him tight. Tears had formed on both their faces.

"Thank you, Father," Lileo said.

"No," Travest whispered as he held his son close. "What I would have missed . . ."

Inwardly, he felt changed for the miracle he had witnessed. A God who could work such wonders was capable of infinite wisdom and love. Travest was certain of this.

What he felt appeared to have been shared by the other witnesses to the event. Many had been on their knees, praying with their eyes squeezed shut. The images that Travest had beheld with his eyes were pressed into the minds of those who did not see, those who could not see, because they were blind, or their view had been obstructed. All had shared in this. The excitement they felt at the rapturous event they had just experienced together calmed even the most resentful of hearts.

"We should go," Lileo said.

"Don't you want to stay a little longer?" his father said,

staring at the sparkling wall of mists just ahead.

"There are many who say they will not go at all. They don't care if they starve. Just to be near the City of Heaven is enough for them. But I'm hungry, and I wish to be off to our new home, wherever that may be."

"God will grant us wisdom and we will find our way," Travest said. He hadn't spoken words like that in many years.

The family that had watched the event from atop Travest's wagon came down, thanking the man once again.

Lileo climbed up to their perch as Travest removed the spikes he had planted in the ground to anchor the mounts in the event they went mad in the unnatural splendor of the Convergence. The former tailor joined his son and guided his wagon onto the road. Many of the Arrow Riders sat about, staring with trembling lips at the shimmering wall. No one got in the way of Travest and his son.

The wagon had traveled no more than several hundred yards along the road when Travest thought he spotted something lying upon the ground. Suddenly, he heard a sound and jumped as an insect buzzed right past him. For an instant, Travest had a decent look at the bug. It was like nothing he had ever seen before. It had a coiled, wavering body, with tiny arms, several heads, and three sets of wings. Nothing like that existed. He squeezed his eyes shut and forced them open. The thing was gone.

Now he was seeing things. . . .

"Did that bug get you?" Lileo asked.

A bee, he thought. *It must have just been some kind of bee.* His mind was still overwhelmed with the miracle he had just witnessed. His imagination had gotten the better of him, that was all.

No. Something else gnawed at him.

"It's too cold," he said distantly.

Lileo laughed. "We travel on a road that leads away from a city of miracles! Look around you. The trees are now covered in leaves!"

It was true. Where these trees had been barren before, they now bore leaves of every color and description.

Why hadn't he seen this before?

Travest laughed. It was best not to contemplate such things.

Enjoy them, that was the key. "I love you—" he began. His words were cut short as the wagon suddenly rose up on one side. Travest felt a sudden bracing fear. He reached out for his son, letting go of his reins. The wagon came down hard, its weight crashing fully upon the left front wheel, which crackled and shattered!

The wagon suddenly pitched to the left, the side on which Lileo was sitting. Travest reached out to grab Lileo, but he couldn't reach his son in time. He heard Lileo gasp in surprise as he slipped away and was flung onto the road. The wagon pitched completely over, tossing Travest free. There was a loud, wrenching, thunderous crash. Then Travest struck the ground and rolled on his side several times until he left the road completely and came to a stop beside a thin, spindly tree.

Scrambling to his feet with no regard to any injury he might have sustained in the fall, Travest looked back and saw his son lying facedown in the road. Only Lileo's head, shoulders, and one arm were visible. His other arm and the rest of his body was pinned beneath the overturned wagon. The mounts were gone. The assembly and the harness holding them in place had been snapped apart.

The tailor saw something out of the corner of his eye. Lying in the road was a blacksmith's anvil. One of the looters had dropped it in the road. Clearly it had become too heavy to carry, too impractical a prize; this is what had shattered the wagon wheel and caused the accident.

Travest struggled to take in the sight before him. Overcoming his shock, he raced forward and knelt before his son. The former tailor tried to call the boy's name, but his mouth hung open and no sound would come. He reached out and touched Lileo's exposed hand. The boy's fingers curled around his.

"He's alive!" Travest shouted. He was vaguely aware that other wagons were riding around the wreck, that many people were on the road, aware of what had befallen Lileo. Travest made eye contact with one of them, a broad-shouldered youth with long dark hair. "Help me, we've got to get him free."

"It is . . . God's will. . . ." the man said without meeting Travest's gaze. He kept walking.

Travest looked to another, then another, begging for help.

One by one, the travelers either ignored him or refused him.

These people were in some kind of fog, just as he had been! Somehow, he had to make them come to poor Lileo's aid.

Travest rose up and grabbed another man, this one around his age, but more firmly built. "God does not want my son to be taken from me. If he did, he wouldn't have allowed this accident to happen with so many people around who could help!"

The man detached Travest and shoved him back. "God's desires are for no man to interpret. I grieve for your loss. I will pray for your boy's soul."

"He's not dead!" Travest screamed. This was a nightmare. It couldn't be happening.

Finally, he returned to the wagon and tried lifting it, but his efforts were wasted. He tried to pull Lileo loose, but the boy was pinned.

Travest held his son's hand as he fell to his knees and yelled, "We are in Your shadow! Help us! Do not turn a blind eye, help us!"

A sudden brilliance shone upon the road.

Travest looked up to see three shining forms shaped vaguely like men floating just above the ground.

"Please," Travest said. "Help us."

The angels eased in Travest's direction. One formed a shape in its hand that resembled a sword. Travest suddenly felt afraid.

The soldiers of the Lord did not always look like this. Usually, they resembled men, albeit with a handful of glaring differences. For weeks the angels had been performing arcane rituals that had transformed them into fiery weavers of creation.

The sword wielder lashed out with his weapon and the overturned wagon exploded in a hailstorm of wood shards and scraps of expensive clothing. Miraculously, none of the onlookers were hurt by the flurry of jagged wooden shards, or by the steel needles and other tools of Travest's craft.

Travest was about to fall upon the body of his son when an overwhelming *presence* moved between him and the boy. One of the other heavenly creatures put out its arms. Lileo's broken body gently turned over and rose into the air. The boy sank into the waiting arms of the shining man.

"You can heal him," Travest said.

"Yes," replied the Being.

Travest waited. A terrible silence passed between him and the unearthly entity. "Please, heal him."

"Very well." The Being turned and began to drift away in the direction of the City of Heaven, bearing in his arms the child who had been Travest's life for ten years.

"Wait," Travest said, confused and all the more terrified.

The sword bearer turned to face Travest. The others continued on. Travest watched as the displaced people of Hampton parted for the shining men.

"We have agreed to do what you have asked. Consider yourself privileged."

"I have to go with him," Travest said.

The Being considered his words. Its features reconciled into those of a man. His smile contained a cruel mockery of pity. "No."

"What do you mean, *no?*" Travest said, realizing full well that with very little effort, this being could take not only his life, but his soul. "He's my son, I have to be with him."

"You may not follow." The entity turned and drifted in the direction of his brethren.

"You can't do this!" Travest screamed, running after the fiery embodiment of God's love and His fury.

The angel did not reply.

"Damn you, you can't do this!" Travest cried.

All three of the shining men stopped suddenly. The sword bearer gestured and said, "Go on."

Absolute horror descended upon Travest as the shining man raised his sword and flew in his direction.

What have I done? the tailor thought. *I can't help my son if I'm dead.*

The Being stopped directly before Travest. Its rage was evident. Its eyes were narrow slits, its mouth a darksome pit.

Travest fell to one knee before the arcane warrior.

"Choose your words carefully," the Entity said. "You would seek to damn me? You?"

"Lord, please, my son—"

"The power of those words is not in your frail little mortal form," the creature said, spitting out each word. The intensity of its flaming body rose with its anger. "If I damn you, you *will* be damned for all time. Do you know the true meaning of damnation? It is to have lost the caring eye of God. To no longer be recognized by the Almighty. To be exiled from the Kingdom of Heaven forever. I can do that to you, no matter what good you may have done in your life until this moment. Speak one more word to me, any word, and that will be your fate."

The auburn-haired tailor trembled. He could not speak.

"You may wait here, if you like. Perhaps word will come one day of your child. Perhaps. If the love you profess for the child is true, you will one day be reunited with him." The angel hesitated. "I wonder about the depth of your true feeling. To my eyes, your love is for yourself. It is your own needs you seek to fulfill."

Travest reached out imploringly to the sword bearer.

"If you have it within you to face this test of your love, then by all means do it. If you do not, then turn and never think on this boy again, never mention his name, and never speak of what you have seen here today. Your salvation—or your ruin—is in your own hands." He raised the sword. "So that you will never forget my words."

Travest raised his hand as the sword descended. Its flames were like ice. He felt them ripple across his hand and tear a gash across his breast and his other arm.

A pain unlike any Travest had ever imagined surged through him and he fell. He was unconscious before he struck the ground.

Night had fallen when Travest finally woke. He was still on the road. The only illumination was from the pale moon overhead.

He was alone.

Travest's first thoughts were of his son. The terrible scene with the avenging soldier of eternity entered his mind the same moment the pain of his wounds announced their presence. His stomach ached from hunger and he was freezing.

A rustling came from the forest off to his side. A voice

called out, "Does that hurt? It looks as if it would."

Travest spun and the effort brought him greater pain. He could see no one in the darkness. As the voice went on, its point of origin seemed to shift constantly. One moment it was on the left-hand side of the road, then the right. Directly before him. Whispering in his ear. Or twenty paces behind him.

"Foolish man. You dared interfere with the Grand Plan, didn't you?" The voice was low and deep, resonating with malice.

"My son, they took—"

"I know all about it. Others who crossed my path told me of the incident. After I convinced them."

"Who are you!?" Travest hollered. He looked down and saw a ragged scar across his chest. His clothing had been sliced apart.

"Your name is Travest Mulvihill. Do you know what your last name means in the Chronicles of Heaven?"

He did not.

"You are grandson of Maolmhichil. Servant of Saint Michael. A fine name, if a tad ironic under the circumstances."

"Show yourself."

"When you give me cause," said the unearthly voice. "For tonight, I will give you only one thing to think about. You may not enter the City of Heaven to bring back your son. I can and I will. Provided you first pledge to serve me in all things."

"You're a demon sent to tempt me."

"Or an angel sent to *test* you. I know. I assumed you would react this way. For that reason, our meeting tonight was by way of introduction, nothing more. I will come for you again tomorrow night. Think hard upon what I have said. The offer will be made three times, no more."

With that, the voice was silenced, leaving Travest alone in the darkness.

The next day, he tried to approach the City of Heaven. The exiled city dwellers who had swore to remain behind had all left. As he moved toward the shimmering wall, his thoughts became muddled. The next thing he knew, he was wandering around in the woods, several miles from the city that had been Hampton.

He tried all day long to enter the City of Heaven, coming at the city from many directions. Each attempt met with failure.

Keeping himself alive had been a simple matter. The trees closest to the City of Heaven bore strange fruit and many brooks lay nearby with fresh waters. He became used to the odd tastes of the purple-and-white-spotted fruits, the yellow-and-black spores, and even the plump bodies of the six-winged insects. Questioning where all these oddities had come from was beyond him. All he cared about was finding sustenance so that he could go on with his quest to retrieve his son from the heavenly creatures that had born him away.

In the sparkling waters he cleaned his wounds. They were ragged and they sparkled with the divine energies that had made them. That would fade in time, he hoped.

The odd voice returned just after nightfall. This time it was accompanied by a fleeting shape that seemed to change constantly, elongating, shrinking, growing appendages, rising to towering heights, or appearing small enough to perch on his shoulder.

Madness, utter madness.

"How are you feeling, Travest? A little frustrated, perhaps?" the voice asked.

"You are no servant of God."

"I was."

"Then you are one no more."

"It depends on how you define God, I suppose. And which God you mean."

Travest shook his head. "You are not one with the Host."

"I am what they made me!" the voice roared.

For several moments, Travest was convinced that he was alone. He loathed this creature, whatever it was, but he hated the idea of being alone even more.

There was a sudden chill and the voice returned. "This is your second opportunity. Serve me and I will go into the City of Heaven and bring back your son."

"They said they would tell me of him," Travest said. "That I will be reunited with him—"

"They *forget* their promises instants after they make them. I tell you this from experience. If the Being who took your son met you on the road even today he would ignore you. Unless you angered him. Then he would probably damn you. Or—wait, I forgot about your scar. Goodness, do you suppose He has damned you already? And that is why I have appeared to you?''

"Leave me."

"As you wish."

The shape did not return to Travest for five more days. At first, Travest had been grateful that the tempting voice of the darksome thing had not announced itself. Then the days went on and his solitude tore at him. Loneliness and despair overwhelmed him. The idea of never seeing his son again terrified him.

The shape came back.

"This is the last time I will make my offer," the voice said. This time, the voice was accompanied by a darksome figure, a walking shadow. "Serve me and I will retrieve your son."

On that final day, Travest had met several of the angels, and they had ignored his pleas, just as the shadow had predicted.

Though Travest had been prepared in his heart to accept the shadow's terms, he could not find voice for his desires. Instead, he heard himself falling into a child's prayer.

The shadow left him.

Two nights later, when Travest was on the brink of madness and despair, he fell to his knees and prayed for the shadow figure to appear.

"You said you would only offer three times. You said nothing of how many chances I would have to accept. Appear! Appear! I will do whatever you say!"

From the darkness came a cruel laughter.

The shadow appeared. "There is one I would have you find, a creature such as I was. A Being such as the one who took your boy."

"An angel?"

"Yes."

"I will tell you all about Him, and about what I want you to do when you find Him. He will be traveling alone."

"No entourage? No squires?"

"Alone. I have already seen to that."

"Yes, lord."

"By my estimation, he should now be arriving in a village named Hope. You will not go there. I have a good idea where he will be headed, and that is where I wish to send you."

"I will go. My boy—"

"We will discuss this after."

"After?"

The shadow laughed. "After you have killed Him for me, of course."

Travest nodded, his hand absently touching his scar, which no longer pulsed with the light of Heaven.

"Surely you can have no compunctions about such an act now. It is not only your kind they persecute, but their own. We are brothers of a sort. Bonded by hate."

Travest could feel the truth behind those words, and knew then that he was truly damned. . . .

One

TOM KEEPER WAS THE FIRST TO HEAR THE VISITOR'S APproach. He sat in his room by the open second story window, staring out at the clear night sky and the glowing crescent moon. This had been his mother's sewing room until the Scourge took her early last year. Half-sitting in his lap, half-hanging out the window, was a collection of posters anchored by a wooden board. The posters had been tacked up throughout the village, advertising the future arrival of a wondrous carnival, until he went out and tore them down in the middle of the night. Tom knew the carefully printed legends were not to be believed. The carnival promised dark thrills, chilling revelations, and miraculous cures. All it would really provide was a momentary distraction. For the people of Hope, his hometown, that would be enough.

The posters were only marred on one side. The other could be used for his one great love, sketching. Coal sticks were cheap, but paper was expensive. If thieving was the only way he could support his habit, Tom considered the violation a right and honorable thing. Provided he didn't get caught. So far, he had been lucky.

Tom had captured the night sky on the back of the poster, exaggerating the size of the crescent moon so that he could etch his mother's bemused profile into its confines. After she died, Papa said she was still with them, watching over all she had been forced to leave behind.

Papa had warned Tom many times to be discreet with his art. The man's words came to Tom: *If They see that you're special, if They see that you're different in any way, They will take you from me. After losing your mother, I couldn't bear that.*

Tom sometimes wondered what his life might have been like in the days before the angels had come. Tom had studied the past—as much as he could, considering he had been taught to read in secret and books were scarce—and he was convinced that in an earlier time, his desire to draw would not have brought undue attention to his family. In any case, he didn't want to become an "artist"; he simply wanted to create art. In his mind, there was a difference. *Artists* were trained by the angels in special schools. They were given rules to follow, commissions to complete. Only a handful of artists had ever been allowed to leave that highly regimented lifestyle behind and walk the earth, painting what they pleased. Roger Hughes was such an artist.

Conflicting stories abounded regarding how Hughes had earned his *leisure*. The Prostinks, as everyone referred to members of the Protestant Liberation Front, had even written an underground play on the subject. All Tom knew was that he loved to draw. It gave him a release from the hard work of the day.

Hope was on the direct supply route between two major cities in the New World Territories—Visitation and Deliverance. Seventy years ago, Hope had been a rest stop for travelers. The purpose of Hope had not changed when it grew into a thriving township of twenty-two hundred people. If anything, the nearness of the natural splendor of the Blue Ridge Mountains and the settlements of the Naturals, as they preferred to be called rather than the misnomer Indians, had drawn both the curious and the hardworking. Pilgrims—or *tourists* as they were sometimes called—kept his father's inn full at all times. That left Tom, his older brother Gus, and his sister Kat, with more than their share of work.

Tom yawned and looked down at his drawing. He wondered if he was being foolish. After all, the purpose of art, of any form of creation, was the sharing of visions and ideas. Tom could not keep a collection of his work. Night after night he would stay up late sketching, then he would feed his work to the fire. Keeping the drawings around where someone might find them was far too risky. The unmarred posters were another matter entirely. He could easily say he objected to the carnival on grounds of faith and he had taken the posters to keep innocents from falling prey to the lewd temptations of the entertainers. If he was asked why he didn't just burn them, he would respond that he was told not to in a dream by a shining man who breathed fire and rose into the air on shimmering heavenly wings.

He had it all worked out.

Tonight, Tom made four drawings. He felt strangely driven to defy the quota he had placed on himself—one poster per night so that we would not go through his supply too quickly.

A sound came from outside: The whinny of a horse that startled him. The posters and the wooden board he leaned on flew out the window as Tom jumped back in his seat. Panic gripped him. Clutching the windowsill, he leaned out and saw the last of the stolen sheets gently touching the ground.

The man below was dressed in black, his clothing made of leather and steel, stylish, expensive. Red jewels glittered on the hilt of a broadsword belted around his waist, and a half dozen rings adorned his long, thin, pale hands. He was strongly built and wore his raven hair in a ponytail.

Tom gasped as the man looked up and revealed himself not to be a man at all; He was one of *them*.

An angel.

Tom recalled the Teachings. When an angel was cloaked in mortal flesh, it was not a sin to think of Him as a man.

Even so, this man's features were chiseled and more beautiful than any man's had a right to be. His flesh seemed to shine with only the barest illumination. His brows were arched, his thin white lips pulled back in a smile. All these attributes could have belonged to a human, but the angel's blazing crimson eyes and slightly pointed ears gave him away.

There was another name for the angels. One that was never spoken to their face:

The Elven.

It seemed that some races had myths of ashen-faced beings like the angels. They were called Faerie Folk. Magical beings.

The angels explained that they had walked among men in many ages, but they had never announced their true natures, or their divine purposes. At the time, myths and legends about them were encouraged. It had been too soon for the truth.

Tom considered calling to the angel, but he didn't know what to say. Instead, he watched in growing horror as the Being dismounted and gathered up the drawings with a bemused smile. The angel looked up sharply as sound came from the inner door to the Keeper House. The weather had changed and the door was swelling, making it difficult to push open. The angel shoved the posters into a small space beneath the porch then rose and backed away.

Katherine Keeper emerged from the doorway with her father, Saul. She was blonde, willowy; her father, barrel-chested and wild-haired. Both fell to their knees immediately.

"God is merciful, God is good," Saul Keeper said. "He has granted our prayers and delivered unto us the glory of His messenger to honor us with His presence—"

"Please," the angel said. "The Recitation is not necessary. I'm very tired."

Kat and Saul exchanged worried glances. Somehow they had tried the patience of this superior being. Saul looked up imploringly. "Lord, if there is a penance I may perform—"

"No," the angel said quickly, "forgive *me*. Your efforts do nothing to offend. Quite the opposite. I'm—what's the phrase you people use? 'Dead on my feet.'"

Tom couldn't believe he had heard the angel correctly. This was a Principality, a warrior of the Almighty, and he was *apologizing* to mere *humans?*

The angel gestured. Saul and Kat stood.

"Whatever you need," Saul said, "ask it. It will be done. Your entourage—"

"I'm alone." The angel's brow furrowed. "I sense an emptiness in this house. A void. A great sadness."

"My wife," Saul said in a low, halting voice. "The Scourge—"

The angel raised his hand to keep the grieved man from reliving any more of his loss. Looking away, the shining man glanced down the main stretch of road that bisected the village, taking in the sorry array of shops and falling-apart houses. Many had been damaged in the last great storm. At least Hope hadn't been hit the way the neighboring Charity had been. A hundred people had died in Charity, and the village was now little more than wreckage to be picked over by the survivors.

"Your wife is with God," the angel said. "She is in a better place."

"Yes."

Kat leaned forward, shifting her attention toward the street that had arrested the angel's gaze. "It's not usually like this. The Beautification Committee is working hard to restore Main Street. There were so many lost in Charity that we've had to spend all our time helping them before we could worry about fixing up around here. I hope the sight is not too unpleasant."

"No," the angel said. "Why would it be?"

Saul averted his own gaze in shame. "The Curacas has shown his displeasure in how long the repairs have taken. He refused to grant a union between my daughter and her betrothed. The young man was sent away to work his Mita as a soldier against the heathen Goths."

The angel nodded. The Mita was a mandatory service that all able-bodied young men had to perform when they reached a certain age. Five years in the direct service of their Lord, either as a soldier, a road-builder—whatever was necessary.

"I prayed for him to remain with us," Kat said.

"I know," the angel replied softly. "God answers all prayers; sometimes, the answer is 'no.'"

"On to happier things," Saul said brightly. "I will make ready a room. It will take only a few moments. My daughter Kat will keep you company as you wait. My son Gus will tend to your mount. If that is acceptable, lord . . . ?"

From his vantage two stories above, Tom frowned. He knew what his father planned. The Keeper House was full. Tom would have to give up his room for one of the guests and sleep on the floor in Gus's quarters. Then the finest room in the house would be made available to the angel. Free of charge, naturally.

Tom looked over to the collection of posters peeking out from under his bed. He would have to burn the other posters so they were not discovered. Though he had a reasonable story to tell regarding why he had taken the posters and hoarded them, the presence of the angel changed everything. The newcomer could look into his heart and know the boy was lying— or so Tom had been taught. Great shame would fall upon his family if Tom was branded a sinner by one of God's chosen. He was not so selfish that he would put his own needs before the happiness of his loved ones.

Even so—the angel *had* hidden Tom's other drawings. What possible reason would he have for helping the lad conceal his talents?

A reasonable explanation came to Tom. The angel said it himself: He was tired. The shining man had no wish to deal with all the complications that would come about if it became known that a mortal was hiding talents that might further the angel's cause. The Crusade of Understanding was still under way in many parts of the world. God's Chosen Warriors had caused humankind to see that all the world's religions were flawed variations of the One True Faith. Those who resisted the solemn word of God had to be purified. It was hard, but necessary. The Thirty Years War had ended the worst of the resistance, but Heretics were always springing up in some part of the world.

Tom had the honor to live in the 333rd year of the Millennium—the Thousand Year Reign of God's Army. During these trying times, the wicked were being weeded out and one day only the righteous would remain. Those who refused to bow to that one simple truth had only themselves to blame when they fell before the might of the angels.

Turning from the window, he set about the unpleasant task. Worried that he might be spotted with the posters in his hands, Tom wrapped the posters in an old cloth that had to be thrown out anyway. He left his room and trudged to the fireplace at the end of the hall. With a heavy sigh, he tossed the posters onto the flames. Fortunately, none of their guests had yet woken to learn of the angel's visit. Sounds came from the foot of the stairs. Heavy boots, thundering his way.

Father was coming! Tom shifted his gaze to the fire. The cloth had fallen away. The posters were exposed. Their edges were curled, blackened, but the pictures of the carnival were in plain sight. The posters bore no writing. Most who would attend would have felt put off by anything other than pictures.

Tom watched the fires licking at the papers. *Burn faster*, he thought. Father's heavy footfalls were growing louder. He scanned the fireplace, found the poker, and stabbed at the post-

ers. Two fell into the back, out of his grasp unless he wanted
to risk getting burned.

The moan of a warped board told Tom that his father was
only three steps from the landing. The man would reach the
landing, turn, and see Tom only a few feet away, looking
guilty and panicked before the fire. There was no time left.

Suddenly, the fireplace roared and a brilliant flash of white
light exploded outward. For an instant, Tom thought he saw
odd shapes in the light. Runes. Laughing faces.

Dropping the poker, Tom shielded his eyes. He felt a sudden
wave of heat that quickly ebbed.

"Tom?" a low voice called. "What are you doing there by
the fire?"

The boy turned to see his father. Saul Keeper stared at him
strangely and rushed forward.

"What was that light I saw?" Saul asked.

Tom looked back to the fireplace. All remnants of the posters had been consumed by the flames.

"I—um—dropped a rag into the fire. It was a little damp.
Maybe it had lamp oil on it. I'm not sure."

Saul reached out and fussed with his son's hair. "Be careful. I wouldn't want to see those good looks I was kind enough
to pass along to you ruined by the flames. It's easy to have
an accident. I know."

Tom smiled and nodded. Unaware that Tom had seen the
stranger's arrival, Saul told his son of the angel's plans to visit.
The preparations were detailed and Tom went to work.

Ten minutes later, when the confusion had died down, Tom
returned to the fire. He had not been truthful with his father.
If the angel discovered him in the lie, the ruination Tom feared
might still come to pass.

And yet . . .

That fire had hardly been of natural origins. There had been
no lamp oil on the rag he discarded. True, someone else could
have tossed something strange on the fire moments earlier, but
that seemed highly unlikely. Even if it were true, it didn't
explain the bizarre shapes he had seen in the flames.

No, a voice within him whispered, *you have your already
overactive imagination for that.*

Tom was still before the flames, this time ready to greet the angel with his older brother Gus, when Saul and Kat led the warrior up the stairs and to the landing. The angel stopped for a moment, fixing his gaze first on Tom, then the fire. With a brief wink, the angel turned and walked away.

Tom watched him go.

Stunned.

Two

THE ANGEL STAYED AT THE KEEPER HOUSE FOR NEARLY a week. He refused an audience with Ben Turpin, the local Curacas, casting in doubt the man's firm belief that he would be Hope's chief administrator for the rest of his life. Several people approached Saul Keeper, most calling in favors that had been owed for years, desperate for a chance to plead with the angel to speak with God on their behalf. Saul turned them all away. He knew his boarder was in no mood to deal with such foolishness. The Church had been clear on the matter of culling favors with God's soldiers: *Ask not.*

Two simple words. In theory, commoners understood this command and swore to all they would practice it. But when faced with the overwhelming presence of an angel, they often forgot their vows and acted foolishly.

The Visitor, as he had come to be known due to his reticence to give his name, was hardly the first of his kind to arrive in Hope. A handful of angels had made brief visits over the years, leaving their cloistered Cities of Heaven to walk among men. This one was different. Unlike other angels, he kept to himself, taking meals in his room, sending for supplies with more than ample amounts of gold. Tom was sent to procure the paper, quills, and ink the angel demanded. One day, his father was too busy dealing with a drunkard in their taproom to deliver a meal to the angel on time. He sent Tom instead.

The boy went to the angel's room. People were gathered outside it. Many hoped to glimpse the angel. Tom sent them away before he would even knock on the door.

Inside, Tom set the tray on a small table. The angel sat at a desk that had been hauled into the room for his use. Sheets of paper by the dozens were piled up around him. All bore his florid script. Tom did not try to read any of them, though he was sorely tempted.

Few people in Hope knew how to read. It was a skill mostly reserved for those in the holy orders and the scribes. Mother had wanted Tom to become a scribe, an honored profession in their society, and he had briefly attended a university in Visitation. But the boy had been tossed out of the school for daydreaming. He had learned something about reading, and a friend who had not left the calling taught him the rest. Even so, his knowledge meant nothing without the proper accreditation. Tom hid his knowledge as best he could. People were made nervous when those who were not scribes or holy men possessed the skill. It was sometimes thought to be the work of the Enemy.

Tom changed out the angel's chamber pot, recalling the words of his sister, who had been charged with that task twice already during the angel's stay.

"Heavenly?" she had said. "The stench is heavenly! They might be one with God, but their *you know what* still stinks."

Tom understood that the angels had to take mortal vessels to move among mankind. Even so, these heavenly creatures could never be confused with a normal man. Tom had been taught that they wielded forces beyond imagination, and that transgressions performed against their persons brought punishment not only upon the guilty party, but also their family, friends, and even strangers. They could cleave the soul from a man and force it to do their bidding. Or they could unite loved ones who stood on either side of the veil. Ultimately, there was only one truism about the angels: Their motives and their desires, even after three centuries, still seemed alien to most people.

Trust in God, the people were told. Trust in the Great Plan.

Tom was about to leave the room when he found he could not depart without saying anything. He was now firmly convinced that the angel had made the fire blaze, destroying the posters that might have gotten Tom in trouble with his father. The boy had gone to the small space under the porch in search of the drawings the angel had hidden. The sketches had vanished. Tom guessed that the angel had disposed of them.

Realizing he might never have another chance like this, Tom whispered, "Thank you."

The angel set down his quill. His crimson eyes seemed less frightening in broad daylight. "Aitan Anzelm. Tell them."

Fear surged within the boy. "Tell them what?"

"Tell them I chose *you* to reveal my name to the people. That I chose *you* to carry my words to them. Tell them."

"Just your name?"

"It will be enough."

Tom nodded. His heart thundered and his hands shook.

"You'd best take that out of here before you drop it," the angel said, nodding toward the picked-clean plates and the heavy chamber pot Tom carried.

The boy did as he was told.

For the rest of the day, Tom was brimming with excitement. He passed along the angel's words to his father, his brother and sister, his friends, the many travelers staying with them, and all their neighbors. For the first time in so long he felt important. Special. No one had truly voiced their disappointment with him when he had been returned from Scribe's Academy, but the air of expectation was gone. His potential as a person of worth had vanished. The cheeriness and pride with which he had been regarded by so many had departed along with it. The next day, Tom's father approached and said, "Lord Anzelm has requested that you bring his evening meal."

"Really?" Tom asked, suddenly quite afraid.

"You should be happy. It's an honor."

"Oh yes, I know."

Saul smiled. "You know that Gus will be leaving soon to perform his Mita."

Tom nodded.

"This bond you're forming with Lord Anzelm has the people of Hope very excited. You will be my right hand in running Keeper House when Gus is away. Now there will be no question that the people will accept you. Did you see the way Dina, that little curly-haired serving wench, was giving you the eye?"

"Father!"

Saul laughed. "It's true."

"She's older than Kat."

"Yes. All of seventeen, perhaps. But I'll tell you this: Experience counts for a lot in this world."

Tom felt his cheeks flush. He knew it was sinful, but he thought about sex all the time. Mostly, he dreamed about Dina.

His father had an uncanny talent for seeing right into the thoughts of his lastborn, just like an angel. Tom wanted to ask his father if the man was sure he didn't have angel's blood in him from somewhere along the line, but he wasn't sure how the man would take such a remark. Everyone knew angel and humans could not procreate.

"Go on," Saul said, hugging his son. "I know you have work."

Tom busied himself.

As the day went on, Tom found himself becoming increasingly nervous. His excitement and anticipation at the thought of seeing the angel once more had turned to fear. All manner of odd, paranoid scenarios occurred to him during the day.

Had the angel been testing him? *Go on, tell everyone that you have been chosen to reveal my name. Then I'll sit back and wait to see if you commit the sin of pride.*

If that were the case, Tom had no defense.

Worst of all of Tom's imaginings was the possibility that this time, Aitan Anzelm would say nothing to him at all.

The moment finally came. Evening had fallen. Tom was in Lord Anzelm's room, the serving tray in his hand.

"Set it down," the angel said. "Come in."

Tom could discern nothing from the angel's tone. The man gestured toward a seat next to the bed and commanded Tom to sit. Tom waited as Lord Anzelm rummaged through his growing mound of papers. The angel stopped suddenly and looked sharply over his shoulder.

"Tomorrow, I need you to get me something to bind all these sheets. You can manage that, can't you?"

"Of course," Tom said, relieved that his voice hadn't broken. He was so tense he had found locating his voice very difficult. "Yes."

With a sharp nod, the angel went to his papers and pulled

out a handful of posters for the Carnival of Wonders.

Tom's heart felt fit to burst at the sight of what must surely be his drawings. The angel set the posters down on the bed without turning them over to reveal Tom's sketchings.

Odd, Tom thought. There were five posters. He had only made four drawings.

"I've reviewed your work," Aitan said.

"My—"

"The drawings. Your art."

The boy had to fight off an urge to tremble.

"Do you want me to tell you what I think of them?" the angel asked softly. "Or do you think you would rather snap both your own ankles first?"

Tom looked down suddenly to see that he had channeled his tension down to his feet in an attempt to look more relaxed up above. He had one foot crossed behind and around the other. His feet were straining at each other, looking as if they were trying to wrestle. With great effort, Tom pulled his feet apart and forced his legs to relax.

"Now your back," the angel said with a grin.

Tom was sitting at a painful angle, his back nowhere near the chair. He had seen a hunting dog lean forward like this once. Settling back into the chair, he mumbled an apology.

"Perfectly acceptable. After all, I have just laid your future before you. A little nervousness is to be expected."

Tom looked at the posters in confusion.

"One of these posters does not bear an original Tom Keeper on its reverse side. I want you to tell me which one that is."

"Excuse me?" Tom asked. "Lord Anzelm, I—"

The angel shook his head. "Unacceptable. In here, my name is Aitan."

Tom swallowed hard. "This is what I have to do before you'll tell me what you thought of my drawings?"

"No. I'll tell you *that* right now. I think your work is very good. And I know something about art."

"Ah," Tom said in a tiny whisper.

"You have great heart, great potential. But no technical training. You are all style, with no skill. There are ways to fix that, of course."

Oh, God, Tom thought. He had been a fool not to see this possibility before.

The angel wanted to see him delivered to an Academy of the Arts. There, Tom would learn the *accepted way* of painting a portrait, the *prescribed method* of the First Church of Rome's artistic masters in representing Divinities, the rigid, proper, and *horribly dull practice* of learning by copying others rather than developing a style of one's own.

"You look as if you're about to lose your dinner and your lunch," Aitan said. "If that is the case, you know where to find the pot. I don't like messes when they can be avoided."

Tom glanced over at Aitan's dinner. "That'll get cold."

"I'll warm it," the angel said. "Like I did the fireplace the other night."

"Do *that* and there won't be anything left to eat," Tom muttered.

"I can show restraint," Aitan said soothingly. "Now, are you certain you're up to this? It can wait, if you'd like."

Tom crossed his arms over his chest. "Why do you want me to do this? What did you mean about my future?"

"You would deny the request of one who has achieved my station?" Aitan asked in a low, quiet voice.

The fear rippling through Tom became that much greater. "No, I'm sorry, Lord—"

"Aitan."

"Yes. Aitan." Tom realized he was sweating. "I was drummed out of one academy already. The shame my family would face if that happened again—"

"This isn't about your family; this is about you. This is about what *you* want."

Tom felt twinges in his cheeks. A nervous laugh threatened to escape. "I—I don't know what I want."

"Yes, you do. You have a fire in your eyes that will one day run its course if it is given nothing to feed it. I know. I saw that fire in my own eyes, once. Just to be clear, I have no intention of relegating you to one of those boorish academies."

"You don't?"

"No."

"Then what do you want?" Tom asked.

Aitan smiled. "Now you're feeling bold."

Tom dropped to the floor on his knees, clasping his hands before him and dropping his gaze down to the floor. "Lord Anzelm, I beg you please do not chastise me for my impertinence."

Aitan sighed. "Are you quite finished?"

Tom looked up. Embarrassed, he dragged himself off his knees.

"There is no reason for you to be afraid of me," Aitan said. "I have something I wish to offer you. Before I do, I need to see that my instincts about you are correct. I need for you to see that, too."

Tom sat down. He looked at the posters. "All I have to tell you is which ones I drew?"

"Yes. Without coming any closer to them."

"Then you're going to offer me something?"

"Yes."

"What if I don't want it?"

Aitan shrugged. "You're a free man, you may do as you like."

Tom raised a single eyebrow. No one had ever called him a *man* before. "All right."

Leaning forward, Tom thought, *This should be fairly easy. I lean in hard when I use a pencil. I should be able to see patterns even from the opposite side of the one I drew on.*

"No," Aitan said. "Close your eyes."

Tom looked up at the man, regarding him strangely. "Then how can I tell?"

"You'll know."

Tom shook his head. "What you're talking about is luck. Like when Janne Bridges and I used to play Snakes and Ladders. I mean, Moksha-Patamu." The Indian named sometimes escaped him.

"More than that," Aitan said. "But if you're not interested, I can always find someone else."

"I'll do it." Tom squeezed his eyes shut. "Can I touch them?"

"Only to indicate which drawing you wish to select."

Exasperated, Tom reached out with his hand. He thought about each of the four drawings. One had been a silly sketch of a dopey-looking boy being chased by his own shadow.

His hand fell on a poster.

"Eyes shut," Aitan said sternly.

The poster was removed.

He thought of the other drawings. Two had been of Dina. In one, she was half hiding behind a large solid column, one hand reaching up and touching the top, the other gently resting on its center. She wore a loose-fitting gown and grinned wickedly.

Oh, no. There's nothing suggestive about that, he thought, slightly embarrassed.

His hand touched a poster. Aitan took it away. He kept his eyes squeezed shut. The other drawing of Dina had merely been of her face. She was smiling in her usual playful manner.

Again, he touched the poster. Again, it was removed.

There were only two left. Tom considered giving up right then and there. He had probably selected wrong by now, even though the odds were with him.

What was it Aitan had said? That it was about more than luck?

Tom thought of the last drawing. It was the image he had been working on when Aitan had arrived. The drawing of his mother, framed in the half-moon.

He had loved her so much. If only he had said it more.

His hand sagged, just a little.

He felt something. . . .

Tom gasped and yanked his hand away. He spun out of the chair, turning toward the wall. Terrified.

For a fleeting instant he was certain he had touched something other than a piece of paper. His fingers had brushed against the smooth, soft flesh of his mother's face. She had reached up and touched his hand.

"No," Tom said, shuddering. Days had passed when he had sworn that he would kill to feel his mother's hand on his once more. Her death from the Scourge had been agonizing. She had screamed for days. Blood had sweated from her pores.

Tom heard a noise. Aitan Anzelm was behind him. The angel placed one hand on the boy's shoulder and said, "Look."

Slowly, Tom turned. On the bed, all four of his drawings

were laid out in exactly the order he had thought of them.

"Now," Aitan said. "What are the odds of that?"

Tom was speechless.

"Now sit down," Aitan said, "and *listen* while I make my offer. . . ."

Three

"SO YOU'LL BE LEAVING US," SAUL KEEPER SAID TO his son.

Tom didn't know what to say. It was only an hour since he had taken Aitan Anzelm's dinner to the man's room. So much had happened since then. He now stood in the kitchen with his father. The cook and the other servants had been dismissed. All that remained of their chores was cleanup and preparations for the morning.

"I don't know," Tom said. "I wanted to talk to you about it first."

"Before you come to any decision, you mean."

"Yes."

A weary smiled crossed Saul's face. "I think you've made your decision. I think you're here to say good-bye."

Tom's hands hung limply at his sides. His entire body seemed to droop. Wide-eyed and miserable, he tried to think of something to say and failed.

Saul shrugged as he placed several pots in a large vat to soak. "It's not every fourteen-year-old who gets a chance to become a squire in God's Army. Especially with no formal training. And at your age."

"Papa—"

"I had *thought* you wanted to stay here." There was no bitterness in the man's voice, only mild surprise.

"I don't know," Tom said, hating the whine in his voice.

"I think you do. I think it's just a matter of saying it."

Tom tried. He could not find the words.

His father cleared off a cutting board that had been used for onions, tomatoes, green peppers, and carrots. Seeds from the peppers and cores from each of the vegetables had clung to it.

"I like to cook," Saul said. "I miss doing it for myself."

"I know. The running of this place keeps you pretty busy."

Saul sniffed the air and twisted his face up in disgust. "Can you smell the ginger?"

Tom nodded.

"When I was your age I loved ginger. Gingerbread, ginger cookies, ginger tea. It was in the days just after the embargo was lifted and spices flowed freely. I swear, boy, my day was not complete unless the rich odor of ginger had found its way into my lungs in one form or another."

Tom smiled.

"Nowadays, everyone's cooking with ginger." He sighed. "I'm not saying there's anything wrong with it, but it's no longer to my taste. And here I am, in a kitchen reeking of ginger."

The fourteen-year-old stared at his father expectantly.

"I suppose that should lead to something profound and wonderful," Saul said. "Something quite fatherly."

Tom stroked his father's back. Hugged him. "No, Papa."

Saul eased away from his son and busied himself with a collection of knives waiting to be cleaned. "If you go, you'll be missed. I can't tell you if you should go or not. That's up to you."

"I just want you to know why I'm saying 'yes.'"

Saul wiped the sweat off his forehead. He left a trail of soapy water in its place. "You have no other choice. One doesn't refuse an offer made by a Principality."

"I would," Tom said. "You know me well enough. I'm an ornery, stubborn little cuss. That's how you raised me."

"Ah, yes. I thought there was something familiar about you."

"It's my art."

Saul squeezed his eyes shut and pressed his lips together. "Your art."

"My drawings. I—I know you asked me to stop, but I couldn't."

"I knew that. We all did. Posters missing from the street.

'Lost' menus. That stack of scrolls that just happened to vanish from the office of the Curacas.''

"They were going to be burned anyway! They were seditious.''

"Did you read any of them?''

"A few—'' Tom caught himself. "You knew about that, too? That I could *read?*''

"I overheard you practicing one night, years ago. You liked to read aloud. I envied you. The Church says that the word of God is for holy men and scribes. No others. Frankly, I would enjoy hearing His words verbatim now and again. Not filtered through the narrow minds of our local clerics.''

"But if you've never read the Holy Word—''

Saul put down the collection of knives and met his son's gaze. "I'm not a young man. I have been to many places. Over the course of my life I have heard the same verses spoken a hundred different ways depending on the views of the reader. It doesn't take a great scholar to know that God's word has not reached us as it was meant to.''

"You sound like a Prostink!'' Tom said with a laugh. Then his smile faded. "Are you telling me you're a Prostink? *You?*''

"I know people. And it's Protestant, just so you know.''

Tom shook his head in amazement.

"Let's get back to what's really important. When do you and Lord Anzelm ride?''

"Tomorrow morning.''

Saul gestured toward a pair of stools. When they were seated, he said, "Tom, I've never lied to you—''

"In one breath you're telling me you're a Sympathizer and in the next you expect me to believe you've never lied?'' Tom asked. He looked deeply into his father's eyes and expected to see anger. Instead, there was only a touch of sadness.

"I may have hidden some truths from you. Its not the same. Now about this matter of you attending another academy. . . .''

"It's not going to be like that. Lord Anzelm wants me at his side. He's going to tutor me privately.''

"Is he? Does he have permission of the Host for such a course of action?''

Tom shrugged. That hadn't occurred to him. *"I'm* not going to ask him.''

"No, of course. I'm being foolish. I just worry about you."

Tom said, "Word might come of me one day. And—I didn't want it to be a complete shock to you, that's all."

"Word that you're now a famous artist? You're *that* confident in your future?"

"No," Tom said. "I have no idea what Lord Anzelm sees in me."

"I do," his father said. "What I've always seen in you. Loyalty. Trust."

"What worries me is Gus. He's going away, you'll be left with just Kat."

"Just Kat? Oh, I'll be sure to tell your sister this is how you think of her. An incapable woman."

"I didn't mean it that way."

"Besides, with her beloved gone for five years, Kat will be thrilled at having a larger interest in Keeper House. She wants her time to be occupied. Everything will be fine. You worry too much."

"What about Curacas Turpin? He could make life difficult for you."

Saul grinned. "While my son is squired to a soldier in God's Army? Think about what you're saying." The older man's mood darkened abruptly. "There is one thing we should talk about. You've never traveled far from Hope. You don't know what the world can be like. The avatar of the Almighty, Lord Anzelm, he's mortal. Flesh, like us." Saul grabbed his son's arm and gave it a light squeeze to illustrate his point.

"I know my life may be in danger if I ride at this man's side," Tom said. "I also know I'm never going to find what I need if I stay here."

Saul patted his son's arm. "You're probably right. I've worried about it myself. Though you and Dina have barely exchanged a dozen words, I can already see where it's going."

"You can?" Tom said, sitting up a bit straighter.

"Oh, yes. A playful flirtation to begin with. Then before you know it the two of you will be naked and sweating and you'll be thinking that you've got her right where you want her—but the truth will be just the opposite. Before long, she'll be with child, and you will be trapped."

Tom's eyes were starting to glaze over at the possibility of a tryst with Dina. Not that he would have any idea what to do, but he had a feeling she would guide him. Then the full import of his father's words struck him. "Are you saying that's how it was with you and Mother?"

"No. I was spared that by the Mita. By the time I returned, the woman I had left with child had gone with another."

"Left with child?" Tom cried. Saul shrugged. The fourteen-year-old felt his excitement at the prospect of an engagement with Dina a little less enticing now. "I have a half brother?"

"Or sister."

"When were you going to tell me?"

"Never. What business is it of yours?"

"I—" Tom stopped. The man had a point. "Gus? Kat? Do they know?"

"No. But I told your mother."

"And she married you anyway?"

"Tom," Saul Keeper said in a low, forceful tone.

"I'm sorry, it's just a lot more than I really wanted to know."

"That's the way of things sometimes. Now go upstairs and start readying yourself. You have a lot to do before morning. . . ."

That night, Tom paused before Dina's door. It was slightly ajar.

If he had heard even a single noise from within, he would have lost his resolve and forgotten the pledge he had made to himself to leave Hope free and clear.

No sound came.

Tom stood there a long time, until the door was finally pushed shut from within.

Four

THE ENORMITY OF THE DECISION TOM KEEPER HAD MADE only became clear to him the next morning, when he was several hours' ride outside Hope. The travelers passed willowy trees carrying bushels of green and yellow leaves. To one side of the road a grey stone wall of mountains rose up to great heights; on the other was a brown field with patches of grass that led to a sharp drop into a valley. A series of lush rolling green hills were in evidence on the horizon, reaching back and becoming blue-grey, seemingly immaterial as they leisurely stretched toward the horizon.

It was fall and there was a soft breeze. The sun was hot, but not unbearable. Tom rode a mount the angel had purchased for him, a fiery-tempered stallion that had only recently been broken.

Leaving Hope had been easier than Tom had expected it to be. He had few belongings and packing them had been the work of a half hour. His father had spoken with Kat and Gus. Kat had been a little tearful, but she could see this was what Tom really wanted and so she had been happy for him. Dina had stayed in her room, claiming to be too ill to see him off.

Aitan spent a little over an hour with the townspeople of Hope, listening to their problems, nodding and saying, "God will answer you in His time."

Then they were gone, easy as that. Only—nothing was that easy. Tom might have only been fourteen, but he was old enough to know that much about life. He made the decision to ride with the angel based on a moment of wonder and mystery. Had the angel guided his hand when he was picking out the posters bearing his artwork? Or had another force been at work?

Tom had been told by Cleric Tsuemeon, a fiery-skinned man recently arrived from some southern state in Aztica called Meheeco, or something along those lines, that "Believers in chance worship at a sacrilegious alter. There is a plan and a purpose to all that occurs. Putting yourself above God's great unseen design is vanity and sin."

If Tom was to subscribe to that line of reasoning, then embracing the notion that he had selected the posters in exactly the right order by chance would be wrong. Minor miracles of this sort were often attributed to the subtle workings of the angels, or to some basic element of faith. Tom had believed that he had witnessed a showing of the latter, but now he was not so certain.

"You seem lost in thought," Aitan Anzelm said.

Tom looked sharply to the left. A moment ago, the angel rode several yards ahead. Now he was at Tom's side.

"Forgive me, lord."

"My name is Aitan. Remember?"

Tom nodded uncomfortably.

"What's wrong?" Aitan asked.

"May I speak freely?"

"Yes. Always, when we are alone."

"It just seems disrespectful to call you anything except 'lord.' That's how I was brought up."

Aitan sighed. "I understand. A man reaches a certain age and it becomes difficult to do away with preconceived ideas. If it is that much trouble to abide my wishes—"

"No," Tom said. He shrugged. "I had no problem with it last night. But last night, everything seemed different. Unreal. Like I was in a dream or something."

"Are you nervous about traveling so far from your home?" Aitan asked.

"I don't know. How far are we going?" Tom blanched. "If I'm not being too forward. I don't wish to offend—"

Aitan reached and placed a comforting hand on Tom's shoulder. He squeezed gently, then let go and said, "You worry too much!"

"Sorry."

"And you apologize far too often."

Tom downturned his gaze.

They rode past several turns in silence. Aitan suddenly gathered up his reins and said, "Hold."

Both horses came to a graceful halt. Tom looked down at his mount, wondering how much he really had to do with guiding the animal.

"The rocks are about to fall just ahead," Aitan said.

Before Tom could speak, he heard a rumbling, then saw several grey boulders tumble loose from the wall on their right. They crashed down to the road just ahead of the travelers and rolled until they were lying in the field off to the left.

"All right, then," Aitan said, coaxing his horse forward. Tom followed, stroking the mane of his stallion. He didn't bother to ask how Aitan knew when the danger would arrive, or when it might pass. God was in all things, and the angels were attuned to His ways.

"Now," Aitan said. "How far have you traveled from your home in the past?"

Tom wanted to give some impressive answer. He was beginning truly to like Aitan Anzelm and he wanted the man to think highly of him, too. But lying to a Principality was a great sin, much worse than deceiving one's fellow man, and so Tom told the truth. "Not far. I've been to Pautock twice, Deliverance a few times. Went to school in Visitation for a while. Papa took all of us to the Chimú settlement on the other side of the divide once. We saw them sitting this dead guy up and putting him in a mummy bundle. I thought it would have been creepy, but it was just kind of interesting."

"Yes, I know that settlement. The Chimú were brought here from the south to help with irrigation. Very good farmers. They love cats."

"My sister loves cats. If it was up to her, Keeper House would be Kat-House." Tom waited. No more than a soft, pleasant smile broke on the otherworldly chiseled features of his companion. Well, it wasn't much of a joke, what could he expect?

"We'll be traveling far. Perhaps taking some less traveled roads." Aitan shifted his gaze back to Tom. "You'll be safe. You have my word."

"I wasn't worried," Tom said honestly, though he wondered if he should have been.

"You still haven't told me what's troubling you," Aitan said.

Tom wondered how much he should reveal to the angel. Papa said there was a big difference between lying and not telling the entire truth. Still, he was now in the presence of a creature who had stood in the company of the Host, who had perhaps seen the true face of God.

"You're probably wondering what duties will be expected of you as my squire. Is that right?" Aitan asked.

That was part of it, Tom thought. He also wondered why Aitan had arrived in Hope with no squire, no entourage. Had something happened to his former vassals, or had this particular angel simply preferred to travel alone? And if that was the case, why had Aitan suddenly decided he wanted a companion?

Tom nodded. It was the safest thing, until he knew more about what kind of Being he was with. Tom's instincts told him that Aitan could be trusted, that he was good and kind. Nevertheless, Tom had learned over the years not to rely solely on his instincts. Common sense had to enter the equation sooner or later.

"For now, I will expect no more of you than the duties I've seen you perform at Keeper House. Grooming and watering our horses. Seeing that they're fed and well rested. Helping to prepare our meals. Have you ever handled weapons?"

Tom said, "Hardly ever seen them."

"I carry a broadsword, as I'm sure you've noticed, and a collection of weaponry. I will show you how to clean and sharpen each article properly. Eventually, you will be charged with maintaining my armor and helping me into it. I can do it alone, but it's easier when one has help.

"You look fit, and I will want to find out exactly how fit. For this reason, though we are on the road to Deliverance, we are going to take a less conventional route and bypass the city entirely. We'll be heading east, toward the shoreline. Don't worry, we're not traveling to a City of Heaven. Not yet, anyway. My business takes us to Paridian first."

Tom was overwhelmed. He had expected the angel to be

much more mysterious. That Aitan had been so forthcoming made Tom feel a little more relaxed, a trifle bolder. He said, "Have you ever been forced to *deliver* anyone?"

It was a less blunt way of asking if Aitan had ever taken a life.

"I have," Aitan said, suddenly kicking into the flanks of his mount and spurring his mount on until the angel had rounded the next corner. Tom kicked at his stallion, but the horse lumbered on, refusing to alter its leisurely pace. For the next hour, Tom caught glimpses of Aitan as the man rounded bends in the winding mountain road, always keeping several hundred yards in front of his newly made "squire."

Finally, Tom edged around a corner and found Aitan waiting for him. The angel had dismounted. He sat off to the side of the road, gazing down at the treacherous fall leading to the valley below. Tom's mount trotted to the side of Aitan's black horse and came to a stop.

Realizing that he must have committed some great breach in etiquette by questioning the angel on so personal a topic, Tom dismounted and hesitantly made his way to the angel's side. Aitan sat with his knees drawn up slightly, his shoulders slumped forward. His arms encircled his knees and one hand was clasped on the opposing wrist. Suddenly, he grasped a stone and hurled it into the yawning drop before him. The fall-off was sharp, but it angled downward and was not totally steep. One could try to climb down, but it was likely that the earth would shift beneath one's feet and send one plunging to one's death.

The rock fell a thousand feet, striking with a sharp crack.

"What happened was *infantile*," Aitan said.

Tom fell to his knees and planted his gaze firmly on the ground. "Lord, I humbly beseech thee—"

"No!" Aitan roared as he turned to face Tom. He reached out and gently tilted the boy's head so that Tom was now looking at him. The angel said, "I'm not impatient with you. I'm angry at myself. I'm trying to *apologize* for my rude behavior."

Tom was a shade more prepared for this statement than he had been the first time he heard Aitan apologize the other night, but it was still jarring. The effect was heightened because this time, *he* was the recipient of an apology from a soldier of the Almighty.

He was about to call his companion "lord" and stopped himself. "Aitan, there's no need to say such things to me. I've agreed to serve you."

"In return for enlightenment."

"Regarding my art, yes."

"There are other issues upon which you must be curious. I would be, if I were in your position."

A ragged gasp escaped Tom. He sat back and looked to the sumptuous valley below, then to the sky. It was a perfect powder blue. The clouds were white puffs forming myriad shapes. A few large bugs flew in close, then became aware of Aitan's presence and sailed away quickly.

"You've entrusted your life to me and yet you know nothing about what kind of a man I am," Aitan said.

"Man?" Tom said in confusion.

Aitan stretched his gauntleted hand before him. "I am flesh and blood, like you. Mortal on this plane. It is the sacrifice my kind makes to walk among you."

Tom nodded.

"As such, I was born a child, and raised to manhood, just as you were. Though I'm sure my surroundings were markedly different." The angel hesitated. "I need to ask something of you."

"Anything."

"Give me some time to gather my thoughts, to choose a proper starting place for my tale, and I will tell you enough to set any fears you may have aside. Is that acceptable to you?"

Tom shrugged, amazed. "Yes. Of course."

"No, not 'of course.' That implies you have no choice. If you are worried that you travel with a madman or a fool, I will begin my tale this moment. But I would prefer to contemplate the ideal starting point for a time. Perhaps tomorrow I can tell you my story."

"Yes," Tom said, his heart racing with excitement. "I can wait until tomorrow."

Suddenly, a caravan appeared. There were laughs and

shouts. No one seemed to notice the two strangers off to the side of the road.

Aitan sighed in relief once the caravan had passed. "You see, I have other reasons for wishing to travel on more lonely roads. We'd have been stopped here for hours if those people realized there was one of my kind anywhere near."

"Your privacy means a great deal to you," Tom said.

"It does."

"But you're willing to tell me everything?"

"No. Not everything. Only enough."

Tom nodded. It was more than he could have hoped for, in any case. "Can I ask one question?"

"You can ask."

"Is there supposed to be some kind of ceremony to make me a squire? A swearing-in of some kind?"

"You mean during which you pledge to remain in my service until one of us is dead? In which you swear to die in my place if necessary, or to carry my bloody weapons into the halls of a City of Heaven though it means you will never again be allowed to walk among your own kind? *That* kind of ceremony?"

Tom realized he had stopped breathing for a moment. He took a sharp breath, let it out, and said, "I guess that's not really necessary."

"I loathe ceremonies," Aitan said. "And I loathe commitments based on fear or some need to believe that there are others in this world who are inherently superior. You are with me because we have worked a deal together. I have taken you from your home, certainly a jarring and frightening experience, so that you may serve me. In return, I have promised to help you hone your skills as an artist. It seems like a reasonable trade to me."

"I was thinking," Tom said, "that book you were writing, or whatever it was . . ."

Aitan did not tense at the mention of the tome he had locked himself away for close to a week to create.

"Would it help you to have drawings to go along with it?" Tom asked. "I'm not trying to pry—"

"I'll consider that," Aitan said. He looked around. "We should get back to the road. There is a forest many miles from here with which I am well acquainted. I would like to reach it by nightfall so that we may make camp.''

Tom rose and looked back to Winding Way. His gaze went to the mountains in the distance and off to one side. The road could be seen even there, a light golden brown band twisting and turning until it could no longer be seen at all.

They had a long journey ahead of them.

Five

NIGHT WAS FAST APPROACHING WHEN AITAN AND TOM made it to the woods. The trail Aitan chose was narrow and covered in a blanket of beautifully colored leaves. The trees were spaced closely together. Tom looked up. The branches high above crossed each others' paths and seemed to fold together like the arms of lovers. Intense white and yellow streaks of light pierced the spaces between broad coverings of leaves and filtered downward. Tiny chirps sounded from birds nearby. Soon crickets would wake and create their own music.

"This place is beautiful," Tom said. "It's so quiet."

"I feel a deep sense of peace here," Aitan said.

Twigs snapped beneath the hooves of the mounts and the animals chuffed. Tom felt drained from the ride. All he wanted to do was make camp and get something to eat. Then he would be ready to plunge into unconsciousness. He wasn't used to hard days like this one.

Soon the shafts of sunlight diminished, then faded altogether. Above, a deep blue sea dotted with bright stars came into view. Tom had a difficult time seeing more than a few feet before him, but his mount did not seem to share in his weakness. The animal seemed to know exactly where to go.

They came to a clearing and Tom leaped off his mount. He rolled on the soft earth, not caring what the dirt was doing to his pale garment. It felt so good no longer to be in motion.

"There's a brook about fifty yards in that direction," Aitan said as he pointed westward. "Take the horses."

Tom tried not to groan as he lifted himself up off the ground. He removed the saddlebags then the saddles themselves from each mount and led the horses away. By the time he returned from tending to the animals, Tom was surprised to see a small camp already set up. The bedrolls had been laid out, a fire had been set. Aitan sat cross-legged, one hand propping up his chin. He looked tired and bored as he stared into the flames.

Warming himself by the fire, Tom reached into his bag and drew out a coat. He knew how cold it could get in the mountains at night.

Aitan said, "I want you to get us dinner."

The fourteen-year-old's mood brightened at the prospect. He went to another of the supply bags. "That will be my pleasure! I know we stocked up on food pretty well at the Keeper House before we departed. I'm not the chef my father was, but I'll do my best. We have several kinds of meats, herb rubs, marinades. I packed cheeses and sweetbreads. Fruits. Even a flask of wine for when the temperature really drops. What would you like me to break out first?"

"Nothing."

Tom stared at the man blankly. "What do you mean? I packed everything that was on your list, and a few things that I liked, too. Did I do something wrong?"

"I want you to go into the woods and bring back dinner."

Tom was certain the angel was joking. "We have plenty of food."

"Are you to be my squire?" Aitan asked.

"I thought I already was," Tom said, his cheery mood fading.

"If you are to be my squire, then you must get to know my moods. Right now, I'm of a mind to be taken literally. I would like for you to go into the woods and hunt for live game."

Tom was at a loss. He was the son of an innkeeper. The only thing he knew about securing food was that Wednesdays generally meant the delivery of fresh poultry while Friday signified beef and pork. What did he know about hunting?

"You're not moving, I see," Aitan said with a wan smile. "Then I suppose you're not hungry."

"I'm, um, um, I'm *starved,*" Tom stammered. "We have food. If you send—" he stopped himself. "I'm not, I've never *hunted* before."

"Best time to learn. While we have supplies aplenty and our survival is not at stake."

There was no longer any doubt in Tom's mind that Aitan was serious. Tom said, "I'll try."

"Good."

He went a few feet into the woods, then stopped and turned. "Shouldn't I take something with me? A weapon of some kind?"

"I didn't ask you to kill anything, Tom. Just catch some small animal and bring it here."

"Yes, lord," Tom said wearily, deciding there must be a point to all this.

Tom waded into the woods. He could barely see where he was going. Soon the darkness became even deeper and Tom had to move very slowly to avoid tripping on low-lying branches or roots. On several occasions he began to get impatient and found himself nearly slamming face first into the body of a tree.

Though it had been unearthly quiet only moments before, the woods were now alive with odd sounds. There were creatures moving up all around him. Every now and then he saw a blur of movement, a dark stain against the deep grey of the woods.

He suddenly thought of something his mother had told him about love: *Sometimes the harder you chase that which you most desire, the farther it will run from you. Try to be very still. Be at peace with yourself, be grateful for all you have, all you are. The object of your affections will become curious, and will come to you in time.*

Tom knew that it was silly to think this motto would apply to the matter at hand, but he felt he could stumble around in these woods most of the night and fail to achieve the task that had been set: Capturing a beast with his bare hands. Aitan either had a great deal of confidence in Tom or he was testing his new squire. This had to be about something other than Tom's hunting skills. He had been honest enough on that subject.

Finding a comfortable spot, Tom sat down and waited. He recalled a free lesson in acting he had won at a carnival some years back and tried to apply what he had learned.

I will be a tree, he thought, attempting to ignore how foolish the sentiment may have sounded had it been spoken aloud in the company of his friends. He pictured a tree, then tried to imagine what he must look like to the small creatures of the woods. Using his artist's imagination, Tom changed the image he held of himself, melding it with that of the tree. He slowed his breathing, forced away all conscious thought.

Several minutes passed.

Suddenly, he felt a tiny leathery tongue licking his finger. He had been so entranced by the exercise he performed that he did not jump at the unexpected sensation. Instead, he waited and felt something small and furry climb into his lap.

Now, he thought, and made a desperate grab for the animal that had fallen into his trap. His fingers closed on something soft, like a pillow. Its heart thundered as it wriggled free and leaped away before he could get a proper grip. Tom jumped to his feet and ran in the creature's direction. It was a hare. They would have rabbit stew tonight!

Tom ran exactly four feet before his foot caught on a twisted root and he went down, his face mercifully falling in a nest of leaves. He felt ridiculous.

Other concerns came to him. What would happen if he broke his leg out here? Or if he was walking and one of these damned branches snapped back and tore a gash in his face?

He felt the first icy touch of true fear and did his best to banish it. Aitan said nothing would happen to him. He had to have faith in the man's words.

Faith.

There it was again. This was another test of Tom's faith. One of the first prayers he had learned was a simple one: *Yea, though I walk through the valley of the shadow of death, I will fear no evil. . . .*

Picking himself up, Tom repeated the prayer in his head until he managed to force away his fear. He suddenly felt that he wasn't alone. Two small orange orbs sat before him in the darkness. Tom strained for a better view and realized that it was the hare.

A part of him said, what difference did it make? The only way he was going to capture an animal was if he fell on one by accident and managed to knock it unconscious.

Refusing to give in to such pessimism, Tom lunged forward. The animal evaded his clumsy attempt to catch it and Tom fell face first on a downed branch, bruising his forehead. The hare skittered deeper into the woods.

"No you don't!" Tom cried as he scrambled to his feet and gave chase. He ran after the hare, somehow managing to keep it in sight while avoiding the tree trunks that kept leaping out at him.

The chase lasted for several minutes, until the hare disappeared beneath a collection of thick roots. Tom leaned against a nearby tree, out of breath. The fourteen-year-old froze as he suddenly realized that he was lost. Until he saw the hare, he had been cataloging his movements so that he could find his way back to the clearing. His maniacal determination to catch the animal had driven all such thoughts from him.

Suddenly, Tom felt light-headed. He lowered himself to all fours before he could fall and hurt himself again. What color he could detect in the forest retreated. His vision improved radically, as if the sun had impossibly chosen this moment to appear. Tom's breathing slowed and became much deeper. The clothing he wore felt horribly oppressive. Overwhelmed by an urge to be naked, Tom stripped off his clothing.

His skin felt almost unbearably sensitive. New sensations cascaded over him. A light breeze blew in from the north. The scent of decay wafted up from the dead leaves on the ground. The sound of crickets and a chorus of other night creatures swelled to a crescendo before returning to a manageable level.

What was happening to him?

Thought came slowly and with difficulty. He felt hunger and could smell prey somewhere close. The hare appeared.

He could hear its heart beating. As he concentrated, the noise became louder. The creature moved and Tom matched its every step. The stink of fear reached Tom and made him angry. He wanted this food. A dark, animal side of him, the existence of which he had always denied, rose up, and he ran for the hare, though he couldn't see it yet. That didn't matter. He could hear it, and he could smell its blood. His own footfalls were graceful and elegant, his scent lovely and pure, blending in with the strong but wonderful smells of the forest around him.

Instinct allowed him to select the proper spots on the ground for his feet and hands so that he would not snap any twigs or rustle any leaves as he chased his prey. The hare tried to run up the side of a tree. Tom leaped high into the air, grabbed a branch, spun, and kicked at the bark just above the creature's head. He could have struck the hare, but that would have brought the chase to a close far too easily.

Finally, after more than ten minutes of stalking the meat, Tom closed for the kill. He feinted to one side, then moved in the opposite direction and snatched the hare from the ground. His hand closed over its neck and—

—the madness that had gripped him faded as suddenly as it had arrived. Tom looked down and saw that he was naked.

"Oh," he whispered, refusing to let go of the terrified little hare. "Oh, merciful Lord."

His heart still thundered. He had no idea what had just happened to him. Then he knew.

It had been a miracle.

Looking around, Tom saw that he had chased the hare back to the clearing's entrance. He could see a slight flickering ahead that was certainly Aitan's fire. For a moment, Tom considered if he should try to find his abandoned clothing. No. Even if he did, he would have to give up his prize.

Tom looked down into the hare's pink eyes. The creature quaked with terror. Tom made a decision.

Kneeling, he let the animal go. Then he backtracked until he found his clothes. Soon he was fully dressed and back at the fire. Aitan had just finished cooking a pair of chicken breasts.

"Lightly seasoned," the angel said. "With spices from my city. I hope you approve."

They ate together in silence. Tom no longer felt tired. He was so energized by his experience he wondered if sleep would even be possible tonight. Perhaps Aitan would allow him to sketch for a time. He knew the best way for him to record what he recalled of the incident in the woods was with images. Drawings would convey not only what he saw, but his feelings about all that had occurred.

After Aitan and Tom had shared a chunk of sweetbread and

each taken a swallow of wine, the subject of Tom's adventure in the woods was finally broached.

Tom told everything that had happened. "I thank you, lord, for the spiritual lesson you saw fit to bless me with. For a time I felt what it was like to live purely on instinct. Now I understand what it is truly to be a man and have a choice. I know that when a lion kills, he does so for food. Not because he is evil. Men always have choices."

Aitan nodded. "So you no longer believe I simply had a craving for rabbit stew?"

"Of course not. We had food. To kill when we had food is a sin." Tom waited for some kind of response. When none was forthcoming, he added, "That's right, isn't it?"

Aitan looked down at the remains of the chicken breasts. "Did you like it?"

"Yes," Tom said. "The spices you mentioned were very strong. I'm glad you were sparing."

"Not as good as rabbit stew, in my opinion, but it served its purpose, I suppose."

Tom felt his stomach tighten. Had he misinterpreted all that occurred tonight?

Again, Aitan winked. Then he gestured and said, "Get some sleep."

Tom fell back, darkness enveloping him. An unknowable power took hold of him, thrusting him headlong into sleep, and the strangest of dreams. . . .

In the dream, Tom visited a beautiful crystal chamber. He levitated in midair. His body was covered in symbols similar to those he had seen Aitan writing in the tome he prepared in his room at Keeper House. A being shaped vaguely like a man carved from flames stood before him. Beyond the sentinel was a gateway, a swirling vortex of light and sound.

"What is your purpose here?" asked the flame guardian, in a deep, thunderous voice.

Tom heard himself reply. It was as if the words were spoken by someone from afar. "I seek the ways. The wisdom. The light."

"You know nothing."

"Teach me."

"First you must leave your preconceptions behind. If you wish me to consider becoming your Patron, I must know that your imagination is up to the task before it. For without imagination, your kind may never pass beyond—"

There was a shocking sensation of being wrenched away, of reality shattering like broken glass, followed by a terrible pain. As abruptly as it began, the dream ended.

Tom woke suddenly. Though a blanket had been laid over him, he was freezing. Some instinct that until tonight had been dormant within him told the fourteen-year-old to lie still. Pretend he was still asleep.

He heard voices. None of them belonged to his companion. Tom found himself lying on his side. He opened his eyes cautiously and saw Aitan sprawled on the ground. Above him stood three men wearing black hoods with holes cut out for the eyes. A crimson symbol had been woven into the hoods: a snake eating its own tail.

They were Anarchists. Madmen. Members of an order that did not accept the righteous rule of the angels.

One of the men carried a heavy wooden club with a splatter of crimson on one end. His leggings were torn, his boots worn through near the toes. Tom shifted his gaze to Aitan. The angel was facedown in the dirt. The dying embers of their fire cast just enough light to show a wetness on the back of Aitan's skull.

"That's it," one of the assailants hissed. He wore a heavy brown coat that reached to his knees. "We did it. Killed the stinking Elven. Now let's go."

The Anarchist carrying the blood-soaked club was shaking. He looked as if he might fall at any moment. "Aw—" he cried, "aw, no, we shouldn't a done this."

"It's over. Let's get out of here."

The third man, who wore thigh-high leather boots and a dark green tunic said, "What should we do with the boy?"

All three were silent for a time.

Tom could not believe any of this was happening. He continued to watch the strangers. Not one looked in his direction. There was a chance he could spring for the woods before they even realized he was gone, but the chance was very slim. They were only a few yards away, and they were taller than the fourteen-year-old. Longer legs, greater strides.

Anger surged through him. Aitan appeared to be dead. Clubbed like an animal. And for what?

Tom would never know. In that moment, the man with the club tossed his weapon on the dying fire. There was a hissing, a tiny roar, and a single burst of flame, then the weapon began to burn.

The trio walked away, yanking their hoods off, stuffing them into their pockets. Their backs were turned and Tom could not get a decent look at any of them. For a few moments, their voices could be heard as they made their way through the woods.

"I can't believe you talked me into this. I can't believe it. . . ."

"We should hit him again. Use a rock or something. Make sure."

"*You* hit him, if you want. I nearly peed myself just sneaking up on him."

"I'm not going back there. . . ."

Tom sat up and pulled off the blanket. He tried to walk to Aitan, but his legs were watery. Instead, he made it to his companion's side on his hands and knees.

"I'm sorry," Tom said, laying the blanket over the upper half of the angel's still form. Tears stung his eyes. "I should have done something. I shouldn't have just let them go. . . ."

The figure beneath the blanket shuddered, then rolled onto his back. The blanket slid off him.

Aitan Anzelm opened his eyes. "You did the right thing."

Tom ran for the wine that had been left out. He brought it over and put it to Aitan's lips. The angel forced it away, spilling some on his cheek.

"No," Aitan said as he sat up. "I need to be clearheaded."

"I was scared, I thought—"

"It's all right," Aitan said. He put his hand to the back of his head. "It would take more than that to kill me."

"You were just pretending. Like me."

"Yes."

"What would you have done if they had come for me?"

"They didn't."

"But if they had—"

"Tom," Aitan said firmly. "I promised that no harm would come to you. Tonight I almost died because I was lax. It's been so long since any human dared raise arms against me that I did not take the proper precautions before . . . well, before. That will never happen again."

"Are you all right?" Tom asked, gesturing at the back of his own skull. "I mean, your head."

Aitan ran his hand over his face. He seemed weak and tired. "I have rituals I must perform. Healing magics. Then I will be fine."

"Can I help you?"

"No. It's best—it's best that you're not involved. I want you to lead the horses down to the brook. You may hear me cry out. Ignore it. The healing itself can be painful. It's something of an irony. No matter what you see or hear in the distance, wait at the brook until I come for you. Be very alert." The angel found one of his supply bags and fished out a small jewel-encrusted blade and handed it to Tom. "Hold it with the blade in your palm. At the first sign of trouble, squeeze your hand down on the blade hard enough to draw blood. I'll feel your distress and I will come for you."

"Really?"

"I know. It's a bit . . . primitive . . . and I apologize."

"Primitive? It sounds amazing."

Aitan smiled, enjoying the boy's excitement. He wished he could feel that enthusiasm again, but so much had happened since he had been taught the ways of magic. "It's all I have ready at the moment. I'll work out something a bit more refined tomorrow or the next day. When I'm up to it."

As Tom readied the horses he said, "Aren't you angry? Those people tried to kill you for no reason."

"It wasn't me they wanted to destroy," Aitan said. "They're frustrated with their lives. Convinced that my kind are the cause of their every sorrow. They are to be pitied, not hated."

"Yes, but you could have died. I don't know if I could be as calm as you if they had gone after me like that. Me, I'd probably want to—"

"No," Aitan said. "Don't think that way. My attackers will

answer for all they've done. God's judgment comes to all, in time.''

Tom led the horses down to the brook, marveling at the forgiving nature of his companion. Tom was a mere human; he could only strive for the nobility and the divine mercy inherent in God's Chosen Warriors.

Tom tried to recall the details of his odd vision. There was a burning man, something about "the ways," whatever they were. . . .

It was gone.

As Aitan had warned, strange cries came from deep within the forest, accompanied by flickers of light Tom could just barely make out. One final burst of illumination came from even farther away. Close to an hour later, Aitan rejoined Tom. The wound to his skull had vanished.

The next morning, Aitan led Tom back to the road. The teenager had dreamed that he was an animal once more, sharing a pleasantly erotic adventure with Dina. His dreams had often been tortuous reenactments of his departed mother's final hours as the Scourge tore through her. So many had died from the disease. If only God saw fit to put an end to the suffering. This dream of Dina had been a pleasant change.

As they rode, Tom was so engrossed in thought he barely noticed the odd glance Aitan gave to a grove of trees off to their left. If he had, he might have noticed the three curiously shaped trees that had not been there the day before.

Or the twisted faces screaming in agony in the knots of each tree.

Six

"I PROMISED THAT I WOULD TELL YOU MY STORY," Aitan said as they continued along Winding Way. The sun was pleasant and a cool breeze drifted through the mountains. "And now I shall. Unless you would prefer to begin your art lessons. I have been lax in that regard."

"We had other things to deal with last night," Tom said.

"True enough. You didn't answer my question."

"My drawings can wait. I want to hear about you."

Aitan nodded. "First I must tell you that the Cities of Heaven have names. Chalkydri was the land of my birth, so named for its founders, the once-winged Angels of the Sun, the singers of morning, the weavers of dawn and creation. I will not reveal to you the circumstances of my birth, though they were most extraordinary. I will say only that I am the last of a once-great line. In happier times, I lived in a shining palace that touched the sky. Clouds lay outside the window to my quarters and when storms came I sat and watched for hours as lightning grew within them, coiling, preparing to strike.

"I was always more interested in learning of the past than most of my contemporaries. While they pursued the pleasures and glories of which I may not speak to a human, I labored over tomes and tried to make sense of the many different tellings of ancient tales among my kind. I traveled and made pilgrimages to the first Cities of Heaven, many of which now lie in ruins. There I sifted through primal matter, cataloging mysteries.

"Such was my fate it seemed, to live only for the past, to be an observer, not a participant in this transient blessing

63

known as life. I was content. Then *she* came into my life, and from that moment on, nothing was the same.''

''You had a girlfriend?'' Tom asked in amazement.

Aitan shrugged. ''We are flesh, like you. We have desires, we have appetite.''

''I've never seen or even *heard* of a female angel.''

''They exist. Many fear that mankind is not ready for their presence, and so they remain in the cities. But you are mistaken. Rachiel was human, not an angel. Once, she had even been alive.''

Tom drew up his reins and brought his mount to a halt. Aitan went on for a few more yards, then circled around to face the boy. Tom asked, ''She was a spirit?''

''Yes. Human spirits are often brought to us in the cities. We are meant to learn from them, to gain a better understanding of those who are meant to be our charges. Rachiel's story was a tragic one. To understand who and what I am now, you must first listen to her tale.''

Tom brushed the hair out of his face. ''This is an awful lot to take in.''

''We can stop if you like.''

''No, it's just—'' Tom paused, straining to find the right words to express his fears. ''Am I *supposed* to be told all this? I mean, lord, don't take offense, but it sounds like you're telling me secrets I have no business knowing.''

''Are you afraid?''

''Yes.''

''Then we should stop.''

Tom shook his head. ''That's just it. I don't want to stop. I just don't understand why you're telling me these things.''

''You will, in time. Shall I go on?''

''Please.''

''We must ride while we speak. There is still a great deal of ground to cover, both in my narrative, and on this road.''

They resumed their ride along Winding Way. Aitan said, ''In life, Rachiel had been a dancer. Her work as a ballerina lifted the spirits of man and God's Chosen. To my mind, she was the embodiment of discipline, hard work, and determination. She was also very much in love with her husband and together they conceived a child.

"In the world of dance, it is understood that when a dancer becomes heavy with child, her career is over. In the sixty-year history of her company, no dancer had ever returned to the stage after giving birth. Rachiel was determined to become the first. Despite all the obstacles placed in her way, from a husband who thought she would at last give up on her calling and devote herself exclusively to him and their child, to the jealousies of other dancers and the pressures placed on her by the theater director, she regained the lead in one of the most haunting pieces of work ever to grace the stage: *Giselle*." Aitan glanced over at Tom. "Are you familiar with this ballet?"

"I've never seen a ballet. I've heard—"

"No, it is a relatively new work, it has probably not graced these shores. It debuted at the Palace of Versailles, a conservatoire for the arts."

"Near the City of Heaven where—"

"Where Paris had been. Yes. That city is Chalkydri, where I was born. I frequented Versailles and had seen Rachiel perform the ballet on more than one occasion; that is why her spirit was bound and given on to me. The ballet's author had labored in obscurity, producing ribald tales and satires of the Versailles supposed 'ruling class'—an unnecessary pursuit, as the marquis and his fools did the job of making fools of themselves so well. The marquis has never understood—and does not to this day—that his presence is tolerated only for the amusement his antics bring to the masses. But I am wavering from my task, and I apologize for that.

"Rachiel had been a student of Jules Joseph Perrot, and though she never succumbed to his advances, there was much she could learn from the man who had unofficially choreographed the solos for his mistress, the Italian ballerina Carlotta Grisi, one of the most famous dancers to assume the role of Giselle. Perrot had another student, a young man named Gustav Marchosias. He took on the role of Albrecht, the disguised cleric with whom Giselle falls in love, and over whom she goes mad and dies when she sees that his first allegiance will always be to God, not to her."

"Sounds like a good story," Tom said.

"It's wonderful. Especially when the Wilis appear. They are vengeful wraiths who literally dance young men to death for their transgressions. Giselle is raised up after death to become one of them, and it is only her ultimate compassion that saves Albrecht from the spirits who wish his destruction." The angel seemed transported, as if the dancers were before him. Then he turned to Tom and saw that the boy's attention seemed to be wavering.

Aitan pointed toward a trail. "Down there, that stream. It is as good a place as any to tend to the horses, don't you think?"

"Certainly," Tom said.

Together they made their way down to a sparkling crystal stream. Aitan removed much of his armor, explaining to Tom where to find and disengage various clamps and ties so that the boy could help him in the future. Soon the angel stood barefoot, wearing only his tunic and leggings. He walked into the clear waters of the stream and said, "You're an artist, Tom. You express yourself visually. You think in terms of pictures and actions, not dry words. For most of my life I was just the opposite, and I forget that not all are stirred by words the same way I am. Some need to be shown a thing to understand its grandeur. So watch closely. . . ."

Aitan gestured and whispered an incantation. Suddenly, the waters at either side of him churned. Aitan continued to weave his magic and soon the figures began to take shape in the waters. A half dozen forms that looked like kneeling young women manifested from the flowing waters.

Tom stared in wonder as the figures rose up and began to dance around Aitan. Each was a perfectly delineated living statue formed from the waters of the stream. They had long wild hair and mischievous smiles that soon turned to malicious grimaces as they danced each in turn with Aitan, who matched their grace and power with his own movements. From somewhere, Tom was certain he could hear music!

When the performance was over, Tom finally understood. Aitan, who was near breathless, came and sat beside him. After he had rested for a few minutes, Aitan said, "You cannot judge this great work of art by the paltry copy I just created from my memory. It is far more impressive. Believe me."

"I do," Tom said.

The faraway look returned to Aitan's eyes as he continued

his story. "Rachiel made such sacrifices for her art. Not that she neglected the duties and responsibilities of being a new mother, either, and that was her most amazing accomplishment."

"You were telling me about that fellow who was trained by the great master. . . ."

Aitan's features darkened. "Marchosias. A less deserving creature had never before been blessed with such talent. For a time, I knew him only from the stories Rachiel told me. He had been jealous of the attention Rachiel was getting for her return to the role of Giselle. He had labored all his life in a desperate attempt to become the greatest dancer the world had ever seen, but his accomplishments in this ballet, which might have otherwise ensured his place in history beside the name of his mentor, were overshadowed by Rachiel and her incredible story. Night after night he performed with her, his jealousy and hatred of this amazing woman kept firmly locked away until the evening he followed her home and murdered her."

Tom stared at Aitan in shock. "He killed her?"

"He made it look as if she had been attacked by Anarchists, like the ones that tried to take my life last night. The monster went so far as to place a torn shred of cloth with their symbol in her hand."

Tom backed away from his companion. The man's flesh seemed to be growing brighter, and his crimson eyes no longer showed any vestige of white, only red that appeared to drift into the air, threatening to spill and flow like lava. Tom stared at the man as if he was looking at an elemental creature, forgetting that it was supposed to be bound by the laws that govern all other beings made of bone and flesh. Aitan glanced Tom's way and suddenly his appearance was entirely normal once again.

Had it been some kind of illusion? At that moment, Tom didn't want to know.

Aitan went on with his tale as if nothing had happened. His anger now seemed contained. "The murderer's plan was childishly simple. No investigators were called. Everyone assumed Rachiel's death was exactly what it appeared to be, a senseless act of violence. Marchosias's whereabouts at the time were never called into question.''

''He got away with it.''

''For a time.'' Aitan stared off at the distance. ''I knew Rachiel for three years. I have no idea exactly when I fell in love with her. If she had feelings for me, other than perhaps those of tender friendship, she never expressed them. From her I learned many things about your world.''

''You said you'd already been to the ballet several times,'' Tom said, a little confused.

''Yes, I had walked among men. I just never understood them. You have to understand, until I met Rachiel, I had been the consummate scholar. I had never known love, I had never experienced hate.''

Tom nodded in sympathy.

''I had reasons for shutting myself off. One day I'll try to tell them to you. Not today.'' Aitan rose up and rummaged through his travel bags until he found a towel. As he dried himself, he said, ''Love and hate. Desire. Fear. These were things I read about, but never felt for myself. Not until I knew Rachiel and I came to understand that I had fallen in love with her.''

''A spirit? A human spirit?'' Tom said, trying to grasp how anyone could love someone who was dead.

Aitan nodded. ''Your reaction is kind compared to most I received when my affections for Rachiel became public knowledge. I'm getting ahead of myself.'' The angel pointed to his armors. ''Help me with these. Last night I had considered that they were mainly for show, but now I see there are dangers in these mountains for which we must show a healthier regard, yes?''

''Yes,'' Tom said. First they slipped the arming doublet over Aitan's head. The boy tugged on the padded garment. ''Doesn't this get awfully hot?''

''I don't feel heat or cold the way humans would,'' Aitan said. ''Start with the cuisse, then the poleyn.''

''Hmmmm?''

''For my legs and knees.''

''Yes,'' Tom said, rummaging through the steel plates. They

were hot to the touch and the boy winced from the searing heat, but he did not complain.

Plates were tied around his upper thighs with waxed thongs Aitan called "points." The angel's boots were steel-tipped and already fitted with greaves and sabatons for his lower legs and feet. The mail skirt was attached next, then the back plates and breastplates with their waist straps. Tom was amazed at how quickly it all fit together. Upper arm guards called vambraces and elbow and shoulder plates followed next, followed by Aitan's leather gloves and steel gauntlets. His sword belt and dagger followed, finishing with his sword. Moving with surprising grace, considering the weight of his armor, the angel took to his mount. Soon Aitan and Tom were back on Winding Way.

"What happened to Marchosias?" Tom asked.

"Yes, that is what all this has been leading to, isn't it? I killed him, of course."

Tom blanched.

"Oh, it was a fitting vengeance. I used my power upon him, causing him to dance himself literally to death. The fate he was spared in the ballet he suffered in life. And beyond."

"Really," Tom said, fear rippling through him, matched with a strange excitement. He had wanted divine justice to come to the murderer, though he knew it was a sin to wish harm upon his fellow man. "What do you mean—beyond?"

"I took his soul and exiled it to a realm far worse than any hell mortals have ever envisioned. There he will dance for mad creatures throughout eternity. No rest. No mercy." He shrugged. "It's possible that I was being a little extreme."

"He killed the woman you loved!"

"Yes, well. Her murder happened long before I met her, and she had come to terms with it. I was like a child, hoping to please. When I told her what I had done, she did not thank me. Instead, she turned from me and I haven't seen her since, though I know where she resides. . . ."

Tom waited. He looked to the blazing sun in the distance and the soft rolling hills off to one side.

"I can't say much more about this," Aitan said, his voice choked with emotion. "I'm sorry to disappoint you. For a historian, I fear I am not very illuminating. I will tell you that even for such as myself, there are rules to follow, procedures and petitions to undertake. I didn't care about any of that. Instead, I satisfied my own urges, and that led to a judgment against me. I was cast out of Chalkydri and told I would be sent for when I was once again fit to enter a City of Heaven. As I cared so much about humanity, I was told to walk the earth and observe mankind in all its suffering, in all its wayward confusion, but do nothing.''

"That must have been pretty hard."

Aitan hung his head. "Impossible, as it turned out. My disobedience led to my being exiled from the eye of God."

"You were *damned?*"

"Not exactly. And the judgment that was made against me, that had been meant to last an eternity, instead only held for six years. An incident took place in the city of my birth, a terrible wrong that only I could right. I was told that in return for this service I might once again gain my status and restore honor to the memory of my family.

"I'm not telling you this to alarm you. When I said you were in no danger, I meant it. I have not yet decided to undertake this mission of vengeance. I'm not sure I have the will for it, the heart. If I choose to do what has been asked of me, then the two of us will part company. As friends, I hope."

"We're going to see her, aren't we?" Tom asked.

"Yes."

"So that she can advise you?"

"And strengthen my resolve, perhaps. She is in Paridian, in the keeping of a man I am sure you'll want to meet. His name is Roger Hughes. He is known as one of the most influential painters of our time.

"With your permission, I intend to offer you to him as an apprentice, in return for a single hour alone with my lost beloved. . . ."

FIRST INTERLUDE

❧

THE PEOPLE OF TRINITY HAD NO IDEA A STRANGER MOVED among them. There was no obvious reason for anyone to feel alarmed.

When the stranger chose to appear, it was always in a pleasing form. To a husband, he would appear as his wife or child. To the women he coveted, he would look deep into their souls, find an image of all they desired, and become it. Then he would take them, brutal and swift.

Only the briefest physical contact was necessary, of course. A touch on the cheek, the brush of a hand. He had a gift to give these people and he had to reach every single one of them. It would have been terrible for his statement to be misinterpreted as a random tragedy, a bizarre act of God.

Casual contact was not satisfying to the stranger. Far better to learn the secret hopes and uncover the long-buried dreams of these people. He would use that knowledge later. The stranger was pleased at the idea that he would leave the good people of Trinity, all 217 of them, with their weaknesses clawing at them, their needs right at the surface.

Inflicting suffering was an art to the stranger and he considered himself a talented amateur, one who acted out of love, as opposed to a desire for personal gain. Very few of Trinity's residents would remember their encounters with the stranger as anything more than a dream, or passing fantasy.

Such was his power.

There were only five left. Two children, a married couple, and Rosanna Craig, one of the most physically appealing young women the stranger had ever met. He found it quite amusing when he learned that the pale, blue-eyed nineteen-year-old had decided to squander her womanly charms by devoting herself to holy service. If she had her way, no man would ever touch her. The stranger would see to it this day that Rosanna knew what it meant to be a sensual, physical being. Deep down she dreamed of it. Desired it. He would unleash her passions, make her every fantasy a reality.

Then he would kill her.

Just as he had murdered everyone else in Trinity, though the fools didn't know it, yet. His touch was death, his desires lethal.

In a day or two, after he had left Trinity behind, the first of the residents would double over in pain. Soon after, they would find themselves in the grip of a horrible fever. Finally, the blood would begin to ease from their pores and they would know that they were damned. Every last one of them.

The stranger wished he could be there to see it, but he could not afford the delay. He had miles to travel and many, many people to visit.

Death's work, it seemed, was never done. He wished he could thank the demon-shadow that gave him this power. There had been a price, of course. He could no longer recall much of his earlier life. Why should he let that bother him, when he now had such a grand and glorious mission to fulfill?

Smiling, the stranger went to visit the first of the five he had not yet touched, his mind firmly fixed on the prize awaiting him when his labors were at an end. . . .

Seven

O VER THE COMING DAYS, AITAN CONTINUED TO AVOID the more well traveled roads. He found an old covered bridge, its bright red paint chipping, its foundations solid, and asked Tom to make a sketch of it. They rested on a soft bank off to one side of the bridge. A gentle breeze wafted toward them, carried above the sparkling waters of the stream below. The sun was bright. It felt like a warm hand brushing away the chill of morning as it caressed Tom's face. Mist drifted across the surface of the stream. Tom listened to the smooth flow of the waters and wished he could sleep right there. For the past few nights he had been restless, and during the days he felt drained.

Lately, he had been unable to remember his dreams. That had never happened to him before. All he knew was that he would wake in the middle of the night with strange longings that he was certain had nothing to do with sex. It was as if something he desired above all else was directly before him, but he somehow couldn't bring himself to reach out and take whatever it was. So very odd. . . .

Tom took out the paper Aitan had procured for him before they left Hope. He had never been allowed to draw on fresh clean paper before and it felt odd, almost sinful, to waste these pages on his meager sketches. That didn't stop him. His excitement at the opportunity to learn more about his chosen craft was more than enough to keep him going.

Staring at the dark maw of the covered bridge's entrance, Tom imagined it to be some great and fearsome beast he would fight at Aitan's side. He could almost see it lifting itself off its underpinnings and writhing like a snake. Feeling a little playful, he drew the bridge exactly that way.

Aitan looked at the drawing and smiled. "That's how I saw it, too!"

Tom laughed, then said, "Tell me what you really think."

Aitan's smile diminished. Clearing his throat, he raised his chin and bunched his shoulders, assuming what he hoped would look like a more authoritative posture. In truth, he simply looked uncomfortable.

"Yes, well," Aitan said, his tone growing slightly more formal. "I'd *definitely* say you're coming along."

Tom waited. When he was relatively certain the angel would not add anything more, he said, "Do you like my use of line?"

The angel pursed his lips. He seemed hesitant to give an honest opinion.

"It's all right, I can take it." Tom wasn't entirely sure this was true. No one had ever really criticized his work before and he was terrified. Still—Aitan thought Tom was good enough to apprentice to Roger Hughes, so what was he worried about?

"I like the fanciful imagery. It shows the same blatant disregard for the school of realism that first attracted me to your work. I would say that the line work is a bit on the crude side and could be strengthened."

"Yes," Tom said, his heart sinking a little. He told himself he would not get depressed, even if the man tore his work to shreds. "How do I fix it?"

"The current masters of illustration would all have different opinions, I'm sure. I wouldn't want to presume. I'm sure Mr. Hughes will wish to instruct you and I don't want to fill your head with theories he will only have to extract."

"Please," Tom said. He couldn't understand why Aitan was being so modest.

"All right," Aitan said, swallowing hard. "What's really bothering me is something about your use of positive and negative space. Have you ever seen the work of Frederick McAlline?"

Tom shook his head.

"Elsidon? Falco? Mermelstein?"

The names meant nothing to the fourteen-year-old.

"Oxnam? Scolaro? Pictaro?"

Tom tried to place the names and failed. "What does their work look like?"

Aitan sighed. He listed a series of techniques that meant nothing to Tom and attempted to describe each of them. He was in the midst of making a groping attempt at defining chiaroscuro when he gave up, his shoulders falling, a frown forming on his handsome face.

"I might as well attempt to describe fornication," he groused.

Tom's mouth opened wide in shock and amusement. He couldn't believe he had just heard such a base term from the lips of an angel.

"Sorry," Aitan said. "I don't mean to offend."

"It's okay," Tom replied. "I've heard the word before. I know what it means. Kind of."

Aitan smiled. "You've been thinking of Dina?"

Tom downturned his eyes. "No, lord. Impure thoughts are not appropriate for one who serves a soldier of God."

"You talk about her in your sleep. Especially about a particular spot on her neck, right here," Aitan said, tapping his own neck right above his left artery. "Either she let you kiss her there once, or you wished she had let you."

Tom was mortified. "Lord! I beg of you, think more highly of your servant!"

Aitan shrugged. "Do you want to know what my first lover told me?"

Looking up sharply, Tom said, "I don't want to presume—"

"It was just before we were about to, well, you know, and she said, 'It's easy to become lost to sex when you've never known love. And even then . . .'"

Tom got to his feet and started pacing. He mumbled, "*Culpam poena premit, culpam poena premit, culpam poena premit. . . .*"

"Swift justice follows sin. I know the phrase. It is the backbone of study at the Scribe's Academy, yes?"

Tom nodded. "They made us repeat that phrase every day. All sorts of things like that in Latin."

"You must understand, my bringing up the topic of carnal relations—"

Tom shifted uncomfortably, hugging himself.

"—wasn't meant as a test of your moral character, Tom. I was just talking with you. I never meant to make you feel uncomfortable." Aitan thought about it. "Or maybe I did. I believe I wanted to get off the subject of your art."

Tom felt stricken. "Is it that unworthy?"

"No!" Aitan said with a hearty laugh. "I am."

"What?"

"I'm no one to judge."

"Lord, don't say such things!"

"Why not? It's true. My education was of a classical nature. I can critique art, perhaps even make some suggestions about what style may fit a particular subject best. I can certainly identify and catalog art. The drawback is—I'm not creative."

"You can't mean that," Tom said. "Look at what you did with the water spirits, making them dance and everything!"

"Yes, but they danced only the exact movements I had seen. I can copy what others originate, but I fear I have no real spark of creativity in me. I'm sorry to disappoint you."

Tom smiled. "Actually, I'm kind of relieved. I mean, you look at my work and you see potential, right?"

"Stunning potential."

"Well, that's all the encouragement I need!"

Aitan gestured with open hands. "Then you forgive my little ruse? That I presented myself as something that I was not?"

"You never did any such thing," Tom said. "You presented yourself as my friend—if I'm not being too bold."

"Not at all."

"That's what matters to me. Look, shouldn't we devote this time to my learning more about how to serve you properly? I have no idea what I should do if we come into contact with other angels and their squires. Or if there was some kind of fight. That's what's really important now, isn't it?"

"Perhaps."

"I've never really fought anyone. I've wrestled with Papa and Gus—"

"And you would have liked to have wrestled with Dina."

Tom nodded, embarrassed all over again. "Yes."

"Forgive me, go on." Aitan could not stop smiling.

"If you fall in battle, what should I do?"

"Run."

"That's it?"

"That's all that's really important. Tom, I don't expect—"

"Neither of us expected those guys to club you in the woods! It could happen again."

"No," Aitan said, "I doubt that." He rose to his feet. "But I suppose we should continue your training as a squire. Let's start by testing how strong you are."

Aitan whispered a phrase as he fixed his gaze on a large stone deeply rooted in the earth. Suddenly, it began to shiver, then it burst from the ground and rose spinning into the air. Tom watched in amazement as the stone, fully a foot across, lazily whirled in midair, about chest level to him.

"Try to bring it down," Aitan said.

Shrugging, Tom went to the stone. At first he couldn't get anything resembling a firm hold on the stone because it was turning, but by putting his full weight into the effort he was able to hold the stone in place and drag it down a few inches.

"All right," Aitan said. He gestured again and the stone fell heavily to the ground. Tom leaped back and out of harm's way. He wouldn't have been much good to Aitan with a broken foot.

"Your reflexes aren't bad. You've got *some* upper body strength. We can work on that."

"Ah," Tom said, sweating and out of breath.

"Now, would you like to consider something that was actually challenging?"

Before Tom could answer, he saw Aitan working his magic once more. A mound of dirt at his feet shuddered and rose up in the form of a man. It had roots for arteries, moss for flesh.

"Try to pin him," Aitan said.

Tom assumed Aitan was talking to him and so he turned, about to object, when out of the corner of his eye he saw the moss-creature dart forward. With a startled cry, Tom fell beneath the smelly, filthy being Aitan had just brought to life. He was pinned in seconds.

"Disappointing," Aitan said.

"This thing's got twigs that are digging into my ribs," Tom said.

Aitan gestured. The life went out of the moss creature. Tom found himself covered in dirt.

"That was wonderful," Tom said. "We both know that a golem can take me. That is what you call a creature like that, isn't it? A golem?"

Aitan nodded. "A creature of the elements filled with unnatural life. You are well educated, I'll give you that."

Tom looked down at the piles of earth surrounding him. He could still see arms, legs, and a smiling head. Just as he was about to ask for another chance at the golem, Tom noticed something odd in the dirt. He fished it out.

"Metal," Tom said. The object he had found was rusted through. It had a handle that fit comfortably in the boy's palm and a cylindrical body that was cracked and falling apart. "Have you ever seen anything like this?"

Aitan took the chunk of metal from the boy. He knew all too well what they had called weapons like this. The trigger mechanism was broken, the hammer falling off.

"It's a relic," he said, tossing the broken weapon several hundred yards away. It splashed as it hit the stream and quickly sank. "A testament to man's willfulness and foolishness."

"Oh," Tom said, surprised. "Yes, lord."

"*Aitan.*"

"Yes."

The angel tested Tom's abilities a third time. A large branch was found that Aitan straightened into a javelin with his power. They climbed up from the bank and stood several hundred yards away from the covered bridge.

"This is to give me an idea of your accuracy," Aitan said, handing the javelin to the boy. "Do you see that horseshoe over the entrance to the covered bridge? Try to hit it with the javelin."

"It's too far away. I don't have the strength to throw it close enough."

"Don't worry about that. All that will matter is if your aim is true."

Tom drew a deep breath, got a running start, and hurled the

javelin! An instant before it left his hand it suddenly felt lighter, as if it was chasing the wind at Tom's back. He watched the wood shaft sail through the air, going farther and faster than he would have thought possible.

"Well, I'll be blessed," he said. The javelin headed exactly where he had aimed it. A second before it would have struck the horseshoe above the entrance to the covered bridge, the javelin froze in midair. Disappointment surged within Tom. "Come on, Aitan! I would have made it!"

The angel did not appear amused. Instead, he stared at the javelin with growing trepidation.

Tom saw the expression on the angel's luminous face and said, "You're not doing that, are you? I mean, you're not keeping that thing hanging in the air, right?"

"I'm not doing it."

"So who is?"

Aitan gestured. The javelin, now once more under Aitan's control, lowered itself slowly, then shot forward into the darkness. There was a horrible roar, then the pieces of the javelin were spat out of the darkness to fall on the road.

"Someone unfriendly," Aitan said. He nodded toward their horses, who were a hundred yards behind them, bound to a stake Aitan had driven into the earth with his magic. "Tend to the mounts. I'll deal with this."

"Yes, lord," Tom said, his fear rising as he saw Aitan draw his sword and walk toward the nightmare black entrance to the covered bridge.

Eight

AITAN COULD SEE NOTHING. THOUGH HE HAD TAKEN only a single step into the shadows, the blazing sunlight at his back had retreated as if a veil had fallen. Looking ahead, he saw no hint of illumination at the far end of the covered bridge. He listened carefully. Pure silence. All sound from outside had been swallowed up by the unnatural darkness.

He tapped his foot. The sound registered. He took that to mean any sounds made *inside* the covered bridge by himself or whatever hostile agency was at work would still be heard. He heard nothing from his opponent, who was clearly standing very still. Waiting.

Aitan gestured and a small ball of flame appeared. The angel saw a figure perhaps thirty feet ahead of him. An oddly dressed person wearing a garish mask. Bright colors. Emerald, orange, crimson.

"No," said a deep, raspy voice. With a wave of his hand, the strange-looking man dispelled the light.

Aitan created a second ball of flame, this one larger than the last. The light was brighter and the figure closer. Fifteen feet. How had he moved so quickly, and without making a sound? Aitan strained for a better look at the other figure. It was not standing still. Instead, it was dancing in place, at least ten inches off the ground.

"I said no."

The light gave out once more, but not before Aitan had a better chance to study the dancing man. He was heavily armored in the eastern style. A black mask that looked like the

80

traditional embodiment of the Enemy, with narrow slits cut for eyes, nostrils, and teeth. A pair of large golden horns curled upward from the sides of the warrior's helmet. Fabric fanned out on either side of his head, bearing beautiful designs not unlike those found on the wings of rare butterflies. A strange cap adorned with straw-colored "hair" rose up a foot above the top of the fighter's skull.

His body was covered in layers of armor and fabric. Pads overlaid with steel and gold protected the shoulders and arms, and his hands were covered by gauntlets. Small iron-lacquered plates laced together with silk and leather hung from the armors, forming exquisite designs. Skirts reached down to the knees in the front, mid-calf in the back.

Most importantly, the warrior wielded a black-and-gold sword that played an important part in its odd stylized dance. Symbols were formed with the sword, mystic runes Aitan had studied from cultures thought long extinct.

Aitan created a final sphere of light. This time there was an oath in a language Aitan did not recognize, followed by a return to the darkness. The illumination lasted long enough to show Aitan that his opponent was forming a spell of binding. Aitan could feel the air thickening around him. If the legends he had read were to be believed, bands of pure darkness would soon descend and wrap themselves around him, crushing his fragile mortal frame.

From birth Aitan Anzelm had been taught that the body was nothing more than a vessel for the spirit, and not to fear the transformation that would occur when death came for him. His teachers, of course, had been referring to a natural death. If he was murdered by another like himself, his soul could be bound and tortured for eternity, or made to serve the ends of another.

With a savage cry, Aitan gestured and loosed a torrent of white fire from his hands. Rippling bolts of energy tore through the air and crackled as they struck the other warrior, sending him several feet into the air. He struck the wood floor with a thud and a grunt. In the brief moment of illumination, Aitan saw a rune hanging in the air, an intricate construct of dark energies. It faded when the warrior's concentration was shattered by Aitan's attack.

Aitan felt drained. Reaching beyond the cloak of darkness enveloping the covered bridge to find the power he needed and bring it there had required more of him than he had expected.

Shuffling sounds came from the darkness. His opponent was on his feet.

"Lightning?" the warrior called out. "That's it? That's the best you can do?"

Aitan heard the warrior coming closer. He tried once again to summon a sphere of flame. It came, but this time it was the size of a man's fist. With a curse, the warrior put it out, plunging them once again into darkness.

Why doesn't he want me to see him? Aitan wondered. *What is he hiding?*

Suddenly, the warrior was upon him. Aitan raised his sword in defense, guessing where his enemy's blade would fall from the manner in which it sliced through the air. There was a clang of steel crashing against steel as Aitan brought his foot up and kicked at where he imagined the warrior's chest to be.

Contact! He drove the swordsman back, throwing him off balance. Aitan came in fast, using the hilt of his weapon as a club. He meant to drive it into the warrior's face, stunning him, purchasing a few precious moments in which he could work some magic of his own.

Aitan fell forward into empty air. He gracelessly slammed face first onto the wood floor and heard his enemy's sword sailing through the air, right for his head! Spinning onto his back, he moved to the right in an effort to avoid the blade. Aitan was startled as the weapon suddenly struck the wood floor directly before his face. Impossible! It had been coming in from the left. Did his enemy have two swords?

"You cannot trust your senses," the warrior whispered. His voice sounded distant, somewhere far behind Aitan. Then it came again, this time from a point directly ahead. "Where does that leave you?"

Though Aitan had devoted his life to the study of antiquity, he *had* also learned how to defend himself. He rose up swiftly, jabbing, retreating, thrusting with his sword at all points surrounding him. His goal was to create a kind of box around himself, an area his enemy could not breach without tasting steel forged in the fires of Heaven. For several precious seconds it worked and Aitan felt elated. Then he realized that he could not continue with such complex movements for long. He was already exhausted, only fear kept him going. Even worse, he could not cast a spell so long as he kept both hands on the hilt of his weapon. He had never been particularly adept at wielding his sword single-handed, but he knew he would have to try if he was going to survive.

Aitan was on the brink of collapse. He did not possess the willpower, the concentration, to create the kind of magic he would need to win this fight. Though it pained him to do so, he envisioned his Patron, the Lord of Heaven who had been his teacher and friend, and pleaded inwardly for his aid. A sudden surge of strength ripped through the angel. He waited for his chance.

"A five-pointed star," his enemy said. This time his voice came from far above. "That's the maneuver you're practicing. Basic, but effective."

Now, Aitan thought, *while the warrior is prattling!* He freed his right hand and gestured, throwing his weight behind the sword as he thrust and retreated, pivoting in different directions at random. The warrior surged forward. The bold ringing of steel on steel sounded and Aitan's blade was swept from his hand. He whispered the word of Power needed to bring forth the first part of his spell and heard his enemy gasp in surprise.

Suddenly they were surrounded by all manner of insect. A thick fog made of bees, hornets, dragonflies, wasps, and mosquitoes filled the air. Aitan had added a spell of protection, making the insects feel repulsed by his presence. He would still be stung, but his injuries would be minimal compared to those of his opponent. Summoning creatures indigenous to earth was difficult for Aitan, especially in his current state. Bringing forth insects from the True Lands, or even the areas where the Cities of Heaven met with the physical realm of earth, would have finished him, and he knew this was nothing more than a diversionary tactic. Now, while his enemy was occupied, he would utilize his last bit of strength to summon a fireball capable of lighting a field at midnight for several miles.

He gestured, spoke the word, then felt something flutter near his lips and nearly fly into his mouth. *Disgusting*, he thought, clamping his lips shut and leaping high into the air. He squinted as the power he summoned lit up the covered bridge. The fireball had been constructed with a hollow at its center. Aitan levitated, keeping himself out of harm's way by holding himself in the fireball's core. A second word of Power caused the flames to radiate out in all directions.

The insects Aitan had summoned to distract his enemy were incinerated as the flames reached out and tore through the mystical shroud of darkness wrapped around the covered bridge. The wooden bridge caught fire. Aitan saw that he stood within a tunnel of flames. Even the floor beneath him was on fire.

His enemy was nowhere to be seen.

The heavy wooden supports of the covered bridge strained and groaned. Several planks fell inward. Aitan used the last of the Power granted him by his Patron and drove himself forward, toward the light of day in the distance, at the mouth of the covered bridge. One of the planks fell and struck his back. He cried out as flames seared his flesh, but he did not falter in his steady flight out of harm's way. In seconds he was once again in the sunlight. His power faltered and he tumbled to the ground.

Tom rushed forward, yanking his own shirt up over his head and whipping it off. Aitan was on his knees, staring at the boy in confusion, when Tom began to beat the rough cloth over Aitan's back. He was on fire!

"We should get you down to the waters," Tom said when the flames had been snuffed out. The boy helped his companion down the slope, where they stumbled toward the cool, fresh waters of the stream. Aitan fell back into the waters and sighed in pleasure as they washed over him. The weight of his armor dragged him down and he rose to a crouch, keeping his head above the shallow waters.

For several moments, Aitan was content to remain in the waters, grateful to be alive. He gave a prayer of thanks to his Patron, who he had feared would not hear his call through the magical darkness his enemy had created. A few hundred feet away, large chunks of the bridge were dropping into the waters, hissing angrily as they struck.

"What happened?" Tom asked.

"It's very simple," said a raspy voice from the bank of the waters. "Your friend dropped his sword."

Aitan turned to see his opponent crouched thirty feet away. The angel's sword was in the warrior's hands.

"Tom," Aitan said, just loud enough to be heard over the rushing waters around them, "remember what I said about running? Now would be the time...."

Nine

THE WARRIOR CAME CLOSER. "THERE'S NO NEED TO BE alarmed. I have no wish to hurt either of you." He looked to Aitan. "I'm sorry about your burns; if you'd like, I'll heal them for you."

Aitan stared at the warrior in amazement. This man had just tried to kill him!

The warrior laughed as he reached the edge of the waters. "Come closer. Look at me. Look carefully, then tell me what you see."

Though he had never actually met an agent of the Enemy, Aitan Anzelm believed in their existence. Today, it seemed, he was to fall before one of them.

Aitan stepped before Tom, ushering him back into the waters. The angel said, "Know this, whoever you are. You may do what you like with me. But I will be *damned* if I'll let you hurt the boy. He's under my protection."

"Damned, eh? Pretty strong words for a soldier of God."

"They are meant to be taken literally."

"Oh, I understand," the warrior said with a hearty laugh. "You have it in you, as do all of your kind, to give yourself over to the Enemy in return for any single wish you desire to see fulfilled. Come now. There are better ways to exile me to eternal damnation than to give up your own soul."

"I haven't the strength for them."

"What of your Patron?"

"That one has limits. I see now that your power could exceed my Patron's limits easily. Now, do we have an understanding?"

The warrior sighed. "You're a very interesting character, my friend. I've never before met a Principality who would suffer to have his soul, his very being, twisted into something unrecognizable just for the sake of preserving a mortal's all too short lifetime. What if I agree not to hurt him and later he falls off his horse and breaks his neck? Such things happen all the time."

"Then it will be God's will, not yours."

The warrior laughed. "You are a fearsome thing, aren't you? Or you'd like to think so. Honestly, there is no need to blaspheme on my account. I have already apologized that my little jest got out of hand."

"Jest?" Aitan asked, surprised.

"Of course. You seemed so haughty, the way you were testing the boy's limits. I thought it only fair to see how you would fare if someone decided to test yours. Now come closer and see me for who and what I really am. You're going to feel very foolish. I promise."

Aitan could see no harm in moving a few steps closer. The sun was in his eyes where he stood and he could not see the warrior at all clearly. And there had been the matter of the fighter wishing to hide his appearance in the covered bridge.

He waded close, the water falling away from him as he got to the shore and soon stood only a few feet before the warrior.

"Christ's blood," Aitan whispered as he took in the man's face and promptly fell to his knees before him.

"That blasphemy is going to get you in trouble one of these days," the warrior warned.

"Humble lord, forgive me," Aitan said.

"Oh, stop blubbering and introduce me to your friend," the warrior said as he gestured toward Tom.

"Come forward, Tom. It's all right."

Tom waded through the waters. As he drew closer, he saw that the warrior was not wearing a mask. Or if he was, it had somehow been grafted to his flesh. "How horrible!" he whispered.

The warrior touched his face, where the slits for his mouth melted into his charred skin. "I'm not happy about it, myself."

"Lord, he meant no disrespect," Aitan said, grabbing Tom and yanking the boy down to his knees.

"Sir," the warrior said, "I seem to recall how much you disliked being called 'lord' by the boy. I share in your distaste for such formality among friends."

Aitan looked up, a look of amazement spreading across his luminous features. "Friends? Never. Not after my behavior."

The warrior held out Aitan's sword. "Well, if you won't accept my hand in friendship, at least take back your weapon."

"No, you misunderstand!" Aitan cried, awestruck and terrified.

Tom could not understand Aitan's reaction, but he was reminded of the manner in which he had behaved whenever Aitan frightened him. Who could this man be to so humble an agent of the One True Divinity?

The warrior sighed and turned to Tom. "Do you think you could get your friend to relax around me?"

Tom said, "I don't know. . . ."

Aitan rose to one knee. He avoided the warrior's direct gaze and said, "False modesty is the same as vanity, lord. Or so I was instructed. If you find me worthy of the mantle you offer, then it would be a sin for me to refuse the honor of being your friend."

"Good. If I had to go and offer it again, I might have gotten annoyed. Now, take your sword and introduce me to your squire."

Aitan gingerly retrieved his sword from the warrior. "Tom Keeper, this is Lord Ainigrim Bosh R'Hayle Skalligrin, former—"

"None of that matters right now," the warrior said as he reached out and clasped Tom's shoulders firmly. The boy felt an odd tingling, as if raw energy were being passed to him with the warrior's touch. "Just call me Grin. I prefer it."

The angel stepped forward. "I am Aitan Anzelm, of—"

"Yes!" Grin cried. "I thought I recognized you!"

Aitan was confused. "We've never met."

"Not that you would recall, no." He tapped the faceplate. "I didn't have this at the time. Believe me, I visited House Anzelm on several occasions."

He knew it was entirely possible that this man had been to his House; visitors constantly frequented House Anzelm when he was a youth. It wasn't until much later that Aitan brought shame and much worse down upon his family.

Off to their side, another flaming support fell from the covered bridge into the waters. The wood sizzled and cracked; steam drifted toward the travelers.

"I bow to your wisdom in this and in all things," Aitan said.

"Wisdom?" Grin said, astonished. "Fah! All I care about these days is having fun. What good is life without fun?"

Tom smiled. He liked this man.

"Is there a reason you have sought us out?" Aitan asked.

Grin rose up and walked in the direction of the horses. "Who said I was seeking anyone? The next thing I know, you'll be thinking it was fate, or God's will that I came among you."

"Was it?" Aitan asked, following the warrior.

Tom trailed closely behind. He saw the blistered patches of skin on Aitan's back and wondered if the angel was still in pain. From the excitement Aitan radiated, Tom guessed his companion was too excited to bother entertaining thoughts of the agony he had suffered. There would be time enough for that later, when the man tried to sleep. Tom knew this from the many times he had burned himself in his father's kitchen.

They reached the horses, both of whom seemed a little unnerved by the warrior's presence. He calmed each with a touch.

"All right," Grin said, caressing the mane of Tom's horse. He turned to Tom. "Boy, have you ever wondered how God makes His wishes known to us, his servants?"

"Through dreams, visions," Tom said. "I'm not really sure. I've never heard a priest talk about it."

Grin nodded. "There are many ways. Sometimes, God appears to us in a corporeal form, a physical body. He manifests. There are nine such manifestations, or vessels. I served the sixth of these for many years."

Aitan said, "Lord Skalligrin is Emissary to the Almighty in his Sixth and most treasured Vessel."

"Emissary?" Tom whispered hoarsely. The boy dropped to

his knees as if he had been struck and began trembling. He had been joking with a being who had stood in the presence of God. It was a miracle he had not been struck down for his impertinence.

Grin sighed. "I'm not with Him now. You can get up. Please get up."

Tom struggled to his feet.

"And look at me while I talk to you."

The boy shifted his gaze to the Emissary.

"Now, all that you have to know is that I was injured in my service to the Lord," Grin said.

"Yes," Aitan said. "In a great battle with the Enemy. There are songs I have heard in your honor. You were—"

"Don't," Grin said, raising his gauntleted hand. "Remembering what happened is difficult enough. Hearing the way my life has been raised up into myth is even worse." He looked to Tom. "When I was injured, these armors you see were made a part of my flesh. In return for my loyal service, I was given my freedom. I now walk the earth, bored most of the time. Except when I come upon interesting company, like the two of you."

"Thank you," Aitan said. Tom echoed the sentiment.

Grin went on, "I would like to travel with you both for a time, if that's quite all right."

"Of course," Aitan said, trying to hide his astonishment.

"I've given you some details about myself to rid us of the need for more questions and answers," Grin said. "I trust you know all you need to about me for the moment?"

"Yes, lord," Aitan said.

Grin shook his head and let out a bellow of frustration. The former Emissary hated to be called 'lord' even more than Aitan. Tom smiled despite himself.

"Now, as to why I am here," Grin said. "In my service to the Sixth Vessel, I learned a very important lesson. Unfortunately, I didn't learn it very well. It's either that everything is random, or nothing is. I always get confused on that point. So—the two of you can think what you like. That I'm acting like one of the Influences—" He turned to Tom. "You do know about the Influences? Spirits who move among mankind, guiding them to their ultimate, happy destinies?"

"My mother believed in them fully," Tom said. "Until she contracted the Scourge."

"She's dead," Grin said sadly. "A thousand sorrows, my friend."

"She's in a better place," Tom said.

"I'm sure," Grin added, his attention wandering. He shook his head. The buffalo horns attached to his helm glinted in the bright sunlight and his mask was almost pure black. He suddenly came back to full attention and said, "We've got a bridge to cross, don't we?"

Aitan looked back to the ruins of the covered bridge. "I don't think we have one anymore."

Grin set his hands on his hips as he surveyed the remains of the burning covered bridge. "We can't leave things like this, now can we? I'm sure that people use this bridge all the time. Local economies may depend on it. Children who need food. The sick, the poor." He clasped one hand on Aitan's shoulder. "So, lad. What are you going to do about it?"

"Me?" Aitan said, startled. "But you—"

"You're the one who burned down the bridge. I was just out for a good time." Grin cocked his head to one side, like a wolf.

Aitan sighed. "I mean that your power is more suited to such a task."

"True. *If* I had a desire to use my energies that way. I do not. Instead, I ask that you fix the mess you made."

Distressed, Aitan turned to the former Emissary and said, "I would have to summon my Patron."

"Then do so."

"I have already called upon that one once this day."

"Yes."

"To do so again would be impertinent. Especially when no lives are actually at stake. The power might be granted this time, or it might not. My Patron could become cross, and deny me later, in a time of true need. I would risk *all* I have invested half a lifetime to build if I do as you ask."

"I suppose there is another alternative," Grin said absently.

"What would that be?"

Grin shrugged. "Humans erected this bridge in the first place. They could fix it. All you would have to do is seek them out and tell them of the blunder you made."

"I am on a journey with a specific purpose," Aitan said. "I had wished to avoid humans if I could manage it. They will slow me down."

"That would follow. All that adoration. Everyone calling you 'lord' and expecting you to fix things for them." Grin looked at the burning bridge once more. "Goodness knows, one of them may have even burned down the property of another and they may wish you to set about fixing it."

"There are other ways to the other side of the waters," Aitan said. "We could take to the air, make the horses grow wings—"

"No," Grin said. "I could do all that for us. And I choose not to. There is something to be said for taking responsibility for your actions. I have come to learn this all too well. Now, if you are so insistent about avoiding humans and continuing your travels, then all you need do is call upon your Patron and we can get on with repairing the bridge."

Aitan sighed. "I don't suppose you know the way to the closest town?"

"As a matter of fact," Grin said, "I do. . . ."

Ten

"Now, about your rather limited grasp of magic," Grin said to Aitan as they rode toward Hartston, a mining town. The former Emissary had no mount of his own and would not explain how he had arrived at the covered bridge or what led him to this area. He took Tom's horse and the boy was forced to ride with Aitan. The path upon which Grin led them rose and twisted as they headed toward the granite wall of mountains just a few miles off.

"I do my best," Aitan said. "With magic, I mean."

Grin shook his head. "Yes, but elemental summoning? If wielded properly, it's effective, I grant you, but the techniques you displayed during our fight are easily countered and practically ineffectual against a truly creative mage. You must know that."

"Yes," Aitan groused.

"By the way, if you're attempting to hide your annoyance, you're not doing a good job."

Tom pressed his face against Aitan's back and smiled.

"I'm making no such attempt," Aitan said. "I seem to be unable to hide anything from you, lord, so why should I bother to try? I thought it would be better to react with complete candor."

"Then I take it back; you're doing a wonderful job." Grin looked ahead. Suddenly he drew up his reins and brought his mount to a halt. To one side of him was a collection of steel grey boulders that rose twenty feet into the air, to the other a drop of several hundred feet. The road continued around the rocks and disappeared behind them.

"We'll be in view of the town soon," Grin said as Aitan and Tom came up behind him. The former Emissary nodded to Aitan and said, "We should stop here and tend to those burns you suffered. It won't do for mere humans to see you in such a state, now would it?"

"I suppose," Aitan said with a sigh of defeat.

Tom could hear sounds drifting their way. A celebration of some kind was going on in Hartston, or so Tom gathered from the laughter and cheers. Aitan asked Tom to help him with his armors. The boy did so, delicately removing one piece of plating after another. The angel said, "We probably should have done this by the stream."

Tom stood behind Aitan. He came to the angel's arming doublet and swallowed hard as he said, "It's stuck to your skin. Do you want me to pull it off real fast or try to peel it slowly?"

Grin took the decision out of Tom's hands. The warrior leaped down from his mount, gently pushed Tom out of the way, and used one of his knives to cut around the section of fabric that was stuck.

"Take it off," Grin said.

Aitan removed the garment slowly. He tossed the doublet to the ground. Tom collected it and set it with the rest of Aitan's armors.

"By the way," Grin said, "did I mention that your brother and I made a raid on the Aerie once?"

Aitan spun in surprise, his mouth partially hanging open. Grin darted back, the strip of fabric that had been stuck to Aitan's flesh dangling from his hand.

"I'll wager you didn't even feel it," Grin said.

It took Aitan a moment to realize what the warrior had done. He reached back and tried to touch his burned skin.

"Don't, Aitan," Tom said, screwing up his features in distaste.

"It itches," Aitan said. He fixed his gaze on Grin. The Aerie was the dwelling place of the female angels. "Did you mean what you said?"

"Of course I meant it," Grin said. "I said it. I meant to

say it. So I must have meant it. The question is, was it true?''

Aitan sighed. "You're trying to distract me again."

"What if I am?" Grin asked. "Is that a bad thing? The boy was right, you know. Don't pick at it and don't scratch it. You've got a couple of little burns on your back, the one you're reaching for is about the size of a fist. It's the worst."

The warrior reached around and drew out a pouch hidden by the folds of his armor. He produced a small black vial filled with what looked like—light. Tom stared at the vial, trying to comprehend what he was seeing.

Grin looked to Tom and said, "There's a lesson to be learned in all of this. What I did with Aitan. Sometimes it's better that way. A clean end to the suffering. Short and sweet, don't drag things out. Remember that."

"I will," Tom said.

Grin held the vial out to Tom. "Apply this to Aitan's back. I'll work on mending his armors."

Tom's entire body tensed as he took the vial. It seemed to throb and he nearly dropped it.

"Careful," Aitan said. "If that's what I think it is—"

"It is," Grin said as he stooped to retrieve the various pieces of Aitan's armor that had been removed. "Be very careful."

Tom watched as the former Emissary found a path between several large boulders and disappeared behind them. The boy asked, "What should I do with this?"

"Take out the stopper, apply the liquid sparingly."

"It doesn't look like liquid. It's so bright."

"The vial contains waters from the River of Healing, where all wounds are mended, where all lives are given a fresh start."

"In Heaven?"

"In Heaven."

Doing his best to keep his hands from trembling, Tom slowly drew out the stopper. The light was blinding.

"Don't look at it," Aitan said.

"I just figured that out," Tom said, applying just a touch of the liquid to his fingers. His flesh tingled and he suddenly felt his heart racing. "I feel kind of strange."

"Ignore it. The waters won't harm you."

Nodding, Tom gently rubbed the liquid into Aitan's wounds. Tom gasped as he saw the wounds vanish the moment the liquid touched them. His fingers moved across the angel's back, producing effects similar to a brush filled with paint touching a canvas. Tom reached the largest burn and drew an X over it in curiosity. Suddenly, there was a perfectly smooth symbol of new flesh over the reddish black wound.

"What are you doing, Tom?" Aitan asked.

"Nothing." Tom quickly finished applying the liquid. He drew back and replaced the stopper.

Grin emerged from behind the large rocks littering the shoulder of the road and set Aitan's armors on the ground. They were perfectly restored. The warrior took the vial back from Tom so that the boy could help Aitan into his armors. Soon, they were back on their mounts, riding around the bend of the road.

The sounds Tom had heard earlier came again, stronger this time. As they turned the corner, Tom saw the mining town come into view. It was located in a valley about a mile distant. The town itself was nothing special, but what lay beyond it was.

"That's a castle," Tom said.

"That's a ruin, actually," Grin said. "They started with the town so the builders would have somewhere to live. They never quite finished with the castle. A long story, I expect."

As they rode toward Hartston along the twisting mountain trail, Tom saw the town and the castle come into bold relief. The castle's walls were sandblasted, and its towers had many sharp angles. The town lay at the castle's base, ringed in by a sturdy wall. Within lay a grid of cobbled streets that divided the land into regularly spaced plots. Close to fifty houses had been built inside the town, and at its center was a marketplace bustling with activity. A tent had been erected and people wandered in and out.

The travelers rode down a smooth trail toward the entrance to the town. The main set of gates sat open and a young man leaned against one of them. He seemed perturbed about something and didn't notice the approach of the strangers until they were within fifty feet of him. Then he straightened up, tugged on his wine-colored tunic to straighten it, and threw his arms open in greeting.

"Welcome, good visitors. Gentle lords. Have you come to see the show?" the young man asked. His hair reached down to his shoulders and his face was covered in stubble. His nose was a little large for his face, which was already becoming jowly, and his eyes were set a bit too close together.

Grin sidled up next to Aitan and nudged the angel with his elbow. "Say 'yes.'"

Sighing, Aitan nodded.

"I wish I could," the young man said.

"What's your name?" Grin asked.

"Michael."

"A fine name," the former Emissary said. "Why don't you come with us?"

Michael shook his head. "There would be trouble. I was told to watch the gates. Wait here in case visitors arrived. Greet them and tell them the way to the celebration. My brother was supposed to come and spell me, but he never showed."

"You don't seem especially bothered by our appearances," Aitan noted.

"You mean that you're servants of the Lord?" Michael asked. "Well, there was a Convoy through here last week. Two other soldiers of God a few days ago. In fact, all sorts of people have been through here recently!"

"You see?" Grin asked. "They're through with fawning. And here you were worried."

"Not worried, exactly," Aitan said.

Tom rode on the same mount as Aitan, with his arms around the angel's waist. He smiled. "Worried. You were definitely worried."

"Listen to the boy!" Grin said. "He's very smart."

"Thank you," Aitan said in a low, defeated whisper.

"Sorry," Tom said, truly saddened at the idea that he might have hurt the angel's feelings, or angered him.

Aitan reached down and patted one of Tom's hands to let the boy know he wasn't really upset.

Michael shifted back and forth uncomfortably. "All you need to do is follow the road behind me. Go about a block, then turn to your left, and at the next corner you find, go right and that'll take you straight to the carnival.''

"The carnival?" Tom asked. "The Carnival of Wonders?"

"That's right!" Michael said.

Tom felt some pangs of guilt over the posters he had stolen advertising the carnival's upcoming appearance in Hope.

"Young man," Aitan said, "I think you should be allowed to see the show. In fact, I think I know exactly how to work it out so you won't be in any trouble."

"Really?" Michael said hopefully.

"I'll need to climb down, Tom," Aitan said. The boy dismounted, then helped Aitan to the ground.

Aitan Anzelm closed his eyes and put his hands out before him. Tom watched as Aitan's hands formed strange shapes in the air. It reminded Tom of when his sister was crocheting. All he could make out of Aitan's whisperings was ''. . . by this Sigil I beseech . . .'' and something about manifestations.

Suddenly, a wind rose up at their backs, matched by another that swept toward them from directly ahead! The arcane winds swirled around each of them, making sounds like whispers. No, Tom realized, they *were* whispers! Now he could hear them clearly.

"Come, good visitors, come one, come all, you are welcome, follow my voice, it shall lead you. . . ."

Michael listened, smiling broadly.

Grin laughed. *"That* was pretty good."

"You see?" Aitan asked. "Now you are free to come with us. Take me to your parents and I will explain all to them."

"All right, I will!" Michael said.

The young man led the travelers to the center of town, where the garishly painted tent Tom had seen from a distance resided. It had been torn in many places. Painted on the tautly stretched canvas were images of creatures he'd dreamed of seeing for real one day. Lions, tigers, rhinos, and more.

A few hundred people were gathered in the town square. Most of Hartston's populace, Tom guessed. Perhaps some from other towns, too. The people had dark circles under their eyes and soot pressed under their nails. Some coughed. Many looked as if they hadn't bathed or groomed themselves in weeks. All that really mattered was that they were enjoying themselves.

Tom saw a strongman working his way through the crowd, challenging one man after another. The strongman was bald, with swarthy skin and a ring in his nose. He had huge arms and legs, practically no neck, and a chest big enough to make two of Tom. His rippling muscles were greased, his chest exposed. He wore only a short wrap around his waist and sandals.

"I can take ya. I could!" the strongman cried in a throaty voice as he thrust his face close to that of a leathery-skinned miner.

"Like to see ya try."

"Wouldn't be worth my time!" the strongman said, citing four other men he could easily "take" before he came to Grin and stopped dead. The fighter thought it over for a moment. "I can't take you." He spun and aimed a finger at a burly man a few feet away. "But you? You'd be nothing. I could take you."

"Big talk!" the burly man shouted. The crowd roared with laughter and approval.

Tom, Aitan, and Grin eyed one another. It was rather pleasant that no one was making a fuss over them. Odd compared to what they had all envisioned, but pleasant nevertheless.

The strongman advanced on the burly man. "Oh, I could take you, all right." He arched one brow and pursed his lips. "The question is, could you take *him*?" The strongman pointed toward a spot in the crowd and everyone's attention went to a man who stood no more than three feet high. He wore a perfectly tailored black suit, a shiny black hat, and white gloves. He seemed quite above it all, from his expression.

"He looks like a dandy," someone said.

"Only pint-sized!" another added, summoning roars of laughter from the crowd.

"This is some kind of trick," the burly man said.

"Of course it is," the strongman said. He tapped his bald pate. "The question is, do you have what it takes up here, in your noodle, to see what kind of trick it is? Or are you a *fool* as well as a coward?"

The burly man's face flushed crimson. "No one calls me a coward!"

"Then stop acting like one. Pay your money, take your chances. Fight the little man. See if you can take him."

"It wouldn't be a fair fight."

"So *you* say. . . ."

Tom stood transfixed. Aitan tapped him on the shoulders. "I must talk with Michael's parents. Enjoy yourself."

Grin leaned in close. *"After* you take care of the horses."

"Oh!" Tom said, feeling quite foolish. He turned from the spectacle, gathered up the reins to both horses, and asked one of the good townsfolk where he would find the closest stable. As he led the horses off, he heard the little man speaking.

"My name is Patrice LaVaughan. I am thirty-one years old. I can see that some of you look at me and are thinking, *Poor man, I should pity him.* Well, don't! It is *I* who should pity *you.*"

That got the crowd's curiosity up. Murmurs and titters of laughter threatened to drown out the diminutive man's voice.

"It's not your fault you were born disadvantaged. I see life from the same level as a child. While the rest of you grow tall and forget what it was like to view all things with awe and wonder, I remain the same. I live in a land of giants and misfits and freaks. All life is a challenge, a mystery, an adventure! While you see a chair to park your enormous rumps—well, they are to me, anyway—"

Laughter came from the crowd.

"You see a chair, I see a mountain to climb! Where you see a tub to bathe in, I see an ocean in which to dive . . . !"

"You're not that small," Tom muttered with a bright smile as he turned the corner and lost the rest of the little man's words. He came to the stables, made arrangements to put up the horses, then recalled that he had no coin on him. He knew the stablemaster's hand would be out when he was done tying up the mounts in the darkened stables. What was he to do?

Go back to Aitan, get some money, he thought. But it was embarrassing.

He made a decision.

When no one was looking, he examined one of Aitan's saddlebags and tried to open it. He couldn't. Though there was no lock on it, something held it closed.

"Magic," Tom whispered. "What was I thinking?"

With a sigh, he tried all the bags on Aitan's mount and on the one Grin had commandeered. He was about to give up, but there was only one bag left and he had come this far. Tom pulled on it and was amazed at how readily the bag opened. He fished inside, found a few coins at the bottom of the bag— and something *else* that made his heart leap!

The vial. He took hold of the elixir Grin had given him to use on Aitan. Its light was a little dimmer than before, but it still made him feel strange to touch it.

How did it get in here? he wondered.

An idea came to Tom. He pictured Grin placing the vial here as a gift. No, that couldn't be right. Why then had he not resealed it?

An idea that might have been considered blasphemy had he spoken it aloud came to him: Perhaps because even those who have walked with God can make mistakes.

Tom held the vial and considered the boys his age and younger who lived in a town like this. Though there had been a flurry of activity during the past week or so, living in a town like Hartston had to be pretty dull the rest of the time. Tom thought of the petty sins he had committed, like the theft of posters advertising the carnival. He wouldn't put it past some stableboy to get curious and go through these bags.

What was he going to do? He couldn't leave the vial unattended.

A scream came from outside the stables. Tom wondered what had happened.

"Squire! Squire!" someone shouted a few seconds later. Running footsteps sounded, growing louder with every passing second.

Tom slipped the vial into the pocket of his breeches seconds before the stablemaster and two of his boys arrived.

"Come quickly!" the stablemaster said. "Your lords have need of you!"

Curious and frightened, Tom nodded and followed them from the stables.

Eleven

TOM RUSHED INTO THE HARSH LIGHT OF DAY, SQUINTING as he raced behind the stablemaster and his boys. They came to the square, where crowds were gathered outside the tent. The strongman and the dwarf stood with the burly man who had been challenged to a fight. The dwarf had a single scuff mark on his black slacks. The burly man looked as if he had fallen down the side of a mountain, slamming into a handful of boulders while tree limbs tore his clothing to shreds along the way. The mystery of how *that* had occurred would have to wait. They held open a flap and Tom bolted into the tent. His eyes quickly adjusted to the muted light within. The interior of the tent was a forty-foot square. Tom saw rows of benches for people to sit upon and a network of ropes forty feet above. The ropes were a mad tangle, a twisted-up spider's web, and someone was trapped in the middle of them. A child. One of the ropes was wrapped around his neck.

Aitan stood on the ground at the center of the tent. His arms were outstretched, his eyes closed. Tom wondered for a brief moment why Aitan did not use his power to lower the child to the ground. Then he saw that something was wrong with the scene before him. Many of the supports holding the tent in place had shattered. The twin towers on either side of the tent leading up to the network of ropes had fallen, making it impossible for anyone to climb up and rescue the boy. By rights, the tent should have collapsed. Some invisible force anchored the broken wood.

Aitan said, "Tom, if I lose my concentration, this tent will collapse and that boy will die. Go up there with a knife and cut him free.''

"Go up there on what?'' Tom asked. There was nothing for him to climb. "What's going on here? Where's Grin?''

There was a rustle of canvas and Patrice LaVaughan, the dwarf, was suddenly behind him. "Lord, my people have brought what you required. I have it here.''

Tom turned to see the dwarf holding a sack filled with saw-dust in one hand, a jagged blade in the other. He took them and turned to Aitan. "I don't understand. What do you expect me to do?''

"I told you, climb up and cut the boy free.''

"I don't see anything. What am I supposed to climb up onto?''

"I've solidified the air in places. There is a walkway. Use the dust in the bag to help you see it.''

Tom looked up at the boy trapped in the ropes, then ran until he was practically beneath the child. Suddenly, his foot slammed into an unseen force and he was sent sprawling. The blade skittered out of his hand and the bag fell but did not open. The diminutive man raced to Tom's side and helped the lad to his feet.

"All right,'' Tom said, "I think I found it.''

Tom yanked off his shirt and used the knife to cut away several strips of fabric. Then he wrapped the cutting edge of the blade with one strip and laid it against his thigh. LaVaughan helped him tie the knife in place with another strip of fabric. Tom opened the bag and poured some of the sawdust into the air. The stepping-stones Aitan had fashioned were now visible. Steeling himself, Tom set one foot on the first stone, then the other. When he sensed that he would not fall, he climbed several more steps, wincing as the stones shifted beneath his weight, teetering first one way, then the other.

On the ground, Patrice LaVaughan wrung his hands and said, "The supports holding up the tent were old, rotten through. We didn't have the money to replace them. Instead, we just kept going. We were idiots thinking this would never happen.'' The diminutive man bit his lip. "I'm sorry. Am I making this worse on you?''

Tom kept climbing. His heart thundered. He was terrified. But he kept climbing. "Go on. It's giving me something else to think about."

LaVaughan said, "That boy up there is an acrobat. Did this whole routine with his sister. It was beautiful. Spider and the Fly they called it. You should have seen Cameron chasing his sister up there, leaping from one rope to another, spinning, falling through the air and catching himself. Amazing. The ropes made a kind of grid. The openings between the ropes were like five-foot-by-five-foot. It wasn't easy, what either of them did. They trained in China. Ever hear of China? This probably isn't the time, is it? Lord, I'm nervous. . . ."

"That makes two of us," Tom said. He was now fifteen feet into the air and the bag of sawdust was more than half-empty. He would have to be even more sparing if it was going to last until he reached the top.

I'm walking the air, Tom thought. It was almost like flying, which he had done many times in his dreams. The experience was terrifying, but exhilarating, too.

Why me, Aitan? Tom wondered. *Why not have one of the other performers do this?*

LaVaughan was shaking. "Look up into the rafters. See those other lines? They're painted black so the rubes can't see them. Cameron and his sister had these hooks they used so they could go up higher, make it look like they were flying, jumping—ah, blast, I'm sorry."

"Where's the sister?" Tom asked.

"She fell. The other one like your friend took off with her, told your friend to help the boy."

So that's what happened to Grin, Tom thought. He took her somewhere to help her and probably didn't want anyone to see the kind of magic he was going to do on her, like when he hid behind the boulders to restore Aitan's armors.

Suddenly, Tom felt the stepping-stone beneath him waver. He gasped as it lost solidity and he fell right through it!

A scream left him and the bag dropped from his hand. His boots struck another "stone" and he dropped into a crouch, clutching at the edges of the stone. He looked down and could no longer see the stepping-stones he had covered in sawdust. They must have lost solidity, too, he reasoned, and the sawdust fell. There was no way to tell if the lower steps were still in place or not.

"Tom, we have no time," Aitan called. "Lord Skalligrin's estimation of my powers as a mage was all too accurate. If not for my Patron, who is none too pleased to have been burdened twice today with my summons, this miracle would not be possible. We must hurry."

On the ground, Patrice LaVaughan fell silent.

Shifting his gaze upward to the boy who was trapped, Tom saw that the child's position was changed. The ropes around him were tighter. Cameron appeared on the verge of being hung by the neck. If Aitan lost his concentration even once more before Tom could reach the child, the ropes around Cameron's throat would probably be pulled taut, breaking his neck. Tom couldn't let that happen.

Reaching forward, he felt another stepping-stone. Standing on one foot, he tapped the air where he imagined the next invisible stone to be. He accidentally caught his boot underneath the stone. For an instant he felt as if he was going to fall, then he settled and placed his weight on the new stone. He found the stone after that without a problem.

Soon, Tom was close enough to see the trapped child. The boy looked unconscious. He wore a costume that was pure white. Easier to see him from below that way, Tom guessed. He looked about ten years old, with long, silky black hair and a handsome, oval face. The child's expression was peaceful, betraying no hint of the danger he was in.

Two more steps and Tom was close enough to reach up and touch the boy. The ropes formed a cradle that held Cameron tight. Tom could cut away at the ropes, but they were the only things keeping the unconscious acrobat from plunging to the ground. Even if he could somehow get close enough to brace the child, cut him loose, and not get thrown off-balance when Cameron sank into his arms, how was he supposed to get down while carrying his burden? Climbing up had been hard enough. Going back down again, feeling with his toes for the next invisible step, teetering in midair with a heavy weight in his arms, or slung across his back—simply didn't sound possible. Not for him, anyway. They should have sent the strongman for a task like this. Then again, the invisible stepping-stones may not have been sturdy enough to support his weight.

"Tom," Aitan called from below, "please hurry. My power is fading."

Fear tried to knife its way into Tom's heart, but he deflected its attack. He would have to sling the child over his shoulder, then sit on the stones and carefully make his way down them, like a tiny child who hadn't yet learned to walk.

Tom felt the invisible stone beneath him tilt suddenly. He reached up and clutched hold of one of the ropes for support. Cameron made a choking sound. Looking up, Tom saw that he was pulling the rope taut, throttling the boy. The stone balanced itself and Tom let go of the rope. The pressure relieved, Cameron stopped choking.

Tom didn't have the time to make his way down the steps slowly and carefully. The only option he could see was to cut the boy loose and make a mad dash downward, praying the stones would be there, praying he would guess the exact location of each invisible step and not falter in any way.

"Well," Tom whispered desperately. "If that's all . . ."

He had to come up with another way down. One misstep and he would find himself falling to the ground with his burden.

An idea struck him. Tom called down to the dwarf, asking if they had any sort of net.

"Sorry," LaVaughan said. "Cameron and his sister refused nets. Said they were insulting. We made one for them anyway, but they sold it when we were on the road."

Tom considered that there was another way. Aitan wouldn't be pleased, but Tom would do his best to make it up to the angel another time. Provided he lived that long.

The lad went up one more step, untied the knife, and took another look at Cameron. The acrobat lay facedown, his arms and legs dangling at points lower than his head. Two tangled ropes were wrapped around his throat. Only a support rope caught under the boy's arms and another wrapped around one leg had saved him from strangulation.

Holding the knife firmly, Tom said a quick prayer then eased one hand between the ropes and the child's neck. Breathing hard with fear, he cut away at the ropes.

"Aitan!" Tom called to his companion. "The way your spell seems to work, you can mold the air into shapes, right?"

"Yes."

"Any form you can imagine?"

"My strength is fading. Don't try my patience."

"In technical terms, Aitan, that was called a question, not a challenge. I don't mean to sound testy or anything, but I'm the one who's in danger of being flattened here. Not you."

The angel's tone softened. "Apologies. Yes. Any form."

"How about a nice soft net? Can you do that?"

There was a brief silence as Aitan thought it over. "I'm not sure. If the consistency of the air is too hard, it would be like falling onto a net made from razor-sharp wires. You and the boy would be cut to ribbons."

"Comforting." Tom pushed his shoulder up into Cameron's torso, easing the tension on the ropes, which he had all but cut through completely. "Let's say we give it a try, okay?"

"Tom? I don't—"

With that, Tom sliced through the last of the ropes. Cameron's still form dropped as Tom thought it would, wriggling past the ropes under the arms and around the one leg like a fish anxious to get free from the bow of a fisherman's skiff. Tom tossed the knife away, then launched himself off the stone and into the air behind the child.

"No!" Aitan cried.

Tom saw the ground race up, heard Aitan curse, and saw the man gesturing frantically. He closed his eyes, believing in the promise Aitan had made, that the angel would allow no harm to befall his squire.

He kept falling.

A wind rushed toward Tom. He opened his eyes and forced back a scream as the ground raced up at him.

He was going to strike. He was going to *die*. Aitan couldn't save him! Worse, Tom would see Cameron die first. He would know that his decision had robbed the child of his life.

Then he saw Cameron's descent falter. Suddenly he felt invisible forces rising up around him.

The net!

Lines of force grabbed at Tom. His momentum slowed, but he was still dropping. The ground reached up like an angry fist—and was frustrated in its attempt to pound Tom into oblivion.

For an instant, Tom hung motionless in midair. Then the net faded and Tom fell a few feet to an ignoble landing. He grunted as he struck the hard earth, then rolled onto his backside and sat up to see the dwarf hurrying toward the fallen acrobat. The strongman was now at his side. The huge, bald man scooped up the child.

"Run!" Aitan cried, racing his way. "Go!"

All of them ran from the tent as the supports collapsed and the tent folded in upon itself. The sunlight blinded Tom for a second as he cleared the tent, then turned to see its fall. After a deafening series of crashes, groans, and roars, the tent finally came to rest, the remains of the supports rising into the air, some piercing the canvas, others poking from underneath it.

Tom and Aitan were surrounded by the residents of Hartston and other employees of the carnival. A cheer rose up as the strongman looked down at the child in his arms and smiled. The dwarf reached up and ruffled the boy's hair.

Aitan clutched Tom's arm. "Why didn't you let me catch the boy first? Why did you jump after him?"

"Because I made a decision that affected him. It wasn't fair for me to stand by and not abide by the same decision."

"That was foolish! You could have been killed."

"I trusted you. I don't see that as being foolish."

The angel allowed a ragged gasp to escape him, then nodded and smiled.

Tom heard the cheering of the crowd suddenly falter as a beautiful young woman with emerald eyes and wild raven's hair came forward. She wore a costume like the acrobat, white, with streaks of glittering clear paint that made her body sparkle in the bright sunlight. Her body was long and lithe, her figure voluptuous. Tom stared at her and could not see anything else.

Grin followed her, clearly unhappy about something.

"Child, don't," Grin said. "It will be too painful."

"Leave me alone!" she shouted. "I want to see my brother!"

The young woman stopped before the strongman. The bald man knelt, the unconscious boy in his arms, and said, "Don't worry, Cameron's going to be fine. He's got a cut on his forehead. Couldn't see it at first through all the hair. Something must have hit him when the tent started to collapse and the two of you fell.''

"He's alive?'' she said in wonder. Then she knelt and touched the side of her brother's face. He stirred, mumbled something. Her hard-set features suddenly collapsed and she began to cry in relief. Looking over her shoulder at Grin, she said, "You told me he would be—''

"That can't be,'' Grin whispered, shaking his head, his mouth hanging open in confusion. "I *saw* him die.''

"Whatever you saw, it wasn't my brother,'' she said.

"I'm happy to be wrong, but it's not possible. My sight is true, my dreams . . .''

The young woman was beyond caring about anything the armored warrior had to say. She held her brother close, crying with joy and relief.

This is the other acrobat, Tom thought. *The one who fell. Grin healed her somehow.*

He had never seen anyone so perfect. Tom decided then and there that even if he never learned this young woman's name, just the knowledge that so perfect a creature had not been destroyed, her spirit lifted from the earth prematurely, would be enough to fuel his imagination and his prayers of thanks for years to come. He was certain of that, though he wasn't quite sure why.

Next to Tom, Aitan looked to the former Emissary. He said, "I think we should go somewhere and talk, don't you?''

"No,'' Grin said, still shaken, "but it is inevitable, I suppose. Just not right now. We are among a people who have a desire to celebrate. I think all that fawning you were so grateful to avoid is about to come your way.''

Just then, the crowd closed in on the heroes, with cheers and more than a few requests. . . .

Twelve

THE AFTERNOON AND EARLY EVENING PASSED IN A BLUR for Tom. It turned out that Aitan's initial response to the collapse of the tent had saved not only the young acrobat, but also dozens of townsfolk who were inside the tent, watching the performance. They had all been evacuated before Tom had arrived.

As the day progressed, the remains of the tent were carted away. Once the debris was gone, Aitan took advantage of the general goodwill to confess that he had destroyed the bridge.

He was about to go into the details when Grin stepped forward and wove a fabulous tale of Aitan's battle with an agent of the Enemy. The people were kept spellbound for close to half an hour. When the story was finished, the general feeling was that it had been worth the loss of the bridge just to hear a story like that. And if an agent of the Enemy had been driven off, then all the better. Besides, the rebuilding of the bridge would give them something other than their daily drudgery to think about. There were other, longer routes to the adjoining towns they would use until the new bridge was completed.

Aitan was uncomfortable with the lie, but he was grateful to the warrior for not showing him up to be a fool.

The people of Hartston took Aitan, Tom, and Grin on a tour of the half-finished castle, telling its history. The building had been meant to be a school for the devout. When extensive mineral deposits were discovered in the hills nearby, those plans were abandoned in favor of a mining operation.

Next, the mines were explored. Tom learned that the mine

contained large amounts of pure kaolin, or china clay, white clay that retained its color when fired and used in the making of porcelain and china. The impure varieties were used for pottery, stoneware, and bricks. The people also mined for othoclase, a feldspar used in the creation of glass. Mineral fibers and gemstones were in abundance, and a good deal of olivine, used as foundry sand and as a flux for making steel. Tom was given a handful of iridescent moonstones and sparkling sunstones, though he had no idea what he would do with them.

A young couple whose child was inside the tent insisted on performing a series of traditional angel sonnets and hymns for Aitan. The angel tried not to squirm for a time, then finally broke down and explained that he had much more of a fondness for folk music from the human lands. The couple seemed relieved and immediately shifted into a host of ballads.

Aitan enjoyed their rousing version of "Tenting on the Old Campgrounds" and seemed genuinely moved by "Bury Me Not on the Lone Prairie." The song had drifted their way from the workers sent to live among the Great Tribes of the West, learning of the natives' cultures while teaching about their own.

"These words came low and mournfully, from the pallid lips of a youth who lay, on his dying bed, at the close of the day. . . ."

While Aitan and Grin sat with the people of Hartston in the town square, Tom wandered around, hoping for another glimpse of the beautiful young acrobat whose brother he had helped to save. Night had fallen and lamps had been set on the street corners. He had seen the young lady half a dozen times that day, but he had not spoken to her once. Each time he ended up staring at her from afar. The moment she looked toward him and smiled, he tensed and found some excuse to get away.

Tom told himself that all he wanted was to know her name, but that wasn't true. He wanted more. He wanted to touch her, to kiss her. Anything more, he knew, would be asking too much. Besides, he had never done much of anything with a girl, though he had been told by older boys about a wealth of unexplored possibilities.

No, he decided, it would be enough for him just to talk with her. Just to know that she didn't blame him for the injury her brother sustained to the head. It had happened before he had arrived, but did she really know that? He also wanted to be sure that she was all right after her own fall, and he was painfully curious about what Grin had done to her. How badly had she been injured?

He had his head down and was staring at the cobbled street, no longer really believing he would see her again, when a voice called out, "You're gonna walk right into me."

Tom looked up sharply. He gasped, certain he was about to swallow his wildly beating heart.

It was she.

She was dressed in a soft white blouse, buttoned-down the front, a red skirt, and sandals.

He thought he was in a dream.

Walking forward, she held out her hand and said, "I was out looking for you."

His mouth was suddenly so dry that it hung open and he thought for certain that he must look like a fool to someone like her. A foolish, lost little child. She took his hand and gently touched her finger to the bottom of his chin, pushing up slightly to close his mouth. He couldn't believe how close he was to her. She smelled like the petals of a rose. Her skin was red-hot, her touch bringing a fire to him that even Dina had never before elicited.

I'm sweating, he thought. *I'm sweating and I must look like a total idiot.*

"You look nice," she said, brushing her hand against his chest. "That shirt we got you fits pretty well. Sorry you had to lose yours."

"Oh," he said, then added a slight shrug. He shook his head, tried to smile, and realized he was twitching. "Oh."

She laughed. "Come here. There's something I want to show you."

"Ah," he said. "Yes. That would be nice."

He couldn't believe he had said that.

She took his arm and leaned close as they walked, occasionally brushing her cheek against his shoulder. Her skin was so smooth, so perfect. She kept talking as they walked together.

Tom couldn't believe he was with her. He had so many questions for her. What would she do now? Would she ever climb up on a wire again or would she be afraid?

Did she like him?

He listened to her talk of the people in town, how friendly they were. She told of a little boy who had seen her fall and thought she was magic because she was back among them. In truth, she felt blessed to have a second chance at life, and relieved that her brother Cameron was well.

Lord, Tom thought, *her voice is so sweet.*

It was deep and rich with a husky edge that made him feel so—*interested.* That was as good a word for it as any.

In moments, they were taking the back stairs up a small two-story building, passing through a doorway, then entering a small room with a bed and a couple of dressers. Moonlight filtered in through a nearby window. Once his eyes adjusted, he could see another door at the far end of the room.

Tom was terrified. He felt a liquid fire building up in his chest and a pressure from *down below* that was painful. His companion closed the door behind herself, locked it, and lit some candles. The soft orange glow made her look even more beautiful.

Forget Aitan Anzelm and his kind, Tom thought. *This* young woman looked like an angel.

"My brother Cameron's asleep down the hall. About four rooms down. There's no one else on this floor. We don't have to worry about making noise."

Making noise? he thought. What was she implying? An idea came to him and he immediately dismissed it. This was a proper young lady he was with, after all.

She was having him on, Tom decided. Just having some fun with him, that's all. He relaxed. What a relief. Sort of.

"What's your name?" he asked.

"Penelope," she said. "But all my friends call me Kayrlis."

"Careless?"

"No." She spelled it for him.

"I like that," he said.

She came forward, placing her hands on his shoulders, and

guided him down to a sitting position on the bed. Sliding in beside him, she whispered, "I like you."

Before he could reply, she surged forward and kissed him hard on the mouth. One arm went around his back. Her free hand caressed the side of his face, then trailed down to his chest and came to rest in his lap. Tom started, but Kayrlis did not draw away. Her lips parted and her tongue worked at his mouth until soon their tongues were entwined. Tom felt her hands kneading him through his trousers. His mind failed to function. All he knew for that amazing instant was her touch, and how he was straining, needing more.

Certain that he was on the verge of exploding then and there, Tom came to his senses and broke the contact. He leaped off the bed, spun to face her, clutching at the handles of the dresser behind him.

"Oh, my," he said.

She frowned. "I didn't get the wrong idea, did I? I mean— you *do* like me, don't you?"

"Yes." His chest rose and fell like a bellows. He was trembling.

She looked down and grinned. "Yes, I can see that. Silly question."

Embarrassed, Tom sank to the floor, bringing his knees up to hide the source of his current troubles.

I want this, I want this, I want this, he chanted in his mind. *I know it's wrong, but I want this. . . .*

Kayrlis leaned back and unbuttoned her blouse. She pulled it from her skirt and left it hanging half-open. Tom had seen women's underthings before. Half the time, he was the one stuck with doing the wash at the Keeper House, and he knew exactly what his sister's "unmentionables" looked like. He had just never seen anything like them while they were still being worn by someone, especially someone like Kayrlis. Her bosom was full and heavy, two generous swells rising up from her corset. She leaned forward, not at all embarrassed.

"We don't have to do this if you don't want to," she said. "I just wanted to show you how much I appreciate what you did."

"Merciful Lord," Tom whispered.

She looked away, tapping one hand on her knee while she

twisted up her gorgeous features in worry. "Don't make this hard on me, please. I'm nervous enough as it is."

Tom's brow furrowed. He felt himself relaxing somewhat, though his desire was still pounding inside him, beating down the walls of his reason, his restraint. *"You're* nervous? Is this your first time?"

"No," she said. "You won't be the first. That alone should take some of the concern away for you. If you are the kind of boy I think you are."

"Well, yes," he said, having no idea what she was talking about.

"The first man I slept with, he didn't know it was gonna hurt me, and he hadn't the first idea about the blood."

"Oh."

"Actually, it was never very good with him." She wrung her hands nervously. "I'm blathering, aren't I?"

"Yeah, but keep doing it. It's helping."

"Is it? Okay." She laughed. "Would you at least sit next to me? I'll cover up if you want me to."

"No, that's all right."

"Can I take my blouse off?"

Tom gestured magnanimously. "Sure."

Smiling, she pulled off the blouse. Tom watched, fascinated by the way her breasts swayed and bounced with her motions. He came up and sat beside her, his hands in his lap. She took off her shoes and said, "I have an idea. Why don't we just lie back on the bed and hold hands? You can take off your boots, if you want."

He removed his boots, turned to see Kayrlis lying back, and lay down next to her. Their hands came together and for a time he looked at the ceiling. His "attraction" to her had not faded in the least. He looked over at her and said, "You're the most beautiful woman I've ever seen."

"I'm not that much older than you are, you know."

"I'm fourteen."

"Seventeen."

Tom swallowed hard. "I know, people get married at our age and stuff all the time."

"Don't get any ideas. I'm not the marrying kind."

"I wasn't asking. I mean—not that I wouldn't. It's funny,

but I *could* see myself spending a lifetime with you."

"Please."

"I'm serious."

She got up on one elbow, stared deeply into his eyes, and said, "I believe you are. I'm not going to kiss you again, you know."

"You're not?" he asked, deflated.

"Nope. You're going to have to kiss me."

He leaned forward awkwardly. Their lips met and he felt his ardor pain him once more. The kiss went on for what seemed like an impossibly long time, then Kayrlis pulled back.

"You *have* kissed a girl before, now haven't you?" she said with a sexy, throaty laugh.

"Once or twice," he said. Honestly, that's all it had been. A few stolen moments with a girl he had a crush on before Dina.

She grinned. "Once or twice. Listen to you."

Tom drew a sharp breath and said, "You don't have to do this, Kayrlis. I didn't go up there and help your brother because I was looking for anything out of it."

She touched the side of his face. "I know. That's one of the reasons I want to make love with you. I really, really want to, Tom. Do you mind me telling you that?"

"No," he said. Lord, how he didn't mind one bit!

"And to be honest, your being handsome as hell counts for a lot, too. If you were ugly, and you seemed like a total idiot, or some conceited fool, the most you'd have to look forward to is a handshake. Maybe a peck on the cheek."

He kissed her again, ignoring her petty blaspheme. Deciding to get bold, he reached out and placed his hand on her shoulder. Again they kissed. He felt as if he could do this forever.

A part of him thought of what he should have been saying: *We can't do this. It's a sin. We're not married.*

He also thought of the warnings his father had given him. Getting a girl with child, suddenly finding himself obligated to her whether he loved her or not.

Then he *knew*.

Looking into Kayrlis's perfect, emerald eyes, Tom said, "I love you."

"I believe you do," she said, leaning forward and kissing him.

"I thought you weren't going to do that again," he said.

She rose from the bed, took off her corset, her skirt, her slip. She stood before him, her hands open, smiling, waiting for him to say something.

"Perfect," he whispered.

Tom had never imagined wanting someone as badly as he wanted her that very moment. He still felt as if he might explode at the slightest touch, and he desperately did not want that. He wanted this night to go on and on, to last forever, if such a thing was possible.

"Take off your clothes and I'll do a lot more," she said.

He found the offer impossible to resist. . . .

Aitan and Grin sat together in one of the towers of the unfinished castle.

"Do you think Tom's all right?" Aitan asked.

Grin said, "Considering the look I saw in the eyes of that young lady who was prowling around after him, asking everyone if they'd seen him, I'd say right about now he's *more* than all right."

"Do you want to explain what's happening here?"

"No. Of course not."

Aitan growled in frustration. "Will you please explain what's happening here?"

"If I must." Grin sighed. "As I believe you've already guessed, I was given a gift from the Sixth Earthly Incarnation of our Lord when I left His service. At least, I assume it was from Him. I don't know who else would have such power to give."

"Prophecy."

Grin nodded. "The proverbial blessing and curse. More curse than anything. You see, the visions I'm granted aren't always as detailed as I might like."

"They told you to seek out Tom and me. Where and when to find us."

"Yes."

"And that we had to come to this place. Hartston."

"Correct again."

"In the tent, when the girl fell, you slowed her descent with your power. You saved her. Doing the same for the boy would have been a simple matter for you. Instead, you took the girl and vanished. When you brought her back, you appeared shocked that her brother was still alive. It contradicted one of your visions, did it not?"

Grin looked stricken. "And such a thing has *never happened before*. You're right, I should have been able to save the boy. But in my vision he died. That told me that if I attempted to save him, something would go wrong. Horribly wrong. Such things have occurred before."

"So you were afraid to try?"

"Yes."

Aitan was surprised. He looked out to the pale moon breaking through the clouds against the midnight blue of the sky. He had not expected one such as Grin to admit to a weakness like fear.

"I was afraid that it would have been arrogant for me to try and contradict a vision sent to me by God," said Grin, "and that I would not be the only one to suffer for such an affront."

"So you took the girl and left the rest to me."

"It seemed the only option. I didn't want her to witness the death of her brother."

"Had she been in your vision?"

"No. I've told you, they're mostly incomplete. Usually, the more detailed a vision, the closer it is to occurring. If a vision is fragmented, odd images of people I have never seen before saying enigmatic things, then it is far distant."

"These visions have always come true. So you left the fate of the boy in my hands, expecting me to fail."

"Yes."

Aitan was silent for a moment. Then: "Have I sinned against God by saving the child? Did I show arrogance?"

"I don't see how. *You* couldn't have known the boy's fate."

Rising, Aitan went to the window and said, "What do you know of my purpose?"

"Very little."

Aitan thought about the task he had been asked to perform. "Your visions told you nothing else about Tom and me? That perhaps I am fated to fail in an enterprise I may undertake?"

Grin issued a slight groan as he hefted his bulky, armored form up off the ground and went to Aitan's side. "I wanted the girl to be spared the sight of her brother's death. I expected you to fail, yes. You surprised me. You defied a vision sent from the Almighty."

"You're certain that's where they originate?"

"Where else?"

Aitan looked at him. "The Enemy *is* real, is He not?"

Grin remained expressionless. "Of course."

"What are you holding back from me, lord? Wouldn't it be easier on you if your burden was shared?"

The warrior's shoulders sank. The fight seemed to leave him. "I have seen things in my lifetime. Things I may never tell anyone, unless I wish to bring eternal damnation down upon myself. All I can tell you is that something horrible is walking the earth. Something that's our fault."

A sudden, stabbing memory came to Aitan. He thought of the mission he had been asked to undertake; of his last days in the City of Heaven, Chalkydri; and of the promises he had made, and how he had no intention of fulfilling them. Not then, anyway.

"Something that will make us question our beliefs," Grin said mournfully. "Something that might be right to do so."

The faces of those he had lost came to Aitan Anzelm, along with an agony he had long been casting aside.

Aitan said, "You've given me a lot to think about. Maybe we should get some sleep. Ride out early in the morning, before those who have spent the night composing lists of prayers and requests have at us."

Grin laughed. "As you say."

Walking toward the twisting stairwell, Aitan turned and said, "Are you coming?"

"I wish to look at the stars for a time."

Aitan continued on alone. As he descended the stone steps, he thought he saw movement from the corner of his eye. Turning, he cast a spell of fire to light the darkness.

There was nothing. Darkness and light. Nothing more.

Why then, did he suddenly feel such a chill? He recalled his childhood, when he had been certain that shadows had secret lives all of their own, that they watched and waited, plotting to take the souls of the unwary if the opportunity was ever given. He had only ever told his fantasies to one other: the one he had been asked to find and destroy.

He dismissed the light.

Foolishness.

The angel did not see the lone shadow that detached itself from the others behind him. It lingered for a moment, watching him. Then an opening formed in what might have been its head, and needle-sharp teeth formed a malevolent smile.

The shadow turned and went upstairs.

It had other things to concern itself with tonight.

Lord Ainigrim Bosh R'Hayle Skalligrin, Emissary to the Almighty in his Sixth and most treasured Vessel, stood in the deserted tower, wondering if he had done the right thing. The world was changing in subtle ways that few truly noticed. The advent of any true technology had been halted, yes. The dreamers of the age had been cast into darkness. Firearms, mostly prevalent in the east, had been removed from the hands of mankind. All was right in Heaven and on earth.

No, that was a lie.

The longer he had known God in his Sixth Vessel, the more he had become convinced that he served a being mired in the depths of insanity. The former Emissary knew that it was not up to him to pass judgment on the most perfect being that had ever come into existence. How could he fathom the will of the Almighty? How could he hope to comprehend the intricacies of the Grand Plan?

He had been a fool, confronting God, railing at the Almighty, and he had paid a dire price for his rash behavior.

When Grin had first become an Emissary, he had been surprised at how few duties he had been called upon to perform. God did not attend his Sixth Vessel very often, and Grin imagined He neglected His other eight even more. When he had no direct responsibilities to fulfill for the Lord, he had traveled the world, doing what had to be done to prevent mankind from taking the path that might one day have led them to insurrection.

It had been on his final Crusade, as his duties as an assassin had been called by the Sixth Vessel, that he had made the

mistake of seeing his victim as anything more than a blight to
be erased from the earth. Grin had assumed a mortal form, a
magic reserved for only the most noble of God's servants, and
he had boarded a ship called the *Beagle*. A harmless sounding
name, but on the small craft was a self-proclaimed naturalist
named Charles Darwin. The ship was nearing the end of a
five-year journey. Soon the voyagers would close on the ports
of N'thrahail, once known as London, and Grin's task had
been to see that they never arrived. He had also been instructed
to destroy all their possessions, and not to listen to their words,
or view anything they would have him look upon.

It had been so odd. The Sixth Vessel had almost seemed
afraid of what these humans had to say, what they had to
show.

Carrying out his task would have been a simple matter if
he had just allowed it to be such. He could have engulfed the
craft in a fire of such intensity that all aboard would have been
reduced to ashes in a heartbeat, along with whatever blasphemous materials they carried. Or he could have summoned a
maelstrom to swallow up the ninety-foot vessel, dragging it
and its occupants to the depths of the sea, where no human
could ever travel to view that which the dead men carried.

Instead, Grin took a human face and planted himself in the
waters where their ship could soon come in sight of him. In
those days, he had not been welded into the armors he cur-
rently wore. He moved among the humans as one of them,
pretending to be the survivor of a shipwreck.

He grew to genuinely like the young Darwin, though the
boy was clearly mad. The daily battles between Darwin and
Fitzroy, the ship's captain, who believed completely in the
literal truth of the Word, as did all who were righteous, was
extremely amusing. Darwin looked upon Grin as a potential
convert to his cause and showed the disguised Emissary his
findings.

It seemed that Darwin had traveled the world over on the
Beagle, miraculously without a mishap. He had skirted the
west coast of Africa, encircled the lower peninsula of South
America, and made many amazing discoveries on the Galapagos Islands before crossing the South Pacific, and venturing
to New Zealand and Australia. After navigating the Indian

Ocean, he journeyed around the southernmost regions of Africa and was now on his way home.

Darwin had intended to enter the Church. He had decided to devote himself to a life of service to the Lord. First, he had to pay his Mita and endure his five years of service to the government as a sailor. He had always been an adventurous man and he relished the challenge before him. When he set sail, he never expected to discover so many things that would make him challenge the very fabric of his beliefs.

The young amateur botanist had been able to spend long periods ashore, making cross-country journeys, climbing mountains, and collecting thousands of specimens. He found bones of extinct monsters, plants and creatures unknown to the naturalist. In the Andes, while climbing at twelve thousand feet, he came across seashells, indicating vast upheavals of the earth's surface.

All this he had put down in his journal. While doing so, he developed many theories about the *true* evolution of mankind. Grin listened to these theories in fascination, while Fitzroy cursed and called both of them blasphemers and madmen. Grin suspected that deep down, Fitzroy was just as interested in Darwin's theories, but they made him afraid.

One day, when Darwin was telling the tale of the giant tortoise he had found and overturned on the Galapagos Islands, Grin came to the sudden realization that they were less than two days away from land. If he was going to fulfill his sacred duty, he would have to be about it soon.

That night, as the men he had grown to consider friends slept, Grin killed them quickly and quietly. He knew how to be merciful, how to ensure that none of them felt any pain. Then he incinerated the ship and all its evidence.

Upon return to his holy service, Grin found himself oddly changed. He was sullen, confrontational. A terrible anger seethed within him.

Why had God suffered this man to live? Why had He allowed such a believer in the Word, such a good and pious man, to be confronted over and over by empirical evidence that theirs was a society founded upon inconsistencies, perhaps even lies? If God knew all things, if God was *in* all things, then why had He set this man on the path to wickedness, why had He placed such damning articles around the world for this man to find?

Grin, who had never before directly questioned the word of God, went to his master and confronted Him.

God, in his Sixth Vessel, blamed it all on the Enemy, a being whom He was not yet ready to confront.

Grin knew that he should have left it at that, but he was unable to do so. All his life he had heard tales of the Enemy. He had trained to be a warrior so that one day he could fight the Minions of Evil, and perhaps one day battle the Enemy itself in his Lord's name. In all his years, he had never once seen any glimmerings of the Enemy. Its handiwork was evident, or so the Sixth Vessel claimed. Everywhere the Vessel looked, He saw the Enemy. Grin had never been so fortunate. Over his lifetime, he began to form a theory that perhaps there was no Enemy. That the phrase was nothing more than a catchall to describe anything the Lord found unappealing or threatening in some way.

He told God this, all this and *more*.

The Sixth Vessel expressed His displeasure by telling Grin that burning in hell would be too easy a punishment for him, considering the extent of his sacrilege and betrayal. He would walk the earth, bound in the armor he had chosen and perfectly preserved for his ultimate battle with the Enemy. The former Emissary would be able to consider his blasphemous claims, but he would be prohibited from ever sharing them with another by a magic powerful enough to scour the universe itself of life, or so the Sixth Vessel had claimed.

That had been over thirty years ago. To most he had become a thing of legend, a myth. He traveled the world over, helping those who deserved help, those to whom he was guided by his visions.

Tonight, Aitan Anzelm had caused him to question once more. It had never occurred to Grin that his visions might have been given to him by someone other than their Lord. Who else would have the power?

Something detached itself from the wall. It was a shadow, but it was alive.

In a low, deep voice the darksome thing whispered, "You know what they say, don't you? That if there was no such thing as the Devil, someone would have to make him up.''

The warrior drew his weapon.

''You would try to destroy me?'' the shadowthing asked. ''Without knowing anything about me? That sounds like something your old friend the Sixth would have you do. Are you still so taken with Him, even after all this time, and after all He has done to you, that you would blindly follow the Ways as He taught them?''

Grin hesitated. The shadow-creature expanded, reaching out to surround the warrior, engulfing him in darkness as it said, ''I thought it was time that the two of us had a little talk. . . .''

Thirteen

TOM KEEPER WAS LOST TO A DREAM THAT HAD POS-
sessed him on many recent nights, a dream he had always forgotten upon waking.

Tonight would be different.

In the dream, he found himself in a glowing, crystal chamber, floating in midair. Symbols like those Aitan had written
in his book at the Keeper House were scrawled all over his
naked body. A man who seemed to have been set on fire stood
before a vortex filled with swirling lights and odd sounds.

The dream began as it always did. The flame guardian asked
Tom his purpose in coming to this place.

Tom knew instinctively what he was supposed to say: *I seek
the ways. The wisdom. The light.*

Instead, he asked, "What is it you guard?"

"The entrance to knowledge and power, to corruption or
righteousness."

"I have sinned," Tom said.

"Not mortally."

"I'm unworthy. Find another."

The flame guardian laughed. "I didn't bring you here. You
came as they all do."

"How is that?"

"You were drawn by your desires, your dreams," the flame
guardian said, "your *curiosity*."

"Was it mine?" Tom asked. "Are you sure of that?"

"What do you mean?"

Tom felt himself advancing. "What you guard is the gateway to magic, isn't it? Humans can't wield magic."

"Human? What makes you think you're human?"

The rapid advance Tom had enjoyed suddenly stopped. He was closer to the guardian, closer than he had ever been.

He was still not close enough. His fear held him back.

"You were human once," the guardian said. "That was a long time ago. . . ."

Suddenly, Tom felt himself being wrenched away from the dream. The flame guardian burst like an exploding sun, blinding Tom, filling him first with light, then with darkness.

"No, no, no," someone was saying. "You can't sleep here."

The boy shook himself awake. His eyes focused and he found himself in the room Kayrlis had rented for the night. He was on the bed, naked and on his side. Kayrlis shook his arm.

"I'm awake," he said. For a moment he couldn't remember the encounter with the flame guardian; then it came back to him. "I was having a dream."

"A pretty scary one, I'd say," Kayrlis whispered. "I thought you moved around a lot when you were awake!"

The memory of the intimacy they shared came to him, bringing a tender smile to the boy's handsome face. He turned over and felt an animal urge to have her all over again. The lad flipped her onto her back and pinned her. "I want to do it again."

"I bet you do," she said wickedly. "No, on second thought, considering what I'm feeling poking at me down there, I *know* you do. Don't you get tired?"

Tom stared into her amazingly beautiful face. "I slept. Let's do it."

"*I* didn't sleep." She cupped his face with both hands and kissed him on the nose. "I'm exhausted. It'll have to be another time."

"The morning."

"No." She eased herself out from under him.

Panic seized him, shrinking his ardor. "What? Why not? Did I do something wrong?"

Kayrlis started to pick her clothes up off the floor. "Of course not. You have to remember, neither of us lives in this town. We're both just visiting. This was nice. What we had tonight was nice."

He noted the past tense.

"It's still dark out," she said. "You only slept for a few minutes. In case you were wondering."

"I had this dream. It's like I've had it over and over for I don't know how long now, but every time I woke up I forgot it again. This time I remembered. Not only this dream, but all the dreams before it."

"I've had that happen."

Tom watched with a sinking heart as Kayrlis took a fine silk robe out of the dresser and slipped it on. The robe was turquoise, with paintings of dragons being bound by the angel. He looked over the side of the bed and found his clothes heaped in a pile. Resignedly, he began to dress.

"Are you sure?" he asked. "We could—"

"Three times is about my limit without some sleep, sweetheart. You'd better get back to your friends. You're a squire, after all."

"I'm no squire," he said. "Not really."

"You tend him, don't you? Lord Anzelm?"

"Yes."

"Then you're a squire."

He finished dressing, doing his best not to pout. Kayrlis came over, held him, and kissed him gently. "Next time we find ourselves in the same town, you just come say hello."

"That's it?"

"What else would there be?"

"You just want me to leave? After—"

"After a wonderful evening. Yes. I told you I'm not the marrying kind. And you said you loved me. If you really meant that, then go."

"You never said it back," said Tom softly. "You never said you loved me."

Kayrlis turned from him. "I said a lot of other things that made you feel good though, didn't I? And I did some things, too. You're not happy?"

"I am, I mean, I feel—no. I'm not happy. I was, but now I feel horrible. I thought you'd come with us, I thought—"

"I never told you that," Kayrlis said as she turned to face

Tom. "I never led you to believe any of that."

Tom touched his chest. "Don't you feel . . ."

"I can't tell you what I'm feeling about you right now."

"Try."

She sighed heavily. "You're the *best* lover I've ever had. You may not know exactly what you're doing, but I've never been with anyone who had more curiosity and willingness to explore than you. And you're creative, that's for sure. And you're young and you're healthy, and you're—there's a *lot* to recommend about you, Tom Keeper."

Tom felt like an ass. He had wanted to run out when she was asleep, get the paper Aitan had bought for him, and come back to make a sketch of her. Of course, that was dangerous. There was always the chance that he would have run into Aitan, who would have said they were leaving now, and then he would have been forced to choose between his friend and the obligation he had taken on and the woman he loved, but that choice had been ahead of him in any case. Or so he had believed.

Kayrlis sat on the edge of the bed. "I'd *like* to make love with you again. But I don't think I want to sleep next to you. It would be too hard. You've got places you're going, I've got my brother to think about—"

Tom's excitement returned in a startling burst. Breathlessly, he said, "Paridian. We're going to Paridian."

"All right. Maybe I'll find you there."

"Do you mean that?"

"Yes."

"I'm an artist. I'm going to apprentice to Roger Hughes."

"Then you must be very good."

"I don't know. Aitan thinks I am."

"All right," she said, nodding toward the far door leading to the stairs at the outside of the building.

Tom was on his feet, backing away. He desperately did not want to leave. He started as he struck the wall with his back, then turned and looked down to see a doorknob. This was the door leading to the hallway.

"Sorry," he said, "wrong door."

"You can use that one. Whatever you want."

"Don't say that. What I *want* is—"

Kayrlis held up her hand. "I know."

"Paridian?"

She nodded. Tom opened the door, suddenly feeling an overwhelming sadness, as some instinct of his warned that if he left her now, he would never see her again.

I'm being foolish, he told himself. *She's given her word. Paridian.*

He was about to look at her once more, but he was certain that if his gaze met hers, he would burst into tears. Not a very manly thing to do. He didn't know what his father would say about that. Or what Aitan would say.

Most importantly of all, he wanted Kayrlis to *view* him as a man, not a little boy.

"I love you," he said without looking at her.

She said something in return, but he had darted out of the room so quickly and shut the door behind himself with such speed that he couldn't quite make it out.

"She loves me, too," he whispered to himself as he walked down the hall. "I know it. I believe it."

His mother had told him that if he believed in something with all his heart, if he truly felt that something was meant to happen, then it would. He saw himself having a life with Kayrlis. Children with her, one day.

One day.

If you really believe that, he told himself, *why do you still feel like you're going to start crying any second?*

He was at the end of the hall when he heard a sound. Turning, he prayed with all of his being that he would see Kayrlis standing at the other end of the hall, beckoning for him to return.

No one was there.

The tears brimmed in his eyes and were about to fall when Tom heard the sound again. A sharp, hacking cough. It came from the room off to his left.

Kayrlis had said her brother was the only other person on this floor. Tom went to Cameron's door, knocked softly. The only reply was a round of coughing, coupled with moans and violent little cries.

Tom had heard sounds like that before. He wanted to turn

from the door, to get Kayrlis, but instead he found himself opening the door and going inside.

The room was dark. The only illumination came from the moonlight filtering in from the main window. Tom walked over to the bed. The child he had saved lay there in breeches and nothing else. He had been under the covers once, but he had clawed his way free. Now he was writhing, his back arched in a bow.

"Merciful God, no," Tom whispered.

The sheets were spattered in blood. The crimson stains looked like a dull brown in the dim light, but Tom was not fooled. He had seen this before, when his mother was dying, and again countless times in his dreams about her.

The boy was sweating blood. He had the Scourge.

I didn't save him, Tom thought. *He's dying anyway. Heavenly fathers, he's dead already. Might as well be.*

How was he going to tell Kayrlis?

He couldn't just leave and let her walk in to find the child like this. That would be too cruel.

Tom went back to the hall. The little sliver of light he had seen from beneath Kayrlis's door had vanished. She had gone to sleep.

She might not be asleep yet, he told himself. *I could wake her—*

Then what? Have her spend the night crying in grief? She would be useless tomorrow, when arrangements would have to be made to keep the boy comfortable during his final days, his last hours. The Scourge did not kill quickly. It was a brutal, heartless murderer that enjoyed playing with its victims. Cameron was in the earliest stages. He would be a week at the very least in the dying.

Tom pulled up a chair. "I'll sit with you. I've done it before."

He took the boy's hand and shuddered as a spasm ripped through the child. The Scourge was not contagious, not like a cold or virus. When the Scourge had first appeared, many had called it God's Judgment on the wicked. But after a time, too many decent people contracted the disease. Too many who had never shown wickedness to anyone.

"God's calling you home," Tom whispered. He knew the

boy could hear him. His mother, in her few lucid moments, had confirmed that. Tom decided that if Cameron returned to consciousness, he would wake Kayrlis instantly. There was no way of telling how much time Cameron would have to speak, and it would be important that his loved ones were nearby.

Tom wondered if Cameron and Kayrlis—or Penelope, as she had been christened—had parents or other relatives traveling with the carnival. It was doubtful. He would have met them, or there would have been some mention of them by now.

He thought of all the things he wanted to talk to Kayrlis about. She had been to China, had learned her skills as an acrobat there. How had that come about? Was she born there?

So many questions.

Images of sitting with Kayrlis, keeping her calm and focused by talking about herself, her life, flooded through him.

That vision was wrong, he decided. She wouldn't want him here. Despite everything they had shared, and how he felt about her, she considered him a stranger, an outsider. She was free enough with her body, but not, he sensed, her emotions.

They would not meet in Paridian. She told him what he wanted to hear so that he would leave. He knew it at the time, but he couldn't bear to accept it then.

His emotions, his hurt feelings—none of it mattered in the face of this horror. And truth to tell, though he loved Kayrlis, he didn't really know her. Perhaps it was her beauty that he loved, her spirit, her wildness. Her body.

He closed his eyes, felt Cameron's body quake over and over.

There was a pail of water with fresh towels set in the corner. Tom went over, wet one of the towels, and set it on Cameron's forehead.

The boy's arm shot out, his hand latching onto Tom's arm like a claw. Tom cried out in pain and surprise, then pulled Cameron's fingers from him. The boy had no control over his body. Tom knew that from experience. Tom had gotten too close, that was all.

Tom knelt at the boy's bedside and prayed for close to an hour. Finally his knees were fiery with pain and he rose, sitting back down on the chair. The towels were all soaked through.

He had nothing clean to use on the child. Then he looked down at his shirt, which he had buttoned wrong in his nervousness with Kayrlis.

I've lost one shirt today, what's another, he thought, and removed the garment. He tore it to shreds without benefit of the blade that had been given to him in the tent. The seams gave easily enough. He soaked a strip of cloth with water and laid it on Cameron's forehead, hoping to offer some relief from the hellish fever the boy faced. Soon the cloth was red and Tom rose to replace it, knowing the futility of the gesture and simply not caring. He needed to feel that he was doing something, not just bearing mute witness.

"I'm so sorry," Tom whispered. "I wish—"

Then he remembered. Digging frantically into his pocket, he found the elixir he had taken from Aitan's bag. Grin's gift.

The vial contains waters from the River of Healing, where all wounds are mended, where all lives are given a fresh start.

In Heaven?

In Heaven.

Tom didn't know if this would be a sin or not. Nor did he care. To allow suffering when it was in your power to stop it had to be the greatest evil of all. He uncapped the vial, pulled out the stopper. The brilliant light exploded in his eyes.

Tom had no idea if the waters would work, or even what the proper method of use would be. He had applied the liquid to Aitan's burns directly and they had healed. The Scourge permeated every fiber of this child. It made blood seep from his pores.

Tom suddenly knew what he had to do. He touched the healing waters to his hand and caressed Cameron's face, his neck, his chest. He reapplied the liquid time and time again, rubbing it into the boy's arms, hands, legs, and back. Cameron's flesh began to exude a golden glow. The liquid shimmered on his body.

Finally, when the vial was three-quarters empty, Tom sat back and waited.

Cameron moaned and writhed. Blood continued to seep from his pores, mingling with the glowing liquid with which Tom had anointed the child.

"Do something," Tom said, watching as the golden light

was consumed more and more by the blood steadily oozing from Cameron's body.

Trembling, an idea came to him. He leaped to his feet and grabbed the vial, nearly spilling the remainder. Forcing himself to be calm, he pried open Cameron's mouth and poured a little of the liquid down the boy's throat.

He waited.

Cameron bucked in his arms, wailing in pain, then he settled.

Others would hear the boy's cries sooner or later, Tom knew. But he was determined to allow Kayrlis some measure of rest before this nightmare was thrust upon her.

He stared at the child, waiting for the miracle he had envisioned.

Nothing.

For twenty long minutes he sat with Cameron, holding the boy down, dampening his forehead, waiting for the elixir to take effect.

The glow from the waters was all but gone now.

"Maybe it only works on their kind," Tom whispered, rubbing his hands on his forehead, not knowing if he was smearing elixir or blood on his flesh. He couldn't believe the amount of blood coming from the child. A part of him understood that it had been this bad with his mother, and that this was only the beginning, but it was still a horror.

Tom waited. He prayed again, this time naming every saint he could think of. Nothing changed.

Finally, he could take it no longer. Tom grasped the vial and hurled it across the room. It struck one wall, then the hard wood floor, and rolled into a corner, unbroken.

"Damn you!" Tom cried, approaching the elixir. "Damn you! What *Goddamn* good are you! Whatever you are, wherever you came from, God *damn you* to hell for failing!"

He collapsed on the floor, the tears he had been holding back falling from his eyes. He shuddered, biting down on his lips to keep himself from screaming again.

The Scourge defied the waters of Heaven. It was of the Enemy. Tom knew that now. But how could God's power be useless in the face of the Enemy? It made no sense!

He heard sounds in the hall. Someone was coming.

Kayrlis, probably. Lord knows, he had made enough noise, and so had Cameron.

He had to face her. He knew that. Yet he couldn't. How could he tell her that he had anointed her brother with waters from the River of Healing, sacred waters, and they had been unable to heal the child?

All that had kept him going during those painful weeks had been the hope that somehow his mother would be the first to earn God's mercy and survive. If Kayrlis knew what had happened here, even that slim hope would be taken from her. She would feel as if her brother had been forsaken—and that wasn't true, as far as Tom was concerned.

God had not forsaken the boy. This had been a test of Tom's faith, and *he* had failed. If he could have just believed, Cameron would have been cured. It was Tom's lack of faith, after having witnessed his mother die of the Scourge, that had damned Cameron to this. Tom didn't know that for certain, but he had to try to make sense of this, and right now, any explanation was preferable to the mysterious ways in which God worked His wonders and His tragedies. . . .

The noises in the hall grew louder. He looked to the window, which was half-open, and scrambled toward it. The window opened the rest of the way easily. He ducked through it, saw a railing, and was out the window and climbing down to the ground below when he heard the door to Cameron's room open. He froze, waiting, then heard the sound he had so dreaded: Kayrlis screaming.

He wanted to go to her, to give her some measure of comfort, but he decided the best thing he could do for her was to run. Never come near her again.

He could still hear her screams as he quickly climbed down into the bushes. Then he ran and ran until his legs could no longer carry him. Finally, he collapsed on the cobblestone street, where Aitan found him just before dawn.

Fourteen

TOM SLEPT WITHOUT DREAMS. WHEN HE FINALLY awoke, it was late the next day. He had been laid across his mount, roped in place to prevent him from falling off. Cloth had been wrapped around his wrists and ankles before ropes had been placed around them, preventing his flesh from being chafed.

His first sight was of the earth beneath his mount drifting lazily along, seen over a dark brown horizon of horsehair. It was jarring, to say the least, and he began to cry, "Whoa! Whoa! Stop!"

The animal was tethered to Aitan's mount. The angel brought his horse to a stop, signaled Tom's mount to do the same, and dismounted. He untied Tom and helped the boy down to the ground.

Tom did not recognize the area. The ground was slightly soft and the trees were tightly clustered. They were in an area just off a narrow road. The sun was low on the horizon, intense and searing. The light it gave was golden and angry, like the light radiating from the waters of Heaven that had been no good at all against the Scourge.

Tom looked away from the light.

Lying on the ground, Tom reached up and touched his face. It was clean and soft. He had been bathed, then clothed in a clean tunic. He watched as Aitan dropped several stones painted with strange turquoise and crimson runes on the ground at several points around them.

"What're you doing?" Tom asked. His throat was raw.

"Something I normally do after you're asleep," Aitan said.

"The laying of the stones. Just a precaution. If anything with hostile intent wanders too close, the stones detect it and intensify the emotions so I can detect them. Are you hungry?"

Tom nodded. The angel brought him some sweetbreads and water, then a little meat, which tasted good though it was cold. It had been cooked in the spices Aitan preferred.

"Where's Grin?" Tom asked when his throat no longer felt so raw and parched.

"Lord Skalligrin bought a horse of his own last night and rode out of Hartston. No one knows where he was heading."

"He didn't leave a note? Or give anyone a message for us?"

Aitan shook his head. "The man was an Emissary. He walked with God. He doesn't have to explain himself."

"I guess not," Tom said. He closed his eyes and wished more than anything that he could just go back to Keeper House, have some soup in his father's kitchen, and play games with other children. When he opened his eyes, he was still in the small clearing and a stale smell was drifting toward him. "What's that?"

"I have no idea. Swamp gas?"

"I don't even know what swamp gas is, let alone what it's supposed to smell like."

"Neither do I. If I hadn't destroyed the covered bridge, we wouldn't have to be finding out, either." Aitan sighed. "I know a little about this area. I asked before we left. You see those trees?"

"How can I miss them?" Tom asked, looking up at the towering sentinels all around them. Many of the trees rose to heights of 150 feet or more. The trunks were massive.

Aitan suddenly tensed. He looked around.

"What is it?" Tom asked.

"The stones."

Tom surveyed the area around them. He saw only trees and the greenish brown blend of the woods in all directions.

The angel stood and drew his sword partway from its scabbard. He tensed, his gaze fixing on something off to his right.

"What do you see?" Tom asked.

Aitan whispered something that might have been a curse,

then laughed. Relaxed, he turned and said, "It's nothing. A natural creature. See there?"

Tom looked to where Aitan pointed. At first he saw nothing at all. Gradually, the form of a small dog came into view. It barked and yipped a few times, then bounded away.

"I knew someone who owned a dog like that," Tom said with a laugh. "Look at him. More hair and attitude than anything. Those rocks of yours are pretty sensitive."

"They are," Aitan said. "That dog may not have been much of a threat, but it was certainly angry at something."

Tom looked around. "Maybe we're in its favorite spot."

"Could be."

"There was something about these trees?" Tom prompted. "Something you wanted to tell me?"

Aitan relaxed with a great sigh. "They're called bald cypress, because they shed their foliage once a year. That we're seeing them means we're near a swamp. If we were looking at them from the waters of a swamp, we would see their roots forming knees that extend above the water. Boat builders use those natural crooks during a ship's construction."

"Uh-huh," Tom said distantly. He was still waking up, but already visions of the odd dreams with the flame guardian, of Kayrlis moaning and crying out below him, and of the dying Cameron thrashing against his horrible fate assaulted him.

"Don't you see?" asked Aitan. "Generally, where there are boat builders, there are boats. I was thinking that maybe we could reach our destination a little faster."

"Okay," said Tom.

Sighing, Aitan said, "I take it you had an *interesting* evening last night."

Tom snapped to full attention. "I'd prefer not to talk about it, lord. If that pleases you."

"It doesn't, but I'll respect your wishes. I know you committed no violence. I would sense it if you had. We've been together long enough for that. No, the blood I found upon you was come by in some other way. . . ."

Tom nodded.

Frowning, Aitan decided his friend was not going to take the bait. He said, "Do me a favor, Tom. Draw something for me."

"I'm not . . . feeling very creative."

Aitan brought Tom's paper and a few pencils. "Go on. Please."

"Of course," Tom said, taking the paper and setting it on the wooden board Aitan had bought for him. At first, he had no idea what to draw. Then it came to him. He sketched slowly at first, then picked up speed as he immersed himself in the portrait of what had come into his mind.

"I have something to tell you," Aitan said.

Tom looked up.

"No, keep drawing. It will make this easier."

The boy felt uneasy about this, but he nodded and went back to his drawing anyway. *I have something to tell you, too. Maybe this picture will say it better than I could.*

"Tom, I told you something of myself, of my origins. I wanted you to understand the kind of being with whom you traveled. I didn't tell you everything."

That makes two of us, Tom thought.

"I believe I mentioned that I had been asked to perform a service, but I gave you no actual details."

"That's right," Tom said. He was no longer in such a hurry to finish his drawing. Aitan sounded very strange and it frightened Tom.

"I think I knew all along that I would do what they wanted, that I *had* to do it," Aitan said, talking quickly, becoming more agitated with every statement.

Though Tom told himself that he really didn't want to know, he found himself asking, "What is it you're supposed to do?"

"Kill a man."

"You've killed before." Tom regretted the words instantly. They were an affront.

Aitan did not seem offended. If anything, he was saddened.

"I killed *once*. Out of passion. Madness."

"The dancer. The man who murdered your love."

"Yes. It was one moment in my existence—other than those I spent at Rachiel's side—when I felt truly alive. When I was something more than a keeper of records, a scholar of the past. The past couldn't hurt me, you see. It couldn't really make me feel anything. That's one of the reasons I loved it so." The angel hesitated, deciding he was veering too far off topic. "All you have to know is that I killed a man and what I did was *wrong*."

"You were avenging an innocent."

"That doesn't matter. Not in the eyes of the Lord."

"It should." Tom shuddered. He lowered his gaze. "Forgive me, lord. The blaspheme was uncalled for. None of us has the right to criticize the Holy Word and the Law. I'm not myself."

"Grin kept telling me that I was blaspheming every two minutes. If I were you, I wouldn't worry about it. I want you to talk freely with me. This is important."

Tom nodded, only slightly reassured.

Aitan needed desperately to be understood. He said, "Tom, I didn't just kill a man. I harvested a soul that destiny wasn't through with. True, when I found Rachiel's murderer, he was evil. Unrepentant for his act. All he feared was one day being found out."

"So what was this destiny he was supposed to have?"

"His fate was to have been for that terror he felt, then just a seed, to grow within him. He was to have lived in unknowable agony for another fifty years."

"Agony?"

"His fear. Just before he died, he was to write what the prophets say would have been one of the greatest cautionary tales in the annals of man. A story that would have served God's purpose in many ways. A fable of debasement, of responsibility, and of salvation. It would have inspired countless millions."

"Did you know that at the time?"

"I didn't care."

"Then you knew?"

Aitan nodded. "I had been warned. I didn't care. I made it so that there would be no second chance for this man. I circumvented the cycle of heavenly punishment and redemption."

"If these prophets you're talking about knew about this story, couldn't they have just copied down the details and given it to someone else for the telling?"

"No. It was lost when he died. When I destroyed the man's

twisted soul. Besides, the work on its own might have had some power, but not nearly so much as when the reader understood that the author was writing about his own life. That this was not entirely fiction.''

Tom set down his pencil and turned the sketch over. ''You said—''

Aitan straightened up suddenly, his gaze moving across their surroundings like a scythe in a ripe field. A shrill cry sounded, startling Tom. He jumped, dropping his paper to the ground. Aitan gestured and a large bird struck out from behind several trees. It was bluish grey, with a black belly. Its head was white, with black stripes running down along the edges of its crown. Its wingspan was close to six feet. The bird rushed over the heads of the travelers with another angry cry.

''What was that?'' Tom asked, feeling foolish for his reaction. He picked up the drawing and set it back, facedown, on his lap.

''A great blue heron, I believe. Another indicator that the swamp is close. That's good. We're going to have to navigate around its borders to reach the road to Paridian.''

''We're getting close?'' Tom asked. ''To the city?''

''Yes.''

''I don't understand something,'' Tom said. ''In your story. You said you sent that murderer to Hell. Some kind of Hell. Why couldn't God just take him back? If you did such a bad thing, why didn't God just undo it?''

''No. There is a balance. A pact between the light and the dark. Such an act on the part of our Lord would have been even more disruptive to the Grand Plan.''

''I still say it shouldn't have mattered,'' Tom whispered.

Aitan knelt before Tom on one knee and touched the boy's arm. ''I know. That's how *I* felt, too. But my feelings, or yours, are immaterial compared to the will and the wrath of God. I should have been *damned* for what I did.''

''Why weren't you?''

''There is a custom among my kind. A way to make amends for trespasses like mine.'' Aitan looked away. ''My family took the blame for me. They accepted that they would be stripped of title, of position. That they would be . . . less . . . in the eyes of God. In the Hierarchy of Heaven. Their ultimate place in the Divine Kingdom was no longer assured."

"They were damned?"

"No. They were stripped of their divinity. Made mortal. And sent among mankind in new bodies. I'll never see them again. Or if I do, I'll never recognize them. And they'll never recognize me. They did all this to save me."

"And you let them."

"I had no choice. It was done without my knowledge, without my consent. By the time I learned of their sacrifice, it was too late. I wanted to curse God that day, but I knew to do so would make a travesty out of all my family sacrificed for me. So I said nothing. I accepted my exile from the city of my birth."

"Then they called you back."

"Yes."

"And you can have it all back again? Your family can be restored? They could be made angels again?"

"Our name could be restored. God's judgment against my parents, my brothers and sisters, still stands."

"They must have loved you a lot to give up so much for you."

Aitan nodded. "I wish I had known it then."

"Forgive me, lord," Tom said softly. "But if all you have to do is kill a man—"

"The one they want me to kill is more than a man. He is an angel."

"How can that be?" Tom asked. The idea of one angel slaying another was inconceivable to Tom, but he had to believe that Aitan would not lie to him. "Are you going to do it?"

Aitan nodded. "You made me remember what I was fighting for. You made me see that there is good in the world. That there is innocence. That certain things must be protected. For a time I believed the Grand Plan to be a lie. Now I see that there is a reason for all the suffering. And I also see that if the price that has to be paid to keep mankind safe from the agents of the Enemy is my purity, my ideals—that's not much to ask. Not really. I told you this because I wanted you to know that *your* life has importance. That you not only can make a difference, but that you already have. With me."

Tom swallowed hard. He thought he understood finally what Aitan was really struggling to tell him. "No matter what happens with Roger Hughes, you're leaving me in Paridian."

"Yes."

Overcome, Tom said, "Why you? Why couldn't they get someone else? What makes you so special? It should have been someone like Grin!"

Shaking his head, Aitan said, "I don't know why I was chosen for this task. I was told I was the only one who could kill this renegade. One of the Vessels appeared to me and told me it was so. How I'm to accomplish the task is beyond me. All I know is that I'm to pray for enlightenment. Hopefully, it will come in time."

A sudden wave of bitterness passed over Tom. "There's another explanation for all this, you know."

"What do you mean?"

"Maybe they sent you against this other angel because they knew you couldn't stand against him. Because they want you out of the way."

Aitan stiffened. The thought hadn't occurred to him. The angel decided that his charge was overwrought. It would be best to change the subject. "Let me see what you've drawn."

Tom looked down at the sheet of paper in his lap. The picture he'd made was facedown, but he could see the heaviest lines very clearly. It was a drawing of the fire guardian.

The angel took a step closer and held out his hand. He was about to step within Tom's reach when suddenly he spun, one hand reaching for the hilt of his sword. He stood frozen for several seconds, then relaxed. The woods appeared to hold no predators.

"Nothing," Aitan said. Shaking his head, he knelt before Tom. "Let me see the drawing."

Suddenly, Aitan felt something sharp touch the base of his skull.

"Don't move," a rough voice said.

Tom looked up and gasped. What he saw was impossible. He could see no hint of anyone standing behind the angel. Even so, they had both heard the voice, and it had come from right behind Aitan. The air behind Aitan shimmered. For a moment, Tom thought he was looking at a man made of glass.

Then the figure revealed itself to be a tall man with short-cropped reddish hair. His features were sunken, his eyes hollow. He held a crossbow. The bolt was touching the base of Aitan's skull.

"My name is Travest Mulvihill," said the man. "I've been sent here to kill you. . . ."

Fifteen

AITAN ANZELM WAS MOTIONLESS. "IS THERE SOME MESsage I'm to hear before I die? Is that why you haven't killed me yet? Or are you afraid of what will happen to you when God learns that you have slain one of His chosen?"

The assassin whispered, "I'm already damned. I think. So don't even bother with that threat."

Tom watched as the red-haired man took a step back. Aitan relaxed as the pressure eased from his neck. The angel stood, then turned to face Travest.

"I just wanted you to know that I could have killed you," Travest said as he lowered the crossbow. "A few weeks ago, I was still human. Now I've been made into something else. I can do things with light. Bend it. Shape it. Make illusions."

"I saw him," Tom whispered. "He wasn't there, then he looked like water or glass, something clear, then he just kind of appeared."

Aitan nodded. "You're a transformed being. It's against God's Law to make one like you. You're an abomination."

"Actually, I'm a tailor," Travest said. "I wanted you to see how vulnerable you are. I thought that way you might actually listen to what I have to say."

Tom allowed the drawing he had made to fall gently to the earth as he rose to stand beside his friend. He thought of the blade Aitan had given him so many nights before. It was secured in a saddlebag. He felt so defenseless.

"Are you alone?" Aitan asked.

"For the moment. The others will come soon enough."

"Take him," said Tom. "Use your magic on him. He's just

trying to hold us here long enough for his friends to come and surround us.''

"No." Aitan looked around. "If that had been the case, he wouldn't have shown himself. We weren't exactly rushing to leave here." The angel looked to Travest. "Who sent you?"

"Like you have to ask," Travest hissed. "Did you really think He wouldn't know that you had been sent to hunt him? Did you really think He wouldn't come after you first?"

"We were friends once," Aitan said. "I assumed he would leave me alone so long as I made no move against him."

"You're an idiot." Travest looked around anxiously. "Not much time." He looked back to Aitan. "Here's what I'm after. The Enemy wants you dead."

"The Enemy?" cried Aitan. "Now he's calling himself—"

"There isn't much time!" Travest said. "He's scared of you, and from what I overheard of your conversation with the boy, it's pretty clear you don't know why. Well, I do. I know how you can kill him. I know why you're the only one who can do it. I'll tell you all of it, but there's a price."

"Of course there is.''

Travest told his story quickly. He explained that he had been forced to leave his home with his son, Lileo, and recounted the details of the accident that nearly took Lileo's life. Then he spoke about the angels who took his son to the City of Heaven, and the shadow-creature that made a bargain with him to retrieve the boy.

"You're willing to betray your benefactor?" asked Aitan.

"I've known all along that he's a liar. I've seen him make deals with people and always find a way to go back on them. Or give what he promised, only it never turns out to be what a person really thought they'd be getting. If I leave it to him, he'll bring Lileo out—then change his face so I won't recognize him and hide him somewhere. Or bring him out, then kill him. Anything's possible with that one. His word is meaningless.''

"And you think I'm better than him," Aitan said.

"I don't know about that. I'm just willing to trust you a lot more than I'd trust him. This is my son's life. I saw the way you were talking to the boy. I heard what was in your voice.

I know that you understand how I feel about Lileo.''

"You're crazy," said Tom. "He was going to leave me."

"To protect you. To make it so you couldn't be used against him, like Rachiel."

Aitan's eyes suddenly became twin orbs of golden light. His entire body glowed as he stormed forward, slapped the crossbow from Travest's hands, and lifted the former tailor up by his throat. *"What about Rachiel?"*

"Aitan, don't!" cried Tom. "You'll kill him!"

With a cry of rage, the angel tossed Travest to the ground. He moved his sword through the air, describing some kind of rune with the weapon. The fires of his anger cooled and he appeared normal once more. "Tell me."

Travest coughed, his throat and face bright crimson. He rolled onto his side and found he was too weak to stand. "The Enemy's been to Paridian. He took Rachiel."

"Now you're the one who's lying," Aitan said, drawing his sword.

"No!" Travest said. "I have proof." He gestured to his vest.

"Go ahead," said Aitan.

"Don't—" Tom whispered.

"It will be all right," the angel said.

Travest unbuttoned one of the inner pockets, then drew out a silver ring. "This was Rachiel's. Her ring of binding, what kept her from leaving the artist. Touch it. You'll feel that it was on her hand."

"She's a ghost," Tom said. "She couldn't wear something like that."

"Hush, Tom," the angel said gently as he took the ring. His hand closed over it, and he gasped. Squeezing his eyes shut, he trembled and longingly whispered her name. Finally, he opened his eyes and fixed Travest with a stare that would have crushed a God-fearing man. "How did this come into your possession?"

"I stole it from Him. Left a duplicate in its place."

"You think he won't notice?"

"Eventually."

"And what do you think he'll do to your son in return for your betraying him?"

"He won't do anything. You're going to get my son back for me, and then you're going to kill that monster. It's that easy."

"Nothing's easy in this life," said Aitan.

Travest glanced about. "They're getting closer."

"What can you tell me about them?"

"I only know the power of the last one, the one that followed behind us and never spoke. He can kill with a touch, but not right away."

"The Scourge," said Aitan.

"Incarnate."

Tom shuddered at the thought of a man who could spread the dreaded disease with only a touch.

"You came with these men?" Aitan asked.

"Who said they were men?" replied Travest. "Three not including the plague-carrier are. Three more are women."

"So there are seven beyond yourself."

"Right."

"You came with them, then went on ahead and told them to wait. I was supposed to be your kill. They were under orders not to interfere, just to make sure that if I escaped you—"

"—you wouldn't escape them. How did you know?"

"I saw him do this before. I don't know what he's become, but his tactics don't seem to have changed especially."

Travest held out his hand to Aitan. The former tailor said, "Do we have a bargain or not?"

Aitan thought about it. Finally, he said, "I don't even know if I could enter that city. I'm not welcome in many places."

"Will you try?" Travest asked. "Will you devote yourself to finding a way to get my son back? On your honor? On your soul?"

Tom stood near Aitan. The lad said, "Don't trust him. Please."

"I don't see that I have much choice," said Aitan. He looked to the red-haired man. "What if Lileo doesn't want to come?"

"He will," Travest said firmly, though he looked desperate.

"No human has ever left a City of Heaven. The Host will not be pleased. You may be reunited with your son, only to be hunted by God's Army until you are dead. Even then, your torments may only be beginning. If I succeed, they will stop at *nothing* to bring your son back. They will damn us both.''

''I don't care. In our ways, we probably both deserve it.''

Aitan gestured to Tom. ''What about the boy? Does he deserve to be punished—''

''I want my son back!'' screamed Travest. ''Help me and I'll help you. Easy as that. If not, you can both die trying to get across the swamp. I don't care about either of you.''

A long, tense moment passed. Aitan lowered his gaze and said, ''You have a deal.''

''No!'' cried Tom.

''We need his help,'' said Aitan. ''We won't survive otherwise.'' He looked around. ''Tell me what you can about the hunters.''

Travest described each of them. He finished by saying, ''You have to release them from His service. Kill them if you have to. But don't take their souls. If you do that, you'll be destroyed, and that's what He wants above all else. More than killing you, He wants to turn you. To make you like Him. Tainted. I can slow them for a time. Give you something of a head start. But I can't go back with them. You understand that.''

Tom watched as Aitan placed his hands behind his back and lifted his face to the sky. The angel closed his eyes and whispered, ''Yes.''

Only the squire saw Aitan's fingers curl and form an odd pattern. Suddenly, Travest slapped at his neck. ''Filthy bugs!''

Aitan crossed his arms over his chest. ''When will we see you again?''

''At very latest, I'll meet you outside the City of Heaven where my boy was taken,'' said Travest. ''When I have my son, you'll have the answers you need.''

Travest turned, picked up his weapon, and left the clearing. He was still rubbing at his neck when he was swallowed up by the heavy woods.

''We should turn around and go back to Hartston,'' Tom said. ''That boy, Michael, he said there were other angels going through there all the time. Maybe Grin will be back—''

''No,'' Aitan said. ''The way to Paridian and the City of Heaven is directly ahead. If Travest sees us doubling back, he'll join with his companions in trying to kill us.''

"We don't even know that there are any more like him!"

"There's no time for this," said Aitan firmly. "Gather as much as you can carry."

"We're not taking the mounts?"

"No. We need them to lay down tracks and lead the hunters away from us. Right now we have to think in terms of dividing their numbers and buying ourselves as much time as we possibly can."

"I don't feel good about this," said Tom as he went to his horse and started rummaging through the saddlebags. "Dealing with someone like Travest is as bad as dealing with the Enemy."

"I swore I'd keep you safe," said the angel. "I promised you a new life. A better one than the one you left behind. I'm not going back on that promise, no matter the cost. Now hurry."

Tom threw one of the bags over his shoulder and went on to Aitan's mount. "Can I admit something to you?"

"Yes," said the angel as he began opening his own bags.

"I wish I was back home."

"Can I admit something to *you*?" Aitan said as he hauled a heavy bag from his mount and strapped it to his back. "So do I. . . ."

Aitan used his magic to set the mounts on a route that would take them far from their masters. The angel and his companion set off, neither paying any attention to the drawing Tom had made. The sheet of paper lazily drifted back and forth in the clearing, a slave to the changing winds.

SECOND INTERLUDE

❧

LILEO WOKE TO A CITY OF MIRACLES AND WONDERS. THE last thing he remembered, he had been riding out of the city with his father. Their wagon struck something in the road and he had been pitched onto the ground. There had been a horrible roar, a sudden and terrible pain, then nothing until a few moments ago, when he woke to find himself lying on a soft white bed surrounded by billowing pale blue curtains. He wore a simple white garment, nothing more. Examining himself, he found that he appeared to be in perfect health. He parted the curtains and saw that he was in a chamber formed from mists. Objects hung in the air. Pedestals, statues, thrones. The sheer size of the room was overwhelming to the boy. It was as large as the Curacas's courtyard. The domed ceiling was decorated with ever-changing images portrayed by the swirling mists that rapidly solidified, then dissolved into smoke once more.

He touched the "floor" with his bare feet. The mists rushed together, forming a surface as hard and ornate as marble beneath the lad. Lileo watched as a path was made by the mists. It led to a large window at the far end of the room. He went to the window, looked out, and nearly burst into tears.

The City of Heaven lay before him. The shimmering, brilliant light, the oddly shaped buildings, the swirling spires, the towers rising from the clouds—all these and more he had briefly glimpsed during the Convergence. They were not what moved him. It was the people. So many people, like him, but in this blessed place, they were much more. Lileo gasped with delight as he saw human beings rising into the air and dancing with angels. Men, women, and children laughed and played, their every word, their every gesture, a sign of love to the God who had made them. No one was unhappy here. Lileo could feel the emotions of the people washing over him, filling him with their happiness.

"Enjoying yourself?" asked a warm, compassionate voice behind Lileo.

The boy spun, falling to his knees as he lowered his head and squeezed his eyes shut.

"No need for that. Rise and let me see you."

Forcing his fear aside, Lileo looked up and saw a being composed entirely of smoke. The longer he stared, the more detail Lileo could make out. It was a young man, with a lean, strong body, handsome features, and a confident smile. His long hair dissolved into the mists from which he sprang. His flesh was like porcelain. The mists made clothing unnecessary.

"I am to be your guide, your teacher," said Lileo's companion. "My name is Elohi."

Streaks of lightning flashed within Elohi. He bowed slightly.

"Where's Father?" asked Lileo.

"It was not his time."

Lileo blanched. "I died on the road, didn't I?"

"You came close."

"I don't understand," said Lileo. "If I'm still alive, why am I here?"

"You have a very special destiny to fulfill. All will become clear in time. For now, all you need to know is that when you call my name, I will appear. When you need something, ask and I will get it for you."

Lileo did not want to seem impertinent, but Elohi *had* offered his help. The lad gestured toward the window. "When can I go out there?"

"As soon as you've learned our ways. In the meantime, there are other matters that require my attention. Just relax— and enjoy the view...."

With that, Elohi burst into a sparkling cloud of sound and color that gently dissipated until every trace of him was gone.

Lileo turned back to the window. He missed his father and

wanted to ask more about him, but felt the time wasn't right.

Besides, he thought as he looked out onto the splendor and magnificence that was the City of Heaven, how could his father be anything but thrilled that he was in so wonderful a place?

Outside Lileo's chamber, looking in at the boy through a small window in the door to his chamber, was an angel. Two others flanked him. The flames that had engulfed them had nearly run their course.

"I don't like this," the first angel said as he turned from the door and shut the small window.

The tallest of his companions, the sword wielder who had held the boy's father at bay with his flaming sword and his promises of damnation, said, "Do what you're told."

The first angel thought about what he had seen when he looked into Lileo's chamber. The boy had been sitting on the floor of a cold stone chamber, staring at a grey wall as if it was a gateway to some fabulous wonderland. "How can he be of any service to the Host when he has no grasp of reality? We show him what he wants to see, not what he must see if he is to one day become something more."

The sword wielder turned on the first angel. "Do you think I'm *happy* that one of his kind, not one of ours, has been chosen to become the next Emissary? Do you?"

Lowering his gaze, the first angel said, "Of course not. You're right. We must do what we're told. That's who we are. What we are."

The angels walked away in silence, the sword wielder in the lead.

An hour later, as night fell upon the City of Heaven and a bitter rain drenched the streets and avenues, the sword wielder took to the sky, his sword raised above him. A bolt of lightning reached across the heavens for him. He took its energy, its fire, and held it within himself despite the pain it caused. He had been doing this for months.

The sword wielder, whose name was Malkiyyah, did this to punish himself for the arrogance of his own thoughts, the wickedness of his desires. He could not see the need for beings such as himself to subvert their true natures, to serve the mortals when all the fleshlings deserved was a fiery death, a purge they themselves had long prophesied.

Malkiyyah, the Angel of Blood, fell to the earth and began to weep. Such sentiments were wrong. He knew that. But he was angry and he felt betrayed. As he cried, every human within miles of the City of Heaven bled from old wounds. Only Lileo was exempt. The reason for this was simple: The boy was no longer entirely human.

And in his lonely chamber, Lileo stared at the grey stone wall, laughing and waving at the happy people he saw through a window that only existed in his mind. . . .

Sixteen

"WHO IS THIS ANGEL THEY WANT YOU TO DO AWAY with?" Tom asked as they trudged, waist deep, through the swamp. It was night, but Aitan sensed that their pursuers would not wait until day before they attacked.

"Someone I was friends with when I was a child," said the angel. "His name would mean nothing to you."

Tom coughed from the stench of old moss and decay crowding into his lungs. His every movement sent ripples through the stagnant waters. Soft moonlight filtered through the tangle of leaves and vines above. Even so, Tom found it difficult to see where he was going.

"Swamp goes on forever," said Tom. "It's like walking through a pot filled with someone's—"

"This will be the worst of it, I assure you," Aitan said. "Once we make the crossing, we can take to solid ground again. I just want to be sure they won't be able to track us."

Tom heard the flapping of wings. Herons swooped down out of the darkness. Bullfrogs croaked strange songs. Something in the distance cried out, long and mournfully.

"Yes, lord. Forgive my impatience." Tom sounded drained.

"No, forgive *mine*," said Aitan. "Do you want to talk about what happened last night? Maybe I could help."

"No," Tom said sharply. He wished he could erase the edge from his voice. "That's not what's bothering me. Really, it's stupid, what I keep thinking about."

"Tell me."

They sloshed through the cold, thick waters. Tom felt as if

154

his legs would go numb if he didn't keep moving. He said, "My pictures. Your book. We had to leave them behind."

"You can draw new pictures. I can write a new book."

"I know it's crazy," said Tom. "If what that Travest fellow said was true, then Roger Hughes is probably dead. I just can't believe it, that's all. We've been through so much, and now we've got all these people after us, and I just keep thinking about how much I wanted to hear Roger Hughes tell me my work was all right. That maybe one day I could be like him."

"I wanted that for you, too. If it's at all possible, I'll see that dream come true for you. I promise."

"I'm curious," said Tom. "What was that book for, anyway?"

"Rachiel," the angel said stiffly. "I wanted her to know all that had happened to me after we parted. I felt certain I would get no more than an hour with her."

"Why? I always heard Roger Hughes was a good man. He must be. You were going to leave me with him. Why wouldn't he let you see her whenever you wanted? Why only an hour?"

"Rachiel's soul is undergoing the Withering. She was not bound to this plane well. Soon she will be unable to appear to the living. Time with her is precious."

"You make it sound like she's a doll you take out of a box."

The angel was silent.

"Why was she with Hughes in the first place?"

"Too many questions."

Tom looked down at the icy muck and wondered if he would ever be able to wash off this terrible smell. Changing subjects, he said, "I really liked that fly business."

"Pardon?"

"What you did with Travest. Making that bug bite him and keep buzzing after him. It was funny."

"It was far more than that," said Aitan.

"How so?"

"That 'bug' was a magical construct. It had a part of my basic essence within it. By biting Travest, it instilled a part of my being inside him. It will follow him and do the same with all the other hunters. We'll know when they are near."

"You're not serious, are you?"

Aitan thought about it for a moment. "No, I don't expect that I am."

Tom smiled, despite the cold.

"Frankly, I had second thoughts about the spell I had been attempting and so I stopped conjuring. The appearance of the bug was a coincidence."

"What kind of spell was it?"

The severing of his soul, Aitan thought, *so that I might learn his secrets.* "Doesn't matter."

A freezing wind sliced through the swamp. Shuddering, Tom hugged himself and said, "I was thinking about something Grin told you. Remember when he was teasing you about your power? About how you use magic?"

"I remember."

"I don't think he was doing that to be mean. He was trying to make you angry, sure, but he was doing it to make you start thinking about the possibilities."

"Excuse me, Tom, when exactly were you trained as a mage?"

Anger flashed within the boy. "They're gonna kill me, too! You're telling me I don't have a right to say anything?"

For an instant, Aitan was taken back by the ferocity of Tom's response. Then he laughed. "*Something* happened to change you last night."

"I suppose."

Aitan said, "Let's say you're right. Tell me what my years of study have failed to inform me."

"You can control the elements."

"To a degree."

"You can feel the pain of other living things."

"That is my birthright. We were Angels of Sorrow. Ours was the task to bear the grief of others."

"Your family, you mean."

"My family. Once their load was much heavier to bear, their responsibilities severe. After many centuries, they earned the right to a proper title and Powers."

Tom said, "I think if you worked at your magic some, you could do incredible things."

"Such as?"

Suddenly, a branch snapped overhead. Aitan gestured and

sent a fireball into the air. It spiraled in place, sending a burning white light over the glistening surface of the swamp. Tom looked up to see a beautiful young woman crouched directly ahead, some twenty feet in the air. She had creamy brown flesh, short hair, and an angular face. Her smile revealed a maw filled with jagged teeth. Her black tunic revealed lean but muscular arms and legs.

Tom heard something brushing against the bright green vines behind her. Then he saw that she had bone white wings, sharp and angular, and her hands looked like talons!

"All this trouble over two little creatures like yourselves," said the woman in a husky voice. "One might wonder if our liege has overreacted."

"You could have attacked in silence," Aitan said. "Are you alone? Do you want something?"

"I'm alone," she said. "The others got tired of waiting for Travest to return. I was sent to go on ahead. Find the two of you if he had not killed you, and guide you to a killing ground we chose this morning."

"I notice you're not doing that," said Aitan, hoping he could negotiate with the hunter. "What do you want?"

The woman's response did not come in words. In a lightning-quick motion she rose up, unfurled her wings, and whipped them forward. Suddenly, the air was filled with hundreds of ivory shards, each as sharp and polished as a dagger. Aitan spun and shoved Tom down into the waters. He heard the knives sailing past him, felt their breeze, heard them rip into the waters at either side of him.

Not one struck him.

Looking over his shoulder, Aitan saw the woman laughing. Tom struggled out of his grip, gasping for air as his head cleared the rancid muck of the swamp. The waters rippled where the daggers had vanished.

Tom's eyes went wide as the daggers flew out of the waters, returning to their source. He stared in wonder as the woman spread her wings once more, welcoming the daggers back. Her wings looked like a cloak with hundreds of tiny cuts for sheaths, but they were made from bone and flesh. The bone-knives fitted themselves neatly into her wings and from a distance looked like feathers!

Tom doubled over, spitting out the waters he had swallowed.

"I just wanted to see you both afraid before it was all over," she said. "That would be right about now!"

With a shrill cry, the hunter jammed her wings forward. Tom saw that Aitan was already gesturing. The angel was going to make some kind of shield by hardening the air, Tom guessed.

"No!" Tom hissed. "Catch them! If you don't, she'll just keep sending them until you're too weak to make another shield!"

The bone-knives sailed toward Aitan and Tom once again. The angel understood Tom's plan and changed his incantation midstream. He knew that such a move was dangerous. If he made even the slightest error, the bone-knives would slice through both of them!

Tom watched as the knives slowed, then stopped and hung in midair. Aitan grunted in satisfaction. Suddenly, the blades spun, their sharp points facing the hunter. The same force that had dragged them back to their sheaths was attempting to draw the weapons home. Aitan struggled, focusing his will entirely on holding the weapons in place.

"What?" cried the hunter. She trembled as a force beyond her understanding, beyond her control, began to pull at her.

Aitan whispered, "No. . . ."

Suddenly, the hunter flew down from her perch. Her flight was not smooth and elegant as one might have expected. Instead, she seemed to have been yanked down from the branch that held her, dragged forward as if the hand of God had taken hold of her.

In that moment, Aitan saw how easy it would have been to kill this woman. All he had to do was hold the weapons tight and she would have been impaled. There were other hunters yet to come, other struggles, and he felt drained already.

With a cry of incredible effort, Aitan pushed with the wall of hardened air that he had created and forced the points of the daggers down. The hunter was suddenly upon the angel and his companion. She came in fast, clawing with her talons. The hard flats of the daggers pummeled her entire body, driving the wind from her, cracking against her skull. She moaned and her eyes rolled up into their sockets. Unconscious, she struck Tom and Aitan, her weight and the sheer breadth of her wings dragging all three down into the bilious murk of the swamp.

For several tense moments, Tom Keeper thought he would drown as Aitan struggled to free them from the winged hunter. Then he felt Aitan's hands on his shoulders and he was hauled from the swamp.

Tom stumbled a few steps, his legs weak. He thought he might pass out, but he somehow managed to hang on.

"Help me with her," commanded Aitan. "I don't want her to drown."

Together, they dragged the winged hunter out of the waters. A heavy branch leaned out from the shore. Aitan and Tom allowed the woman to sag forward, the branch catching her in the stomach. Her face skirted the edge of the waters, but did not sink below them.

"I know what we should do," said Tom, breathless, exhausted. "I bet those knives or whatever they were are going to come back to her when she wakes up. And with her wings, she could fly right for us, catch up to us quick no matter how much ground we've covered, how much of a lead we've got on her. Or even worse, she might go back to her friends and lead them right to us. Just because we went out of our way not to kill her when she was trying to slice us up—what's that gonna matter to her?"

"I understand," said Aitan slowly. He couldn't believe what he was hearing. Was Tom advocating murder?

"We can't, though," said Tom. "We just can't be like them."

Relief flooded through the angel. Aitan knew that killing the hunter would have been the practical decision for most. Grin probably would have done it without a moment's hesitation. But Aitan had another way of making sure the woman would not come after them. There was a spell he could use to bind her.

He thought about the last time he had used the spell. It had been the other night in the woods, when the Anarchists tried to take Aitan's life. The angel had not wanted Tom to see what he had planned, and so he sent Tom ahead. He couldn't do that now. Even without the hunters, the swamp held too many dangers.

The angel said, ''I want you to understand something. What I'm about to do will not kill this woman. She'll be all right in a few days or maybe a week. But this may be—disturbing to you.''

''Do what you have to,'' said Tom. ''I can't stay innocent forever, right?''

''I wish that you could,'' Aitan said. The angel lowered his gaze to the hunter and began conjuring. He doubted that his Patron would deny him, considering both he and the boy were in mortal danger.

Reaching out with his power, Aitan summoned his Patron. With that one's help, he began to conjure.

Tom watched as the hunter's flesh rippled and changed. The woman's skin hardened and became the color of the branch she lay upon. Her clothing and her wings also changed. Bark formed over her and her limbs became spindly, stretching to intertwine with other nearby branches.

Aitan was making her into a tree!

The boy was startled as he looked at the woman's face and saw that her eyes were open. She was aware of what was being done to her.

Suddenly, Aitan bellowed and stumbled back, nearly falling into the stagnant waters of the swamp. Tom went to his side and helped steady the angel.

''What happened?'' asked Tom, frightened.

''I don't know,'' Aitan gasped. ''My Patron was with me, the spell was almost done. Then I felt a pain, a shattering, and the power I needed was snatched away. I can no longer feel that one with me.''

They both turned as a moan sounded from the partially transformed hunter. The woman was staring at her hands in horror. She now looked only vaguely human, a wood carving of her former self come deliriously to life.

''It won't last,'' said Aitan imploringly. ''You *will* be human again. I don't want to fight you. Please.''

The waters bubbled and churned. Suddenly the vast array of bone-knives tore themselves from their watery grave and flew at the hunter as she unfurled her wings. The knives were now dark and knotted, but their edges were every bit as sharp. With a hiss they sank into their resting places in her wings, ready to be dispatched at a second's notice.

Aitan gestured quickly and brought the fireball he had created down until it floated between him and the hunter. "You are vulnerable now. Stand down. Leave us. I don't want to take your life."

For a moment, the hunter's shoulders relaxed. She took a step back and a terrible crackling sounded. The woman looked down. With the light of the fireball, she could see far enough into the waters of the swamp to understand that she had been *rooted* to this spot!

With a maddened cry she sent her wings forward.

Aitan lashed out with his power, sending the fireball sailing forward to engulf the hunter a second before she could unleash the deadly collection of knives from her wings. The hunter opened her mouth but had no time to scream as the fires consumed her. She fell into the waters, her brittle wings shattering, her body twisting and cracking as the waters hissed to receive her flaming form. She spasmed, her wooden form breaking in places, then settled into the waiting arms of death.

Tom and Aitan stared at the woman's charred body for long moments.

"God forgive me," Aitan said. "I could think of no other way."

"We should pray for her," said Tom. "Pray for her soul."

"Yes."

They recited several prayers for the hunter, and a few for themselves.

Finally, the angel took Tom by the shoulders and steered him away from the gruesome sight of the charred and blackened hunter. The boy was shuddering. He couldn't believe what he had just witnessed. Aitan felt numb. He had had no desire to hurt the woman, but there had been no choice.

They walked deeper into the swamp until the night swallowed them whole.

Seventeen

THEY REACHED THE SWAMP'S NARROW BANK AND RISKED a few hours' sleep before morning came. As the sunlight bore down on them, Aitan wove a spell to cover their tracks. Tom kept looking over his shoulder. His footprints vanished as the ground rose up to obscure his tracks. Broken twigs mended, branches made their way back into place after being brushed aside.

Their supplies were waterlogged, much of their food ruined. Neither had much of an appetite. They contented themselves with a handful of small red custard apples Aitan found that were called pawpaw fruit. Each took a swig of fresh water, then they continued on their journey.

The area they needed to cross was known as the Great Dismal Swamp. Not an inspired name, perhaps, but certainly an apt one. The swamp bordered the Carolina and Virginia colonies.

As he walked with Aitan through an evergreen shrub bog, Tom saw something that made him smile. He stopped and held out his finger to the edge of a large green leaf. A frog barely larger than Tom's fingernail edged close, then took one look at the angel and leaped the other way.

"Sorry," said Aitan. "I didn't mean to scare him off."

"I know. You're using your magic to keep the crocodiles and the alligators away."

"The bugs, also."

"Which I appreciate," Tom said. "You should see the way I swell up."

"We should keep going," Aitan said.

Tom agreed. The long walk continued. They saw bobcats, yellow-bellied turtles, white-tailed deer, and river otters. For hours they pushed and shoved their way through thickets of white cedar trees, Aitan using his sword to cut away the heavy shrubs that gathered like mist at their feet. The trees looked like a collection of wraithlike sentinels to Tom, who tried to force away his fear by concentrating on the details of the swamplands. He was determined that one day he would sit down and make a book of drawings detailing his days with the angel.

After an hour, they came upon a small road. It bordered one of the great ditches cut into the land meant to lower the level of the swamp. Less than one hundred yards ahead, a yearling bear rose up from the swamp forest undergrowth. Aitan stopped, his sword still in his hand. The bear did not seem to notice the travelers. It ambled down the road for several hundred feet, then disappeared into the forest.

Aitan and Tom walked cautiously ahead until they found where the bear had gone back into the woods. Hundreds of bees and flies buzzed around a clump of pepperbush shrubs and swamp magnolia saplings. Tom saw a number of bees stuck to foliage that looked glazed. Aitan motioned toward fragments of a honeycomb nearby.

"Well, we know what *he* was after."

Above, bees swarmed around the hollow of a large shattered branch. The tree trunk bore heavy ragged wounds made by large, angry claws.

Tom was embarrassed to hear his stomach rumbling.

"Take some," Aitan said, pointing at the dripping wet bits of honeycomb. "I'll keep the insects away."

Tom bent down and watched as the honeybees abandoned the bits of comb. He picked up two large chunks, gave one to Aitan, and tasted the honey. "Wild honey. It's wonderful."

They walked on, Aitan's magics masking their tracks. Finally, Tom said, "It's not true, is it?"

"Pardon?"

"What they say about killing people. That it gets easier every time."

Aitan bowed his head. "I didn't want to hurt her."

"I know."

"I'm sure that for some people it gets easier. I hope it never does for me. When I took vengeance for Rachiel—no, for *myself*—I knew that man. I knew so much about him. I hated him for what he'd taken from the world. For hurting the only woman I'd loved. Last night . . . I never even knew that woman's name. That in itself should make things easier, I suppose. I don't know what dreams she had. If she had friends. What kind of games she played as a child—"

"Aitan," warned Tom, "don't."

The angel shuddered. "It doesn't make it easier. I keep seeing her burning in agony."

"She would've killed us," said Tom.

"I should have been able to *think* of another way to stop her."

"You're not God," cried Tom. "You can't be responsible for everything!"

"No, but I am responsible for that woman's death," the angel said. "Besides, I am of God. I answer to a higher standard than most."

"We're *all* of God."

"I'm one of His chosen. I was born in His paradise."

"Which the angels are bringing to earth, a little at a time. I've heard people say that there's going to come a day when we're all the same. Maybe *that's* the Grand Plan. For Heaven and earth to be one and the same."

Aitan walked a little slower. He said softly, "You mentioned ways that my magic could be made more efficient. That my skills could be put to better use and maybe no one else would have to die."

"I just have a few ideas, that's all."

Aitan considered this. Despite his training, he wasn't a warrior. He had no idea how to keep his calm in the midst of battle, how to maintain reason as chaos threatened to overtake him. He had read about great battles. He understood the single-minded need to survive and conquer that was present in true warriors. It was a quality he did not believe he possessed.

"We were lucky just to have survived last night," the angel said. "I've never been one for quick responses. I'd rather take time and reason out a problem. I also don't have much imagination. You do. It shows in your art. If you've thought of ways to help keep us safe, then by all means, let's hear them.''

Tom described some of his notions as he walked at the angel's side. The boy finished and Aitan had to admit that he was intrigued.

"The real issue, I suppose," said Aitan, "is control. Take this idea you have for creating a barrier of hard air around an attacker's head to suffocate him until he passes out. Too much pressure and you could crack a man's skull.''

"We could find something for you to practice on,'' suggested Tom. "If we were back in Hope, I'd get some melons from storage. I'm sure we could find something else along the way.''

"There's no time. We have to keep moving. If we had a few months ahead of us and no one out to kill us at our heels, I'd be a lot more interested. All I can say is that your ideas are good ones. If the opportunity presents itself—and I hope it doesn't—I'll keep everything you said in mind.''

"All right," said Tom. It was all he could ask.

"Though I will add that your notion about controlling the blood of an enemy the way one might the waters in a stream was entirely gruesome! Lethal and gruesome!''

"But imaginative. That's what you wanted, right?''

"Yes. I sometimes worry about what goes on in that mind of yours, that's all.''

Suddenly, Tom heard something rustling in the woods. He tensed.

"It's just the bear," said Aitan as he pointed. "You can see him from here, look.''

Tom looked in the direction the angel had indicated. He saw the bear peeking through the trees at them. "That's it! You can go after that bear!''

"Pardon?''

"I'm serious. You can try everything we talked about on him.''

"Including rending the earth and dropping him into a pit after I've pummelled him with fists of solidified air and drawn the breath from him with the wind?''

"Absolutely.''

The angel stopped and looked over at Tom. For a moment,

the boy seemed to actually mean it. Then a grin spidered across Tom's face.

"I might try it, too!" said Tom. "Get down on all fours. *Wrassle* that big old bear. He'd remind me of my dad!"

Aitan laughed, placed his hands on Tom's shoulders, and propelled the boy forward. "Keep making jokes like that and I may practice on *you.*"

"As if you would know how to get along without me!" Tom cried.

"Did I mention that when I made that net for you the other day, the one that broke your fall and saved your life—"

"I remember that."

"Did I mention I was just *guessing* when I decided on the consistency of the air? That I might have easily torn you to pieces with it?"

"Well, you messed up. Now you have to keep listening to me!"

Aitan sighed and followed the boy down the long, featureless road.

The day wore on. The travelers heard sounds up ahead. As they came closer, they heard the rough voices of men. Tom could make out swearing.

"First one of the day. Bring it down!" one of them cried.

A crackling sounded and Tom saw one of the trees in the distance fall.

"Loggers," Tom said excitedly. "I'd bet you anything."

"Which should mean horses we can buy."

"Thank the Lord."

They went ahead cautiously, aware of the possibility of a trap. After observing the eleven men who made up the logging operation for close to an hour, Aitan chose to reveal himself.

The tree cutters fell on their knees before him. For once, Aitan did not make a self-effacing display. He was their sovereign, a messenger of the Almighty, a warrior dispatched to route the evils of the Enemy. That he was also covered in filth from the swamp, exhausted, and in dire need of two mounts was immaterial.

No mention of gold was ever made.

Aitan had the tree cutters tell him where they took their lumber. It turned out that there was a lake relatively close. The loggers explained that normally they would wait to chop down trees until the winter. They had horse-drawn sleighs for pulling the logs across the snow. In the event of a thaw, they floated their bounty to the lake. An unusually high demand for wood that could be used in the shipbuilding enterprises of the newly arrived City of Heaven had prompted the men to start early this year.

A boat was already waiting in the lake. One that could take them out to sea, and away from the hunters. It was large and slow-moving, but it would more than suffice.

Aitan and Tom were about to depart when one of the loggers, a lean young man with bright green eyes and close-cropped brown hair said, "I'm telling you, it's a sign we'll be spared."

The angel turned. The man who had spoken stood with a friend, a black-bearded, thickly built man.

"What's your name?" asked the angel as he walked toward the thinner of the two men.

"Trip," said the woodcutter as he bowed nervously. His friend backed away and went to stand with his fellows.

"Spared from what?" asked Aitan.

"The holocaust. The plague."

Maintaining his aura of authority, the angel said, "Tell me what *you* know of it."

One of the other woodcutters said, "He's angered the deliverer and tempted God's wrath!"

Aitan looked sharply at the assemblage. These men were terrified. Why?

"Tell me," said the angel. "No harm will come to any of you."

The woodcutter bit his lip and said, "Seven towns so far. All here, in the colonies. No one knows what's happening in the southlands, or to the west and north, where the Naturals live."

"And in these seven towns?"

"Everyone's dead. All of them taken by the Scourge." Trip hesitated.

"Go on."

"At first, people were saying this was God's punishment. The people must have been wicked."

"At first," said the angel numbly. Tom stood at his side, taking in these revelations.

"It's just that the people who died *weren't* wicked. They were devout. So now it's being said that this must be the work of the Enemy. The war's begun."

Aitan knew all too well what the human meant. A war between the forces of darkness and light, a war to test man's faith and judge his worthiness to enter the kingdom of God, had long been prophesied.

Attempting to hide his shock, Aitan asked the men to kneel. He said a blessing over them, then joined Tom near the horses. The angel instructed the loggers to claim they hadn't seen him or the boy if any came inquiring, then he went off with Tom at his side.

Tom looked over at the angel as they rode. "Travest said one of the Enemy's men could kill with a touch. He's a plague-carrier. The Scourge incarnate, that's what Travest said."

Aitan nodded grimly, understanding the implication.

They rode on in silence.

Travest Mulvihill had been relieved of his duties as point man. He had returned to the other hunters bearing a gruesome prize: The head of the angel, Aitan Anzelm. Of course, he actually possessed no such thing. The powers granted to him by the man who was the night allowed him to bend and shape light into any illusion he could imagine. In reality, all he held was a large stone which he had slipped into a bag.

He had tried to talk the group into beginning the long journey south, to the colony their liege had converted to his own, but one of their number was missing.

Kristiana, the flyer, had not rendezvoused with her fellows. Her husband, Sabiere, was another of the hunters. A tall, pale-skinned and powerfully built man, Sabiere had shaved his eyebrows and most of his skull. A single fount of long black hair rose up from the center of his head and was twisted into knots that reached down to the center of his back. Lodged at the very end of this rope of matted hair was a single eye that blinked and followed the movements of all who walked behind the hunter. Beneath the eye was a maw filled with needlelike teeth. He wore a cloak with a tiny hole when he wished to conceal this oddity. His wife had done the same when she needed to walk among the *unenlightened*.

Travest knew the other hunters only by name. Like him, their odd abilities were not hinted at by their appearances. Unlike him, however, they had abandoned their true names for more fanciful appellations. The man who walked at his side was known as Sinistari, a name that had once belonged to a noted Franciscan friar and author of a text on the Enemy. Sinistari was one of the most beautiful men Travest had ever seen, other than the angels. He had long golden hair and rich midnight blue eyes. His features were like those of a lion. He wore black leggings and boots, and a red shirt over his heavily muscled frame.

His lover was Lilith, who took her name from the Assyrian temptress Lilitu. She was swarthy-skinned, raven-haired, voluptuous, and desirable. The clothes she had chosen were violet and black, tight and functional.

Close to Lilith was Rose, a gaunt, hollow-eyed woman. Rose's hair had been dyed green. Nightmare black vines with tiny thorns pricking her skin covered her bare arms and legs. She wore a simple white frock that was now covered in filth and looked more like a burial shroud.

Two others completed the group. The plague-carrier looked *different* each time Travest gazed at the man. At times he appeared handsome with tightly curled black hair, at others, he was the image of what Travest imagined his son Lileo would look like as a man. The former tailor tried not to look at the disease bringer, who always followed ten steps behind the others.

Finally, there was Shax, who had the look of a man ravaged by too many years of hard drinking and relentless sin. The man's brow was furrowed, heavy lines ringed his sallow features. His long black cloak and hat hid the tattoos that covered most of his body. He seemed to be lost to private wanderings, mumbling warnings to people who weren't there. Despite his apparent delirium, there was a sense of power about him, as if he was so out of touch with this reality because he was focused on another infinitely more powerful inner world.

They had been searching for Kristiana since nightfall the

previous day. The swamp where she had been stationed in the event of Travest's failure bore no trace of her. The hunters had searched for the missing woman long into the night. Once daylight had come, they returned to the swamp to take another look around.

"There were tracks," Travest said from the bank of the swamp. He stood on the knotted fingerlike roots of a bald cypress. "After I killed Anzelm and the whelp, their horses rode off in fear. Kristiana might have heard the horses and followed them. She could have gotten lost—"

Sabiere spun on him, the long tangle of his hair flashing before him. Travest heard the clicking of teeth an instant prior to being confronted by the chittering maw and crimson eye that rested in the clump at the base of his hair.

"She would never leave me!" Sabiere bellowed.

"Of course not," said Travest as he backed away. The eye and its razor-sharp maw withdrew and Sabiere flipped the rope of hair over his head, slapping it against his back. "It's just that I *must* bring this trophy back to our liege. If you wish to take some of our numbers with you and continue your search, I'm certain our master wouldn't begrudge you. He must be informed that the threat He feared is at an end."

Sabiere considered this. "Yes. Fine. Take Shax and Rose with you. See if you can get our silent companion to follow."

Travest nodded. He motioned to the sullen duo, who started his way. The plague-carrier did not move. Just as well. Travest needed to divide their numbers. Killing Shax and Rose would not be especially difficult, he decided, so long as he took them by surprise. The plague-carrier might be a different matter. Sabiere's decision to keep the most powerful of their lot at his side to continue the search only helped Travest. He really didn't know what had happened to the winged hunter, but he guessed that she had decided to face the angel alone and had paid for her foolishness with her life. With any luck at all, he would arrive at the City of Heaven where Anzelm had promised to meet him while Sabiere and his crew were still searching for Kristiana.

He had only gone a few feet before he heard Sinistari holler, "I've found something!"

Travest motioned for Shax and Rose to follow quickly. "This is no concern of ours."

Neither moved. Returning his gaze to the swamp, Travest saw Sabiere take hold of something the blond-haired man offered. It looked like a charred black wooden mask of a woman's screaming face.

Lilith was also in the swamp. She said, "I see something near the bottom. A leg. Part of a wing."

"They turned her . . . into . . . a tree," Sabiere said, he broke into hysterical laughter. "Then they set her on fire!"

The hunter screamed and laughed. Travest was debating on turning and running or attempting to attack all of them here and now when *something* struck the side of his head! He stumbled back, tripped on a root, and fell. The bag he carried came open and the stone rolled out. He was too dazed to maintain the illusion that it was the angel's head, the prize he had been sent to collect.

"You lied to us, little tailor," said Sabiere.

Travest looked up and saw Shax staring at the ground a good twenty feet away. The man's cloak was open and one of his tattoos, that of a large, gripping hand, had come to life! The hand had reached out from his flesh, stretching until it had covered the distance separating its wielder from Travest, and punched him in the side of the head. Now the hand was withdrawing, but Shax's flesh wriggled and a host of other tattoos were slowly gaining substance. Travest saw tentacles, claws, and talons writhing about his body.

Rose came closer. The vine along one of her arms moved like a snake, cutting her. She whipped her arm forward, a few drops of her blood splattering on him. Travest felt as if he had been sprayed by acid! Her blood was some kind of corrosive.

The others were rising out of the swamp. Travest had no time to think, only to react. He had command over light. Drawing down into the deepest reservoirs of power granted him by the Enemy, he looked up at the sun and willed himself to become its avatar. Suddenly, he was engulfed by blinding white light. Fear struck at him. Had he set himself on fire when all he had meant to do was blind his opponents?

Panicked, he drove the light from him with an explosive force that left him all but drained. He heard the others screaming and moaning. Strangely, he felt nothing but a fiery ache that spread throughout his body. His vision was a white tapestry with outlines of objects in yellow. He turned and ran. Unaware of the extent of the damage he had done to his former allies, he pictured a thousand different versions of himself running from the swamp. Then he saw it. Phantomlike shapes racing in every direction.

He *had* managed to create the illusion! Hopefully, the images would confuse his enemies long enough for him to make his escape.

Moments later, on the banks of the swamp, the survivors gathered. Each had been told that Travest had been made into one of their liege's most powerful warriors, but until this moment they hadn't understood the truth of that statement. The light wielded by the former tailor had rippled forward in waves that tore through the ranks of the hunters. It was as if they had been attacked by swords made of fire, capable of cutting through *anything*.

Sinistari was dead. He had been neatly cut in half by Travest's power. The man had been in mid-transformation when he had been killed. His body was no longer that of a handsome, lion-maned human. Instead, he looked like a half dozen terrible beasts stitched together haphazardly. The heads of a bull and a ram jutted from his shoulders, his legs looked like the limbs of a cock, and his back was graced with gossamer wings like those of a fly. His face had become feline and his belly had ruptured to show the gaping maw of a ravenous beast.

Shax had also fallen, his tattooed form a mass of smoking black cuts. The plague-carrier had vanished. Only Sabiere, Lilith, and Rose remained.

The right side of Sabiere's form had been singed black. The long tassel of hair topped with an eye had been burned away completely.

Shuddering with pain, he saw that Lilith did not appear hurt, though her clothing lay in a pile around her. With a slight smile, she crouched to collect her singed garb.

"How did you—" Sabiere began.

"Hush," whispered the raven-haired woman. "One has to have one's secrets."

Sabiere looked down at Lilith's dead lover. "You're not going to mourn him, are you?"

"Lovers come and go. I have what I wanted. What I always wanted. Our liege has seen to that."

"What I want . . . is vengeance."

Rose stood. She touched her arm, where she had cut herself with the vines, and the bleeding stopped. The earth around her had been melted into glass. She had been quick enough to step behind a huge tree and use it as a shield. Little remained of the tree, but she had not been hurt.

"Our liege has made us into what we are to further His purpose. To bring truth," said Rose in a surprisingly authoritative voice. "Nothing may distract us from our task. Fortunately, it was certainly our quarry who killed your lover, Sabiere. By keeping a cool head, you will get what you want—and we will all find favor with our liege. Your injuries look severe. Can you go on in your present state?"

"No," said Sabiere as he focused his will and began to shed his wounded skin. "And there's no reason why I should have to. . . ."

Rose nodded, watching Sabiere transform. She vaguely recalled a time when she would have been frightened by what he was becoming.

Now all she felt was a rising satisfaction.

Later that day, in a clearing far from the swamp, the plague-carrier came across the campsite Aitan and Tom had abandoned. He had known all along that Travest had not killed the angel. If someone had asked him, he might have mentioned it. As it was, he was not interested in the petty dealings of his liege's other soldiers. He had been told to go with them, nothing more.

The others were lesser beings than himself. Only Travest Mulvihill, the light-bearer, possessed power that rivaled his own. But Travest Mulvihill was clinging to his humanity and that made him weak. The light-bearer would not look deeply into his soul and confront what he had become. Instead he hid from it. Why his liege had transformed a man with so little taste for change into one of his highest-ranking lieutenants, the plague-carrier had no idea.

All that worried him was that he had been taken away from

the task he had been born to perform while there was so much work left to be done. He had decimated only seven human towns and had been about to move on to one of the greater cities when he had been recalled without explanation.

"You must follow my orders without question," his liege had said. "This is a matter of faith. All will become clear in time."

The plague-carrier had done as he had been asked. His liege had shown him secrets, given him answers to questions he hadn't even known to ask. Now the plague-carrier knew the Truth, and his victims knew it, too. He did not consider himself an entirely cruel being. True, he sated his desires, many of them centered on sex and violence, in the course of delivering his victims. A simple touch seemed—insulting. He considered their suffering, which many had not even been fully aware of at the time, adequate payment for the enlightenment his victims received when they were in the final stages of the disease and could no longer communicate with others. In this way, they understood their part in the Second Grand Plan, and they knew that their deaths would help to one day bring the Truth to all who lived on this world, human or "divine."

The time he had spent with the lesser soldiers had been tedious. He searched through every event, looking for some clue as to why he had been asked to follow his inferiors. Then, as the others had been searching for some clue as to what fate had befallen their comrade, he felt a strange yearning. He left them and walked until he came to this place. The angel and the boy had been there. The same wild talent that had allowed him to be the deliverer of more than two thousand human souls in recent weeks told him this was so.

He looked around, praying he would find the answer he needed so desperately. Without a purpose, he was nothing.

On the ground, he saw a single piece of paper. Picking it up, he turned it over and stared at the picture Tom Keeper had drawn of the flame guardian. In that moment, everything became clear to him. He knew the boy's dreams—so much like his own—and in so knowing, understood what fate intended for the child.

From this moment on, his existence, and that of Tom Keeper, would be bound as one. All that could sever the bond he now realized they shared was death. His death—or that of the boy.

For the first time since he had been made into something more than human, for the first time since he had been given the name Rogziel, in honor of the first of the seven angels of punishment his master had slain to achieve his current power, the plague-carrier wept.

He was no longer alone.

Eighteen

TOM KEEPER SLEPT, AND THE DREAM CAME UPON HIM once more. He was in the crystal chamber, floating naked before the flame guardian. Tom looked down at the symbols painted on his body. He understood that these were runes. Sigils. Angelic script.

"Why have you come here?" asked the flame guardian.

For the first time since the dreams began, Tom felt no compulsion to follow lines that had been written by someone else, lines—he sensed—that were the translation of the symbols elegantly painted upon his flesh. He felt a chill and suddenly the Sigils vanished. Tom fell to the cold floor of the chamber.

"I'm here because you brought me here," Tom said. "That's right, isn't it?"

The fiery man was silent.

"So much of what you've told me is a lie," said Tom.

"Is it?"

"I think it is."

The flame guardian laughed. "In this place, thinking makes it so."

"So who are you? Why do you keep coming after me in my dreams?"

"I am what you've been seeking."

"I doubt it."

The flame guardian gestured at the swirling vortex of light and sound. "I stand before the gateway to fulfillment. I offer power and delight."

"That's really nice for you. Last time you said something about being my Patron. You also said I wasn't human anymore and so I could wield magic. I thought about that. It's what made me see you're nothing but a liar.''

"What is, what was, what will be. In this place, they are all the same.''

"I don't believe you.''

The flame guardian bellowed, "I can give you your *heart's desire!* I can make *Kayrlis* love you.''

Tom blanched at this. It was his heart's desire. He would give almost anything for it. "You know a lot about me.''

"Practically everything. There is a spell I can give you. You will need a white lily and a crystal goblet. I will tell you the 137th Psalm, if you do not know it. You will need a piece of cypress that you will dip in oil and tie to your arm. And the name of the angel Anael. Once you have—''

"I don't want to know any more.''

"Of course you do.''

"Maybe. But what do I have to give up in return?'' Tom asked. "My freedom? My soul? My humanity?''

"You are a dramatic young lad, aren't you?''

"That doesn't answer my question.''

"All I want is something you have no further use for.''

"What's that?''

"You decide.''

The flame guardian gestured and a brilliant flare of light engulfed the chamber.

Tom woke to find himself on a ship towing a large, slow-moving barge. Night had fallen. Tom looked past the huge white sails to the barge's load, a collection of heavy logs meant for the dock outside the City of Heaven.

A dozen men operated the vessel, which made stops all along the eastern coastline. The crew of the *Emalle's Bliss* was a mixture of Naturals and Dutch. The ship's captain had considered the presence of the angel and his squire as a blessing and a sure sign that they would encounter no ill winds or choppy waters. So far, that assertion had proved correct.

Tom lay on a blanket near one of the sailing ship's great masts. An oil lamp had been hung nearby, casting an orange glow on the deck. Aitan was nearby.

Other than offering the captain's quarters and a decent meal for the travelers, the crew had left Aitan and Tom alone. Aitan preferred to rest above deck. He wanted to be able to see if any other boats approached. It would be morning before they cleared the Great Dismal Swamp completely. The banks of the swamp were well within the range of fire arrows. An attack could come at any time, though Aitan felt fairly confident they were safe from the hunters.

The deck was cold. Tom wrapped the blanket around himself and positioned himself closer to the angel.

"Look at this," said Tom as he blew into the air. A tiny cloud formed in the air. "Can you see your breath?"

"It's getting colder. Winter's coming."

Tom noticed a waterskin hanging on a rod near Aitan. He gestured and the angel handed it to him. The water was fresh and tasted wonderful.

"You were having a nightmare," said the angel.

The boy did not try to deny it. "I've been having them ever since we've been together. I thought you were giving them to me at first."

"You thought I'd be giving you nightmares? On purpose?"

"Well, they weren't really nightmares in the beginning.

And I kept forgetting them. A few seconds after I woke up, the dreams would be gone from my head. It wasn't until Kayrlis and me, until we . . ."

"When you and Kayrlis slept together."

Tom looked sharply to the angel. "You know about that?"

"I've known all along."

Shifting, drawing the blanket closer, Tom asked, "What else do you know?"

Aitan dug into his leathers, pulled out a dark vial that had only a flicker of light left within.

"So you know everything. Why didn't you tell me?"

The angel put the vial away. "It wasn't my business, really."

Tom couldn't believe what he was hearing. "How can you say that? Grin left that vial for you, in case you were hurt. I threw it all away. If something happens—"

"We'll deal with it, if something happens. What matters is, you tried to save the boy. It was a good and honorable thing."

"Does Kayrlis know?"

Aitan nodded.

"I thought she'd hate me."

Aitan frowned. "She was—too busy worrying about her brother. Adjusting to the idea he would die."

Tears threatened to fall from Tom's eyes. He shook as he said, "We went through so much to save him."

"I know."

"I mean, what good did it do anyone? We saved Cameron from a quick death so now he can suffer for weeks. It's just some big joke."

"This is why you've been angry?"

"Wouldn't you be?" Tom could restrain his tears no longer. He drew his knees up, buried his face, and cried with great, racking sobs. The angel put his hand on Tom's back, waiting for it to be over. Finally, Tom raised his head and wiped the tears away. There was a hardness to his features.

"Tom—"

"I thought it would change everything," said Tom. "Becoming a man."

"Sleeping with a woman doesn't make you a man."

"I love her."

"Don't confuse love with sex. Or love with gratitude."

"I'm not."

"Good."

"But she doesn't love me."

"Do you know that for a fact?"

"No."

"While there's life, there's hope."

"I used to think that. After everything that's happened, I'm starting to think that hope is the enemy."

Aitan breathed out heavily. He looked up to the starry night sky. "I heard the final words of a heretic once. He was about to be put to the Question and he asked us to think about something. He proposed three things. First, that God was all-good. Second, that God was all-powerful. And third, that terrible things happen. He said any two of those propositions worked together, but not all three."

"I don't understand. What does that have to do with me?"

"His theory was that there could be a great and all-powerful God who allows horrible things in the world, but then God couldn't be all-good. Or that if God was all-good and these horrors still happened in the world, then God couldn't be all-powerful. He said the existence of evil was the best argument against the existence of God.''

"That's—that's—" Tom sputtered.

"Shocking, heretical. Yes, I know. God is good. God is just. But this man wanted us to think. And I've never quite been able to put his words out of my mind. Not even after he had died screaming, recanting his earlier statement in a desperate bid for mercy on the soul my brothers damned and cast out for eternal punishment.''

"Merciful God," whispered Tom.

"All I'm saying is that there are no easy answers. It's all a matter of faith. Of belief. Right now, we're going through terrible trials. I took a life I might have spared had I been able to think a little quicker.''

"That wasn't your fault," said Tom.

"Maybe not. We're all as God made us. Imperfect. Limited. Capable of horrible mistakes and wretched choices. All I'm trying to say to you is that none of this is easy. All we can do is try to hold on to our faith and believe that there is a Grand Plan, that everything that happens is for a reason.''

Tom thought about this. "You know, my mother told me something once. She said the reason God allows bad things to happen is because in the beginning, man had paradise. He had everything handed to him. And he got lazy, and he got bored, and he got surly. Before too long he got himself cast out. She said that man can't really learn anything if God's making it easy for us all. He can't really learn to appreciate the good unless the bad's there, too.''

"God responds to all prayers, sometimes the answer is no.''

"Exactly.''

"Your mother was a good woman. I'm sorry I'll never have a chance to meet her.''

"You will," said Tom brightly. His dark mood seemed to have lifted. "When we're all in Heaven, I'll get the two of you together. How would that be?''

"I'd cherish it," said the angel. "Now, tell me about the dreams.''

Tom told Aitan all that he could remember about his nocturnal visits with the flame guardian. When he was finished, he waited for Aitan to respond. The angel appeared perplexed, but not overly concerned. Tom had a sense that the man was hiding something.

"It's him, isn't it?" asked Tom finally. "The one who's calling himself the Enemy. Your friend."

"We were friends once," said the angel, "a long time ago. And even if it is he, you've handled yourself well in these encounters. Even offering you what you wanted more than anything in the world wasn't enough to sway you."

Tom said, "It wasn't easy, turning him down."

"It never is." Aitan ran his hand through his long, raven's hair. "I'm trying to think of what I can tell you about him in case he appears to you again. Anything that would give you an edge."

"How did you know him? What's his name?"

"Fair enough questions," said Aitan. "All right. His name is Komm Kyriel. He is descended from the Guardians of the Gates of the West Wind. His family, all of whom he has slain, were among the governing bodies of the Mansions of the Moon. As to how I knew him, it was when we were children. He was dark and magnificent. Tall and strong for his age. It was at a time when very little could distract me from exploring the ruins of the first cities of God."

"Ruins?" asked Tom, alarmed.

"There were conflicts. Wars among our kind."

"Over what?"

Aitan shook his head. "I can't tell you. All I can say is that I had gone to an ancient city and climbed the highest spire I could find. I'd often found telling evidence of secrets in the hardest places to reach. I was in a small chamber, about to lay my hands on a treasure that I could hardly believe existed. One of the ancient Grimoires, the Mysts Arcana."

"What, it was some kind of book?"

"An ancient tome, yes. I was certain the answers to all the mysteries lay within its pages."

The ship creaked and moaned. Tom found its subtle movements relaxing. "Someone just left this lying around?"

"No. You couldn't see it, only sense it. To find the book, I had to use a spell I had scared up in a desecrated crypt."

"What kind of crypt?" Tom said, becoming enthralled.

"The crypt held the remains of several warrior angels from a time before the creation of the world. I touched the Mysts Arcana, but only for a second. The tower I was in collapsed. I fell for what seemed like an eternity and was crushed beneath a mountain of stone. I should have died. I didn't, though I was unconscious for a time. When I awoke, Komm Kyriel was there. He had dug me loose. Healed the worst of my wounds."

"What about the book?"

"I saw it—sensed it—for a moment through my pain. Then I felt the earth trembling and saw the sky turn to blood. Daggers of lightning fell from above. Komm Kyriel risked his own life to fly me from that place before it was swallowed up by the earth. I went back much later, but all that remained was a dark, stinking pit."

"The two of you became friends."

"For a time. He was very clever. Outgoing. He could make an ally of anyone, end disputes that had raged on for centuries. I'd never met anyone I found quite so perfect until I first saw Rachiel."

"When did you stop being friends? What happened?"

"Nothing, really. He was sent away. I never knew why. We never saw each other again."

"That was it?"

"Yes."

"But you told Travest that you had been studying him, that you knew everything about him!"

"I *did* study him. In texts and scrolls. From stories about his valor as a soldier of the Lord. He was called the Most Favored for a time, even above those who now hold the Name and Rank of Michael and Gabriel."

Tom looked around. The night sky seemed to be deepening, the stars fading from the sky. He saw a canopy of trees reaching over the swamp just ahead. The gentle, soothing rhythms of the ship made him feel like taking another nap. He was bone weary from their travails.

"What happened to him?" asked Tom.

"I'm not sure," said the angel truthfully. "I've been told that he went mad. That he turned on all of us, and that every attempt to bring him to justice has failed."

Tom hugged himself. He felt a cold wind slicing through

him. "Aitan, you can't do what Travest wants. If you go against your own kind, you'll be like Komm Kyriel. Hunted."

The angel glanced over at Tom and smiled. "I suppose I shouldn't be so oblique."

"Pardon?"

Aitan laughed. "I thought with your imagination it would have been obvious to you, and that's why you never brought the matter up before now."

"I don't—what?" Tom was completely confused.

"I told Travest he had a deal. I didn't say he had one with me."

Tom stared at the angel in stunned silence. "He had a deal. The one he already made with Komm Kyriel."

"When we get to the City of Heaven, I will have others of my kind come for Travest. They will take from him the secrets we need to know. I would have done it myself, but I sensed a Power within him, one I didn't dare stand against alone. If Grin had been with us, it might have been different."

Finally, a smile broke on Tom's young, handsome face. "You really are a corker sometimes, you know that?"

"I'll take that as a compliment."

"Still," Tom said as they cleared the canopy of trees and the stars shone brightly once more, "I can't help but wonder about the kid."

"Travest's son? I'm sure he'll be fine."

"He'll never be allowed to leave the City of Heaven."

"Have you ever considered that maybe the reason no human ever leaves a City of Heaven is that they don't *want* to go?"

Tom thought about that. He said, "I've been thinking about what happens to me when we get to the City of Heaven. I know I can't go in there with you. And once you speak with the Emissary, or one of the Vessels, or whatever—they'll probably give you an army to command or something. Your whole life is going to be devoted to stopping Komm Kyriel."

"Tom," said the angel in a pained voice, "I know I made promises to you. If it is no longer possible to gain an apprenticeship for you with Roger Hughes, then I will see that another artist who is at liberty takes you on."

"No, you don't understand," said Tom excitedly. "I *want*

to go with you on the Crusade against Komm Kyriel. I want to be your squire. For real.''

Aitan was stunned. ''You can't mean that.''

''I do. With your power and my imagination, we can do anything!''

''What about your dream of becoming an artist?''

''Well,'' Tom shrugged, ''I've got to have *something* to draw and paint, right? When it's all over, you can put the story down in words, I'll do the same in pictures. That way, people will really know what's it's like to stand against the Enemy and live. It'll inspire people who are questioning their faith.''

''And your fame will make you irresistible to young Kayr-lis?''

''No!'' Tom said with a laugh. ''That would be nice, but . . . I just want to be at your side, that's all. I feel like I've earned the right.''

''Maybe you have,'' said the angel. ''Let me think about it?''

Tom nodded.

Suddenly, the ship was rocked, as if it had struck something in the waters. Tom and Aitan stood. He saw the crew members coming up from below, rippling across the surface of the boat in fear.

The waters around the sailing ship churned, rocking the craft one way, then the other. Tom stood transfixed as a wave appeared from nowhere and rose up before the ship. When it fell, the wave would engulf the boat, pounding its surface and all those present with its hammerlike force.

The impact Tom anticipated did not come. The wave was *frozen*. It sat, some twenty feet above the craft, foaming like the maw of an insane animal. Three figures appeared at its crest. A man, flanked by two women.

The hunters had arrived.

''Greetings and salutations,'' cried Sabiere. ''An old friend sends his regards.

Tom saw that the hunter who had spoken was not human. Though the light was dim, and Sabiere was not very close, Tom could see that the man's body seemed to be composed of a host of smaller entities that glittered and swam in the overall outline of a man.

The boy looked over and saw that his companion had not been idle. Aitan was gesturing, forming some kind of flaming rune before him, as Sabiere allowed the wave to break. The waters came crashing down. Tom looked away, waiting for the jarring, crushing impact. He heard it, but felt nothing. Turning back, he saw that Aitan had erected a shield of solidified air above them. The wave slammed upon it, delivering the worst of its terrible power. Tom and the angel were spared. The crewmen were not so fortunate. Some were crushed instantly, the others swept overboard.

Suddenly, the trio of hunters were upon them. Tom stood beside Aitan. Sabiere approached Aitan directly. The women circled around Tom and the angel. This time, Tom could see the transformed man clearly. His entire body writhed with snakes, bugs, silverfish, and glistening energies rushing through his bodies like tributaries.

"You carry a sword," said Sabiere to the angel. "Fight me with it."

Rose and Lilith closed on Tom.

"Fight me or I'll have my beloved companions *do things* to the boy. Things he won't like."

The network of thorns crawled over Rose's body. She bled and droplets of acid fell hissing upon the slick surface of the ship. Tom looked around. Aitan gestured once more. A wall of mist suddenly surrounded Lilith. It hardened and became clear. She seemed startled, as if she had suddenly been trapped within a chunk of ice.

"End this now or I'll crush the life from her," Aitan said. "It won't take much. Just a little pressure."

"Wrong victim," said Sabiere.

Lilith smiled and walked out of the trap Aitan had set. Tom could see right through her, as if she were a phantom. Before the boy could react, Lilith rushed forward, her hands reaching for Tom. Aitan spun, unsheathed his sword, and moved between her and the lad.

The hunter went through Aitan and put her hands on Tom. He shuddered as he felt Lilith's hands move into his body. He had never felt anything so chilling.

"No one moves," Sabiere said. "If she makes herself solid

again, the boy dies. Her hands, I believe, are wrapped around his heart.''

Tom stared into the woman's violet eyes. She felt nothing toward him. He could tell.

Sabiere laughed. ''I thought you would attack the one who seemed most vulnerable. Cowards are always predictable.''

Aitan waited.

''Fight me,'' said Sabiere as he stepped away from the group.

The hunter spread his arms. ''Raise your sword and try to kill me. Go ahead. But at the first sign of magic, Lilith takes the boy's heart.''

Tom could feel her icy touch. His heart raced. He began to tremble.

Only moments before, he had pleaded with Aitan to let him stand at his side.

Your power and my imagination.

The words seemed so hollow now. He couldn't think of a single thing that would get them out of this.

Aitan moved forward with his weapon. Sabiere didn't move. The angel said, ''You're unarmed.''

Sabiere raised his arms. They suddenly fused into rapierlike appendages. ''Hardly. Even so. Come on, pretender. Try to hurt me.''

The angel whipped forward with his blade, expecting Sabiere to counter with his movement in some way, or at least try to leap out of harm's way. Instead, the man stood there, arms spread, while Aitan's blade sliced through him, entering just to the left of his neck and cutting a neat, clean diagonal path to his hip on the opposite side before exiting.

Sabiere grunted as the blade went through him, then he smiled and looked down at his own body. The wound Aitan had made was filled with the sparkling waters. It healed instantly.

''Scared yet?'' Sabiere said. ''You ought to be. You killed my lover. Remember her? Wings, dark skin. Something of a temper.''

The angel held the man's gaze. He understood there would be no reasoning with the hunters now. Blood had been drawn.

This was about more than following Komm Kyriel's orders; this man wanted vengeance.

Suddenly, Aitan spun and brought his sword across Sabiere's throat in a sweeping arc, beheading him. The man's headless torso caught his falling head and slapped it back in place. Again, the waters flowed and Sabiere was restored.

A few feet away, Tom thought about the powers Aitan had invoked. Tom had seen the angel make dancing men and women from a stream without calling upon his Patron—or so the boy assumed. The angel had also called forth a swarm of insects when fighting Grin in the covered bridge, and he seemed to be able to control animals and bugs. By rights, Aitan should have been able to destroy Sabiere easily. The hunter was made of all the elements over which Aitan had mastery. But the man would not act so long as he was in danger. Somehow, he had to get away from Lilith.

"I want you to know how Kristiana felt," said Sabiere. "I want you to understand what it means to go up against forces you cannot possibly defeat. I want you to die in despair."

Rose took a step forward. A few more drops of her blood struck the deck and hissed. Lilith snapped, "Keep away from me. You know what could happen."

"I want to end this," said Rose.

"Not before I have my fun," cried Sabiere.

Tom was intrigued. Why would Rose's particular ability so frighten Lilith? He could think of only one reason: Rose's blood was steeped in some kind of magic.

Suddenly, with the same perfect clarity that descended on him when sat down to draw and an image came into sharp focus in his imagination, Tom knew what he had to do. First, he had to try and slow things down a little.

"What do you mean, 'pretender'?" asked Tom.

Sabiere laughed. "He didn't tell you, did he? I wonder if he even knows."

Aitan glanced in Tom's direction. The boy hoped that the determination in his eyes would be enough to signal Aitan that he had something planned.

Sabiere said, "It's all a lie. Your friend here's no more touched by God than I am."

No, Tom thought, *you've been branded by the Enemy.*

"They're not angels," Sabiere went on, "they're *Elven*. The old legends had it right. The Faerie Folk. Where they're from isn't Heaven, either."

"Blasphemer," Aitan said, his anger rising.

"You really don't know," Sabiere said delightedly. "You have no idea how your people plundered their own world of its very soul, of the source of its magic. That's why the True Lands are in chaos and ruin."

Aitan blanched. None of this could be true!

As Sabiere raved, Tom reached to the small of his back, where he kept the enchanted blade Aitan had given him days ago, when they had been attacked by the Anarchists. Ever since the encounter with the winged hunter, he felt better having the knife on him. Carefully he drew it out of the sheath he had made on their journey. Then he sliced open his palm. The pain was sharp and intense. Suddenly he felt a fiery power reach out from his own mind and latch onto the consciousness of his friend. It was as if he had thrown a rope to Aitan that had been caught and pulled tight, a mystical bond connecting them in a way Tom had never dreamed possible.

He heard the Elven's thoughts in his own mind, a strange ethereal presence: *Tom, whatever you're thinking, don't do it. I'll offer myself to them on the condition that you be set free.*

No, Tom replied. *The second I get away from her, do what you have to so we can survive. And if I die, avenge me.*

Tom had an idea how Aitan could rid them of the hunters. It passed between them instantly, then their connection was severed. The boy saw Aitan start for a moment, then look back his way and nod solemnly as he lowered his gaze.

Sabiere was still talking. "That's why you've come here. To take our world, one piece at a time. And why you created the Scourge. You want to wipe out our kind."

Aitan's lips curled in disgust. "Madness. It's Komm Kyriel who's using the Scourge to kill humans. He's destroyed entire villages with the monster he created!"

Snakes writhed in and out of Sabiere's chest. "Our liege is moving up the timetable, that's all. He's making it so that the people can no longer ignore the Elven's plans for us. If a few innocents have to die now, rather than later, to save us all— so be it!"

Tom reached out suddenly, his bloody hand touched by magic penetrating to the center of Lilith's cold, wraithlike form. She gasped, and suddenly he felt her withdraw. Tom turned and ran for the boat's railing, the blade slipping from his hand.

"Now, Aitan, now!" Tom screamed.

The angel was already gesturing as Tom closed on the ship's railing, Lilith behind him. Aitan knew that these people were deluded and should have been pitied, not destroyed, but he didn't have the power to risk an extended battle with them. He had to end this quickly, and Tom's idea made sense.

Sabiere shuddered as Aitan took control of the countless creatures that made up his form. The lightning fires binding the hunter together writhed and hissed as Sabiere was pulled apart.

"Do what you will!" Sabiere cried. "Scatter me to the ends of the earth, I'll form again. I won't stop until you're both dead. I won't—"

Rose came forward, the vines tearing her flesh, exposing her enchanted blood.

The angel saw Tom leap over the side of the ship. Lilith was no longer in sight. The boy was safe.

"God forgive me," Aitan whispered as he used his power to send the thousands of creatures making up Sabiere at Rose. They attacked her with the ferocity of a thousand hungry blades. She was sliced apart, there was a horrible, crimson explosion, and her blood consumed and dissolved the myriad sea creatures.

Aitan stood behind a shield formed from solid air that had been rocked and nearly crumbled as Rose's blood came for the angel.

It wasn't over. The angel stared at an undulating spiral of lightning. This was the energy holding Sabiere's soul a prisoner, the binding force that would retreat into the swamp and find new creatures to use as a host body for the hunter.

Aitan dropped his shield and performed the Spell of Severing. The energies rebelled as Aitan's sorcery attacked them. The lightning sparkled and crackled, lancing across the deck of the ship, sailing toward the angel.

He completed the spell and heard a soul cry out in despair.

The energies lost their form and purpose as Sabiere's essence was severed from their control. They rose up, slapping across one of the ship's masts, then filled the sky. Aitan heard a cracking, saw the mast and the sails attached to it falling, and leaped overboard. He was vaguely aware of lightning filling the sky at his back and a terrible crash as the mast fell. Then he was bursting through the surface of the dark waters.

Free.

He swam back to the surface of the waters, burst through, and took a swallow of air. Suddenly, an icy hand grabbed him by the throat and yanked him back in the waters. He felt a knife slide across his throat.

"Gruesome," Lilith said in a throaty whisper. "Clever, but gruesome. Now—I'm well aware that you know my weakness. Stepping through the magical trap you laid for me before was far more painful than I let on. If I so much as think that you're about to work magic on me, I'll cut you. Understand?"

"Let Tom live," pleaded the angel. He was drained, unable to conceive of enacting another spell.

"I have every intention."

The knife came away from Aitan's throat. He felt Lilith take his wrist and slap the blade into his hand.

"You're not going to kill me?" Aitan asked.

"I don't share the fondness for our liege that my fellows did. Besides, you and the child have *potential.* Another time."

Spinning him to face her, Lilith kissed Aitan, then dissolved into her ghost form and vanished beneath the waters.

Nineteen

HALF OF THE SHIP'S CREW HAD BEEN PULLED UNDER THE
waters, their bodies lost. The rest survived to help Aitan and Tom repair the damage to the ship's masts and
bring the craft out of the Great Dismal Swamp. No longer
feeling particularly blessed, the crew treated Aitan and Tom
with respect, but not reverence.

An hour after dawn, they reached a port just south of the
City of Heaven, where they were confronted by another craft
bearing angels. Aitan met with the group, eight in all, and
agreed to make the remainder of his journey with them.
Strangely, the angels were alone on their craft. Aitan recognized many of their number, and acted humbly in their presence.

Mounts were secured for the angels in the port town and
the riders set off. Within hours, they entered the woods leading
them to the holy city. Aitan rode up beside Sandalphon, an
angel who had inherited the title and Power of the Angel of
Tears. Many such highly placed persons were among the ranks
of the travelers. Sandalphon was handsome, with dark hair and
flesh that appeared clear as glass, revealing his inner fire.

"I'm surprised to see lords of your station traveling alone,"
said Aitan. "Your squires? Your attendants?"

"Dismissed."

Sandalphon spurred his mount and rode ahead of Aitan, who
fell back and rejoined Tom at the end of the procession.

Aitan and Tom had talked long into the previous night about
the outlandish claims made by the Enemy's soldiers. Aitan
was certainly willing to admit the existence of many perplex-

191

ing mysteries in the universe, but the solution offered by the transformed beings was insane. They came to the conclusion that the minds of the enemy's soldiers had been twisted when they took Power from him. But the claims of Komm Kyriel's trackers would not be dismissed so easily. They preyed upon Aitan and Tom.

Aitan had not shared Grin's final words: *Something horrible is walking the earth. Something that's our fault. Something that will make us question our beliefs. Something that might be right to do so.*

The angel had believed Grin to mean the Enemy. The True Enemy, not Komm Kyriel, who now masqueraded in that guise. It had not occurred to Aitan until recently that the two could be one and the same. Had Komm Kyriel been possessed by the Enemy? That would certainly explain his actions.

Questions, endless questions . . .

Aitan knew that before he reached the City of Heaven, he would have to convince at least a few of his fellows to stay behind with Tom. Unfortunately, though the others were willing to tolerate Aitan's presence, they were not of a mind to be sociable. Aitan assumed that at least part of their attitude stemmed from his lack of status. After all, he *had* been cast out of the city of his birth, and only a handful knew of the chance for redemption that had been offered to him. Nevertheless, he was confident that before journey's end, he would be able to prevail upon Sandalphon at the very least to stay with Tom when he entered the city and attempted to summon the Second Vessel.

As they rode, the weather turned foul. The sky became steel grey, the winds tore at them, seemingly from every direction at once. Aitan used his power to lessen the effects of nature, which endeared him to the other angels, whose province was chiefly over emotions, not physical laws.

"Anzelm," muttered Pahadron, Angel of Terror and Trembling. He had nightmare black flesh and eyes like crimson coals. "Your line was once sword bearers to the Angels of the Four Winds, Michael, Raphael, Uriel, and Gabriel."

"Once," said Aitan.

Tom, who rode at Aitan's side, stared at his companion in

amazement. He noticed one of the other angels watching him and so he shifted his gaze downward.

"What brings such an esteemed company of angels such as yourself to the city?" asked Aitan.

"The Event," said one of the other angels. "The Unveiling. You hadn't heard? You weren't Summoned?"

Aitan shook his head.

"Then it's not our place to tell you!"

"Perhaps not," said Aitan, choosing this moment to play his hand, "I suppose the Vessel would have mentioned it to me if He had wished me to know."

"A Vessel?" cried Sandalphon. "You have been addressed directly by a Vessel? Not through an Emissary?"

"I was given a Task," said Aitan, feeling pleased. He glanced over at Tom and saw the boy shivering. Though he didn't want to see Tom suffering, he knew this was a result of Pahadron's losing control over his emotions. The Angel of Terror and Trembling was convinced. He alone would make a fine guardian for Tom.

With a confident laugh, Aitan said, "Ingethel was upset, true, but it is not up to me to question the Vessel."

"Ingethel," an angel muttered. "Emissary to the Second."

"Perhaps the Vessel thought it amusing to keep secrets from the Angel over Hidden Things," said Aitan. He glanced around and saw that none of the other angels found this particularly funny.

The angels believed Aitan's story. Telling lies about the Vessels was a mortal sin. Only a madman or a fool would dare such an affront.

Aitan told the absolute truth. He *had* been visited by the Second Vessel, and later by the Emissary Ingethel.

Rising up in his saddle, Aitan said, "My squire fought bravely at my side. He has aided me in the Task. When we arrive at the city, I will need you, Pahadron, and you, Sandalphon, to stand with him while I enter ahead of you."

"I'll not miss the Event," cried Pahadron.

"Of course you won't," Aitan said gently. "I'll have others sent to relieve you immediately."

The Angels of Trembling and Tears regarded one another, then nodded.

"I have your Solemn Word?" asked Aitan. Each vowed to do as they had been commanded. Aitan heard an odd sound and looked over to see Tom weeping. The boy looked perplexed. Sandalphon, this time. The Angel of Tears was clearly not pleased. Aitan went on to give a description of Travest Mulvihill. He instructed the angels on how to deal with the man: "Just tell him that Aitan Anzelm will soon return with the one he seeks. And don't listen to his lies. I would sooner forfeit my soul than perform the task he begged of me. We just can't let him know that!"

As the company of angels neared the outskirts of the holy city, nature quietly went mad. The road upon which they traveled lurched and trembled.

"Pahadron!" cried one of the lesser angels. "Is this your doing?"

Laughter came from the rest of the company. The Angel of Trembling did not deign to answer.

The winds screamed and words could be heard. Horrible obscenities. The trees wept. Insects and small animals, many not indigenous to Tom's world, rose up and died in the road. Aitan, still unable to contact his Patron, was able to do little to settle nature's fury. The angels bore these indignities in silence. It was well-known by their kind that the earth often attempted to reject the presence of a heavenly city. Apparently, this was happening outside this one.

The angel rode into the lead, Tom at his side. Suddenly, Tom felt weak. He felt something moist on his upper lip. Wiping away the moisture, Tom looked down at his hand and said, "Lord, I'm bleeding."

Before Aitan could respond, Pahadron spat, "Malkiyyah must be in a snit again!"

Aitan understood. "The Angel of Blood is near, and he is being careless with his Power."

"One of his Powers," cried another of the angels, this one thin and yellow-haired.

"Hush, Marifiel," said a taller angel who rode near him.

"Yes, Lord Narcoriel."

These two were Angels of the Hours of the Night. Aitan guessed that they were both soldiers and magic wielders.

"It will pass," Aitan said. "It's only because we're close to the city."

As they rode, Aitan confided in Tom that he had not been able to gain an audience with his Patron.

"Do you think something's happened? Could your Patron be hurt?"

"I pray not."

"Who is this person, anyway?"

"A gentle being I helped once, who has been helping me ever since."

"An angel, like you?"

"A fellow exile. We met when I first left Europe and arrived at St. Johns. Newfoundland. It's a long story."

Suddenly, the winds became deafening. Conversation was no longer possible for the last part of the company's trek along the dirt road that wound its way through the forest. The madness ceased as they broke from the forest and beheld the shimmering wall that hid the City of Heaven from the view of mortals.

Aitan saw two people sitting about one hundred yards off. At first, he worried that Travest had found a shorter route to the City of Heaven. The angel wanted a fitting reception waiting when the former tailor arrived.

"It's Grin!" Tom shouted.

The former Emissary raised a single gauntleted hand in greeting. Tom broke rank and rode to Grin's side, Aitan following him. All the other angels, except the pair who had vowed to guard Tom, rode into the mists and vanished.

Tom dismounted and raced to the warrior. With a joyous laugh he cried, "Where have you been?"

Grin gestured at the man who sat beside him. "Don't you want to say hello to my companion before you start hurling questions at me?"

Tom glanced at the man. His clothing had been reduced to tatters. His flesh was bruised and scarred, blistered red in places. He had long dark hair, a scraggly full beard, and the look of a man who had just stared into the Book of Judgment only to find his name listed among the damned.

"No offense, gentle lord," said Tom. "Hello, sir."

The ruined man looked over at Tom. His haunted eyes never quite seemed to focus.

Aitan made it to Tom's side. He gasped when he saw the man beside Grin. Then he dug into his vest and withdrew Rachiel's silver ring. The man cried out like an animal and held his hands up imploringly.

"Just let me touch it," he moaned. "Let me feel her once more."

"Merciful Lord," whispered Tom. He looked closer into the once-strong and handsome features of the man and knew in that instant that he was in the presence of Roger Hughes.

Aitan handed the ring to Hughes, who clutched it to his breast and cried as he gently rocked back and forth with it.

Tom thought he would feel devastated if he learned that Hughes was dead. Looking at the man, Tom sensed that Hughes had suffered a fate far worse. His spirit had been broken, his creative fire put out.

The boy felt only pity. His own path, he was certain, was set. He would ride with Aitan, be his chronicler. Aitan hadn't agreed to this yet, but Tom felt it was only a matter of time.

Aitan bowed before Grin.

"Not this again," said the warrior.

Rising, Aitan asked, "Why did you leave?"

"Why did I leave?" the warrior groused. "Why did I appear? I do what I want. What I must. And what is foretold."

"That's not an answer."

Grin shrugged. He looked to Tom. "I know about the boy."

Tom lowered his gaze. He had thought often about Cameron, wondering if the child was still clinging to life, and what Kayrlis would say to Tom if and when their paths ever crossed.

"I'm sorry," said Grin. "I honestly wished that my vision had been wrong."

"Vision?" asked Tom.

Grin glanced over to Aitan. "I would have thought you'd tell the boy everything."

"No. I didn't think it was my place."

The former Emissary explained that he had been granted the Gift of prophecy.

"God honors you, though you no longer serve him directly," Tom said.

Grin nodded sharply. "Yes. God in his infinite mercy and wisdom, I suppose."

The former Emissary hardly sounded convinced. Anxious to change the subject, Grin set his armored hand on the artist's shoulder. "I found this poor wreck wandering the road. I doubt he would have survived if I hadn't looked after him."

Aitan said, "Has he said much about what happened to him?"

"You mean that Komm Kyriel savaged him and took Rachiel's spirit from his keeping? Something along those lines?"

The angel sighed. Grin hadn't changed.

"No, nothing like that at all," said the former Emissary.

The artist handed Rachiel's ring back to Aitan. "There's no hope if this stays with me. Help her."

Aitan took the ring. He said, "You know that I hated you, don't you?"

"Yes."

"Because you got to be with her."

The artist loosed a hollow laugh. "I hated you, too."

"Why?"

"You were all she talked about. All she thought about."

The angel was stunned. "Me?"

"I've got no reason to lie," Hughes said, "especially now."

Tom wondered if he would ever know all that passed between Aitan and this man.

"I met your friend," said Grin. "Komm Kyriel. Or what had been Komm Kyriel, I should say."

"Is he possessed?" Aitan asked. "Does the Enemy have him?"

"That or he's insane. Or both."

Aitan looked to his companion. "Tom, I need a few moments alone with Lord Skalligrin. Would you see if Mr. Hughes needs anything? Get it for him, if you can."

"Sure," said Tom. "That's not a problem."

Aitan led Grin away from Tom and the artist. When they were out of earshot of the others, Aitan asked, "The woods around here. Is that your doing?"

"Mine or his. Both. Maybe neither."

"Well, you're certainly as enlightening as ever," Aitan said.

Grin laughed. "I chased the Enemy here. We fought. He entered the holy city."

"You let him enter the City of Heaven?"

"I would have gone in after him, but he worked some kind of magic on me, keeping me out. I had to wait until it wore off before I could make the crossing."

"And now?"

"I'm ready to try again." Grin shook his head. "I suppose if you're someone like him, the best place to hide is in a city of your own kind. Especially when you can look like anyone."

"He can change his form?" Aitan asked.

Grin shuddered. "He can become things the likes of which even I have never seen. I *think* they're just illusions."

Then how do I know it's you, and not him *in disguise,* Aitan thought. "That would make sense. One of his agents could do the same."

Without warning, Aitan sprang forward and hugged the former Emissary. He pulled away, satisfied.

"What was *that* for?" Grin spat.

"An illusion will fool the eyes," said Aitan. "I had to know that it was really you. If what I touched had not been short, round, and heavily armored, I would have known that I was in trouble."

Grin shrugged. "That's a good plan. When we go inside, we'll tell everyone to hug. That way, we'll be able to find the Enemy in no time!"

Aitan stood before the former Emissary with a stony expression. When he could stand it no longer, he smiled. "It might work, actually."

"Fah!" said Grin. "Now, from what I could see, he has a very difficult time maintaining a mortal shell. He prefers to be one with the shadows."

"We live in cities of light," said Aitan. "He should have very few hiding places."

"Everything has shadows, even the cities where God can be felt most strongly. Without shadows, there is no form."

"All right," Aitan said. "What did he tell you?"

"He talked madness."

"Tell me."

Grin recited the catalog of apparent lies the Enemy's soldiers had leveled at Aitan and Tom the previous night.

"I've heard all this," said Aitan.

"There's one more. It's the best of all. It concerns the Vessels. According to Komm Kyriel, there is no God."

"Blasphemy."

"I'm just repeating what he said. It's what you asked."

"No, I mean—"

"It's heretical, I agree. I'm amazed we're able to speak such words without bursting into flame, quite honestly. Do you want to hear the rest?"

"Yes."

"He says that we come from a world of mad gods. Nine of our kind who found the means to transform ourselves into creatures without limits. They are the Nine Vessels."

"I see," said Aitan. "And if this were so, why would there be only nine? Why wouldn't each and every one of us be attempting to cheat mortality and become like the Vessels?"

"Because the Vessels don't want any more like them. They prevent others who try to follow their path. They subvert the knowledge necessary for the journey."

"I don't believe any of this," said Aitan. The angel was shaken. "Where does he get these lies? Fever dreams? His imagination?"

"He claims it was all spelled out in a book he found. The Mysts Arcana."

Aitan thought of the falling tower when he was a child, and the daring rescue Komm Kyriel performed to save the young angel's life.

The book had not been buried, Aitan realized. Komm Kyriel had it the entire time. Or he went back for it.

Merciful Christ, Aitan thought. If through its lies that book contained a means for allowing the Enemy to come into one's body, then it easily could have been *Aitan,* not Komm Kyriel, who had become a slave to the Enemy.

Grin spoke up. "I left you and Tom to go after that walking shadow because I had been granted a vision of the three of us reunited in this place. I knew you and Tom would be safe at least this long. And considering some of the things Komm Kyriel said about you, I thought it my place in the Grand Plan to chase that devil and keep him away from you.''

Aitan briefly recounted his encounters with the soldiers of the Enemy and the ''deal'' into which Travest Mulvihill attempted to force him.

''Then I was a fool,'' said Grin darkly. ''He was leading me away so that you would be put in a position where you might have been brought down to his level.''

''I survived,'' said Aitan.

''At what cost? Did you harvest the souls of the beings who attacked you and the boy?''

''No,'' said Aitan.

''Let's hope you didn't.'' The former Emissary turned and was about to walk over to the angels who stayed behind to safeguard Tom. The Angels of Tears and Trembling could not seem to avert their gazes from Grin and it clearly annoyed him.

''Lord Skalligrin—a question,'' said Aitan.

Grin stopped.

''Did his words test your beliefs?'' Aitan asked.

Grin shook his head. ''Until I met him, my faith was wavering. Now I know there is such a thing as the Enemy. Whether it is he, or he is just a servant of its darkness, I don't know. But I now believe in the Word and the Ways as I never have before.''

The former Emissary spun and called out to the pair of angels who had been staring at him. He went to them, bellowing, ''What city is this?''

The angels exchanged worried glances.

Aitan rushed forward. ''We don't need to ask that—''

Grin raised a single, gauntleted hand to stop the angel. ''I don't care if you're worried about looking stupid. I'm standing before one of our cities and I have no idea which one.'' The warrior pointed toward the wall of mists. ''Would one of you fools kindly stop gaping at me and tell me the name of this place?''

The Angel of Tears cleared his throat. ''This is Abaddon, one of our most cherished cities. So named for the Destroyer Angel who binds the Enemy for the Millennium and will return to scour the earth in the Apocalypse. Once neighbor to the city Araboth, home of the First Angels of Love, Fear, Grace, and Dread.''

"Abaddon, huh? That figures."

"What's wrong?" Aitan asked.

"Abaddon is where I'm fated to die. That's why I've always avoided it in the past. Ah, well." Grin looked up at the sky and shrugged. "Better get on with things!"

With that, he turned and stalked toward the wall of mists. Aitan gave hurried instructions to Tom's guardians and stole one last look at the boy. His squire sat beside Hughes, who was busy eating an apple Tom had found for him.

"I'll be back for you as soon as I can!" Aitan called.

"I'll be here!" responded the lad.

Aitan looked over at the angels. "That had best turn out to be true, or else the Vessel may be extremely displeased."

"We've made our Vow," the charcoal-skinned angel said. "What do you want? Our blood?"

"No," Aitan said as he waved to Tom one last time. "Just be careful. Treat the man I told you about with respect if he arrives. He must not suspect anything."

The Angel of Trembling yawned.

Praying that he was doing the right thing, Aitan turned and ventured into the mists.

The plague-carrier saw it all.

He watched the angels vanish into the borders of the city. He was so close. The fools had no concept of the many gifts his liege had granted so that he could carry out his blessed duties. Distances meant nothing to him. The Powers of the Elven, who masqueraded as angels, meant nothing to him.

Rogziel waited.

The time of judgment would be at hand.

Soon.

Twenty

AITAN ANZELM WAS HOME. TRUE, THIS WAS NOT THE city of his birth, but it would do. Stepping out of the mists, he experienced a few moments of disorientation stemming from his sojourn in the purely physical realm of the humans, but now he could fully register the splendor of Abaddon. Aitan and Grin stood before a small bridge stretching over the Lake of Memory. He looked into the waters and saw nothing but a reflection of the city's celestial spires and narrow, twisting walkways. In a few hours, he would be able to come back here and see a reflection of all he had experienced since arriving in the city. If he chose, he could then leap from the bridge and swim through those memories, examining them from new vantages for enlightenment on how he was perceived by others and how his behavior might be altered so that he was acting more in accordance with the Ways of the Lord.

Beyond the bridge lay pathways that might take them to the city's farthest reaches in a few seconds, or only a few feet in a matter of hours, depending on the measure of urgency one held in his or her heart. Some angels flew from one destination to another. Others walked up the sides of buildings, while others passed through solid walls without hesitation. Aitan saw a cathedral shaped like a sparkling crystal candelabra and realized how long it had been since he had sung praises to God. Above, a great stone building floated in the air. It looked like a butterfly with orange-and-black wings. Aitan had spent entire days in apocryphas like that one, sitting on the gently flapping wings while reading an obscure text or engaging in a friendly debate with other angels. Ahead, a porcelain tree whose roots could have filled an ancient coliseum wavered slightly in the breeze from on high. Its branches reached out and wrapped around hundreds of buildings. Within its hollow core, beings endowed with the souls of the greatest composers of the ages, human and angel alike, created new works. If one was pleased by the sounds, they would fill the heart with uplifting, almost mad glee. Aitan was not of a mind to hear these many concertos and symphonies, and so he politely declined the music. It retreated to a trembling he felt under his feet.

Grin said, "If you're done basking, I'd suggest we seek out an Emissary."

"Yes," said Aitan, pleasantly overwhelmed.

They crossed the bridge and set themselves on one of the blinding paths through the cities. A dizzying array of sights, sounds, and ideas flashed past them and suddenly they found themselves in an onyx courtyard patrolled by several three-headed dogs made of jade. The dogs could not make any sound as they were little more than statues come to life, but they bared sparkling diamond teeth and ruby nails that left grooves in the floor as they stalked forward. Surrounding the courtyard was an array of greyish black storm clouds riddled with flashes of lightning. Suddenly, a fount of sparkling water descended toward the center of the courtyard and stopped, transforming into a beautiful ice sculpture. The ceiling was also made of ice.

A flurry of snow burst upon the room, covering the jade statues of the three-headed dogs and freezing them in their tracks. Three silver balls materialized before the angels.

"I wanted something different today," said a voice driven by the icy winds. "I needed a change."

The silver balls transformed into prisms, then tympani that rang with deafening crashes.

"Must I command you to take your true form?" cried Grin.

The odd shapes vanished. In their place appeared a young, silver-haired angel wearing a black silk robe. He had grey eyes and a sullen expression.

"I don't get many visitors," said the young angel. "My name is Shakziel."

"With dominion over snow and ice, I presume," said Grin.

"That would be it, yes."

The warrior looked to his companion. "I envisioned an audience with the Emissary or his attendants."

"So did I."

"The Emissary?" cried Shakziel. "Oh, no. That won't happen. Not just yet."

"Why not?" asked Aitan.

The Angel of Snow seemed perplexed. Dazed. "I don't know. I'm not told many specifics. I don't get many visitors. . . ."

Frustrated, Aitan and Grin willed themselves back onto the path. The chamber of the snow angel vanished and the jarring motion along with a new array of wonders flashed before the angels. Most went by too quickly to be assimilated, but Aitan was certain he saw a chamber filled with writhing crimson snakes and giggling angels, and another in which a burning tower was engulfed by darkness and the howling of many-eyed children.

Finally, they were deposited in the center of a solemn meeting. Four groups of children sat in a luscious garden with several fountains spewing wine. Rainbow-colored fish with heads on both ends floated in the fountains. The children ate them raw. Each of the four camps of children was made of exactly five members. Above one group was a banner bearing a red cross. Each of these children wore crowns of rose flowers and wore white. The next group wore red satin. Their heads were adorned by crowns of red gillyflowers. Both of these groups consisted entirely of boys. The next quintet was all girls, dressed in green or silver. Their crowns were bay leaves, and a pleasant perfume radiated from them. The last batch was comprised of older boys who were still very small. They wore black robes mixed with green and passed a trembling white bird among them. It took Aitan a moment to notice that each of the children sat a few inches above the ground. They had been staring at each other. Now their gazes were fixed firmly on the intruders.

"This is a sign," said one of the children in black triumphantly. "I am destined to be September's child."

"Are not!" cried another of the white-robed children.

"Am, too!"

A girl stood up and said, "All you stupidheads do is bicker.

We're here to negotiate Change. If you have something to offer, get to it!''

"Excuse me," Aitan began.

"Let him decide!" cried one of the black-robed older boys as he pointed at the angel.

"We're looking for the Emissary," said Grin.

"How come he gets special treatment?" asked a boy in red satin.

"No one's getting anything," the girl said pointedly, "unless the Covenant, the Sigils, and the Paradox are aligned."

Another of the children rose up. "I'm tired of being the Sixth hour of the Sixth day of the Sixth month! Do you know what that makes me sound like? Do you know the kind of Summonings I receive? The Reverence? It's horrible!"

Grin buried his hands in his face. "The Altitudes. They're swapping appointed hours."

The Angels of the Altitudes could only be invoked by mortals who knew their proper hours of the day and the month. They were also called the Chora.

"If you decide that I should be an Angel of September, I'll take you to a consecrated hall!" said one of the boys.

"March!"

"December!"

The girl cried, "I have followers who have pledged Devotion all their days to me. Give me an offer that makes sense or quit this whole stupid thing!"

"Elomina's being mean again!"

"Do you think this is Komm Kyriel's doing?" asked Aitan. The former Emissary sighed. "An eatery?"

"That should be safe enough."

They willed themselves to be gone. Again, there was a fantastic rush of images and suddenly they found themselves in a lavishly decorated feast hall. Dozens of angels sat at long marble tables surrounded by ten-course meals.

"That's better," said Grin.

Aitan and the warrior found a vacant table. It was long and black, with crossed silver blades melted into its surface. Neither had a true appetite. If they had, whatever food they desired would have appeared upon the table.

"I've spoken with many humans regarding their views of

Heaven,'' said Grin. "So many times it comes down to food. 'It would be heaven if I could eat all the sweets I like and not become fat.' 'My idea of heaven is lying with my lover, feeding him all his desires.' Fah. *I'd* say that my idea of heaven is to be on the Wild Hunt, to slay and eat my prey raw, except that if I so desired it, my wish would be granted. Humans had no idea all they gained when they were booted out of paradise."

"You envy their misery, heartbreak, and hunger?" asked Aitan.

"I don't know," said Grin. "How can anything be special if everything is within your grasp?"

The former Emissary noticed that many other angels were staring. This time he chose one at random, pointed, and motioned for the angel to come over and join them. The angel, whose mortal form was blurred by a pulsing light that arose from deep within him, had hair down to his feet and wore a white robe.

Grin said, "The way to the Seven Celestial Halls is not open to us. Is Abaddon in some way tainted? Is this the only of God's Holy Cities without the proper spells of Opening, without the Seals and the Sigils and the Righteous Ardor to bridge the Way?"

"No!" cried the angel. "Of course not!"

"Why then should this be so?"

The angel quivered. "The Event. The Unveiling."

"What Unveiling?" Grin asked angrily.

"No one may speak of it," the angel said. "To speak of it is against Holy Law. So it is Writ. But if you wait, and not long, the Summons will be upon us and all your questions will be answered."

"Do you know who I am?" Grin bellowed.

The angel lowered his head. "I know who you were."

Grin settled back and dismissed the angel. He said, "The Wardens and the Warders. They must be behind this. There must have been criticism."

Before Aitan could reply, someone came up behind him and laid a pale hand on his shoulder.

"Patience is a virtue," said a decidedly feminine voice.

Aitan turned and saw a female angel standing before him.

She was beautiful beyond compare, her features constantly changing behind the gossamer veils that hid her lean, dark form. Her flesh was a dark blue, almost black. Eyes riddled her body, dozens up and down her arms and legs. The eyes appeared and vanished as they opened and closed. Her hair spread out before her, twisting into odd, grasping shapes, strands reaching over impossible distances to steal food from the tables of other angels lost in her sensual, rapturous appeal. A piece of fruit was delivered by her lush hair. She took a bite. Her teeth were sharp.

Aitan had to fight with his body not to respond to her. Beside him, Grin said, "Turn from her."

"But—"

"Do it!"

Closing his eyes, Aitan turned away. His heart raced. The females very rarely came down from their Aerie. Only when they had been commanded by God to go forth and beget children were they supposed to appear. This woman's presence signified that an angel somewhere in this city was to be rewarded with an heir.

At times, the females appeared to the men privately at night, taking into themselves the Lust of the men, a powerful source of their sustaining magic. This was supposed to be a sin, a forbidden act, but it happened all the time and the males simply didn't talk about it, except with their closest confidants. The males understood that they were the inferior beings. Children were always left in the East Midian, with one of the pious Gatekeepers beyond mortal lusts.

Aitan felt movement as he was spirited from the eatery and into a white marble room where shimmering waterfalls of sparkling divine energies bathed the walls. An angel dressed entirely in butterflies' wings sat behind an ornate desk. Several tomes and scrolls were spread out before him. The angel's chubby face was bathed in the light from the waterfalls, an ever-changing mix of soft blues, greens, and golds. He was a Cherubim, a keeper of records. In the hierarchy of the heavenly Host, his line was second only to the Seraphim before the Vessels.

"We Petition thee," Grin said to the angel.

The Cherubim grunted. "Who doesn't?"

Aitan said, "Our Wishes are not being granted. We think of where we wish to go and we are instead hurled about to random locales throughout the city. Why should this be so?"

Finally looking up, the Cherubim said, "Where were you trying to go? Who did you want to see?"

"Any of the Emissaries. Preferably the Emissary to the Second. The way to the Celestial Halls—"

"I know." The Cherubim sighed. He opened a huge tome on his desk. "Here's what I can do for you. There were to be no more appointments scheduled, but I received word of a cancellation on the 311th day from today. Would that suit you?"

"A plague of darkness grows in this city, an agent of the Enemy is here to work dark magics!" cried Aitan. He really had no idea why Komm Kyriel had come to the City of Heaven, but this was as good a guess as any. He also thought it sounded impressive.

"Let's not resort to hysterics or fantasies, it won't do you any good," said the Cherubim. "And don't blaspheme. It's so childish."

"To speak the name of the Enemy is not blasphemy when there is cause," said Grin. "We do not have to see the Emissary to the Second. Any Emissary will do."

"So I had assumed." The Cherubim gestured. "I no longer find your theatrics amusing. Your audience is hereby denied. You two are dismissed."

Their surroundings shifted again. Aitan and Grin found themselves back at the feast hall. The female angel was gone.

"Madness and death!" Grin cursed.

"Agreed."

Grin went to the quivering angel he had bullied earlier. "The Angel of Blood resides in this city, yes?"

"He does."

"Is he still a sword bearer?"

"Of course."

Grin touched Aitan's arm and pictured not a place, but a person. In seconds they were taken by the energies of the city to a dark, bleak tower that was comfortingly devoid of furnishings and strange magics.

The Angel of Blood sat on the floor, his sword resting on

his knees. The fire that had consumed him had nearly burned away, revealing a frighteningly handsome angel with dark soulful eyes. He wore leathers cut away to reveal his muscular arms and legs. His long hair was black except for a single red streak that matched the sash he wore around his waist. Beyond him was a descending circular staircase. If he had looked more attentive, he might have been taken for a guard, keeping the curious from venturing lower in the tower. Instead, he appeared apathetic.

Grin whispered, "Hello, Malkiyyah."

"I should have known you'd come," said the angel. "What business do you have with me?"

Aitan spoke out, "An agent of the Enemy has entered the city. Komm Kyriel."

Malkiyyah appeared unmoved. "Impossible."

"We have to find him," said Aitan. "I don't know what he's planning, but it can't be a coincidence that he's here right at the time of the Event, whatever it is—"

"You don't know?"

"No."

The Angel of Blood shrugged. "Can't help you."

Grin stormed forward. He kicked the sword from Malkiyyah's knees. It went crashing down the stairs. With a hiss, the former Emissary grabbed the front of Malkiyyah's tunic and hauled the angel into the air. "The greatest evil our world has ever known stalks this city and you can't help us?"

Malkiyyah's eyes burst into flame. "I was relieved of duty. Unhand me or I will change the blood in your body to ice."

"You would be damned for such an act."

"I think I already am."

Grin released the angel, who landed on his feet and reached out in the direction of his fallen sword. There was an explosion of light and the sword flew into Malkiyyah's hand.

Aitan was about to draw his sword when a sound like broken glass echoed through the tower. The angels felt a pain, a horrible tearing, and their surroundings changed as they were ripped from the tower and deposited in a vast public square. Thousands of angels surrounded them. The entire Hierarchy was present: Closest to the center of the gathering was the Seraphim, the Angels of Love, Light, and Fire. They were the most Holy of Holies. The Cherubim, the Keepers of Celestial Records and Bestowers of Knowledge surrounded them. Then came the Thrones, the Avatars of Justice. The Dominions, carrying their Scepters of Power, made up the next circle of spectators. The Virtues, the Bestowers of Grace upon Earth, those who worked miracles for the betterment of man, stood behind the Dominions. The Powers and the Principalities, sworn to fight the Influence of the Enemy, were next, followed by the Archangels. Finally, at the outer rings of the gathering, were the angels without high rank and purpose. Aitan, Grin, and Malkiyyah were among them. Aitan and Grin looked around.

"He could be any of them," said Aitan.

Grin closed his eyes and willed himself into the presence of Komm Kyriel. Nothing happened.

Malkiyyah was still beside them, the fires of his sword extinguished. The weapon had a cold blue aura. "I was one of those who spoke against this. I felt it my duty. So much of this is my fault, a result of my pride and arrogance."

"What are you talking about?" Aitan growled.

The Angel of Blood gestured toward a white marble stage that floated several feet above the ground. Suddenly, the sky darkened and the heavens were torn asunder. A voice that was millions of voices all at once cried, "Behold!"

"I recognize that voice," said Grin. "The Fourth Vessel. My lord, the Sixth, met often with Him."

Aitan found that he could not look away from the stage. A brilliant light appeared and a figure was traced in air. At first, the figure had the vague form of an angel. Then something formed behind it. Lightning struck the figure from every direction and suddenly it stood revealed.

Grin shuddered, and around him, the crowd gasped as one. The figure standing before them was not one of them. His skin was the healthy rich bronze of human flesh. He wore armor of silver and gold. Around him was a flowing crimson cloak.

"A man," someone cried hoarsely, "it wasn't heresy, it was true, the Vessel's chosen a *man.*"

Behind the man was the greatest travesty of all. Rising up majestically from his well-developed back was a pair of wings.

"His name is Lileo," said the Vessel. "Treat Him as you would treat Me. He is my Emissary and His word is Law. . . ."

Twenty-One

OUTSIDE THE CITY OF HEAVEN, TOM KEEPER SAT IN THE presence of a man he had worshiped as the greatest living artist in the world. He thought he would feel awe. Instead, all he felt was pity for the man.

The angels who had been left to guard Tom paced back and forth outside the city. They were upset about something. As a result, Tom felt fear, and he couldn't stop crying. He knew why he was reacting this way, but his companion was apparently not so well versed in the Powers and the Ways of God's soldiers. Hughes asked if there was anything that could brighten the lad's spirits.

"I'm fine," Tom said. He nodded toward the angels. "That's a sight, don't you think? A pair of angels circling like expectant fathers."

Hughes said, "It's not proper to ridicule the chosen of the Lord."

"No, I suppose not. I didn't want to sound mean or anything. It's just that I've been with Aitan for a while, and even though I've seen him make miracles, the longer I know him, the more I start to think of him as being just like us. All the angels really aren't that far removed from us."

"Don't blaspheme, boy. You might be overheard."

"I'm not talking blasphemy. They really don't mind. They don't want us to be afraid of them. We need to respect their power, and know that they have our best interests at heart, but not fear them."

"Interesting," said Hughes. "You have a very different way of looking at things."

"I just wish we still had some of the things we left behind when we were being chased. Aitan got me all this paper. Good, clean paper to draw on."

"You're an artist?"

"I try. It's what I want to be."

"You either are, or you aren't. You might be good or bad, talented or talentless, but you can't be wistful about it. Now, are you an artist?"

"Yes."

Roger Hughes went to the edge of the forest. He retrieved a large bag. In it was a board with a fresh sheet of paper tacked to it. He handed Tom a drawing stick, graphite mixed with only a little clay encased between two pieces of cedar wood.

"Sketch something for me," said Hughes.

Suddenly, Tom's fear escalated into terror. He saw a flicker of the man he had journeyed so far to meet and the very idea that his work would be judged in such a light, that this man could destroy his hopes and ambitions with nothing more than a cruel word and a disappointed glance—

No, Tom thought. *I'm not going to do this to myself. Hughes is entitled to his opinion. I know this is what I want to do with my life. If he can help, fine. But he can't have this kind of power over me. Aitan taught me better than that.*

Tom set the board on his lap and began to draw. He created a whimsical sketch of the two angels, one holding a human infant wrapped in blankets, the other looking on adoringly with his hands clasped together in delight. His nose started to itch and Tom felt a sudden heat on his upper lip.

"Not this again," Tom said, straightening up a moment too late. A drop of blood suddenly fell from his nose and landed on the drawing. "I don't believe this."

"Tom?" asked Hughes.

"The Angel of Blood," Tom said as he snatched up some grass and wiped his nose with it. "He must be at it again."

The artist cocked his head slightly to one side, like a wolf. "I don't understand."

Tom looked at the artist. It suddenly occurred to him that Roger Hughes had not bled at all. Even now, he was not bleeding. The power of the angels was complete, according to Aitan. Anyone human within miles of the city would be affected.

Hughes did not bleed. He had not shown the least bit of fear when the Angel of Trembling became careless with his power. Nor had he wept for the Angel of Tears.

No one human.

Panic seized Tom. He hurled the drawing and the wooden board at the artist, who leaped for Tom. The board struck Hughes in the face, slowing him. Tom scrambled to his feet and ran toward the angels as if he were being chased by the Enemy. He screamed for the angels to help him. They turned and looked his way, then glanced around to see what had frightened the boy.

Sensing their confusion, Tom cried, "It's not him. It's not Hughes!"

The angels drew their swords as Tom ran behind them. They angled their weapons toward the approaching artist.

"The boy's gone mad," Hughes said. "Look at him. He's got some kind of fever. He's bleeding."

"Try to use your Power on him," Tom said. "It won't work. He's been changed."

The angels turned on the boy. The charcoal-skinned Angel of Trembling snarled, "Don't presume to order us!"

In that moment, Roger Hughes leaped forward, his bare hands outstretched. He placed his hands over the faces of the angels; each of whom stiffened and writhed beneath his touch.

"This isn't mercy," Hughes said, "so don't get confused. It's expediency."

The angels fell to their knees. Tom saw their flesh turn crimson, saw them sweat and shiver as blood poured from their skin. They screamed, then fell forward and lay still.

"I thought you were Travest," Tom said, backing toward the wall of mist behind him. The artist advanced on the boy, his hands glowing like hot coals.

"No."

"Thought you were him in disguise."

Hughes laughed. "I'm Roger Hughes, one of the great artists of the day. You've heard of me, now haven't you?"

Tom felt a sudden dizziness overtake him as the cool mists swirled around him. He knew that he could not enter the City of Heaven, but he hoped that he would be safe in the mists, that a follower of the Enemy would be burned by their touch.

Hughes walked toward him, unaffected. "Now I'm an artist of a different kind. I even have a new name. I'm Rogziel, one of the new Seven Angels of Punishment."

"Who—who are you punishing?" Tom asked, backing deeper into the mists, which were making it hard for him to think clearly.

"Man. For his ignorance. And the Elven, for their deceptions."

Tom thought of the still bodies of the angels. "You're the plague-carrier."

"Oh, yes." Hughes smiled. "I was watching you at the carnival. I saw how you rescued your little friend. That's why I went to him while you and the girl were rutting. He was only the first. I specialize in *wholesale* destruction, you see."

No, Tom thought. *All those people. Kayrlis—*

Tom took another step back and stumbled. Hughes flung himself forward and took Tom's hand, steadying him. Tom felt a terrible heat rise up in every part of his body.

"How long it takes is up to me," said the death-dealer. "It can be over in seconds, as it was with the Elven I destroyed. Or I can make it drag on for months. Years even, or so I understand. Even a lifetime."

Tom wrenched his hand from Rogziel's grasp.

"Now," the plague-carrier said, "now, you're mine. And if your precious friend wishes to see you live, he will offer himself to me."

"Why?" asked Tom. "Why did you give in to the Enemy?"

Rogziel shrugged. "I didn't want to die. This was my alternative. Until I passed through those woods, so much of my past has been hazy to me. Then I remembered all I had, and all I lost. The Enemy can make Rachiel live once more. He can save her from the Withering and make her love me. He's said as much and I believe him. So you understand, I want to please Him. And I want to see the lies dispelled."

Tom thought of the pain that would come from the disease, the horrible delirium. "You didn't have to do this."

"I think I did. You saw the flame guardian, too."

"Did he make you into this?" Tom asked. "Is he Komm Kyriel?"

The plague-carrier pursed his lips in confusion. "I suppose that not all of it has come back to me. I really don't know. I just remember seeing him in my dreams, and I recall his offer of power. Now I have power. Draw whatever conclusions you wish."

Tom felt the fires spreading through him. "How long?"

"A day before you can no longer make your wishes known to others. Less than an hour before the true suffering begins. But it's all right. You're not going to die."

"I'm not," Tom said.

"No, I've reasoned it out. I know why you've seen the flame guardian. It's all so clear to me now. Every evil must have its opposite number. My liege has Aitan Anzelm. I have you. We share a grand destiny."

Tom stared at the madman in horror.

"Don't you understand?" Rogziel wailed. "You are fated to bring salvation to the people, to bring an end to the Scourge when my time is done. You are to bring an end to me."

"There's no cure for the Scourge."

"There will be. I've seen it in my dreams. Someone who can cure with a touch, who can heal the same way I can kill."

Tom shuddered. The former artist's imagination was still at work, creating these wicked fantasies, these twisted fevered dreams. There had to be a way to turn the man's wild imaginings against him. He knew the plague-carrier's ravings had no basis in fact. He had tried to cure Cameron with the waters of Lethe, the River of Healing in Heaven, and it made no difference.

"You will survive and you will bring about an end to all I have done," said Rogziel. "Now come. We must enter the City of Heaven."

"What?" cried Tom. "We can't."

Rogziel looked at the mists. "Not this way, no. But my liege granted me many powers." He gestured and it was as if a tear had been created in the fabric of reality. Tom saw a gateway to a brilliant land, a shining city so bright he could not look at it without hurting his eyes. The plague-carrier grasped his arm, then stiffened and threw his head back as another light ripped forward from his chest. He sank to his knees and fell back, smoke rising from a charred black wound in his chest. Tom couldn't believe it. Rogziel was dead! The plague-carrier had been destroyed!

A voice behind Tom said, ''I don't know how long it'll stay open without him. Go!''

Tom hesitated, then he felt hands upon him, shoving him forward, into the portal of light. He fell through the gateway and suddenly felt as if his world were being torn apart.

Tom burst through the portal on the other side. Within the City of Heaven he fell face first onto what looked like stone, only it whispered, undulated, and buzzed. Frightened, he tried to rise. Another figure stepped through the portal beside him. Tom looked at the man next to him and thought he was going mad. It was Travest Mulvihill and yet—it wasn't. The man's shape was distorted, stretched to impossible lengths one second, squashed flat the next, his features at once human and bestial. Averting his gaze, Tom found that nothing was as it should have been. His senses were askew. Incredible, bizarre sounds assailed him except when he closed his eyes. He opened them again and the noises returned. When he looked at Travest, he heard a large bird crying out. Turning his gaze to the bridge ahead, he heard metal screeching against metal. The sky elicited a horrible roar. The buildings in the distance brought forth eerie laughter when he glanced at them.

''What's wrong with you?'' Travest asked. His senses functioned normally. ''Yes, it's very strange, but what would you expect of a city from another reality?''

''Stop, stop, stop,'' Tom moaned. Even with his eyes shut, the madness could not be blocked out. Not only could he hear sights, now he could *see sounds.* Every tone summoned a bizarre vision that struck him whether his eyes were open or not. Lines, spheres, and triangles of every color, size, and intensity burned themselves into his brain with each sound. He was forced to cease his own moaning, as that brought fresh agonies.

A new torture began. He began to feel odd textures as if objects were brushing up against him. But nothing was near him. He felt scalding water assailing his skin, a rush of air that made it nearly impossible for him to breathe, a crushing pressure as if he was being squashed between huge boulders, his mind and body splintering.

This is what happens to our kind in the holy cities, Tom thought. *This is why we aren't allowed to come here. We can't survive. Only the dead can exist here. The angels and the human dead!*

He felt the feverish rush of the Scourge upon him. The pain was coming early. He screamed, then stopped as a thousand fiery daggers raced at his eyes, brought forth by the sound.

Travest looked down at the boy in contempt. He couldn't understand what was wrong with Tom. The boy would be useless now, even as a hostage. He would slow Travest down and call far too much attention to him. An angel traveling with a squire seemed an appropriate disguise. He thought of the angels the plague-carrier had killed and decided to assume the visage of one with charred black skin.

Travest's power, which he had been laboring to master on his journey back to the City of Heaven, was stronger here than on the mortal plane. That made sense. This was a city of light, and he had dominion over light.

He bent the light to form a shell around him that he was confident would fool his hated enemies. No one had seen him the entire time he stood in plain view of Tom, the plague-carrier, and the Elven. Then he had merely wrapped light around himself to keep himself from being seen. This illusion would be even more impenetrable, he was certain. The only problem was that he knew nothing about the being he was impersonating.

"Tell me what you know of this one!" Travest commanded.

Tom's hands were over his eyes.

"Look at me!" Travest commanded. When Tom did not respond, he reached down and pulled the boy's hands from his face.

"Pah-pah—"

"Come on!" cried Travest.

"Pahadron," Tom managed to get out, "ah—ah—Angel of Terror and Trembling."

"So I make people tremble with fear, do I?"

"Pahadron does. Mortals. Just mortals."

"I suppose it's good I didn't leave you behind," Travest said angrily. "You've served some purpose after all."

In the guise of an angel, Travest left Tom behind and

crossed the bridge, entering the full domain of the holy city. From what he had observed in the mortal lands, the Elven were not particularly friendly toward one another. That would serve him well. His fearsome disguise would make the thought of approaching him even more unappealing.

There were no angels in sight. He searched a dozen oddly shaped buildings and found no signs that anyone occupied this bizarre place. Not that he wanted to encounter other angels. All he desired was the speedy return of his son.

As he left a building that looked like a long length of pipe twisted upon itself a dozen times or more, creating a strange labyrinth within, something nagged at him. He thought about the way Tom had collapsed. Would most humans who entered what the Elven called the True Lands react so violently? Travest had been transformed by the magics of his liege. Perhaps he had been made immune to the more disruptive effects of the city upon the frail mind of a mortal.

Had Lileo reacted that way when he had been brought here?

Suddenly, there was a shimmering in the air before him and a group of angels appeared. They brushed past him without a greeting, which relieved Travest. He looked down the narrow lane upon which he had been walking and saw the angels appearing in several other places.

No, not angels, he had to remind himself. Elven. Creatures from a dying world.

His first hope had been that he could find his son without actually engaging any of the city's residents. The best course of action was to get an understanding of the city, listen to the people, and see if anyone mentioned his son.

He couldn't bear to be that patient, that methodical. Not when he was so close, and not after he had given up so much of himself to reach this place.

Turning, he saw an angel sitting alone upon one of the winding porcelain branches that seemed to make their way through all parts of the city, delivering bright, inspirational music. The angel was staring at the ground, shaking his head. He was burly, with square features and a shock of crimson hair that fell to his dark armors.

Steeling himself, Travest approached the angel. In a booming voice he said, "I am Pahadron, Angel of Terror and Trembling."

"How nice for you," the angel muttered.

"Excuse me?"

"God is good. God's love be with you in all things," the angel said defeatedly. "The righteous are the blessed, the wicked the accursed."

"There is no end to it, is there?" Travest asked, attempting to be conversational. "Punishing the wicked."

"No end in sight." The angel looked up. "Just arrived?"

"You could tell?"

"Your spirit seems high. That means you must not have been present for the Fiasco."

"Tell me," said Travest.

The angel gestured at the space next to him on the massive branch. "I'd rather not shout."

Travest turned and was about to sit down when he suddenly caught a blur of motion, heard a terrible crackling, and felt a sharp pain in his head. He had been struck!

"Ahhhh," Travest moaned, his concentration broken, the illusion cloaking him fading. He fell to the ground on his stomach and felt someone drop onto his back. Before he could summon his power, his hair was grabbed and his head was slammed into the street. There was a searing pain—then nothing.

Sitting on Travest's back, N'mosnikttiel, the Angel of Rage, jammed his victim's head into the stone walkway one last time, though he could sense that the human was already unconscious. Yanking Travest's head back with only a touch of restraint, the angel put his lips near Travest's ear and said, "There are more senses than just sight, you stupid little fool. Did you think you *sounded* like one of us? That you *smelled* or *walked* like one of us?"

A host of angels came running. They were startled to see the unconscious human. N'mosnikttiel told them what happened.

"In all my days, I've never put my hands on a true agent of the Enemy," said the Angel of Rage, "but I think this one qualifies."

"What should we do with him?" asked another angel.

"I don't know," said N'mosnikttiel with a laugh. "I'm sure we can think of something. . . ."

Twenty-Two

$\mathbf{A}$ITAN, GRIN, AND MALKIYYAH WATCHED WITH GROW-ing horror as the upper ranks of the Hierarchy crowded upon Lileo to welcome him as one of them.

"Travest's son," Aitan said softly.

"The tailor. I remember him," said Malkiyyah. "I threatened him with damnation. I think if he saw what had become of his boy, he would feel that sentence preferable to living with the knowledge that his son had been made into this abomination."

Grin said, "The Emissary's going to be sent into the world, isn't he? To be seen by all mankind. The first true link between their kind and ours."

The Angel of Blood said, "So one would assume from the talk recently."

Suddenly, an angel broke from the crowd and threw his arms open in greeting. "Anzelm! I suspected an event like this would draw you."

Aitan looked at the angel, trying to remember him. The angel had ashen skin, steel grey hair, and aquiline features. He wore armors similar to Aitan's. A soft green cloak had been thrown over his shoulders. The angel stopped suddenly, sighed, and said, "This always happens to me."

"Purah," Aitan said finally, "the Angel of Forgetfulness. I'm sorry, at first—"

The angel smiled. "I know. I have one of those rare Powers that can affect other angels."

Grin said, "You are known as the Lord of Oblivion."

"My father's title. It will be willed to me when he passes

into the Final Kingdom and his blessed bones lie in the Crypt.''

The sword bearer said, ''You have something to do with the Sabbath, or so the humans claim.''

Grin looked down at the slender new angel. ''I've heard it said that you are the angel who dissipates God's light.''

Aitan wondered why Grin was being rude to the new arrival. Then it occurred to him that this was not necessarily the Angel of Forgetfulness standing before him. It could easily be Komm Kyriel. Malkiyyah, even Grin, could be someone other than who they appeared, despite the test Aitan had given the former Emissary.

Purah smiled. ''Really, Aitan. If I didn't see you soon, I was going to have you Invoked.''

''Why don't we go somewhere more private?'' asked Aitan. ''We could talk.''

''My house is vacant,'' said Purah. ''Father will be here for hours. Bring your friends.''

This could be a trap, Aitan reasoned, but he had Grin and Malkiyyah with him. ''Go ahead, we'll catch up.''

''As you will.'' Purah gestured and quickly vanished.

Aitan turned to the sword bearer. ''You'd like a battle, wouldn't you?''

''All of my kind relish the chance to fight for the righteousness of the Lord. But I have been chastised. I was the one who brought the boy to Abaddon. I had been sent to find a child by the Fourth Emissary. I didn't question. Not then.''

''What did you *think* He wanted a human child for?'' asked Grin.

''I believed the time had come for the Innocent to be sacrificed,'' Malkiyyah growled. ''The Lamb to be taken. You understand. You were an Emissary once. The Vessels are prophets. Those who are fated to commit evil acts are often harvested when they are young, still closest to God. If I thought anything at all, it was that this child did not bear the face of evil, but then again, who was I to judge? I had a mission and so I fulfilled it.''

''What swayed you?''

Malkiyyah looked around. Though they were on the outskirts of the crowd, it was not inconceivable that some of the angels might be using their personal magics to eavesdrop on the conversation. It happened all the time. "Let's speak of this in the tower. There are too many eyes and ears in this place for my comfort."

Aitan and Grin agreed. Each willed himself to be returned to the tower. In seconds the noise of the crowd had vanished and the trio could speak in peace.

"Are these walls secure?" asked Aitan.

"No magics can penetrate," said the Angel of Blood. "None that I do not allow."

Aitan nodded. The angels could travel to any place in the holy cities by sheer will alone—*provided* no seals of privacy had been evoked. An angel's personal seal could be shattered only by a Vessel or his Emissary. The Hierarchy of the Host meant nothing in this regard.

"What happened to the last Emissary to the Second?" asked Grin. "The one Lileo replaced?"

"He was sent on," Malkiyyah said. "Songs will be sung of his willing sojourn to the body and the soul of the Almighty."

Grin shook his head. "Were *you* given the order to kill him?"

"Yes," said Malkiyyah. "He had no idea anything was amiss. The Vessel spoke to me directly."

"Almighty God," whispered Aitan. "Cruel in Your mysteries."

Malkiyyah looked at his companions with a sharp, vicious smile. "You honestly believe the slayer of angels to be loose upon this city?"

"Yes," said Aitan.

"How would he have passed through the mists? They are enchanted, after all. Humans aren't the only ones the mists expel. Those of us who have sinned most grievously, those angels who are damned, are also kept from entering."

Grin said, "He has greater magics."

Malkiyyah shrugged. "I'm bored with contemplating my sins. If you want my help in trying to locate this one, why not? If you're right, then maybe we can all regain our place in God's heart by bringing this creature to justice."

Aitan felt relieved. He didn't care if the Angel of Blood

was only humoring him, or helping because it would mean a pleasant diversion from his inner miseries. They needed allies.

Grin and Aitan told Malkiyyah all they knew of the angel who was now calling himself the Enemy and his plans.

"I've heard of the plague towns," said Malkiyyah. "They are a cause of great concern. But the Scourge is a mystery to us all. How could any angel claim mastery over it?"

"I suspect the answers are in a tome of Forbidden Lore called the *Mysts Arcana*," said Aitan. "I searched for it, once. Such was my duty as an antiquarian. Komm Kyriel found it. Whatever he learned in the book shaped him into something beyond our comprehension."

Malkiyyah raised his sword and set it ablaze. "Scholars and magicians," he said contemptuously. "I prefer this."

The fires engulfing the sword gave Aitan an idea. "Some kind of test *is* in order. From what I've gathered, his assumed forms can't stand up to light."

"That would make sense," said Grin. "He has given himself over to the darkness. He has claimed the name of our Lord's opposite number, the embodiment of the Void."

Malkiyyah pointed his sword at Aitan and the former Emissary. "The wicked cannot face these flames."

"Then sear away all evil among us," said Grin. "God knows, I'm sure we could all use some cleansing."

Aitan nodded. Malkiyyah gripped the flat of his blade with his free hand and did not flinch. Aitan followed. Only Grin hesitated. Finally, the former Emissary wrapped his hand around the blade. The fires grew bright enough to blind any mortal, then faded.

Nothing had changed.

"Well," said Grin. "Now we know it isn't any of us."

Aitan was incredibly relieved. "I'm worried about Purah."

"Let's put him to the Test," said Malkiyyah.

"No," said Aitan. "Not yet. If he *is* Kyriel, he approached me for a reason. Let's hear what he has to say. At my signal—"

"I will sear the evil from him," said the Angel of Blood. "Provided he is Kyriel."

Malkiyyah nodded. The trio willed themselves to the House of Purah and were taken to a crystal tower high in the clouds, where the burning light of the sun seemed to set the great House and its furnishings ablaze. Aitan saw that they were in some kind of receiving chamber. Revenants surrounded them, bowing and pleading for some task they could perform for their lord and his esteemed guests. Purah held a drink. Some kind of nectar.

"Go play in the clouds," the Angel of Forgetfulness said. The spirits, beings made of smoke and whisper, hurried off, vanishing through the walls, slipping through the floor. "Annoying, aren't they?"

"They've willed themselves into our service," Aitan said. "Postponing their eternal reward to serve our needs instead."

Purah gestured dismissively and laughed. "The ancient argument between us, yes? It *is* good to see you again."

Aitan took Purah's hand. He had known this angel many years earlier, though they had never really been friends. Aitan said, "I was petitioned by the Second to perform a service for Him. Now I cannot get His attention."

"You know what they say," Grin said with a laugh. "When you make a deal with the Devil, there's no end to dealing with Him."

The other angels were silent in the face of such a shocking blasphemy. Aitan knew that Grin was attempting to draw out their host, trick him into revealing if he was really Kyriel.

Purah smiled. "The Devil. What a grand and anachronistic concept. Fallen angels. Lucifer. Hell. Have you people been reading the forbidden books again?"

"Every chance we get," said Malkiyyah uneasily.

The Angel of Forgetfulness said in a conspiratorial tone, "I don't know how it is outside Abaddon, but you wouldn't believe the kind of bartering that has to be done to get ahold of one these days." He sighed. "So, what did you people think of the Unveiling? That was something, wasn't it? Just don't see that kind of thing every day."

"Certainly not," said Malkiyyah.

"These are strange days," said Grin.

"There's a rumor going around that—" Purah hesitated. "Do you promise not to tell anyone where you heard this? It is heresy, after all. Not of my creation, I assure you."

"You have my word," said Aitan.

"It's about the Vessels."

"Please," added Grin.

"Word is that the Second Vessel, where the aspect of God's Forgiveness is the strongest, and the Sixth, the vessel of His Vengeance, argued with the Fourth, Creation, that He was no longer necessary. That is why this atrocity has been committed. The Fourth decided that he had been too complacent and new things must now exist in the world."

"Do you believe that's true?" asked Malkiyyah.

"I believe all beings gossip and angels are the worst in that regard." He shrugged. "There *could* be some element of truth in what's been said."

Aitan looked to Malkiyyah and nodded. The sword bearer drew his weapon and willed the flames of righteousness to engulf it.

"No!" screamed Purah, who fell to his knees and clasped his hands together in prayer. "Don't kill me! Heavenly Father, save me!"

Malkiyyah brought the sword closer to the angel crouching before him. "What are you afraid of?"

"I've sinned."

"Haven't we all?"

"My sins are mortal. I've blasphemed. And worse, I've done things with the females. I had a vision of the Aerie recreated upstairs. Father and I even brought along a few Revenants—"

Malkiyyah touched his sword to Purah's face. The angel wailed and cried, but he was unharmed.

"It's not him," said Aitan.

The Angel of Blood withdrew his burning sword. "Perform whatever Penance makes you happy. We're done with you."

The trio turned and left Purah on the floor, shuddering and crying for his sins. They returned to the outskirts of the public square and watched as the crowd continued to prey upon the new Emissary.

Grin said, "I remember when they made such a fuss over me. The fools. Despite what they think, an Emissary can do nothing without the leave of his Vessel. Nothing at all."

"What if it's different this time?" asked Aitan.

"An Emissary with free will? I don't think so." Grin wove

a series of spells and secured the area from eavesdroppers. "We can talk freely."

Aitan considered Purah's statements. "Elements of God's nature at war with one another. It's an absurd concept. Yet if one were to accept that the nine Vessels were not the receptacles of God's varied nature, that instead they were Elven gods, one only has to look to the mythology of the humans for precedents. Their storytellers were always writing about warring gods."

The sword bearer fixed his dark gaze on Aitan. "Are you saying that Kyriel influenced the Vessels? Or one of Them influenced him? Madness. To think that an angel could sway a Vessel."

"I agree," said Aitan, "it doesn't sound possible, but how else could Kyriel have become so powerful unless he had an ally among the Vessels?"

Grin nodded. God turned a blind eye to much, this was true, and He left the responsibility of policing the True Lands and the Human World to the Host. Highest among the Hierarchy was the Vessels or Aspects. There were many times in history when the Aspects directly interceded in the affairs of man. Why would they act then, but not now? Why would they allow Kyriel to become such a monster? Such a threat to their rule?

"You're thinking too much," said Aitan. "I know that look of yours."

Grin laughed. "Sounds like something I'd say to you. So what's our plan? Terrorize every angel in the city until we're caught by Malkiyyah's friends and bludgeoned for our crimes?"

"I don't know," Aitan said. "We have to make our brothers understand the danger they're in."

Malkiyyah hissed, "What danger is that, exactly? What is Kyriel here to do?"

"I don't know," said Aitan. "You wouldn't think he'd want to harm the new Emissary. The kind of chaos that will come to the world once Lileo goes forth seems to be what he thrives on."

"If he is here, as you've said, it has to be for a reason," said the sword bearer.

"I know," Aitan growled. "I—"

Aitan Anzelm froze. Walking before him was a raven-haired angel carrying a small wooden box. The box was adorned with a lock and a seal in the shape of a black lotus. The angel was dressed in a red silk robe. His long thin hands bore rings with gemstones of every color.

"What is it?" Grin asked.

Aitan tried to speak, but couldn't. Instead, he launched himself at the angel carrying the box.

The angel turned in surprise and cried, "What—"

Aitan's only reply was to pluck the box from the angel's hands. Spinning, Aitan brought up one steel reinforced boot and planted it in the angel's stomach. The angel was driven back. He fell to the ground in a heap.

"Aitan!" cried Grin as the warrior ran to his friend's side.

"Test him," Aitan said.

Without hesitation, Malkiyyah willed his sword to burst into flame.

"No!" cried the angel on the ground as he tried to cover his face with his hands. Malkiyyah tore one of the angel's hands away and touched the flaming sword to his victim's face.

Nothing.

Malkiyyah unhanded the angel and drew back. A crowd had already gathered around the altercation.

"What is the meaning of this?" an angel cried.

"Violence? On this most holy of days? In this place?" said another. "Do you all wish to be damned?"

Aitan held the box close to his chest. He looked down at the fallen angel. "Where did you get this?"

The angel struggled to his feet. Malkiyyah's flaming sword kept any of the angel's potential allies away, though it would not do so for long.

"Tell me!" Aitan screamed.

"Found it," said the angel clutching his stomach. "Why did you do that?"

"*Where* did you find it?" asked Aitan. "Was anyone near it?"

"No. I was at the apocrypha, studying one of the rare tapestries, trying to see if I could understand the weave—"

"And?" said Aitan.

"I looked over and there it was. No one else was around. They had all gone off to the Unveiling. I had—" The angel swallowed hard. "I became so engrossed in my studies that I forgot the time."

"You didn't feel the summons?" asked Grin.

The angel shook his head.

Aitan took a closer look at the angel and saw how much the youth looked like him a decade earlier. Komm Kyriel used to tease Aitan about his studies. He said that true knowledge couldn't be found in any book. It seemed that times had changed.

The angel who had fallen said, "I was going to present the box as a gift to the Emissary, or one of his attendants. I hoped it would please him and I would be forgiven for missing the event."

Aitan nodded. "I'm sorry." He turned to the sword carrier. "We were tricked. Kyriel knew that the sight of this box would drive me to madness. I'm behaving just as he planned."

"What's so special about the box?" asked Grin.

Suddenly, a blinding light exploded into existence above their heads. Every angel present turned from the light. Aitan thought he had been blinded. He heard the beating of wings.

"It contains a Key of Summoning," said a calm, soothing voice. "With it, one can reach a spirit who resides in Mydian and may soon be sent Beyond."

Aitan's vision cleared. He looked up and saw Emissary Lileo floating above his head. The crowd stared at him with a mixture of awe and fear.

"The three of you," said Lileo. "The Vessel wishes to see you. He wishes to see you right now. . . ."

Aitan could hear the sound of chimes and waterfalls with the Emissary's every word. Lileo was no longer human. There could be no doubt.

"Give me that," Lileo said, gesturing at the box Aitan held. Suddenly, the box flew from Aitan's hands. It tumbled through the air and came to a gentle rest in midair before the Emissary. A wicked smile played across his face. The man's eyes melted into shimmering pools of blue-white light. "Oh, there is love here. Secrets. Unfinished business. And many lies. This would be delightful."

"No, please," Aitan said.

"You don't want me to have it as a gift?" Lileo asked. "But everyone wished me to have gifts. Look at all the gifts I've been granted already. My wings, for instance."

Aitan cared about nothing except the box.

Lileo's eyes widened. He caused the box to spin in place. "Pretty butterfly. Pretty, pretty, pretty."

"Be careful, please," Aitan whispered.

"Here," said Lileo as he tossed the box over his shoulder. "Take it."

Aitan gasped as he saw the box fall. If it shattered and the Key was destroyed, Aitan would lose what he treasured most in this life. Suddenly, a cloud of mist rose up and took the shape of a young man. Arms formed. Hands caught the box and pulled it into the cloudy and vaguely human form. Then the box vanished with the Revenant.

"Now, if you play nicely with me, I might give it back," Lileo said with a high, shrill laugh. "Elohi can hold it now. He's my servant. My teacher. He tells me when I can make miracles. Isn't that nice? I was thinking of making something new. A horse with two heads, maybe. I thought it might be fun."

Lileo looked around to the crowd. He suddenly became vexed. "That sounds like fun, *doesn't it*?"

The crowd cheered in desperation and terror.

He's insane, Aitan realized. *What did they do to him? Why is he so much older, a man, not a boy?*

Malkiyyah could not look at the Emissary. Grin could not turn his gaze away.

"ELOHI!" the Emissary screamed.

The man shaped from mists appeared.

"Why does your kind always hide away? I want to see them in the city."

Elohi bowed his head. "As you command, lord. Anything for your pleasure."

"That's what I like to hear." The Emissary trained his gaze on Aitan. "My teacher told me that knowledge is power. Odd, isn't it, that I have the Power of knowledge? I have only to look at you and I can see so much about you."

Aitan felt an uncomfortable presence in his mind, something cold and hateful. Then it vanished.

"Oh, you *do* have a story to tell, now don't you. And you've *suffered* so on your journey." Lileo shrugged. "Come on."

Aitan, Grin, and Malkiyyah exchanged worried glances.

"And none of this willing yourself from place to place. I want to see Elohi's handiwork," said Lileo.

With that, the angel rose into the air. The trio walked away from the crowd, which followed at a distance. In the streets were the dead, the spirits given over to serve the angels. Hundreds of grey figures dragged themselves out and paraded themselves before the new Emissary for his pleasure.

Aitan felt ill. How had he never seen it before? This was a city of the dead.

After a few minutes, Grin turned to the Angel of Blood and said, "What path leads to the Celestial Halls?"

"I have no idea," Malkiyyah said. "I've never had to do this."

Many souls swept aimlessly through the city. Some of the fresher Revenants danced about with happy motions, but their eyes were dead and cold.

After fifteen minutes of wandering, Lileo said, "I'm bored."

Suddenly, the trio found themselves standing in a vast receiving hall. The ceiling was so high that clouds formed in the room. A golden glow filled the hall. Pillars rising from the earth to the sky moved about lazily, forcing the small group always to keep in motion, and they created an ever-changing maze.

The pillars came to rest. Figures appeared on either side of the group. Two sets of twins. One set had flaming red hair, the other gold. They wore no clothing, and their bodies pulsed with energies that writhed like snakes.

There was a thunderous roar and the floor vanished. The trio did not fall. Instead, they stood suspended in midair, looking down at a terrifyingly beautiful vision. At first, Aitan thought he was looking at a rose composed of light and fire. A blinding light could be seen at its core. Arcane winds made its petals quiver. Then Aitan heard a sound so frightening that he thought he was certainly damned.

Angels wailed in pain. Thousands of them. Tens of thousands.

Aitan looked more closely at the fiery rose and saw that it was composed of living beings. Angels wearing crimson cloaks. They writhed and screamed in unbearable agony.

"There's some mistake," said Grin. He knew this place. So did Malkiyyah.

The fluttering of wings came from above. They looked up to see Lileo hovering over them. "No mistake. Save for the one you made when you made pacts with this man."

Lileo pointed and a golden fire seared the air, tearing open a portal through which a beaten, bloodied man fell. A burly red-haired angel followed him, catching the mortal before he could fall into the pit.

It was Travest.

"I must see the Vessel," said Aitan.

"You will see no one except the caretakers of this place. They will be your companions until one such as I decides it is time for you to pass Beyond."

Aitan looked down at the pit once more. "They're dead, aren't they?"

"Heavenly Revenants, yes," said Grin. "Angels who have sinned irretrievably. Captured, tortured souls."

"You sent quite a number this way," said Lileo. "Now didn't you?"

The two sets of twins moved forward. "Behold the Ring of Punishment. This will be your dwelling place."

No, Aitan thought, fear consuming him. *I can't bear this. I've done nothing to deserve this!*

"We are the Qaddisin," said the first pair of twins.

"We are the Irin," added their companions.

The four angels positioned themselves around their prisoners and said in unison, "We are greater than all the children of Heaven, and none are our equal among all the servants of God. For each of us is equal to all the rest together. We are the supreme council of justice, the servants of God's Court."

Aitan knew nothing of these beings. How could he have never been made aware of their existence?

"It's over," Grin said. "Over before it began."

Travest Mulvihill stirred. He looked up, saw the winged man, and trembled as he recognized this mad creature as his son. "No!"

"You have him?" asked the Irin.

The Angel of Rage nodded and kicked Travest in the side. The man moaned. "His power is great, but I'm keeping him distracted."

"Good."

Lileo descended. He folded his hands together and cocked his head to one side. "Father, you have become Unclean. You have lain with the Enemy, taken evil into your soul. There is nothing I can do for you, and if there was—I would let you suffer. This is what you have brought onto yourself."

"Shall we begin?" asked the Angels of Supreme Judgment.

"No," said Lileo. "Judgment will be made upon them some other time. This blessed day will not be spoiled with blood."

Terrified, Malkiyyah stepped forward. "I was not in league with them! Do not punish me as you would this filth!"

Lileo laughed. "Of course not. Why should I? You were only shepherding them my way, making sure their mischief was kept to a minimum. That is so, isn't it?"

Malkiyyah realized he was sweating. He couldn't remember the last time he had sweated for any reason. Though it was a lie, he said, "Yes, lord. That is so."

Lileo gestured and a doorway appeared. The Angel of Blood lowered his head and passed through it quickly. The door vanished. "The rest of you may be tried and punished on the morrow. Until then."

The Emissary rose into the sky, flying until he was swallowed by the clouds in the high ceiling. Lightning forked within the clouds, then they became dark.

Aitan was about to turn and face the twins when suddenly he found himself in a small, stone cell. Grin was with him. There were no doors. No windows. He looked down to see if the Ring of Punishment was still there. No, it too had disappeared.

"I suppose we've been allowed to keep enough magic to create air to breathe," said Grin. "And there's light. The walls glow so we can see. Thank Heaven for the little things, eh?''

Aitan looked around. Travest was not with them. Aitan said, ''How could they think we were in league with that creature?''

''The human believed it. As far as he knew, you made a pact with him. You were willing to set yourself against the legions of God for him.''

''Lileo was inside my mind. I felt him. He must know the truth.''

''He may not care. Madmen seldom do.''

Aitan shuddered. He thought of Tom, and hoped that the boy had not been harmed. Sinking to the floor, he realized for the first time in his life that he had no desire to pray.

They sat together in silence. Finally, Aitan said, ''They *don't* care, do they? Komm Kyriel could bring it all crashing down on their heads and it doesn't matter to them at all.''

''It'll matter to them when it's happening,'' said Grin. ''But they're arrogant. I've always thought that would be their downfall.''

''I know it will probably be pointless, but we should see how much of our magic is left to us,'' Aitan said.

''Agreed.''

The mages attempted to summon various spells to raze the walls and free themselves, but the only magics they could perform were those meant to shield them from harm. Exhausted, they settled back. The night would be long and tedious, but compared to the suffering ahead of them, it would be a fond memory.

Aitan noticed something—a fine mist forming on the floor of the cell. He rose to his feet along with Grin. The vapors took on the shape of a man. Two arms appeared, holding a small, wooden box.

''Please,'' said Aitan in sudden desperation.

The box was handed to him. Elohi's form took even greater shape and he said, ''Who would have known that you prisoners commanded such magic as to seize this from its hiding place without my knowledge. We do have an understanding, don't we?''

''Yes,'' said Aitan. ''Anything for this.''

''Don't say that,'' said Elohi. ''It's like signing your soul away. I should know.''

The Revenant vanished.

Aitan stared at the box for long moments.

"Well," asked Grin. "Aren't you going to open it?"

The angel nodded. He strained with the lid until the lock shattered. Then he withdrew a black-and-crimson ring which he held to his chest.

The mists returned. This time they took the form of a lovely young woman with long, flowing hair and eyes that burned like twin suns. She went forward, touching the side of Aitan's face gently. He touched her hand, comforted that he could still feel some of her essence. Tears formed in his eyes. Grin watched it all with growing wonder.

"You must be strong, dearest heart," said Rachiel as she stood before Aitan. "We haven't much time. . . ."

Twenty-Three

TOM KEEPER LAY QUIETLY UPON THE BRIDGE. HE HAD no idea that if he fell from the bridge he would have drowned in the Lake of Memory. Just as well. The idea that he might have been able to relive the chaos and madness that had engulfed his senses for the last hour might have been just enough to push him past the brink of sanity.

He could feel the dark magics of the plague-carrier at work within him. Strangely, as the fever and the racking pain had come over him, his senses had cleared. Struggling to his feet, he looked over the marble railing at the waters beneath. His first thought was that he had found Lethe, the River of Healing. The waters of Lethe had done nothing for Cameron, but Hughes maintained that there was a way for Tom to save himself.

Of course, that had been before Hughes had been struck down by the dark magics of Travest Mulvihill. The former tailor now had the power to mold light into fiery, raking shapes. He could cut a human into pieces the way he used to slice apart garments.

Tom had thrown one leg over the marble railing and was about to drop into the waters below when a voice called to him, "It's not what you think."

The lad tensed. He knew that voice. He had heard it in his dreams many times. Turning, he saw the flame guardian standing on the bridge before him. It was startling to see the man here, and not in the crystal chamber.

The flame guardian laughed. "Haven't you guessed? You created the crystal chamber, the portal. The entire vision was

235

of your design. It stemmed from your art. You may lay down
your quill and never sketch, lay down your brush and never
paint, but your art informs everything you do. It affects the
way you look at the world and what you give in return. I
remember when I had such a great sense of wonder. I miss it
terribly, though I know it's not lost—just misplaced.''

Tom shuddered as a racking pain moved through him. He
nearly lost his grip and fell into the waters. Shaking, he
climbed back onto the bridge and fell to his knees. ''You know
what's in my thoughts.''

''I've been in your dreams. It would follow that I would
know what you're thinking.''

''The Sigils. The runes I had painted on my body in the
dream—''

''Remember them. The symbols have meaning, one that you
will only begin to grasp some time from now.'' The flame
guardian cocked his head to one side. ''Have you thought
about my offer? I could make Kayrlis love you.''

Tom hugged himself. The pain was excruciating. ''Not interested.''

''Or I could make the pain go away.''

Tom sat back. He took in the wonders of the City of
Heaven. It was beautiful beyond compare. He had never
dreamed of such visions. ''Without the pain, I couldn't see all
this. It's the magic from the Scourge that's letting me see
clearly, right?''

''Yes, but the disease is killing you. Do you want to die?''

''No one wants to die.''

''Don't be so sure.'' The flame guardian held out his hand.
''I've come one last time to make you an offer. I can give you
power, Tom Keeper. Power to make your every dream come
true. Think of it. Consider the forces that would be at your
command. I know what you could do if the power of Aitan
Anzelm was within you. Nothing would be impossible. Think
of the good you could do. Anzelm is destined to fail in his
final conflict with the Enemy. Where he fails, you could succeed. You could have mastery over all the arts. Not just drawing and painting. You could shape reality. You could have
what they all want. You could be what they all *dream* of
becoming.''

"What's that?"

"God. Or as close to God as any mortal can ever really be. You could end the Scourge. No more like your mother. Or Kayrlis's brother, Cameron. No more misery. No more death. You could stop the suffering and the pain."

Tom tried to stand. The most he could do was rise to one knee. With a courage and a conviction that startled even him, Tom said, "My father told me about the days he fought in the wars. He said he would fight for God. He would lay down his life for God. But he would never want to *be* God." Pain surged through Tom. He gasped. "Wasn't his place to think of something like that, even though he'd heard a lot of men wish they had that power. They wanted to end the suffering. That's a noble cause. A good thing. But it wasn't their place to want to be God. I guess that's how I feel about it, too."

The flame guardian's arms sank down to his side.

Tom looked past the flame guardian, wondering if any of the other angels would come from the city and cross the bridge. He wondered what they would think of this little mortal, dying alone of a mortal disease on the threshold of their paradise. Would they cast him out? Leave him to die in the Human World? Or would they carry him through the city and let him see the fine works of the Lord before he died?

He thought of Aitan and hoped the man would not grieve too heavily. Tom was all right with the idea of dying young. He had seen enough wonders for any lifetime. His only wish was that he could thank Aitan for all the man had done.

"Your answer," said the flame guardian, "is 'no'?"

A stabbing pain plunged deep into Tom's stomach. He nodded. "Afraid so."

"Even though it means you will die?"

Tom closed his eyes and nodded sharply.

The flame guardian threw his head back and laughed until the sound of his laughter became deafening and Tom was forced to look up at him.

"*Good lad!*" cried the flame guardian. "I was worried about you for a while there. I feared you would be as weak as the last one. He answered wrongly and I cast him out."

"What?" Tom asked.

"Roger Hughes. The first artist I chose. You see, it must

be an artist. Only one whose creative spirit is alive and not tampered with can fulfill the destiny I have in mind.''

"Wait,'' Tom said, "what are you—''

The flame guardian did not wait. Instead, he gestured and the swirling vortex of light and sound appeared. This time, it manifested *between* Tom and the guardian. The burning man no longer blocked Tom's way to the light.

"I don't know,'' said Tom, "I don't want—''

Before Tom could say another word, he felt himself being pulled forward by an irresistible force. His flesh seemed to shimmer and transform. Suddenly, he was yanked ahead, into the vortex, his body, mind, and soul becoming a streak of light and fury, a fiery sword that pierced the vortex and became one with it.

Tom tried to reason and found he couldn't. All he could do was try to grasp what he saw.

No, that wasn't right. He wasn't seeing anything. He was experiencing the wonders all around him without benefit of the traditional senses. If he encountered a castle made of light that swam in a sea of stars, then he became that light, understood it, and was filled with love for it. Moving forward he was embraced in greeting by a race of beings who were nothing but sound, hymns of wonder and grace, and he, too, was sound, a song of eternal life and hope. Strange creatures sprang from amazing chrysalises, part-human, part-insect, part-animal. He reasoned with them, flew with them, hunted, killed, and made love with them. Everywhere he turned, such wonders.

Suddenly, it all stopped, and he found himself floating in a featureless void. He looked down and saw he had a human body and again he was naked, his skin covered in bizarre runes. The darkness ahead of him split and an object came into being before him. It was made of blue flame and radiated a coolness that alarmed and excited Tom. He reached for it as it reconciled itself into a sword with three blades sharing a common hilt.

"Don't be hasty,'' said the familiar voice of the flame guardian. "What you see before you will set you on a course from which there will be no turning back.''

"Is there a price I have to pay?'' Tom asked.

"Like your soul, or your decency?" asked the guardian. "No. But if you choose this weapon, if you choose life over death, you also choose misery, pain, and loss to go along with love and potential victory. You have a hard road before you. The sword is a tool meant to make your life a little easier. But only you can decide if walking down your destined path is worth the effort. Many have stood at the crossroads that face you. Only a few have dared to go beyond."

Tom hesitated, then grasped the sword's hilt.

Suddenly, he saw a burning sky filled with winged angels, and he stood upon the glowing jade ground of a world unlike his own, with a dozen warriors of God surrounding him, waiting for his command. He saw Kayrlis standing before him, tears in her eyes.

And he saw Aitan Anzelm, lying dead on a battlefield.

Tom withdrew his hand. He felt himself being pulled back, his mind, body, and soul rent asunder without pain. There was a blissful rush, then it was over.

Opening his eyes, Tom found himself on the bridge. The flame guardian stood before him. The portal was gone. Though he could still feel the Scourge within him, he was stronger now, able to stand. He felt strange. Something that had not been there before now resided within him, a cold and glorious power not meant for any human.

"What did you do to me?" Tom cried. "Did you make me one of them? Like Travest?"

"No," said the guardian. "I gave you a Gift. There is an infinite gulf between the carriers of righteous glory, the Gifted, and the Transformed Beings."

"There's—there's—there's something *inside* me," Tom stammered. He was terrified. "I can feel it. I can do things. Just like one of *them*!"

"The difference, Tom, is that they are damned and you are not. You are Blessed."

The young man trembled. All he could manage was a soft, "Oh."

The flame guardian turned.

"Wait. I saw something when I touched the sword. A bunch of things."

"Some of what you've seen will occur. Some may be pre-

vented. Remember a simple prayer. 'God grant me the ability
to change the things I can, accept the things I cannot, and the
wisdom to know the difference.' That wisdom is often the
hardest to come by. Now go to your friends. They need you.
One comes who can show you the way.''

''Who are you?'' Tom asked.

The flame guardian opened his arms. ''A friend.''

Tom watched as the guardian vanished. A sudden pain
coursed through him, doubling him over. He heard footsteps
on the bridge and looked up in time to see a sword-carrying
angel rushing his way.

Tom looked at the vast City of Heaven. He wondered if his
power as an artist had something to do with his ability to
reconcile the impossible sights and sounds before him so they
wouldn't drive him mad. At first he had believed this to be a
result of the dark magics of the Scourge moving within him.
Now he was not so certain.

''Who are you, boy?'' asked the angel who stopped before
Tom.

Tom straightened. ''Who are *you*?''

The angel seemed startled. He laughed. ''Malkiyyah, Angel
of Blood.''

''Tom Keeper.''

''Aitan Anzelm's squire?''

Tom nodded.

''No wonder you're not writhing on the ground. He must
have given you some kind of ward to keep you sane.''

''Something like that,'' Tom said, noncommittally. ''By the
way, thanks for the nosebleeds. You get upset and every mortal within five miles pays for it.''

They stared at one another for a moment and the belea-
guered angel shook his head. Malkiyyah said, ''I'm leaving
this place of madness now, while I can. If you want, I'll take
you with me.''

''Where's Aitan?''

''You don't want to know.'' The angel stared long and hard
into Tom's eyes. ''Or maybe you do. Your lord has been accused of conspiring with the Enemy. If you try to help him,
you'll share his eternal punishment. There's no hope. No way
to save him. None that I can see.''

Tom felt an odd sensation. A prickling cool that moved through his entire body. Suddenly he understood the nature of the Gift he had been given. He knew the limits and the possibilities of his newfound power.

"You're lying," said Tom.

"What?"

Fear flickered within the lad, but he held to his conviction. "That's not meant as an insult. I know when people are lying. It's a Gift I was given."

Malkiyyah drew his sword and willed it into flames. "Touch this and I will know if you are Unclean."

Steeling himself, worried that the Scourge's presence within him would make him seem like an agent of the Enemy to the angel's sword of righteousness and purity, Tom grasped the fiery blade. An array of blue flames leaped forward, engulfing Tom, dancing around and through him before returning to Malkiyyah's sword and shattering it.

Tom was unharmed.

The angel shuddered and dropped the hilt of his sword. He fell to one knee before Tom. "Gracious lord, I beseech thee, forgive me for my doubt."

Tom could not hide his shock at Malkiyyah's reaction. Fortunately, the Angel of Blood was staring at the ground, not at him.

Calming himself, Tom said, "Please stand up. I need your help, not—this."

Malkiyyah rose to his feet.

Tom tried to think of how he could explain all that had occurred. He said, "If only I could make you see what I've just been through."

Malkiyyah looked to the Lake of Memory. "If that is what you desire, and my knowledge would help you, then there is a way. A simple way. . . ."

Less than an hour later, Tom and Malkiyyah emerged from the waters. Darkness had fallen on the City of Heaven, but the city continued to burn with a golden flame that permeated every building.

"We both may die if we go back for them," Malkiyyah said at last. "Wouldn't it be better to live so that we can tell others what we've seen?"

"I can't leave them," said Tom. He was haunted by the vision of the Ring of Punishment. He would rather risk eternal damnation than allow Aitan to suffer with the other angels.

"I know. Now that I've seen what you've witnessed, and know what you are—which even *you* don't understand—"

"Explain it to me."

"I'm not sure I can. I don't know that I can find the words. But I'll search for them, and do my best." Malkiyyah went back to the bridge and tossed the broken shards of his sword into the lake. He returned to Tom and said, "I suppose I have no real choice either."

They stood for long moments, staring at the spires of God's creation, then walked silently toward a building in the distance.

Twenty-Four

AITAN ANZELM STOOD IN THE PRESENCE OF THE ONLY woman he had ever loved. The very concept of mortal love was strange to his kind. Caring for mortals, shepherding them—this was expected. But the only true love they were expected to feel was for God. Animal urges, of course, were another matter entirely. The females came down from the Aerie, and some male angels even found ways to summon them. Procreation was regulated through the females so that their cities were not overrun. The rearing of children was the sole dominion of the males.

To love any other than God was a sin. Aitan had sinned and he didn't care. His family had paid the price so that he could stave off damnation. Now he faced eternal suffering anyway.

Aitan looked into Rachiel's heart-shaped face and told her that he loved her. She nodded, leaned forward, and kissed him. Her lips were cold, but he could feel them.

"There is so much I have to tell you," Rachiel said. "I've learned so much. It's important for your kind and mine to know the truth."

"I don't care," said Aitan. "I just want to touch you."

He reached for her, but his hands touched only mist.

"I can't," she said. "I'm dying again."

"No."

Lord Skalligrin, who had been all but forgotten on the other side of their cell, said, "It's true. She doesn't have long. The Withering is near. Let her speak."

"What do you know of it?" snarled Aitan.

"He's right," Rachiel said, putting her hands to his lips.

Aitan felt a chill, nothing else.

"Komm Kyriel fears you and I must tell you why," said Rachiel.

Aitan said, "Did he hurt you?"

"No. *Listen.*"

The angel was silent.

"You told me of the day you went to the Ancient Cities of Heaven. The tower where you found the Grimoire and the collapse of the tower. How Komm Kyriel saved your life."

"Yes."

"What you don't know is *how* he saved your life. What he sacrificed for you."

Aitan's brow furrowed. "Sacrificed? Rachiel, did Kyriel work magic on you?"

"No. He came to the house of Roger Hughes. Roger had been having visions. Strange nightmares of a burning man. He told me of them, then became cross when I had no answers for him. I was made to dance. What I loved most in life has become my punishment in the hereafter."

"Rachiel, I—"

"No," she said. "It was my choice to go with him."

Aitan tried to touch her again. Failed.

"Komm Kyriel took me to a place of darkness, a place Beneath. It is his realm of power. From there, he can go to any point on earth—except the Holy Cities. He cannot enter them."

"Then he's not here."

"He is. I can feel him."

"Then how—"

"I don't know. You must let me finish. There isn't much time." She closed her eyes. "You know that I would never hurt you."

"I know that."

"And that I could never lie to you."

Aitan nodded slowly.

"I'm sorry, but it's true. What Komm Kyriel claims, that your people aren't divine. It's all true."

The angel stepped back. "*Are* you Rachiel? Or are you some vision sent to taunt me and torture me in my last hours?"

She turned away. Tears of mist gathered in her eyes. "I only have the strength to touch you once more. Don't make me waste it on proving what you already know."

Aitan shuddered. "I'm sorry. Why do you believe his lies?"

"They're not lies. I read the Mysts Arcana. It offers proof."

"The book is a thing of evil," said Aitan. "It twists the reader, invades their soul—"

"No. It's just words. The book isn't alive, like you seem to think."

Aitan covered his face. "I can't listen to this."

"Please, Aitan. I do love you. You've always known that."

The angel looked at her. "I wanted to believe."

"You've always known. You couldn't accept what you knew."

Aitan felt ashamed and hurt, but he knew she was telling the truth. "Yes."

"There are spells in the book. Ways of opening the doors between this reality and many others. Of contacting beings who can offer anything you desire."

He looked up sharply. "Could they make you live again?"

"Yes, but by the time the book is finally in your hands it will be too late. I don't want that, anyway."

"You don't want to be with me?"

"You know that isn't true. I pray we'll be together again. But you have to accept that I'm not afraid of having my bonds to this existence severed. I welcome what may come. I'm tired of being a servant. Of being a captive."

"It wasn't that way with me. You know that."

She did not turn her gaze from him. "It was that way for both of us. *You* know that."

"Rachiel, you can't expect me—"

From the corner, Grin snapped, "Aitan, if she has something to tell us that will help, let her speak!"

A ragged gasp escaped the angel. "Tell me why Kyriel is afraid of me. What was it he sacrificed?"

"A part of his soul. It lives inside you."

"No!"

"It's true. You were beyond saving when he found you as a child. Broken. Seconds from death. He made a decision. The only way to make you strong enough to accept the Healing

Ways he needed to perform was to become one with you.''

"I'm not like him," said Aitan.

"No, you're not. That's the point." Rachiel began to weep. "I'd rather die a thousand times than hurt you by telling you these things. You have to know that."

Rachiel's form became less complete. She was fading into the mists.

"Yes," Aitan said desperately. "Tell me, please, so there's still some time—"

"I will." She wiped her tears away. "Within you is the only remnant left of Komm Kyriel's decency and kindness. The only part of him that remains uncorrupted. He doesn't want you dead. Not yet. If you die pure of soul, he will never achieve what he wishes."

"What does he want?"

"To become a god. Like the beings you call the Vessels. Only more powerful than any of them."

From the corner, Grin muttered, "Merciful Lord."

Aitan asked, "What about this place you mentioned?"

"I don't know. There was so much I couldn't comprehend. In this place was darkness, and at its heart, a greater darkness."

Grin said, "What about the book?"

"Much of what I read made no sense to me. Ancient names were mentioned. The Rephaim, the Essenes, the Key of Solomon, and the Wheels. All of these are important. Do they mean anything to either of you?"

"No," said Aitan.

"The Rephaim," said Grin. "That's another name for the Weavers, the Openers of the Gates between Heaven and Earth."

"Angels," said Aitan.

The former Emissary said, "Once."

Rachiel's form became even more ethereal. "There was a passage I memorized. It said, 'The Elven gods would one day become as the Demiurge, the half-maker who created part of the world, and the Elven themselves would be as the Archons, lieutenants, rulers of the Outer World.' I think that time has come. The Elven devastated their world. They took it for all it was worth. Drew out all the magic there was. They took the soul of the Almighty.''

"Blasphemy," Aitan whispered, but he felt little conviction in his pronouncement.

"God is in all things," said Rachiel. "I'm being drawn closer. I can sense truths I never dreamed of before. You must believe me, magic is one of the Powers of God. Your world had a soul. It was nearly destroyed. The same could happen here."

"It makes sense," said Grin. "And it explains the ruined cities of the True Lands, where magic is unstable if it works at all."

"You said that your faith had been strengthened," said Aitan, turning on the former Emissary.

"My faith in God, yes," said Grin. "It's the Vessels that made no sense to me. Now I think I understand."

Rachiel's essence grew dim. The mists composing her elegant form dissipated.

"No!" cried Aitan. "Wait. There is so much left unsaid between us. You can't leave me."

She drew closer. "No, I can't. You have something of mine. I can't go beyond without it. My soul will crumble. I'll turn to dust."

"The rings," Aitan said frantically as he searched for them, then held them out to her.

Rachiel put her hand before her face. She forced the last vestiges of her will into one final effort and suddenly she was whole once more. Aitan reached out, nearly sobbing with relief as he touched her hand and placed the rings on her finger. One he had been given by Roger Hughes. The other had been in the box. He took her hand and brought it close to his chest.

"No matter what you learn," Rachiel said, "no matter what you choose or may be forced to believe, understand that you will always be an angel. *My angel.* I forgive you for the act of vengeance you took in my name."

Aitan drew her into his arms.

"There is much left unsaid," she whispered. "This is how we'll say it."

Their lips touched. For a single moment, Aitan forgot the world and the punishment waiting for him. He tasted her lips, soft, sweet, and warm. He felt her body crushed against him and prayed to God that he could feel her like this for all time. There was almost no price too high to pay.

Suddenly, the final stages of the Withering struck. Her warmth faded. The strength of her arms around his body lessened. He felt her tremble, then pass into mist.

"Rachiel," he whispered. "Don't."

Then there was nothing. He opened his eyes and saw only a few scattered remnants of the ghostly mist. They faded within seconds.

She was gone.

Aitan and Grin stood together silently for a time. Aitan didn't want to accept that Rachiel was gone, but he knew she was.

Finally, Aitan said, "Well? You're the one who's supposed to know the future. How are we supposed to use the knowledge Rachiel gave us while we're trapped in this prison?"

Grin lowered his head. "Um . . . this might not be the best time to mention it, but since you asked . . ."

"Yes?"

"My visions are gone. My gift of prophecy has faded. I have no idea what's going to happen. . . ."

Twenty-Five

ABADDON, KNOWN IN THE TRUE LANDS AS THE NINE-teenth City of Heaven, hosted a wondrous celebration this night. Few of the participating angels felt any real joy, but they didn't want to disappoint the new Emissary.

In the streets, hymns were sung to the glory and wisdom of God. Prayers were given for the Almighty to watch over and guide Lileo, His new son. Everywhere, there was dancing and music and laughter.

The evening was dubbed the Night of Creation. Lileo walked the streets or flew overhead, accepting gifts from the angels. Some created games or puzzle boxes to amuse the Emissary. Others transformed plants or animals, at times intermingling the two, and treated Lileo to oddities never before seen in the world of man or the Kingdom of God: a feline with butterflies for ears and roses for eyes. Paintings with frames made of golden tendrils that came alive and gently massaged the viewer as he appreciated the art. Elegant robes with images that moved, among which, the Emissary's favorite was a comet racing across a starry sky. Lileo could feel the heat of the comet as it streaked from his collarbone to his hip, wrapped itself around his body, then descended again, altering its course each time. The tiny stars blinked and filled him with warmth.

As angels approached Lileo, the new Emissary held out his bronze hand and said, "Be still, and know that I am God."

His words were never doubted.

Occasionally Lileo appeared distracted. He looked away from the adoration of the angels, his expression forlorn.

Elohi, his servant, asked what troubled the Emissary.

"The eternal silence of these infinite spaces terrifies me," whispered Lileo, then he rose into the air and abandoned his worshipers for a time.

In another part of the city, Tom Keeper sat with the Angel of Blood in his tower. They had been here half the night, performing the arcane rituals necessary to transform Malki-yyah into the fiery avatar who had carried Lileo into the city weeks earlier. The soldier's flesh burned with an inner fire. Many of the rites had been agonizing for them both, the presence of the Scourge within Tom impeding their progress even more. Tom was sweating blood and Malkiyyah's sacred Power had nothing to do with it.

They rested, preparing themselves for the one final act of conjuring before the inevitable conflict would begin. Malki-yyah gestured at Tom's face and said, "I might be able to make the bleeding stop."

Tom shook his head. "You have to keep all your power ready for when we need it. Besides, none of us knows how the Scourge really works. Maybe sweating out the blood is slowing things down. I don't know."

"The one you called the plague-carrier, the artist, Roger Hughes. You're certain he's dead?"

"I'm not sure of anything right now. Except that I hurt real bad. We better keep going."

Malkiyyah nodded. He rose up and began a chant that called a series of flaming runes into existence. Malkiyyah's chest had been bared. The runes rushed forward and tattooed themselves into his skin.

Tom knelt before the angel. His main duty was to clear his mind of all concerns and focus himself fully on his belief in the righteousness of their cause. Any element of doubt could prove disastrous. Malkiyyah fed upon Tom's belief, welding it to his own. No thought could be given to where they might run once they rescued Aitan and Grin. Any concern that they might one day be captured by the Heavenly Host and cast into the Ring of Punishment—or an even darker hell—had to be allayed.

Malkiyyah knew all the various plots within the Torture Gardens. The one that frightened him the most was the Tomb of Madness, where beings who had once been angels chittered and oversaw the torture of mortal souls, a dominion whose doors opened only one way, and from which there was no known avenue of escape. The Angel of Blood had no idea that this was the hell to which Aitan Anzelm had sent the soul of Rachiel's murderer. With luck, he would never go there and find out.

The runes burned into the angel's flesh. In his hand, a new sword of fire exploded into being.

"It's time," said Malkiyyah.

While in a small featureless grey room devoid of light, Travest Mulvihill wept. All he cared about had been taken from him. His son, whom he had raised to be honest and good, had been transformed into a nightmarish creature.

Lileo had been a boy. The Emissary was a man. How had they done this to him? How had they made him age, and how had they twisted him so that no vestige of the beautiful soul that had inhabited Lileo's form remained?

His son was dead. Travest knew that he had to accept this. What he could not accept was that this travesty of Elven sorcery now stood in the mortal frame that had once belonged to his son, an innocent child.

The Emissary had to be destroyed. No matter what torture was heaped upon Travest from now until time itself came to an end, the former tailor vowed that he would suffer it gladly so long as he knew that every vestige of his son had been sent beyond.

"God is merciful, God is good," Travest whispered. These were the first words he had been taught to write when he was a child. He had written the phrase thousands of times in an effort to make his script absolute perfection and please his teacher. In the filth of the cell floor, he wrote those words.

Travest believed in God. Despite all that happened, he was certain that a kind and merciful Lord existed somewhere, and that the trials mankind now faced from the Elven overlords served some purpose. He didn't have to know the nature of that purpose to believe in its existence. There had always been suffering in the world. Perhaps only through suffering could one ultimately achieve purity, and only when one was pure was one worthy of divine intervention.

That meant he had to suffer. *Everyone* had to suffer.

But how could he make it so?

Travest felt a sudden pain. He clutched at his chest. It felt as if it was on fire!

Tearing at his shirt, he looked down and saw a glimmering light rising from his chest. The scars he had been given by the sword-bearing angel when he tried to stop the being from taking Lileo were glowing. As he watched, the scars grew brighter and brighter still, until their light would have been blinding to any mortal man. But Travest was more than human.

Free yourself, a voice whispered in his mind. *The power is within you. Use it well.*

Travest looked around and saw the dilapidated walls of the holding cell. Which of these walls led to a way out?

The voice guided him. Was it Komm Kyriel? Travest didn't know and honestly didn't care. All that mattered to him was vengeance. He laughed triumphantly. The means to achieve his goal had just been given to him.

Readying himself, Travest absorbed the light.

A blinding rush of pain swept through him. He gasped, but he did not try to put an end to his suffering. Perhaps this was only fitting. Using his powers for selfish ends, for evil, had been pleasurable. It only made sense that his attempt to be noble and serve the cause of good by ridding the world of the abomination that had been his son would bring untold agonies.

Travest had heard of men who had been struck by lightning and survived. He knew the way the ground itself could be turned to glass from the intense heat. More importantly, he knew about the pain, the shockingly intense sensation of having the power of the elements coursing through your body, charring your mind and soul.

Until this moment, his wielding of the light had been a simple matter. Each time he used it, the power brought a rush of pleasure without even a trace of discomfort. This time was different. The light flowing out of him was agonizing.

He welcomed it.

Once he felt he couldn't breathe, that he would burn up alive if he attempted to contain the power any longer, Travest turned to the wall the voice had commanded and released a torrent of light that made the walls shudder and could, he was certain, make the heavens fall!

Closer to Travest's cell than either of them would have ever guessed, Aitan Anzelm and Lord Ainigrim Bosh R'Hayle Skalligrin saw the far wall shudder and begin to radiate a crimson haze. The angels had barely enough time to raise spells of protection around themselves before the wall imploded and an inferno of light and fire swept over and around them, striking the wall opposite, and demolishing it as well!

The light faded and the angels turned to see Travest Mulvihill standing before them, the clothing burned from his smoldering form, his flesh charred and blackened. His skull and brow were smooth, his hair and eyebrows having been burned away.

"Take me to my son," Travest said, his eyes and teeth a startling ivory contrast to the rest of his body. Aitan felt a sudden breeze and looked the other way.

The golden light of the City of Heaven was plainly visible. The way to escape was before them.

"We *will* take you," said Grin. "We—"

Without another word, the angels vanished. Travest started forward, screaming in rage, but there was nothing he could do. Instead, he looked out at the City of Heaven. The golden light that suffused every building, and every being in the streets, began to flow into him.

His anger faded and he closed his eyes to welcome the light.

Within the tower of Malkiyyah, two figures stepped from a shimmering light. Aitan and Grin found themselves in the darkened tower, staring at the still forms of Malkiyyah and Tom, who had fallen to the floor in a heap.

Grin bent and pulled the trembling form of the Angel of Blood from Tom. The angel's light had faded, though his sword remained. Tiny red specks covered Tom's face. Aitan sensed at once that this was not Malkiyyah's doing.

"The plague-carrier," Aitan whispered. He turned to Grin, who was helping Malkiyyah to his feet, and said, "How do you feel?"

"If you're asking, 'Are the wards that held my power down still in place,' the answer is 'no,' " said Grin.

"Then we have to get out of here now, before anyone sees

what's happened. We've got to leave Abaddon.''

"I'm not arguing."

Aitan picked up Tom. The angel had a dozen questions, but they could wait. He heard an odd sound, a flapping of wings.

The angel turned—

—and the tower was gone.

Shuddering, Aitan realized that he was back in the Celestial Hall, where he had been accused of conspiring with the Enemy. Tom was still in his arms. Grin and Malkiyyah stood at his side.

The floor was green marble and inlaid with golden serpents. "This is not good," said Grin, looking down. "This is where I saw myself in the vision, lying dead upon *this* floor."

Lileo hovered above him. "A valiant, if misguided effort, gentlemen. And to think, if I hadn't chosen to visit the Angel of Blood and tell him that his sin of speaking out against my creation was forgiven, you might actually have escaped...."

In the streets of the holy city, a figure made entirely of light prowled toward a collection of angels. The laughing angels held sparkling goblets filled with nectar the color of a rainbow. Tallest and the most fierce of these angels was the crimson-haired Angel of Rage.

The angels paid little notice to the shining man. Many of their kind had altered their appearances this night in honor of the new Emissary. Within each of them was the light of truth. To walk the streets as the embodiment of that light was perfectly natural on such a night.

Travest Mulvihill looked at the gathering of angels. The agony he felt was excruciating, but he wasn't going to let that stop him. Raising his hands, he unleashed the forces he had gathered, shaping the light into a gigantic scythe.

Not one of the angels saw the magical construct Travest had formed. They were laughing as Travest cut them down with the scythe, ending their existences as he took their light into himself to replace what he had lost.

The shining man moved on. He found a pair of angels earnestly discussing the ramifications of having a mortal act as an emissary to the Almighty.

Travest went up to them, slapped each on the back, and

allowed his power to rip through them. He felt nothing as the angels shuddered and died, looking down in horror at their mangled forms.

He would do this until someone was able to stop him.

Or until the Emissary was called.

Within the Fourth Celestial Hall, Aitan and his companions were joined by the twins. They linked hands as Grin drew his sword and surged forward, prepared to fight his way from this place even if it meant calling down the wrath of the Vessels themselves!

Lileo raised his hand and said, ''Fall.''

Grin stumbled to the ground.

''Remain there.''

The former Emissary could not move.

Lileo smiled. ''A good power, I think. All I have to do is speak and my will is done. All are powerless to resist. Now, anyone else?''

Aitan set Tom on the ground. Placing his hands behind his back, he began the conjuration of the Severed Soul. He had no idea if the spell would work on an Emissary, but he had to try. Suddenly he felt a cold presence brush across his thoughts.

''Anzelm!'' the Emissary said. ''You forget, I can also see into the hidden heart if I choose to look.''

On the floor, Tom was beginning to stir.

Lileo said, ''You might be able to carve my soul from my flesh. God knows, there's precious little of it left, but what there is, you're welcome to take a stab at. Of course, I'm not alone here. There are the twins to consider. And there is your friend Tom.''

Aitan hesitated.

''I won't tell you what to do,'' continued Lileo. ''All I'll say is that if you stand down, I'll cure him of the Scourge and let him go free. He will endure no punishment.''

''Don't believe him,'' Grin gasped.

''Quiet,'' said Lileo. ''Be still.''

Grin fell silent and motionless.

''As to whether or not you can trust me,'' Lileo said, ''well, look at me. What do you see? I was a boy when I was carried into this city by Malkiyyah. Do I look like a boy anymore?''

"No."

"Time passed more quickly in my chambers. What was for you only several weeks was *seventeen years* for me. I would spare the child suffering simply because he is a human and therefore easily led. On the other hand, your attempt at escape, and Malkiyyah's act of betrayal, simply will not do at all. I am of a mind for vengeance. I wish to see God's work be done."

"The way of vengeance is not the way of the Lord," Aitan said. "Love—"

"What would you know of it?" Lileo screamed as he raised his great and terrible wings. "Love is what did this to me! If my father had let me die, I would have passed beyond pure and innocent. Instead, I'm worse than any of you. The angels promised me miracles. They said I would be the embodiment of joy and love. They lied. My soul has been ravaged and I have been made a horror because of love. Do not speak the word in my presence!"

Aitan was silent.

Lileo grinned. He saw the angel looking to Malkiyyah, who was also attempting to rise. "No, Anzelm. You won't get any more help from him, believe me. Hmmmm. I would wager that you wish understanding, yes? How you escaped was a mystery that gnaws at some part of you. I suppose you *should* know precisely why your night of grace has been brought to an earlier conclusion. Watch."

Images flashed across the surface of Aitan's consciousness. He understood in seconds what Malkiyyah had done. Weeks earlier, when the Angel of Blood had scarred Travest and set his mark upon the man, he had created a connection between them. Malkiyyah knew that he could not approach the Spires of Holding without alarming the guards set to watch Aitan, Grin, and Travest. Instead, he chose to reach across the distance separating him from the prisoners and feed the light he had manifested with Tom's help into Travest. The madman did the rest. Once the otherwise impenetrable walls had fallen, it was a simple matter to will Aitan and Grin to his tower.

"You see, very simple," said Lileo. "Now, do you have a decision for me? Are you going to attempt to cleave my soul from my body, though you might risk the lives of all your little friends in the process? What are you going to do? You've had plenty of time to think about it.''

''I have,'' said Aitan Anzelm. ''I came here to warn Abaddon of an evil that seeks to destroy everything we stand for. I came to accept a task given me by the Second Vessel. You have been in my mind, you know this is true.''

''I know that you believe it,'' Lileo said.

''I came here willing to give up my life in the service of God, if necessary,'' Aitan said, ''but I'll be *damned* if I'm going to see you triumph in your madness and your ignorance.''

Lileo's entire body tightened. His wings drew up sharply. ''Do you understand the importance of what you're saying?''

''If I'm to be damned anyway, then I have nothing to lose. Now summon the Fourth Vessel, and through Him the Second and the Sixth, or I will condemn my soul for all time to the true Enemy—in return for the price of seeing this city and all who reside within dead before dawn. . . .''

Twenty-Six

TRAVEST MULVIHILL HAD SLAIN ONE HUNDRED ANGELS before anyone realized what he was doing. A half dozen warriors of God assembled against him, but none could get close enough to strike him down. Any magics they sent against him merely fueled his fire and were sent back against the warriors with gruesome finality.

"What's wrong?" Travest asked with a crazed laugh. "I'm the light-bringer. I thought you'd be *happy* to see me!"

A battery of archers lined up in the street to face him. They loosed their arrows, but each shaft was burned to a cinder long before it reached Travest and could do him any harm. The shining man reached out with his power, taking the light from the angels and their city at will.

Towers fell. Fissures opened in the earth and rivers of molten fire ran through the streets.

Travest looked about him and said, "It is good."

His son would come eventually. Until then, he had plenty to keep him occupied.

He went about his work.

In another part of the city, one that bordered the True Lands, the Emissary Lileo summoned his master, the Fourth Vessel.

The clouds trapped within the Celestial Hall split and lightning flashed within them. Darkness fell across the sky, then a single brilliant form descended.

Before Aitan's first visitation by one of the Vessels, the angel had often wondered what form God took when He appeared to his followers. That night, Aitan had seen the Vessel as a magnificent and nearly undefinable force, an entity that possessed and became every object in the quarters he had taken, surrounding Aitan with His magnificence, while maintaining an ever-changing phantasmagorical shape that had elements of man, angel, and beast.

What descended from the heavens was not so imperious or unknowable.

It was Rachiel.

Aitan gasped. He tried to understand what he was seeing, and even wondered for an instant if he had finally gone mad.

"Mother?" Tom asked.

The angel looked sharply to Tom. He knelt beside the lad and said, "Tell me what you see."

Tom whispered. "It looks like my mother."

"And I see Rachiel," admitted the angel.

The Vessel hovered a few feet from Aitan and his companions.

Lileo gestured toward Grin and said, "Rise. Don't be disrespectful."

The former Emissary was jerked to his feet as if by an invisible force.

Malkiyyah whispered, "Janos? Brother?"

"Hush," whispered Grin. "The Vessels often take pleasing forms. They appear to you in the form of that you love most upon the mortal plane. Or sometimes what you long for the most."

"Janos was my brother," Malkiyyah said. "He died in battle. I always thought it should have been me who perished instead."

Across from Aitan and his friends, Lileo finally took a closer look at the Vessel. "You're not my Liege."

"I AM THE SECOND," said the Vessel in a voice that shook each of them to the core of their souls. "THE FOURTH AND THE SIXTH HAD OTHER DUTIES. WHY HAVE I BEEN SUMMONED?"

"Gentle lord," Aitan said, falling to his knees, "I beseech you to look upon me and tell the others of the task You yourself set upon me."

The Vessel turned to Aitan. "I DON'T KNOW YOU. YOU HAVE NEVER BEFORE STOOD IN MY PRESENCE."

Aitan was stunned. He didn't know what to say. He looked

down, all too aware that he could not accuse one of the Almighty's nine incarnations of being a liar. Why had his Lord forsaken him?

Then he saw something that made him gasp on the ground before Grin. Though the light of the Vessel was in front of the former Emissary and a shadow stretched away and behind the angel, a second shadow was easing out of him. Sharp black claws sprang from the vaguely manlike form and a nightmarish figure rose up before the Vessel.

"WHO DARES—" the Vessel began, unaware that it had just spoken its last words.

The twins surged forward and Lileo screamed, "No one moves!"

Only the living shadow and the Vessel were unaffected by the Emissary's power. The shadowthing hissed a phrase in an ancient tongue, then thrust both of its claws into the body of the Vessel. Aitan Anzelm watched in frozen horror as the Vessel, wearing the form of Rachiel, arched back and screamed in agony!

A torrent of blinding energies erupted from the Vessel and flowed into the shadowthing. The Vessel placed its hands on the face of the living shadow and released a magic that was toxic to the creature. It withdrew and the wounded Vessel fell to the floor. The moment the Vessel's outstretched hand touched the ground, a jagged fissure opened with a wrenching moan and a river of light appeared.

Powerless to intervene, Tom Keeper averted his gaze from the wounded Vessel. To him, it looked like his mother, dying all over again. Instead, he stared at the heavenly body that had appeared. He was certain that this was Lethe, the River of Healing. Would the Scourge be banished from him if he could somehow make his way to those waters? Cameron had not been cured of the horrid disease, but then, he had not been immersed in the river.

No, Tom thought. Angels from every city had access to these waters. What if the Scourge left his body and contaminated Lethe? It would be better to die than be responsible for destroying a thing of such beauty and perfection.

Ahead, the Vessel struggled to reach the healing waters. The shadowthing would not allow it. A ragged hole appeared in the living shadow's head, quickly filling with jagged, razor-sharp teeth. Its jaws extended, growing wide enough to swallow up any mortal.

With a laugh, it consumed the Vessel.

For long seconds a war was fought within the body of shadows. Light and shadow raged until finally the last flickers of illumination were stilled and the Vessel was gone.

"That's better," the shadowthing said in a low, deep voice that shook the foundations of the Celestial Hall.

Lileo stepped forward. "You are the Vessel now? You have taken His power?"

"Some elements of it, yes. But not all. At best, I've created a void. A vacancy. Time and a good deal of effort will be required to ensure that I'm the one who fills it."

"But I helped you," said Lileo. "When I looked inside Skalligrin, I saw you hiding there. Even he didn't know you had fused yourself to him. I knew what you wanted. I helped you attain it. Now I want something in return."

"What would that be?"

"To die. To be released."

The shadowthing laughed. "Is that all? That's easy enough to arrange. Begone!"

Lileo vanished.

In a chamber far across the city, where a veritable woodland sprang up from the floor and a host of spirits danced about in freedom over the bodies of the angels who enslaved them and made them sing and create music, the Emissary appeared. A being made of light was cutting through the last of a series of angels with a fiery scythe.

"Father?" Lileo said.

The light-bringer slew the last of the angels, then turned to face his son.

Lileo fell to his knees. "Forgive me, Father. For I have sinned."

Travest went to his son. Lileo was crying. For the first time since he arrived in the heavenly city, Travest saw at least a vestige of the boy he had raised. He willed the scythe into nonexistence and stilled the burning fires raging in his heart.

Opening his arms, he embraced Lileo and began to weep. His son's soul was not beyond redemption.

The time had come to leave Abaddon forever. He was about to propose this to his son when he saw Lileo look up at him in fear.

"Father?" Lileo asked softly.

Travest watched in confusion as a strange brilliance rose upon Lileo's face. Then he felt it. The power he had taken from the angels, building up within him, reaching an intensely painful crescendo seemingly against his will.

"No," Travest said as he attempted to force his son away. Instead, Lileo clung to him, though the fires were now raging out of control within the light-bringer.

"Thank you," Lileo whispered as his hair and his wings caught fire and were incinerated. "Thank you. . . ."

A fireball of pure light engulfed them both, its roar drowning out Travest's plea for God to stop this from happening.

Then there was nothing but light.

While in the Celestial Hall, those who had been rendered immobile by Lileo's magics suddenly found themselves free to move again.

Grin wasted no time. He hurled an array of spells at the shadowthing and leaped at the creature with his sword drawn. All his life he had dreamed of one day confronting the avatar of ultimate darkness and evil. His chance had finally come.

The Enemy recoiled from his attack, crying out in fear and surprise! Grin swept forward with his blade, calling forth invocations and conjurations, sending a stream of crackling light and fire into the heart of the living shadow!

Falling to its knees, the Enemy reached up to feebly protect itself as Grin raised his sword overhead and prepared to bring it down upon the abomination. With a sharp, high cackle, the Enemy extended his claws and pierced the man's armors, five ebony blades running through the warrior at once. Grin teetered for a moment, then dropped his blade and fell back. The former Emissary shuddered and held his arms before his wounded chest.

Aitan and Malkiyyah stared at the fallen angel in shock. If a former Emissary could be felled so easily by Komm Kyriel, what chance did they have?

Tom went to Grin's side and knelt beside him. Grin whispered, "Know all that we have learned."

Tom gasped as Grin's gauntleted hand touched the side of his face. Sights and sounds exploded in his head. Suddenly, he was aware of Rachiel's claims and the words of Komm Kyriel himself, spoken to Grin days earlier at the castle in Hartston.

Then the flood of knowledge stopped. Tom looked down to see Grin staring at him, eyes wide with wonder.

"It's within *you*," Grin said to the lad. "I can feel it. The Gift that had been granted me. The power of prophecy. Not as strong, not yet, but it's yours. How could this be?"

Tom thought of the visions he had seen in the realm of the flame guardian. "Long story."

"No matter." Grin fell back.

"No!" Tom cried as he tried to get his arms under Grin. If he could just drag the man to the River of Healing, maybe the warrior could be saved. Grin's armors made him too heavy, and Tom was too weak. He cried out for Aitan or Malkiyyah to help him, but before the angels could make a move in Tom's direction, the shadowthing extended its body and blocked the path to the healing waters.

"Let it go," whispered Grin.

"No, you can't die," Tom hissed. "I won't let you!"

"Remember what I told you and Aitan on the road? When we healed Aitan's wounds?" Grin said. "Sometimes it's better when it's over with quickly. Go to Aitan. He needs you now."

Reluctantly, Tom got to his feet and joined Aitan.

The shadowthing rose up. "Anyone else? This is fun?"

Malkiyyah drew his sword.

"No," said Aitan. "Don't."

Next to the angel, Tom said, "Aitan, this is him, isn't it? Komm Kyriel?"

Aitan nodded.

Suddenly, the four angels of judgment, the two sets of twins, launched themselves away from the Enemy. They sailed into the River Lethe and were quickly gone from the hall.

"They go to bring others," said Kyriel. "There isn't much time. Do the lot of you wish to fight and die, or would you rather hear me out and perhaps keep hold of some hope to save the True Lands and the mortal realm? The choice is yours, good people. Entirely yours. . . ."

Outside the Celestial Hall, the City of Heaven was on fire. Travest had slain his son, though in the end, it had not been his wish to do so, and now he had gone mad. No vestige of his humanity remained. He took the light of the angels, the light of the city, into himself, then released it, tearing down the walls of Heaven, razing the city to its very foundations!

Battalions of heavenly warriors set themselves against him, but their efforts only heightened his resolve and fed him more power. He killed and wrought destruction like a force of nature, brutal—and unstoppable.

Within the Celestial Hall, the effects of the battle outside were finally heard.

"What's happening out there?" Aitan asked with growing dread.

"Travest Mulvihill," said Komm Kyriel. "He's taken the power I gave him and is carrying it through to its logical extreme, as I hoped he would. He is killing angels. He is destroying Heaven."

Aitan almost laughed at the absurdity of the very idea, but Tom touched his arm and said, "It's true. I can tell. Everything he's saying is true."

The boy's touch emitted a fire Aitan had felt only a few times in his life. He looked down at his squire and realized that Tom had been changed. The boy was now an avatar of truth.

Komm Kyriel laughed and his shadow form trembled. "If I know you, Aitan, you probably have so many questions. Ask them quickly. There is little time left."

Aitan had to think of a way to stop this creature. But he needed time and so he asked, "The Second Vessel. Why did He deny me?"

"Easy enough." The shadowthing suddenly transformed into the towering vision Aitan had seen when the "Vessel" first visited him. "Does *this* look familiar?"

"It was you."

"Of course. That's why the Emissary to the Second treated you so strangely. He thought you were mad, but of course, he was always dealing with angels who thought they had seen the true face of God, and so he humored you to an extent— as I knew he would."

The walls surrounding them burst into flame and the sky split and delivered lightning that struck all around the assemblage, but harmed no one.

"Now hurry," said Kyriel. "The twins have alerted others to my presence. The Host is sealing off the sacred ways out of this city."

"They're not going to help?" Malkiyyah asked. The Angel of Blood was shocked.

"No. They feel it better to contain my evil, to see me destroyed even at a cost of this city and all who dwell within it. My compliments to them, really. I wasn't sure they would be this ruthless."

"Yes you were," Tom said, feeling the power rising within him. "You were counting on it."

Kyriel ignored Tom.

Aitan said, "I was willing to damn myself before. You are not the Enemy, despite all you claim. Surrender yourself to the judgment of God. Take us all from this place before it's too late, or I will make good my claim. I will summon the true Enemy and you will suffer."

"Do it," said Kyriel. "The Enemy is a fiction. Nothing will happen."

"No!" Tom hissed. "That's a lie."

Kyriel looked to Tom sharply, distress clearly apparent on his shadowy features. The shadowthing said, "Well, now, aren't *you* anxious to burn for an eternity?"

"It's what he wants," Tom went on. "Rachiel was right. He can't win unless you're dragged down to his level. Unless you become what he is. He won't kill you."

"No," said Kyriel. "But little humans who don't know when to keep quiet can't claim that same protection."

He won't kill me, Aitan thought. *He needs to keep me safe.* Suddenly, the angel knew what he had to do.

"How much of this have you been manipulating from the beginning?" Aitan asked as he began to weave a spell in his mind.

"If it makes you feel better, a good deal of it was happy accidents that I made the most of."

"Why are you doing this?" Tom screamed.

Kyriel shrugged. "Everyone has a right to Truth. Beyond

the world of man, beyond the True Lands and its opposite number, the Realm of Shadow, which our denial has given strength, there are two more higher planes that we can each aspire to. A world of light that is God, and a world that has not yet come into being, in which God and the Nameless, the co-creators of all that has ever been and all that will ever be, will finally come together as one. The weavers of light and darkness.''

''The Nameless?'' asked Aitan.

''The Demiurge, he who created all evil out of spite, because he opened his arms to embrace the light of love that was God a moment too soon and was wounded, scarred for his enthusiasm and delight.''

The angel scowled. ''I can't believe any of this.''

''What you believe doesn't matter. I have seen that paradise *is* possible. And if I have to make the world of man and the True Lands a living hell, if I have to become the embodiment of the Enemy to see that paradise eventually flower, I will do so. No price is too high to pay for redemption and perfection. None.''

''Who are you to make that decision for all of us?'' Malkiyyah asked. The Angel of Blood stood resolute.

A little longer, Aitan thought. *Just a little longer*.

Kyriel said, ''The only one among us with the courage of his convictions, and the willingness to sacrifice all to see God's will finally be done.''

''I don't want to live in your world,'' said Malkiyyah.

''Then don't,'' said Kyriel. He gestured, and Malkiyyah vanished.

''What did you do with him?'' asked Aitan.

''Nothing much. I just sent him to visit an old acquaintance. A simple tailor. Though I doubt fittings and measurements are on Travest Mulvihill's mind right now.''

Kyriel looked to Tom. ''You're being rather quiet. It's just the three of us now. You don't have to be shy.''

''I wasn't. What you've said is true,'' Tom said. ''But it's not the whole truth and you know that.''

Kyriel appeared shaken. He had sensed the Gift glowing brightly within Tom and it frightened him terribly. ''So what *is* the truth?''

Tom looked to Aitan, then back to Kyriel. "Ask God."

A howl of rage erupted from Kyriel. He extended a claw and was about to run Tom through when Aitan Anzelm raised his hand in warning and began to chant.

Komm Kyriel recognized the words of his old friend and froze in terror.

Across the city, Malkiyyah found himself in a Temple of the Sky that had been brought crashing to the earth. In the distance, he could hear angels screaming and abandoning their posts. The trumpeters sounded retreat and Malkiyyah knew that the city was being abandoned. No others of his rank and station would come to his aid.

Ahead, he saw the being that had been Travest Mulvihill. The creature was engulfed by light. It seemed that near-infinite power was his to command. The Angel of Blood thought he would feel anger at the sight of what Travest had become. Here was a mortal who dared to turn the light of Heaven, the very building blocks of paradise, into something destructive and evil.

Instead, he felt only pity for the misguided creature. Malkiyyah guessed that his brethren had retreated for the fortresses and training grounds of warriors in the True Lands. They believed the light-bringer incapable of ever leaving this city.

The Angel of Blood cursed them for fools. Mulvihill found a way into this city. He would find a way out again. And if he escaped into the True Lands, where the light of love and the richness of magic was at its strongest, all of Heaven would be at risk.

No, it had to end here, no matter the cost.

Malkiyyah cried, "Do you remember me? I'm the one who started all of this. The sword bearer who took your son, who wouldn't just let him die."

Travest turned to face the angel, trembling in unholy rage.

With a cry of pure animal hatred, the shining man launched his Power at the angel.

Malkiyyah did not fall. He screamed with agony as the Power of a dozen of his kind was channeled into him, but he took that magic and began to glow with a luminescence all his own.

"That's right," said the Angel of Blood. "Fill me with your

Power. Fill me with your hate. Fill me with all of it. I can stand anything if it means putting an end to you and your suffering.''

Enraged, Travest tore the magic from the earth below. He ripped the light from the city, the sky, and the angels who attempted to flee. All this and more he took and hurled at the angel. Still, Malkiyyah did not fall.

The titans, each a living embodiment of blinding light and incredible power, launched themselves at one another.

Meanwhile, in the fiery ruins of the Celestial Hall, Aitan continued his chant:

''I will arise and go to my father, and I will say unto Him, Father, I have sinned against Heaven and before Thee. And am no more worthy to be called Thy son; make me as one of Thy servants. Make me worthy. Show me Thy light and Thy love. Fill me with Thy blessing so that I may pass beyond and again be blessed with Thy presence. . . .''

''You don't know what you're doing!'' Kyriel screamed.

''He knows exactly what he's doing,'' said a rough, pained voice.

Tom turned to see Grin rising slowly.

''It's called the Spell of Supreme Sacrifice,'' said the former Emissary. ''When it is over, all of us will be swept away.''

Aitan continued to weave his spell. While suicide was a mortal sin that would have resulted in precisely the corruption of the soul Komm Kyriel wished for Aitan, the Spell of Supreme Sacrifice was something else again. God had decreed that giving up one's life when faced with impossible odds so that an agent of the Enemy could be expunged from existence was a good and noble thing.

''I'll take their souls,'' Kyriel swore as he pointed at Tom and Grin. ''I'll send them to their eternal damnation. Open the way to the Ring of Punishment!''

Tom felt the Power rise within him and hollered triumphantly, ''He can't do it! He's lying. The spell's making it impossible for him to harm us.''

''All you can do,'' said Grin in a hoarse whisper as he turned to face Komm Kyriel, ''is die in this place.''

The shadowthing fell silent.

Tom looked to Aitan and said, ''It's working! He knows

he's beaten. He won't attack, he knows it's over." The lad looked over to the shadow-creature. "Get out of here."

Kyriel stared at the child, then began to laugh. "I can't. None of us can. The spell, once begun, cannot be stopped."

Sensing the truth of those words, Tom looked to Aitan in horror. "Why? You said we'd be together. We're friends!"

"Yes," said Grin. "And this is the only way to protect us all."

"Don't," said Tom.

"It's too late," said Grin.

Tom's gaze met with Aitan's. He saw the love Aitan had for him, exactly like that his own father held, and the agony Aitan felt at being forced to make this painful decision. Tom nodded slowly in forgiveness. He knew that Aitan's obligation, his sacred duty to rid all the worlds of the evil that had been his friend, was more important than any of their lives.

Refusing to accept his defeat, Komm Kyriel leaped at Aitan.

Tom saw the living shadow descend upon Aitan. The angel never stopped his recitation, but he managed a flicker of a smile.

The monstrous, twisting form of Komm Kyriel engulfed Aitan, but only for an instant. Suddenly, he was brought down to the size and shape of a man. Tom saw Aitan grappling with the nightmare made flesh. Kyriel's eyes glowed red, and Aitan's form seemed to shimmer and lose its shape, then regain it again.

Aitan looked to Grin, and nodded once.

The former Emissary called upon his magics and suddenly a fiery red pit formed beneath Aitan and the Enemy. Tom recognized the Ring of Punishment and heard the screams of the angels cast into it. It was a burning, reddish gold rose made entirely of angels and their suffering.

Aitan's gaze moved to Tom. He nodded once, very slowly, then turned and dragged his struggling nemesis deep into the pit with him.

Then he was gone. The screams, the flames—all of it— gone.

"AITAN!" Tom cried, rushing forward.

"No," said Grin. "There is no time."

Tom turned. "You sent him to hell."

"It's what he wanted."

"You damned him!"

"I pray not."

Tom looked around. The Celestial Hall was crumbling all around them. The lightning striking from on high was getting closer.

Grin gestured and a shimmering gateway appeared. "Go. This is the last of the paths leading back to the Human World. Go now while I can still hold it open."

"We've got to help *Aitan*," said Tom, tears streaming down his face.

"I will go to him. I promise. I will enter the flames of damnation itself and fight the Enemy. It's what I was born to do. But *you* have to survive."

"I have the Scourge," said Tom. "I'm dying anyway. Let me come with you."

Grin shook his head. "Do you believe in God, young master Keeper?"

"Yes."

"Then believe that God will spare you. Believe in His mercy and you will be well."

Tom clutched at his chest. The pain was growing worse. He felt as if his ribs were being pulled apart, his heart and lungs squeezed by a dark and invisible hand. Blood eased from his pores. He could barely stand. "It's true, you know. What Kyriel said. You're not angels."

"Maybe not. But I've devoted myself to His Glory. One day, He may see fit to raise me up. I can only hope." Grin laughed. "Now remember, names are very important. You are a Keeper. Live up to the titles and responsibilities of that name. Be a keeper of our story. Of our triumph. Tell it in words, and in pictures. Never despair and tell others they must not either."

"Lord, please—" Tom began.

"Pray for me, Tom. Pray for us all," Grin said. He gestured and an invisible force dragged Tom to the portal.

The lad vanished within it.

Shuddering, Grin looked down at his wounds. He meant to fulfill the promise he had made to Tom, and just the knowledge that the vision of his own death had been wrong was enough to make him think anything was possible.

He conjured and the shimmering Ring of Punishment appeared. The former Emissary took a step forward then froze.

Something was coming out. . . .

In the dying heart of the heavenly city, Malkiyyah and Travest clawed and tore at each other. The cloud dwellings plummeted to the earth. One had plunged down and been smashed into dust in the very spot they stood, but neither of the warriors had been harmed.

They manifested swords and daggers, lances and scythes. But no matter what punishment they inflicted upon one another, they each rose up again. Neither understood why they were fighting any longer. Their reason had fled. All they could comprehend was an instinctive need to bring about each other's destruction.

They were evenly matched. Their battle could rage on for a millennium and never be decided. Not without intervention.

Suddenly, the ground shook. The earth beneath them split.

A piercing howl sounded from below. Malkiyyah and Travest stopped fighting long enough to see a flurry of crimson angels flying toward them. Each burned with a light that was no longer pure, that had been corrupted by decades, even centuries of imprisonment and torture.

Malkiyyah's reason returned to him. He knew what he was seeing. These were the souls of the angels cast down into the Ring of Punishment. They had been freed from their torment!

As the crimson souls flew upward, the light with which both Malkiyyah and Travest had been imbued was taken from them. They shuddered and wailed as the light was painfully wrenched away.

The purity of that light cleansed the souls of the angels. They rose into the sky, flying in ever-growing arcs over the ruined city of Abaddon.

Linking hands, they began to sing.

Malkiyyah looked down at his flesh. All vestiges of his Power was gone. He turned his gaze to Travest, who was also weakened and vulnerable.

The former tailor looked around and saw the destruction, the bodies of angels everywhere, the fires that might never be put out. He knew that he was the cause. Worse, he understood that buried somewhere beneath the rubble was a charred skeleton of a boy who had been given wings though he had never asked for them. The body of his beloved son, whose life he had inadvertently taken.

Travest fell on his knees before the angel. "Forgive me, lord. I have sinned."

Malkiyyah studied the man silently.

"Take my life," said Travest. "It's yours. Take it now before I can become what I was. End it here and now. I beg you."

"There's been enough killing," said Malkiyyah. "Enough death."

Travest placed his hands over his eyes. He could feel his Power returning, feel the light being harvested and brought to him.

Malkiyyah saw slivers of light leak from between the man's fingers. Tenderly, he went to Travest, put his hands on either side of the man's skull.

"Thank you, thank you. . . ." Travest whispered, then he began to recite a prayer.

With all his strength, Malkiyyah twisted the man's head sharply to one side. There was a sharp crackling, and Travest Mulvihill's body fell limply to the ground.

Malkiyyah turned away from the mortal's corpse and looked to the skies. The angels were flying faster and faster. He could hear their singing, their chanting, and see odd runes coming into existence.

In that moment, he knew what they had planned for the City of Heaven.

"No!" Malkiyyah screamed as he raised his fists into the air. "NO!"

But in his heart, he knew it was too late. There was nothing anyone could do to stop them.

While outside the city, in the clearing before the woods, a shimmering vortex appeared and Tom Keeper stumbled through it. He saw the body of the plague-carrier in the mists. Though he had almost no strength left, Tom forced himself to run until he reached the edge of the forest. He tripped, fell, and found he had no strength to rise again.

Turning, he looked back to the City of Heaven.

The mists obscured much, but Tom was able to see a surprising amount of the city. There were shapes above Abaddon, figures flying through the air so quickly that they were becoming blurs of light. He saw buildings lose their forms, spires tumbling from the heavens, and clouds filled with crimson flame!

Tom had heard tales about the coming of the Heavenly Cities. He knew of the odd, twisting, ever-changing shapes that appeared on earth and in the sky, and of the Weavers, the angels who brought about the Convergence.

What he was looking at now was strangely like the tales he had heard—yet different. Forms were not appearing, they were vanishing. Tom watched in growing horror as black lightning broke from the gathering of angels above the city and a veil of impenetrable, blinding light wrapped around the city. In the instant before he turned away from the arcane fires that set the night sky ablaze, he was certain that he saw Sigils being drawn in the very air.

He heard a singing that was strangely hollow and eerily beautiful. It grew louder until Tom thought he might go mad from the sounds and the strange shapes that appeared in his mind to accompany the cacophony.

There was a sudden rush of air.

Then silence.

Tom looked back. The mists had been dispelled. All that remained of the heavenly city was rubble and shattered spires charred black and smoking.

"Aitan," he whispered. "AITAN!"

There was no reply. Tom fell on the earth, sobbing and weeping for what seemed like hours, but was really only a few brief minutes.

Then he heard the sounds of footsteps behind him. The crush of fresh grass. And a voice that made him think he was dreaming.

"I see him." Low, throaty, achingly feminine and racked by concern. "He has it. Go to him, hurry!"

Another voice. A boy's voice came next, but Tom was beyond hearing it. For the briefest of instants he was certain that he had heard Kayrlis, but that was utter madness. The Scourge was reaching a new stage within him, Tom decided. He was starting to hallucinate, just as his mother had in the days before she became unable to respond to the outside world at all.

He was dying.

Hands were on him suddenly. On his face, he felt a touch that was cold, yet comforting. At once his pain began to ease, the fever diminish.

Someone turned him over.

"Now I know I'm dreaming," Tom said. Crouching above him was Kayrlis, and her brother, Cameron.

Kayrlis took Tom's hand, kissed it, then held it close to her heart. "You'll be well. Sleep, dearest heart. Sleep."

Tom saw Cameron reaching for him. The boy's hand seemed to glow with a blue white fire.

Then he knew nothing at all.

Epilogue

TOM WOKE IN A STRANGE, BUSTLING CITY. HE COULD hear the sounds of people hurrying about outside his window, and town criers proclaiming the local news.

A smile spidered across his handsome face as he realized that he was in Paridian.

The lad was not alone in the room or in his bed. Kayrlis was with him. Tom lay on his side and she held him from behind, her body pressed neatly into his. A perfect fit.

She was asleep.

For a fleeting second, Tom wondered if he had died, and if he had been sent beyond, to the true Heaven. Then he felt the painful collection of aches and pains that riddled his body and he knew that Heaven could never hurt this much.

Soft golden sunlight filtered into the room. It was morning, just after daybreak, Tom guessed from the coolness in the air. The window was wide-open.

"Kayrlis," he said softly.

The young woman grunted.

Tom reached down and tickled her palm. Kayrlis laughed in her throaty voice and drifted awake. Tom turned over and watched as she opened her lovely emerald eyes.

"Oh no," she said, putting her hands over her face. "I must look terrible." She touched her hair. "It's all stringy." Looking down she bit her lip. "And I'm wearing this stupid frock. I had a dress picked out, wanted you to see me looking just right—"

"Kayrlis," Tom said, stopping her. He gently pried her hands away.

"Uh-huh."

"I love you and you look perfect."

Kayrlis moaned and squirmed. "Blast! I knew this would be a mistake."

"We should both make mistakes like this more often."

Sighing, Kayrlis snuggled into his arms. "How much do you remember?"

"Not much."

"Coming here? We're in Paridian, y'know."

"I know. I heard the crier."

"Oh," she said with a wry grin. "Well, don't let this little arrangement give you the wrong idea. I had to keep you warm somehow. What he does, it takes the pain away, but the cold it puts in a person can kill them just as easily. Gotta be careful."

"What *who* does?" Tom asked.

"Cameron. He cured you of the Scourge."

Tom slowly sat upright, allowing Kayrlis to move off him. "Would you like to tell me that one again."

"How do you feel?"

The lad thought about it. "A little chilly, but that's about it."

"Have you ever heard of the Scourge going into remission?"

"No."

"So what do *you* think happened?"

Tom was wearing a heavy robe. He went to the window. There were two chairs beside it. He sat in one, Kayrlis came to him and sat in the other. He reached out and took her hand without hesitation. She didn't resist.

Kayrlis told Tom as much as she knew. She found her brother dying of the Scourge the same night she and Tom had made love. She knew he had been in Cameron's room, and returned the vial of healing waters to Aitan. For days, there was no change. Kayrlis became resigned to the idea that her brother would die of the Scourge. Then others in Hartston began to manifest signs of the plague. One night, Cameron started whispering something the young woman would never forget:

"I seek the wisdom. The Ways . . ."

The flame guardian, Tom thought. He hadn't been the only one visited in his dreams by the fiery apparition.

"He was touched by God," Kayrlis said. "He woke with the Gift to heal. Even he isn't sure if it's because of what you did with the waters, making him drink them, or if the man he saw in his dreams gave him the power, or if it was a little bit of both. What did matter was that when I got sick, he saved my life. Then I helped him save as many as he could in Hartston, before we moved on."

"How did you know where I would be?" asked Tom.

"The man in Cameron's dreams. He led us on. It was a long ride, I'll tell you that. If I'd have known where we were headin', I could have found a shorter route."

"Best that you didn't," Tom said. "There were things Aitan and I saw—things it's best you didn't come up against."

"I can take care of myself," said Kayrlis.

"Oh, I know." He laughed. "I know."

He told her the story of all that had happened to him since they parted.

When it was over, Kayrlis asked, "Do you think they're gone?"

"I don't know what to think," said Tom. He looked away from the window, into Kayrlis's dark, beautiful face. "That's not true. I still feel him in my heart. I believe he's alive. And I can't forget about what I saw when I was with the flame guardian. Aitan and me on that battlefield. That's still in the future. So Aitan's still alive. Somewhere. And I think he needs me."

Kayrlis leaned forward and kissed Tom softly. "I think I need you, too."

They made love again, tenderly at first, then with passion and without restraint. When they were done, they lay in each other's arms.

After a time, Kayrlis said, "I've got money. Lots of it. We wouldn't have to worry for a long time."

"I want to be with you."

"Just don't expect too much of me."

"I won't. But you know that I have to find out what happened to Aitan. Even if it takes the rest of my life, I have to find him."

"I know. And we can help people along the way. Cameron was given this Gift for a reason. We've got to use it."

He took her hand, brought it to his lips, and kissed her gently. "We will."

Tom knew where to start in his search. Aitan had told him only a little about his Patron, but it would have to be enough for Tom to find him. He would learn why Aitan's Patron had abandoned him, though Tom suspected it had something to do with the machinations of Komm Kyriel.

They would begin to deal with the search soon enough. There was something else Tom had to resolve first.

Looking into Kayrlis's stunning eyes, he said, "I love you."

She looked away from him. "I don't love you."

He felt the Power within him. The fire of truth.

And he knew.

"Well I'll be damned," he said for the first time in his life. "You're lying!"

It can in no sense be said that heaven is outside of any one; it is within. . . .and a man also, so far as he receives heaven, is a recipient, a heaven, and an angel.

—Emanuel Swedenborg
Arcano Coelestia